FINAL RIGHTS

Grateful Steps Foundation
159 South Lexington Avenue
Asheville, NC 28801

Library of Congress Control Number 2014916294
Frank, Tena
Final Rights

Photograph of the author is by Murphy Funkhouser Capps,
Kudzu Branding Co. Asheville, NC.
Photograph of the house on the cover is the Snead-Adams House, used with
permission from the North Carolina Collection, Pack Memorial Library,
Asheville, NC. The Photoshop treatment of the photo is by Cheri Britton.

ISBN
978-1-935130-84-0 Paperback

Printed at Lightning Source

FIRST EDITION

www.gratefulsteps.org

To Linda, who taught me the joy of learning

FINAL RIGHTS

A Novel

TENA FRANK

GRATEFUL STEPS
ASHEVILLE, NORTH CAROLINA

1962

He's prob'ly gonna kill me. This one thought raced a tight track through Ellie's mind as she huddled in the corner of her bedroom. She hoped her ferocity would come when the moment arrived, but she knew she lacked the physical strength to withstand the fury raging in the living room once it reached her. The destruction of her world came to her in sounds— furniture cracking like kindling, bric-a-brac smashing to the floor, potted plants shattering against the walls.

Maybe I can't save myself, but I will protect the girl. Ellie's determination cemented into resolve and she wrapped her arms around her small body to quell her trembling. She went to the quiet place inside herself, the place that had always been her refuge, her salvation. She hunkered down into it and rested for a bit, creating a cocoon of safety where she could think and plan. She could not save herself, she knew that, but she could and would take care of the girl. Just before the bedroom door flew open, Ellie tucked a quickly scribbled note under the pillow, then stood up and faced the inevitable.

"Where is it?"

"It's for the girl. You'll never get it. I swear you'll never get it."

These words came from her depths, and Ellie uttered them with conviction and forcefulness. She liked the sound of them. She felt invincible in that moment even as the blow to her chest sent her crashing to the floor.

She looked up at the face she had known so well for so long but no longer recognized it. She saw a beast there now, inhabiting the body of the son she had once loved fiercely. Only repetitive, devastating disappointments and overwhelming grief had finally broken the bonds created by her love.

The final kick to Ellie's midsection broke a rib, which punctured the atrium of her heart. She spent the final moments of her life in the arms of her husband, extracting from him a promise he would never keep.

ONE
2004

Tate Marlowe huffed her way along the street, barely aware of her surroundings. She jogged until the stitch in her side forced her to slow to a walk. Sometimes the walk slowed to a near-crawl, but she did not stop. Once she got her breath back, she jogged again, determined to quell the anger pulsing through her body. She had a choice, work it out or give into it. Go on a tirade against the unknown creeps who had egged her truck the night before, or push to her physical limits until the adrenaline rush subsided and she could think clearly again.

An hour earlier, Tate had stepped out onto her small porch, breathed in the clean air and stretched out her sore muscles. The warm morning sun and crisp, dry air held the promise of a beautiful day. Tate loved this weather. Last week had been cold and damp, but now late fall ruled, and she looked forward to the day ahead.

Her mood had taken a detour as she headed down the cobbled walk and saw the mess awaiting her. The day after Halloween, and her truck dripped with congealed egg snot. Several garbage cans lay on their sides along her block and the obligatory toilet paper streamers hung from trees just down the street. Miraculously, her motorcycle, parked behind her truck where it had been languishing for over a year, seemed to have escaped all harm.

At least there's always good news along with the bad. Maybe it was just a typical Halloween prank. Maybe it wasn't aimed at me specifically. Tate wished that were true, but she knew better. These childish pranks could easily be blamed on a bunch of recalcitrant teenagers, but it seemed equally as likely to Tate that she had been targeted by some disgruntled neighbor.

She had moved to Asheville, North Carolina, the previous year and purchased two neighboring duplexes on the east side of Broadway, across from Montford, one of the city's most beautiful historical districts. Ever since she had started renovating one of the rental units she owned, her FOR RENT signs routinely disappeared within hours of being posted. The culprit even took down signs from her private property. Obviously, someone was determined to thwart her efforts to find new tenants for the remodeled apartment.

Rather than focusing on cleaning the gunk off her truck, Tate had changed into her walking shoes and headed into Montford. Intent on working off her irritation and preoccupied with who might be targeting her, she had strayed into an unfamiliar part of the neighborhood.

"I don't care what they think. It's my property and I'll do what I damn well please with it." Tate exhaled her declarations along with her breath as she propelled herself past the elegant homes gracing the street lined with towering trees dressed in late-fall color. "They'll just have to adjust."

The stabbing pain in her left side finally forced Tate to stop. She stood hunched over, hands on knees, eyes pinched closed. Her breathing restricted by the spasm in her rib cage, she swayed gently and willfully slowed her breathing. Once she could stand up again, she arched her back, hands on her hips and expanded her chest to allow in more air. The first thing she saw when she opened her eyes was a huge abandoned house sitting at the top of a sloping hill and surrounded by a weed patch that had once been an expansive lawn.

"What the hell is that?" Tate gasped at the sight of the derelict house.

"That's our local eyesore."

Not expecting an answer, Tate whirled around and took a step back when she heard a man's voice coming from directly behind her. "Whoa! Where'd you come from?"

"Around the corner. Saw you about to take a nose dive onto the sidewalk. Thought maybe you needed some help."

The best defense is a good offense. Tate leaned in toward the man a bit and adopted a slightly menacing tone of voice. "I was not about to take a nose dive, not that it's any of your business."

"Coulda fooled me. Have it your way then." The man retraced his route and disappeared.

The threat of being the recipient of a random act of kindness having subsided, Tate turned her attention to the old house at the top of the hill. It could only be described as a dream in ruin. Both outlandish and beautiful at the same time, the house exhibited a hodgepodge of styles from Asheville's architectural history. It somehow managed to reflect its era while ridiculing it at the same time. Tate guessed the house had been constructed in the early to mid-20th century. The pebbledash exterior walls of the first floor crumbled in spots. The soft green of the original paint, now gray from age, looked the color of mold. The second story boasted the cedar shingles common on old Montford homes. The upper-story windows had Tudor-style sashes and trim, now peeling and rotting. With the turrets and gingerbread trim that had been added, the house appeared clown-like, yet sad in its disrepair. In spite of all this, Tate immediately resonated with this disheveled behemoth sitting at the top of the gentle hill at 305 West Chestnut Street.

She walked up the shallow and graceful stairs cut into the field-stone retaining wall decorated with cheap pieces of colored glass. This appealing touch from an earlier day now looked tawdry.

Though mismatched as a whole, elements of the house radiated beauty. A spacious porch belted three sides of the first floor, and the second story sprouted large balconies on each end.

Stepping onto the porch, Tate continued her exploration, peeking through the windows to see the inside, frustrated with the closed drapes that allowed only the smallest glimpses around the tattered barrier they created.

The back section of the wrap-around porch overlooked a large, quiet garden and a dry fishpond overgrown with weeds. As she did at times like this, Tate began talking aloud as she continued her exploration. "This would be a perfect meditation spot! How beautiful. How nurturing!"

She spied a long set of uncovered windows spanning some thirty feet and peered into a massive kitchen at the back of the house. She gasped. The room looked like an abandoned set from a movie, everything perfectly in place and neatly ordered, but now covered with decades of dust. Still, its beauty could not be denied.

"Amazing! This kitchen is fantastic. I want to cook here. So much space! I love the tiled countertops, and those cabinets are incredible! Look at the craftsmanship!"

Whoever had created this house and this kitchen had clearly loved it, she knew for sure.

Tate imagined all the wonderful parties she could host in a house like this—a place to be proud of, with no need to wiggle out of inviting visitors by doing a fine balancing act between welcoming and warning them off.

Tate allowed herself unfettered daydreams as she walked around the entire house again. After half an hour in reverie, while heading back across the lawn, she turned back for one last look. What she saw shocked her. How could she have missed it?

This grand old dame of a house, obviously once a showpiece of the rich owner, had a distinctive front door that so closely echoed the dimensions and design of the door on her simple house in the working class section of town that it left her stunned. There were subtle differences—each had two panels, hers with windows in the top half, this one without windows, and this door had a triangular panel above it that hers lacked, giving it a more imposing appearance. The main exception seemed to be in the craftsmanship. The wood was heavier and more rough-hewn here, and the detailing in the oversized hardware lacked the finesse of that on Tate's house. Still, she knew instinctively that whoever had made this door had crafted the one on her house as well.

Tate heard what sounded like a whisper, then a flash of light flickered through the autumn foliage of a huge maple tree and bounced off the grimy upper windows. She shuddered as a sudden gust of cold wind swirled through the crackly leaves gathered in a corner of the wide porch.

TWO
1916

Big dreams that seem reasonable to the dreamer serve as a common hallmark of early childhood, and even as a very little girl, Marie Eleanor Vance believed she would live a happy life filled with everything she wanted. Her parents had enough of everything to take care of her and her brother. Kind and gentle folk, not given to drama nor attractive to difficulty, they nurtured their children with a healthy balance of love and discipline. Families just like Ellie's populated the quiet neighborhood where she lived. She had plenty of friends and peaceful days sprinkled with sunshine, freedom and security.

Then she entered first grade. She approached this phase of her life with great expectations, just as she did any new adventure. So when little things began to happen that challenged her beliefs about herself and her life, she let them slip by barely noticed. She avoided engaging in battles with the other children. When they tried to provoke her, she smiled sweetly and went to find other playmates. When it rained, she anticipated the sun coming back out. In the heat of the day, she awaited the cool evening ahead. In the cold grip of winter, she bundled up and looked forward to the arrival of spring. Ellie's approach to life worked very well indeed, but even the most optimistic outlook sometimes must give way to reality.

Ellie got her first bloody nose at the hands of a bully. Grace was sorely misnamed by her parents who believed they had received a child with a good disposition following an uneventful and easy delivery. Big and gawky, she towered over most of the other first graders. Bossy, demanding and downright mean-spirited for no reason apparent to anyone, not even Grace, she enjoyed nothing more than making the other kids squirm.

Ellie didn't squirm well. Being an optimist, she took little notice of Grace. For a bully, it is close to unbearable to be ignored or, worse yet, not even noticed. So Grace had little choice, in her own mind at least, but to take all necessary action to get Ellie's attention.

This took the form, one fine morning, of a threat to throw a shovelful of sand into Ellie's face. Ellie had to acknowledge a danger so imminent and personal. She looked up from her play just in time to meet the flying sand head on. It filled her mouth and eyes and slipped under her dainty dress, covering her body with grit. Stunned, she could barely move as Grace dropped the shovel and came at her with clenched fists.

Ellie scrambled away at the last second, heading across the playground. Almost within reach of safety, Grace hard on her heels, Ellie slipped and fell against the swing set, and that's when she got the bloody nose.

Of course the adults in charge had reached her by this time, and they coddled and tended to her. She saw others haul Grace away. Her classmates, uninjured and secretly grateful, cowered on the playground as they watched the scene unfold. They had learned long ago that Grace picked on those who paid no attention to her. Ellie the Optimist had not learned that lesson. So, the fault lay with her, didn't it?

The adults washed Ellie off, cleaned her up and sent her home. The nosebleed stopped quickly with no real harm done—according to the adults in charge, at least. Ellie's parents took the same approach. One of life's little lessons: be more attentive next time, steer clear of trouble, watch what's happening around you, pick yourself up, brush yourself off and move on.

In the world of an optimist, these helpful hints seemed puzzling. Ellie wondered how bad things could happen to a good child like herself, in a peaceful world like the one she lived in, on a lovely day like this one. Many years passed before Ellie began to find answers to these troubling questions. Nonetheless, her life unfolded much as she originally expected it to in the years that followed.

Grace disappeared from school when her family moved on shortly after the playground incident. Ellie settled into first grade easily after that and quickly became a star pupil. Intelligent and creative, she did as well in reading and writing as she did in arithmetic. She participated joyfully in arts and crafts and enthusiastically presented her mother with her macaroni collages and handprints in plaster of Paris. First grade faded into second grade, then third, then fourth, and although small glitches occurred along the way, she typically side-stepped any real harm. As a natural problem solver, whenever little things came up to disturb Ellie's happy life, she quickly found a way around them or through them.

By the time she entered high school, however, Ellie began to understand the flow of her life would not always be as smooth as she had hoped. This realization formed about the same time Ellie became interested in boys. Although popular with all her classmates, Ellie knew the boys she found most attractive did not seem drawn to her.

Dating age arrived for Ellie and her girlfriends with mixed results. Some of them developed breasts and hips and winsome smiles, but not so for Ellie. She retained her little girl shape too long, and when her body finally began maturing, she grew up, not out—no breasts or hips to speak of—but suddenly she towered several inches taller than her friends and, in many cases, taller than the boys in her class.

She wore nice clothes, always clean and neat, but not stylish ones like the other girls. Her mousy brown hair lacked the rich chestnut glow she longed for. Fine, thick and almost straight, it fell short of the wavy, full and luxurious hair of her mother. She could live with all those little shortcomings. With a nice smile, pretty laugh, generous nature and strong, healthy body, only one problem truly stood in Ellie's way: Ellie was almost pretty.

Close-enough-to-pretty meant she had friends. It established her place on the fringe of the popular crowd. It resulted in invitations to parties and landed her a part-time job at the soda fountain at Woolworth's. Close-enough-to-pretty attracted just about everything she wanted except those cute boys who asked girls out.

While her friends began dating, Ellie sat home alone. She studied her face in the mirror. *If only my eyes were not quite that close together,* she thought. *If only my hair were wavy; if only my face was more oval instead of so square.* If only, if only, if only . . .

Then Ellie would quietly cry herself to sleep and hope for dreams of being more than almost pretty.

THREE
2004

Tate's excitement about finding the old house offset her physical exhaustion as she headed back home. In fact, she found herself enjoying her walk now that she took a more leisurely pace. Surprisingly, walking had become one of her favorite activities since arriving in Asheville. She had trudged her way through New York out of sheer necessity, so the notion of walking for pleasure had taken some time to cultivate.

So many things had changed in Tate's life since she left the City. She now owned two properties, both upstairs-downstairs duplexes sitting next to each other on a quiet urban street. She occupied the top space in one of the units, and the upstairs apartment of the building next door sat vacant in the early stages of a major upgrade.

She hoped the carpenter doing the work would be on site when she returned, so seeing his truck sitting at the curb as she rounded the corner made her happy. She popped into the apartment instead of heading directly home.

"Hey, Dave, how's it going?"

"Mornin', Tate. Okay, I guess. Quite a mess they left in front of your house. Any damage?"

"Nothing a trip to the car wash won't fix. I can scrape egg off my windshield, but now I'll have to actually get the truck washed. Been putting that off for weeks." The walk—and the discovery of the old house—had done exactly what Tate hoped. Her anger about the egging had disappeared. "How's the work coming along?"

"Hard to tell at this stage just what you're going to find." Dave's gesture swept the empty room.

Tate looked around. The apartment had been gutted, and the salvage and trash covered the front yard in piles. The floors had been stripped of all covering, revealing an unidentified hardwood coated with grime and aged to a dull gray.

"I think you've got heart pine here," Dave said, indicating the floor.

"Really? Do you think we can save it?"

"Don't know for sure, but it looks pretty good." Dave surveyed the floors, running his hands lovingly over the old wood as if he could feel its soul.

"The wood is solid, not spongy anywhere. It's been cut up pretty bad in some places, but I think we may be able to save it here in this room. This interior has been changed a lot. The doorway to the back used to be over there, I think." He pointed to the now barren kitchen wall. "And it had a fireplace right here at one time." He tapped the floor in front of the hallway entrance with his toe.

Tate examined the room. It ran the full length of the front of the house, over two hundred square feet of open space with natural light streaming in from sunrise to sunset through tall windows positioned midway between the floor and ceiling in groups of three.

New windows would eventually grace the east side of the room, but at this point Dave had progressed no further than removing the inside trim on the old ones. Tate hated to give up that set of original windows but decided to replace them with shorter units in order to create a second wall that could accommodate a countertop and cabinets. By expanding the counter space, she had made room for a dishwasher—one of the modern conveniences she considered essential but still lacked in her own living space.

"I often wonder how old this house really is, Dave. Any ideas on that?"

Dave focused on the room, feet planted firmly, shoulder-width apart, hands on his hips, fingers resting gently on his tool belt. He was a good-looking guy with a gentle, country way about him. His brown hair hung in short, loose curls over his ears, his mouth always arched in a small, permanent grin, his blue eyes smiling as if what he saw always made him happy.

Tate liked working with Dave. She liked being around him, and that always surprised her a little. In fact, Tate had spent most of her life being surprised when she met men she actually liked. She didn't think of men in general as bad people, she just didn't have any particular use for most of them, and she had little interest in getting to know them—except for her clients, of course, back in her social worker days.

She glanced at Dave now, happy to be working with him and aware she trusted him. She welcomed feeling that way about a straight man.

"I'd guess the 1930s, maybe early '40s," Dave said. "It's got these heart pine floors, and the German siding on the porch was very common back then. It was cheap and popular."

"Yeah, I love that wooden porch. It would be nice to have the whole place like that."

"It probably is under the vinyl siding."

"Why do you think they covered the wood up?" Tate asked.

"Vinyl siding was all the rage in the '60s. Everyone wanted it because it was so easy to take care of. You never had to paint again if you put it on your house."

"But it's so ugly," Tate lamented. They had walked outside as they talked, and she looked around the house, trying to imagine what it had looked like when originally built.

"Yeah, it's ugly," Dave agreed.

"Well, maybe next time around I'll try to do something about that. I wish I could afford to have it all removed and give this place a coat of yellow paint."

"Yellow would be nice . . . I guess." Dave seemed skeptical.

"You know, Dave, I was walking over in Montford just before I got here and I saw an old house with a door much like this one. Don't you think that's odd?"

Tate and Dave studied the massive front door which stood at least eight feet high. The wood had never been painted, only sealed, so it retained its beautiful natural color. The bottom of the door sported a solid wood panel framed by delicate, scrolled molding. A similar panel in the top held six panes of old glass mottled with the small imperfections Tate loved. The original lock mounted to the outside of the door needed a skeleton key, which had been lost long ago. A cheap silver deadbolt had been added to provide security. The metal hinges also sat on the outside of the door and matched the old lock, all of them adorned by intricate carvings.

"Yep. It's a bit odd on this little house, but it's beautifully crafted and in great shape."

"Any idea how I can find out who made this door?"

"Why would you wanna do that?"

"I just wonder why this house has such a fancy door. It seems out of place."

—*∿*—

Dave watched Tate as she surveyed the house. He'd seen the same look on her face many times. *Obviously a dreamer.* She had a vision for this place as crystal clear to her as raindrops glistening in the sun after an afternoon thunderstorm. Practical, too, and he appreciated that about her.

When he first began this job, he wondered what to make of her. On one hand, she could be a bit overwhelming, on the other quite forgiving. Though overweight and strongly built, she made no attempt to appear small by hiding her even bigger personality.

He quickly understood that Tate rarely displayed self-consciousness. When she stood near him, it always came as a surprise to realize the difference in their heights. She just acted like a taller woman, if that made any sense, which it didn't when he tried to think about it. But still, he could not deny the truth of it.

Dave knew Tate had a temper. He had seen it brewing on a few occasions over the course of their work together. He also knew she never came close to venting her frustration at him. He found this curious. He had let her down in different ways on several occasions, and this job in particular had been a problem. He had too many things going on to give it the attention it needed. He had done his best to squeeze in a couple of hours here, a morning there, to work on the renovation. But everything remained way behind schedule, and he would soon run out of excuses for the many delays.

"So what's on the agenda for today?" Tate asked.

"Well, I'm hoping to get that wall in the bathroom torn out so things are ready for the plumber. It should only take me a couple more hours."

"That sounds good. Can we be ready for the carpet to be installed in the bedrooms next Thursday? That's when the guys are scheduled to come."

"We should make it by then. It depends on the plumber more than me. He has to rough in the half-bath and get it inspected before I can get the sub-flooring down." Dave braced himself for her response.

"You know I'm concerned about getting this place done, Dave. I was hoping to have it ready for occupancy by the first of next month. Any chance that can still happen?"

"It's possible. We'll have to push it some."

"Okay, Dave. We'll figure it out. I'll need enough time after you're done to paint before getting the carpet installed."

The only hint of Tate's frustration was the veiled comment about painting near new carpeting. Even though he knew he had let her down again, Tate didn't give him a hard time about it. He wondered if she had always been this way and if not, how long her flexibility would last.

Tate left the apartment feeling good about how she had handled things with Dave. Controlling her anger became easier each time she practiced it. Ever since she had escaped from New York and her job working with mentally ill and substance abusing homeless people on the city streets, Tate had been mellowing. A slow process for sure, but now, three years later, she seemed like a different person.

She felt enormously grateful that she had somehow managed to land in Asheville. The move had not been a conscious decision, nor the result of plenty of research and planning. Rather, she came for vacation with the intent of spending the fall riding her motorcycle along the Blue Ridge Parkway, and she simply never left.

Everywhere she went, Tate met folks who had moved to Asheville for the same reasons she had. Nestled in a valley in the Blue Ridge Mountains, it is a small town surrounded by natural beauty. With long, leisurely springs and falls, and short, mild summers and winters, the weather appealed to Tate greatly. Even today, as she had cleaned the dried egg off her windshield, she'd taken time to breathe in the crisp air of the chilly morning and feel it deeply in her lungs. She relished the simple act of being aware of her breathing. She had lived most of her life shutting out non-essentials such as feeling, enjoying and being present in the moment, and she liked the slow, steady change in how she lived her life.

Tate spent the rest of the day cleaning house, reading and trying to push thoughts of the abandoned house in Montford out of her mind with little success. *Wonder who owns the place. Why is it just sitting there vacant?* Those questions and more populated her thoughts and dreams that night.

FOUR
2004

Tate arose extremely early the next morning. At least 8:15 seemed extremely early to her. She forced herself to get out of bed and padded into the kitchen, turning up the thermostat on the wall furnace on the way. The faint click told her the place would be warm in a matter of minutes.

She limped a bit on her sore heel and thought about putting shoes with arch supports on over her fluffy pink and orange ankle socks. She shivered in the morning chill and pulled the fleece robe around herself.

Sunlight flooded in through the decrepit windows that lined two walls of her tiny kitchen, filling the space with a golden glow. The southeastern exposure of the kitchen delighted Tate, and she smiled as she put the coffee on to brew, thinking about how nice it would be to have a kitchen three times as large, with French doors leading to the triangular deck she imagined and glass filling every possible inch of wall space.

She sat down with her coffee at the glass-topped round table she had found at Goodwill and looked around. But now instead of focusing on her vision of what the space could be like, she looked with a calculated eye at what really existed.

"Pitiful," she muttered. Pocket, her cat, opened one eye halfway and looked at her before returning to her nap on the wooden ledge between the table and living room.

"Morning, Miss Kitty," Tate cooed as she reached over and rubbed the old cat's ears. Pocket leaned into her hand and began a soft purring. "How you doing this morning, Babycakes?" Tate continued her gentle strokes. Pocket had lived with Tate since she was seven weeks old, and over the course of their fifteen years together, Tate had given the sweet old cat countless nicknames. Pocket answered to none of them, choosing instead to grace Tate with her presence only when it suited her to do so.

Tate's little house in North Asheville had many redeeming qualities, but she inevitably focused on the multitude of problems it presented—the cramped rooms, decrepit old windows, tiny bathroom—all those things she dreamed about changing.

"Why did I ever buy this place, Pocket? I could have used the money for something already remodeled, or a new place even." A drawn out yawn served as the old cat's only response before she sauntered away.

Pocket's lack of input didn't matter because Tate knew she was not likely to do what others would

23

do given the same circumstances. As much as she believed she wanted an easy life free of complications, she knew in her heart she naturally gravitated toward something much different.

Tate decided to clean up the mess of paperwork on her kitchen table. But try as she might, she could not focus on writing checks and sorting through stacks of junk mail. The house on Chestnut Street kept intruding into her thoughts. She needed help tracking down its history. Immediately she thought of Holly.

Holly had quickly become Tate's first friend after she arrived in Asheville. Tate found her in the local gay newsletter when she started searching for a realtor. Their first meeting on a beautiful Saturday afternoon in October had lasted more than three hours, even though Tate made it clear from the beginning she had no intention of buying property. She just wanted to learn about Asheville and what kind of housing it offered, research in case she decided to settle down at some point.

From the beginning, Tate recognized Holly as a knowledgeable professional who also happened to be gay, friendly and welcoming. Not all realtors met those standards, by any means, so Tate felt grateful to have found her.

After that initial meeting, Tate had become quite curious about housing in Asheville, and she found the low price of real estate very appealing. She heard many people complain about how expensive property had become in Asheville, and she understood that could be true for people who had lived here all their lives. But for Tate, who had become accustomed to the exorbitant cost of housing in New York City, the prices in Asheville seemed amazingly low.

Tate enthusiastically dug into the stack of forms from Holly, plotting out locations of the various listings on her map. She headed out to explore the town. After looking at dozens of properties, she bought the first house she saw.

Not that Tate grabbed the first thing that came along. She did her research, but after three days of going from one place to another, into all of Asheville's many corners, she kept coming back to the little house on Maplewood, actually a duplex with one unit upstairs, where she could live, and another downstairs for a great rental unit. So she bought it, and she also bought the second duplex right next door. While some people might consider her behavior to be rash, Tate knew she had been drawn to Asheville and to these properties by something beyond logical thought, by some mysterious yet driving force that had guided her safely for her entire life. And she knew buying them was exactly the right thing to do.

Even though she expected no answer at this early hour, Tate dialed Holly's cell phone. Holly picked up on the first ring.

"Hey, Tate, how's it going?" she asked, chipper and wide awake. Holly's sweet and mellow voice made Tate smile, as it usually did.

"Okay, but I need your help. There's this house at 305 Chestnut Street. It's not for sale, but I want to know whatever you can find out about it for me. When was it built? Who owns it? Why is it so run down . . ." Tate rattled on at the fast clip so common for her when she became excited about something. Tate loved puzzles and she was already fully engaged in the challenge of unraveling the mystery of the house on Chestnut Street.

"Yeah, I can check that all out for you. I'm headed into the office now. Give me a couple hours, and I'll look at the tax records, okay?"

"Okay. Thanks, Holly." Tate hung up and left Holly dangling on the other end of the line.

FIVE
2004

Long before the advent of Head Start programs, Tate Marlowe had Lee Lou. The oldest by two and a half years, Lee Lou started kindergarten about the same time Tate began to run without falling down. Up until that time, the two had been inseparable, spending their days playing with dolls, making up games to keep themselves entertained and roaming about their thinly populated neighborhood looking for pretty rocks and shiny objects.

Lee Lou adhered closely to the rules set out by their mother. No exploring in the woods behind the tiny house where they lived; no crossing of streets, though the only street they knew about was the narrow one bordering their front yard and it carried very little traffic; no playing with the cooking stove or leaving the refrigerator door open; no taking

27

food without permission; no noise when Mommy is sleeping; no bothering Daddy when he comes home from work . . .

Keeping track of all the rules fell to Lee Lou and breaking them fell to Tate. This proved to be a full-time job for both of them.

"Stop that, Tate!"

Tate sat on the floor in front of the cabinet in the cramped living room, methodically removing all the contents and surrounding herself with them. "No!"

"I'll get in trouble!" Lee Lou began picking up the folded doilies and table scarves her mother had ironed and put away the previous day.

Tate grabbed a crocheted doily and placed it on her head. "Me pretty!"

"You're bad!" Lee Lou shook her finger in Tate's face.

"Me not bad. Me pretty!" Tears started rolling down Tate's cheeks and just before she began wailing, Lee Lou clamped her hand over Tate's mouth.

"Mommy's sleeping. Be quiet!" Lee Lou hissed the command and physically dragged Tate out of the house and down the front steps across the yard to the edge of the lawn where she made Tate sit.

Once there, Lee Lou let go and Tate sat sobbing on the sidewalk. "You can't wake Mommy up! You know that."

"I want Mommy!"

"You got me." Lee Lou plopped herself down on the bottom step, folded her arms over her knees and rested her head on them.

Tate's sobbing quickly subsided to sniffling when she realized she no longer sat in the center of Lee Lou's attention. She closed her hand into a tiny fist and began sucking on her knuckle, tears still streaming down her face. Lee Lou did not respond.

"Lee Lou?"

"Leave me alone, Tate."

"Lee Lou love me?"

"I love you, Tate, but leave me alone a minute, will ya?"

Now on full alert, Tate walked over and wrapped her little arms around her sister, resting her cheek against Lee Lou's bowed head. "Don't cry, Lee Lou." Tate patted her sister's back and began slowly rocking.

Tate learned much from Lee Lou—not just rule-following and compassion, sadness, responsibility, forgiveness, nurturing—but also how to survive in a world with parents whose best efforts to care for her fell far short of what she needed. In a world like that, sisters take care of sisters as best they can.

At the hands of Lee Lou, Tate gained something equally as valuable as the survival skills that buoyed her through childhood. She mastered the fundamentals of education—numbers, letters, shapes, colors, words—long before the time came for her to attend school herself.

All this occurred because Lee Lou hated school. Basically a shy child, she preferred sitting at the desks in the back of the classroom. She never volunteered to answer questions posed by the teacher. When called on unexpectedly, she felt embarrassed and became tongue-tied.

Lee Lou's main problem with school, however, lay in the fact that she found it supremely boring.

At home she had access to the whole world through the magazines her mother bought on subscription. Each week, a new one arrived in the mailbox. Lee Lou preferred LOOK or LIFE to Ladies' Home Journal because they had the best pictures, and she quickly took to losing herself in the magazines long before she herself could read.

As Lee Lou flipped through the pictures, she made up stories for herself and Tate about what she saw. Lee Lou's imagination allowed her to soar beyond the confines of her small world into exotic places with strange animals and vast horizons, and always she was safe there in the world of her own making. So sitting in a kindergarten class hearing about Jack and Jill getting hurt while running up a little hill seemed a silly waste of her time.

Obviously, school was important. Everyone told Lee Lou so and she believed them. She tried hard to pay attention in class, but when her mind wandered, the teachers reprimanded her and she drew even farther into her shell of embarrassment. Her mother scolded her for the Cs and Ds on her report card, so Lee Lou attempted to apply herself even more. The message about the importance of education sunk in, and she figured if it was that important for her, then it must be valuable for Tate as well.

Since no avenue of escape from school presented itself to Lee Lou, she decided to do the next best thing. Each day she trudged home with her assignments in her notebook. She spread the homework out on the floor and insisted that Tate sit and study with her. Tate proved to be an unwilling student, however. Unaware that a child of 2 and 1/2 years lacks the cognitive development of a 5 year old, Lee Lou took Tate's immaturity as stubbornness. Nonetheless, she remained determined to teach Tate. This pursuit required creativity on Lee Lou's part, and she possessed that in abundance. Each lesson became a game in Lee Lou's hands and she played those games with Tate.

Tate remembered big block letters and numbers printed on colored construction paper. Lee Lou taught her to turn those letters into words, like putting a puzzle together. A-T-C became "cat," O-D-G became "dog," and L-L-B-A became "ball." Numbers could be used to count, or to add and subtract. Tate steadily developed the skill to put those pieces of brightly colored paper in the necessary order to make the correct answer to whatever question Lee Lou presented. Tate learned to draw the letters and numbers herself and to keep them on the lines of the paper Lee Lou used for her lessons. It wasn't easy for either of them, but with Lee Lou's persistence and Tate's growing willingness, Tate learned to read, write, add and subtract.

By the time she entered kindergarten, Tate could produce the work expected of a second-grader. She carried this advantage with her throughout her school life. She learned effortlessly in most cases, and when something proved more difficult, her curiosity usually kicked in and she dedicated herself to learning what was being taught. Every challenge became a puzzle for Tate, an invitation to dig in and figure out the answer. It could be a mathematical

SIX
1927

Harland Freeman waited for his opportunity. It materialized on a Thursday afternoon at the end of English class. Ellie Vance rose from her desk at the final bell, knocking her books onto the floor.

———

Mortified, Ellie stooped to pick up her books just as Harlan Freeman approached. Their eyes met as he reached down to help.

Ellie couldn't help it. She actually swooned for a moment—not enough for Harland to notice, she thought, but she recognized the swoon for what it was, and she felt both excitement and shame.

He's out of my league. Of all the thoughts running through Ellie's mind, this one stood out. With only one disappointing date under her belt during her entire high school experience thus far, she knew most boys fit in that category. Harland Freeman and boys like him most definitely did not give Ellie Vance and girls like her a passing glance. But in that moment she allowed herself the dream as he held her gaze, looking deep into her, it seemed.

"Let me help, Ellie," Harland boomed. When Harland spoke, he never did so quietly, never did so with any indication that what he said varied at all from exactly the right thing to say at the moment.

"It . . . it's okay, Harland. Uh, don't bother . . ." Ellie couldn't control her stammering. Dark and deep, Harland's eyes seemed to convey something Ellie had not seen before—the hint of interest she so often hoped for from boys but never felt. Confusion clouded her thoughts. Harland Freeman could not possibly be interested in her, could he?

"Gotta' run. I'm late for practice!" he bellowed as he dropped her books into her arms. "See ya later!"

Ellie's heart raced a bit when she heard that. *See ya later. Does he mean that? No, of course not—just something to say.* But as she gathered her books and herself back together, she felt a little glimmer of hope building deep inside her.

Apparently Harland did mean it. Two days later, he approached her as she stood at her locker at the end of the day.

"Hey, Ellie!" That booming voice again, this time calling out to her. "I'll walk with you, okay?"

"Uh, okay, uh . . . sure." Ellie faltered as she took in the full force of Harland's dark eyes looking squarely at her. "I'm just going home."

"Okay," he said. "Let's go through the park." He nonchalantly took her books and headed toward the door. Ellie followed, half a step behind at first, amazed that she, Ellie Vance, had him, Harland Freeman, for an escort.

As they left the school building, Harland called out to some of his friends who stood in a huddle under the trees at the entrance. He waved brightly. Ellie felt very proud in his company and to be shown off to his friends like that. She barely registered the smirks on their faces as she and Harland passed.

Harland strolled through the park with her. She remained in disbelief that he found her interesting, but he jabbered away as they walked along, and Ellie let herself feel the warmth of his presence flowing over her.

"I've been noticing you for a while, Ellie," he said as he looped her hand around his elbow. The slightest touch from him sent delicious, unfamiliar chills through her body and she longed for more. Though Ellie continued to glow after his announcement, he said little more about her.

The rest of his chatter was about himself—about the current baseball season and his team's chance of taking the championship; about what he had planned for himself after graduation, what he would become in the future. Maybe business, perhaps politics . . . but whatever path he chose, Harland Freeman seemed sure a wonderful life awaited him.

Ellie preferred to believe he shared all this with her because he wanted her to be a part of it. Thrilled, scared and tongue-tied, she had lots of questions for him, but none of them would form fully enough for her to ask. She answered most of them for herself anyway, at least her version of what life as Harland Freeman's girlfriend—maybe even his wife!—would be like. Ellie and Harland living happily with plenty of friends, all of whom celebrated their love along with them. The years of their life unfolding, filled with stories about how they met, how they watched each other from afar before finally becoming a couple, how they dated and courted and fell in love and . . .

But Ellie knew she was getting ahead of herself. In this moment, she enjoyed just walking through the park with Harland Freeman, listening to him talk, soaking up the warm sunshine and cool breeze on her skin. When he asked her to sit with him for a while, she believed this moment would stretch into a lifetime.

They sat under a huge old tree for an hour, Harland talking about himself and his dreams, Ellie captivated and silent, drinking in the essence of him and imagining her life with him. He finally wound down and walked with her the rest of the way home.

"See ya later," he said. No promises. No requests. But Ellie had heard that from Harland before, and he had, in fact, come back to see her later. He would this time, too. She held tightly to her fragile certainty as she watched him depart.

And the next day, her optimism proved to be correct. "How 'bout we get together after practice, Ellie?" he asked as they passed in the hall.

"Yes, of course, I'd love to." She beamed back at him, aware of the curious glances from nearby classmates.

"Great! Meet me in the park, okay? Under our tree? About six o'clock?" His dark eyes sparkling, he smiled that smile of his, the one with all the teeth showing, the one that set her heart to racing.

"Yes! See you then!" Ellie barely contained her excitement. She and Harland Freeman meeting for an evening together—almost a date! Ellie Vance had an almost date with Harland Freeman!

She arrived at the designated spot in the park right on time. All primped and preened, she looked as pretty as she possibly could. She wore her best dress. Not her fancy dress, but her very best everyday dress. She had touched Lily of the Valley perfume behind both ears and between her tiny breasts. Not that Harland would notice, but she wanted to be the best Ellie she could be for their first date.

Harland bounded into the park almost fifteen minutes late. Nearly frantic by the time she saw him taking the steps two at a time, she heard his reassuring apology and melted a bit.

"So sorry, practice ran late. Coach is putting me in first string! Can you believe it? First string! Just in time for the big game! Johnny sprained an ankle in practice today. Damn sad luck for Johnny, but damn good luck for me! I may be the luckiest man in town just now!" he said, and then he leaned down and gave Ellie the first passionate kiss of her life.

She burst into tears. All her dreams flooded into view. Even for an optimist like Ellie, this turn of affairs seemed almost beyond belief. It transported her to a new place, and all her hesitations and worries melted. This boy—this man—mesmerized her! Harland, a real man who loved her! Euphoria engulfed her.

Harland quickly spread out the blanket he had tucked under his arm and pulled Ellie onto it. He wrapped his arms around her and kissed her deeply. She responded in kind. She did not know where her passion came from. She had not experienced it before, but she went with it. She explored his body with her hands, just as he explored hers. She pushed into him when he pulled her closer, and when he rolled on top of her, she surrendered to his insistent hands and mouth.

As the sun slowly descended in the western sky, the shadows deepened under the spreading tree where Ellie and Harland were locked in embrace. Ellie lost all sense of time, all sense of the world around her, all sense of herself except for the captivating, all-encompassing, unrelenting passion she felt for Harland Freeman. When he moved his hand to her thigh and then up a bit higher, Ellie felt her own warm wetness. Terror gripped her, then quickly passed as she felt the delicious waves of . . . what? Nothing she had felt before, but she somehow knew it . . . sexual passion, lust. Unavoidable. Different from romance, more powerful, more dangerous, more luscious, more unforgiving. But she went with it, she went with Harland all the way to where he wanted to go and when he finished, she lay back dazed and exhausted.

Harland rolled off her and laughed out loud. He laughed boisterously. He brushed his hair back off his sweating forehead with a hand rake and let out a deep, audible sigh. He patted Ellie's hand before reaching down to zip up his pants.

"Ellie, my dear, that was quite something!" he said, the jovial tone still evident in his voice. "Quite something, indeed!"

Ellie tried to bring herself back to the moment. Her body still quivered from the tension that had built while Harland gratified himself with her. Ecstasy, not satisfaction. Although confused, she recognized the difference. She wanted more, and shame for her desire filled her. Shame for that and for having done what she had just done with Harland Freeman. She tried to reassure herself. Harland loved her, and their happy life together awaited. He must love her or he would not have wanted her or taken her the way he just had.

"Oh, Harland, that was so . . ."

"Yeah, great!" Harland got up and began tucking in his shirt and straightening himself up. He reached for Ellie and pulled her upright too as she hurriedly put herself and her own clothes back in order. He gave her a quick embrace, picked up the blanket and said, "You can get back home okay, can't you? I have to go." A self-satisfied smile formed on his handsome face, but it did not invite Ellie in.

"I, well, I . . ." Confusion reigned. Didn't they have so much to talk about? Surely he wanted to stay with her as long as possible.

And then she returned abruptly and fully back to the moment. Her body still reverberated from the encounter, but her mind returned to sharp focus and awareness. The romance and mystery of Harland

Freeman evaporated, and Ellie knew what had *really* just happened. Her stomach turned and she thought for a moment she would throw up.

"Yes, well, I . . . yes. I'm fine, Harland." Ellie said this with conviction as she gathered herself up emotionally just as she had done in the past when something bad happened. She closed down the festering passion that clawed at her, shut off her dreams of the future with Harland and set about solving the problem of how to forget about him entirely.

Some problems simply cannot be solved, but Ellie didn't know that yet.

"Okay, see ya around." Harland threw a casual wave in her direction.

Ellie watched as he turned away and headed back up the path to the street, using not his normal walking gait but that swagger she had witnessed occasionally from boys who had just faced and won some kind of challenge.

Harland's words echoed through Ellie's mind. She knew exactly what the difference in his choice of words meant. "See ya around." Not "See ya later." Ellie quelled her tears, set her shoulders straight and walked herself home.

—⁓—

The following days tortured Ellie. She did not expect to see Harland except in passing in the halls. She did not expect that he would seek her out or give her the wide-mouthed, all-teeth-showing smile, or that he would gaze at her again with a sparkle in his deep, dark eyes. But even though she did not expect anything at all from him, it still shocked her when she overheard him bragging to his friends.

"Even easier than I thought! Just a walk through the park, a little bit of talking . . ." When she heard the sniggering and congratulations of Harland's friends, she ran to the bathroom to throw up again.

Strong and resilient, Ellie knew she could hide her shame. She could go about her life in a fairly normal fashion, keep her grades up and spend time with her family and friends. She could move past feeling like Harland's Conquest and get back to feeling like Almost-pretty Ellie Vance who had plenty going for her in other ways. Under most circumstances, Ellie knew she could still live a happy life.

But Ellie soon realized normal circumstances had finally escaped her. She did not have the luxury of time to mend from the damage done to her by Harland Freeman and her own damn optimism.

Ellie was pregnant. Ellie Vance needed a husband, and she needed a husband now.

SEVEN
2004

Cally wanted to go home. She sat in the snarl of Los Angeles traffic, headed to a meeting that could catapult her even farther up the corporate ladder, and she wanted nothing more than to turn around and go home.

A reluctant success. That's how she thought of herself. She had fallen into her career by accident, starting out as a receptionist in a prestigious LA public relations firm right after she graduated from college. The job allowed her to pay the bills while she cast around for something she really wanted to do. Over twenty-five years later she found herself at the same firm with a fancy title, a coveted corner office and a reputation as a driven powerhouse with ethics.

Ethics were not a requirement for a good publicist, but Cally placed personal integrity at the top of her list of the Ten Most Important Things in Life. Depending on her mood, her circumstances and the angle of the moon, her list changed with some regularity, but integrity never drifted from the top, always followed closely by honesty and dependability.

Cally showed up for other people. Whether they recognized it or not, beneath her fierce precision and demand for excellence, she cared deeply about people. She put her own needs after the needs of her clients and the company more of the time than she cared to admit to herself or to anyone else.

But it was all catching up to her. She questioned whether she wanted the recognition and the added responsibility that would come from seeing the name of the firm changed to include her. Pearson, Graystone and Thornton. It had a ring to it, but the price would be high and Cally was really, really tired. She would talk to Laurel tonight. Maybe they could clear their schedules enough to take some time in the mountains. *That would be good.* She inched along in traffic. *That may be just the right thing.*

———∿∿∿———

"We should take a vacation," Cally announced later at dinner.

"We were just on vacation." Laurel seemed preoccupied. Cally noticed how she avoided eye contact and how her usual radiant smile was gone.

"I know, but I've been feeling really tired lately, and I was thinking maybe we could go to the mountains. It would be rejuvenating." Cally watched as Laurel pushed the food around on her plate.

Something's up. And I don't want to know what. The thought had barely formed when Laurel began speaking again.

"I don't think I can do that, Cally."

"You can finagle it, Laurel. I know you can get the time off one way or another. It would just be for a long weekend. The Tetons are beautiful this time of year." Panic caught Cally unaware and she started second guessing herself: *The Tetons are beautiful any time of the year, but it's November. It will be too cold and too wet. Maybe they'll be shrouded in clouds and fog . . .*

"Cally, this isn't working." Laurel let out her breath in a long sigh.

"What isn't working?" Cally stalled. She knew exactly what Laurel was talking about. This discussion had occurred at least four times in the two years since Laurel had moved in with her.

"This. Us." No elaboration needed.

"Laurel, we'll get through it. We always do. Some time in the mountains would help." Cally looked around as she said this, willfully pulling away from the painful conversation.

She scanned the beautiful condominium, now much nicer than it had ever been when Cally lived there alone. Laurel's sense of style had turned a plain box done in neutral colors and bland furniture into a rich tapestry of color and texture. Cally loved the change, and though other areas of their relationship had never blossomed with the same vibrancy as their home, Cally was comfortable with Laurel. They had a good life together.

"Not this time," Laurel said. "I'm leaving."

Cally refocused. Her mind revved into overdrive and her body stilled. She felt a creeping sensation, as if being slowly encased in ice, starting at the top of her head and moving down over her face, to her shoulders, her heart, her stomach, all the way to the tips of her fingers and her toes. She felt like she was going to freeze to death.

I have to do something. There's time. I've got to do something!

But she couldn't move. Fear always had this effect on Cally. First, the dreadful, freezing immobilization and racing thoughts. Then decisive action when she kicked into gear and took charge of everything around her, hyperalert to all the details.

The iciness suddenly lifted, and Cally didn't waste a second. "That's ridiculous, Laurel," she said. *I wish I could say please, please don't leave. I love you so much.*

Laurel's face hardened and her neck flushed. Her eyes flashed rage and Cally realized the magnitude of her mistake.

"Really? Ridiculous? It's ridiculous I would leave you, or it's ridiculous I would want to be happy? Which is ridiculous, Cally?"

"I didn't mean it that way, Laurel, honestly." Cally tried to back-pedal. "I meant we shouldn't . . . give up. We have a good foundation. We shouldn't give it all up."

"I'm not giving up, Cally. I'm moving on." Laurel's anger disappeared, quickly replaced with resolve.

Cally continued to fight the inevitable. "What does that mean, Laurel? How is leaving not giving up?"

"I'm not going to get sucked into one of your philosophical discussions, Cally. This isn't a matter of semantics."

Laurel's strength is beautiful. Cally's love for this woman surged to the surface of her awareness. "You're incredibly beautiful!" Cally blurted this out before she could stop herself.

"What? You are a piece of work, Cally."

"Okay, wait . . ." Cally tried to regain some control. "What I meant was . . ."

At that precise moment, something extraordinary happened. A vast hollow space opened inside Cally's body and from within it came a clear voice. "MAKE THE CHANGE NOW." The words filled her, shaking loose all her ingrained beliefs and creating a new internal landscape. Suddenly she saw everything from a different perspective.

She didn't like the thought of losing Laurel, but Laurel herself was not the issue. Laurel represented what sat at the core of Cally's longing. She represented home and belonging. She represented a resting place, a place of nurture and safety where Cally might someday feel at peace.

It's all my imagination. That's all it is. Cally recognized the past two years as her desperate attempt to fabricate something special with Laurel. Regardless of her wishes and her effort it had never existed with Laurel or any partner she had ever been with. She had experienced what she craved so strongly only once in her life a long time ago in another place, and she knew in that instant she wanted to go home. Nothing else mattered, regardless of what she would find there.

"You're right, Laurel." Cally realized how easy this acknowledgment had become.

Laurel saw the softening, the coming to resolution sweeping over Cally like a warm breeze.

"That's the Cally I fell in love with," she whispered as tears filled her eyes.

Cally knew she had changed since she and Laurel first met. She used to be soft, accessible, and responsive to all the nuances of the new romance. They had played together, spent long hours talking about important and inconsequential things, walking in the woods, lying on the beach, dining in quaint restaurants and taking long drives up and down the coast. But their life together had slowly changed. They had fallen into the comfortable trap of a familiar routine. The magical sex which had drawn them together originally had become a rare occurrence. Cally knew Laurel longed for the missing passion and suspected that as much as she loved Cally, she believed she had to leave in order to open that door again. Cally also knew the truth of Laurel's conviction. The passion between them would never reignite.

"You're right." Cally looked at the woman she loved and knew the end of their relationship was really a good thing, for both of them. "When are you leaving?"

"I've rented a place in Venice. I'm taking time off work and I'll be out by the end of the week."

Leaving Los Angeles had been surprisingly easy. Laurel's move proved uneventful once the initial drama of the break-up passed. They told their friends. Cally helped with the packing and liked the cute apartment on the beach Laurel had found for herself. They would remain friends, which pleased Cally greatly. When she returned to the condo alone, relief filled her. She had the place to herself once again. Now she could move on, too.

The next day she asked for a sabbatical. Pearson and Graystone were both shocked, each believing Cally, a publicity dynamo, had no life outside of the office. They reconsidered their plans to include her as a partner, and after some wrangling through the details, Cally left with the promise she could return to her job in three months. Her huge bank of accrued sick and vacation time ensured she would receive full pay for more than two months. Cally had a sizable retirement fund as well as cash savings and a fluid portfolio of stocks and bonds that earned dividends in up markets and down markets alike, so the continuing paycheck seemed like a bonus for taking care of herself, maybe for the first time in her life.

She packed some clothes and personal items into the Subaru Outback and headed east. Now, two weeks later, she could almost touch home. She had taken the scenic route. She stopped wherever she pleased along the way—small towns with not much to offer, hot spots like Sante Fe, Albuquerque and the Grand Canyon. A few days in Sedona had been plenty for her and left her wondering why so many people seemed to think of it as a mecca. The red hills seemed burnt with little of anything green to be seen. Once she hit the long, dusty, hot stretch of interstate highway through Texas and Oklahoma, she interspersed her favorite music with long periods of quiet time and only essential stops for gas, food and sleep. The trip gave her plenty of time to think, to dream, to reconcile and to sort out her life.

She found the rolling green Ozark Mountains soothing after the long flat stretch through the plains. She took a detour to Hot Springs on her way through Arkansas and knew she would return someday to explore the town in depth. History fascinated Cally, and the little town had plenty of it to offer.

The urge to rush to her destination and the desire to meander through the mountains competed for control of the trip. Cally did a little of both, pushing hard one day, poking around the next, steadily working her way east. When she reached the Tennessee/North Carolina border, her pulse grew faster and getting to Asheville as quickly as possible won out. The exit to Harmon Den beckoned strongly, but she kept driving. Her great-great-grandmother's maiden name, on her father's side, was Harmon. She wondered if long-lost relatives lived in Harmon Den. *I'll have to go back there, too.* And she pressed on.

She reached the Pigeon River Gorge at dusk. Here I-40 snakes through the mountains along steep inclines and declines, forcing traffic to slow down. No more cruise control along straight flat stretches for hours. Instead, every curve offers a new vista, each tunnel opens to the unparalleled beauty of the undulating Great Smoky Mountains. The curvy highway becomes narrow with retaining walls on both sides in places, producing the sensation of sliding through a long chute. Patches of light fog softened everything— sound, light, even the pavement it seemed to Cally.

She turned off the air conditioner, opened all the windows and breathed in the wet, heavy air, filling her lungs with the freshness of the muted emerald mountains. Huge plumes of fog rose like smoke from the valleys around her, stretching into an evening sky streaked with bands of gold, pink and purple.

She had yearned for these mountains ever since being taken from them as a child. She knew now all the vacations to the western and European mountains over the years had been attempts to go home, but only these soft, ancient, voluptuous, rolling green mountains filled the longing in her soul.

Knowing she would arrive in Asheville within a day, she had made reservations the night before at the Princess Hotel. She found her way there and checked in, noticing as she did the magnificent wooden mantel in the sitting room and the welcoming fire burning in the hearth.

EIGHT
2004

A few hours after Tate's early morning call to Holly, the two of them sat at a small table inside Heiwa Shokudo, a trendy Japanese restaurant on North Lexington Avenue.

Tate never let much time pass between thoughts, really no time at all; that's just the way her mind worked, leaping from point to point, and all of it making sense to her. But she had trained herself with great effort to slow down while talking to others, even if she could not help but think way ahead of the actual conversation. So she stopped after telling Holly about the doors on her house and the one on Chestnut and waited for a response.

"What do you mean, it's the same door as the one on your house?" Holly asked.

She thinks I'm crazy, Tate thought. *She thinks I'm just going off on another tangent, pursuing yet another crazy idea I've gotten into my head. But that's not the case. There really is something here, something unusual about those doors. I know it. It's so obvious. It should be obvious to her, too.*

But she said: "You know that fancy door on the house I'm renovating—the size of it, the scroll around the panels, the hardware on it?" She could barely contain her excitement. "Well, this old house on Chestnut Street has a door very much like it. It has the two panels, the scrolls, different hardware, but they are very close to the same in a lot of ways."

Tate finished and sat back, careful not to say everything she thought about what this find might mean.

"Oh," said Holly, "now I get it. You think there's a connection. That's interesting."

"You think I'm crazy, right?" Tate asked, bracing for the answer.

"You're kidding, right?" Holly asked, puzzled. She saw the veil drop just behind Tate's eyes. "I mean about being crazy, not about the door."

"No, I'm not kidding . . ." Tate saw the perplexed look on Holly's face. ". . . about either," she added.

They looked at each other and burst out laughing at the same moment, Tate with her full, body-slam laugh that turned the heads of the other customers in the restaurant, Holly with her fluttering, closed-mouth twitter that radiated love and enveloped Tate in cottony comfort. They laughed until tears ran down their cheeks.

"You are a bit of a nut case, Tate, but you certainly are not crazy. Tell me more about the doors."

As they ate lunch, Tate told Holly everything she thought about the meaning of the doors on the two vastly different houses and Holly shared what she had discovered about the history of the house on Chestnut.

The place had only two owners on file in the tax records. The first, a man named Harland Freeman, apparently had it built in 1940. The current owner, a living trust created in January 1942 for the benefit of Leland Samuel Howard, had taken possession less than two years later.

On her way home, Tate pondered several questions. *What happened to Harland? Why had he owned the house for only two years? Why did it sit vacant and deteriorating? Who, if anyone, was looking after the place? Who is Leland Howard?* These questions ran helter-skelter through Tate's mind, totally preoccupying her and culminating in a massive headache.

Tate enjoyed few things more than an afternoon nap, and a headache like this one provided a perfect excuse. The warm weather allowed her to open the windows in the bedroom, flooding it with sunlight and a fresh breeze. She dropped onto her bed, quickly sinking into a state of deep physical relaxation. But her mind kept working, as it often did during sleep, and she awoke an hour later with Pocket snoozing in the crook of her arm and a plan of action.

Her work in the following days left Tate feeling hectic and exhilarated. She managed to keep tabs on Dave who made slow-but-steady progress on the renovation project next door, but she spent most of her time at the public library on Haywood Street and in the archives of the *Asheville Citizen-Times,* searching for information about Harland Freeman and Leland Howard.

She found minimal, but shocking tidbits. Harland Freeman had committed suicide at his home at 305 Chestnut Street on February 13, 1942. She uncovered only three references for Leland Howard. Two of them mentioned him in passing as a craftsman of note engaged by wealthy Ashevilleans when building their stately mansions. In the third, he appeared as the husband of the deceased, one Marie Eleanor Howard, the victim of a vicious beating in her own home in 1965.

These revelations stunned Tate. The odds that one house had connections to two sensational deaths seemed unbelievable. Far from answering her questions, what she learned only generated new ones, and she became even more determined to uncover the full story of the deteriorating beauty that had ignited her curiosity.

NINE
1927

Ellie's pregnancy put an end to all her girlhood fantasies. She could not finish school and move to New York to find fame and fortune the way she had dreamed for years. Instead, she would get married, have a child, make a life here in Asheville. Several aspects of her new plan plagued her, but finding a husband took top priority.

This problem occupied her totally in the face of her looming pregnancy. She walked through her life, attending classes and dispensing Coca-Cola at the soda fountain at Woolworth's where she worked part-time after school, but all of it she did in a fog.

One afternoon, as she walked to her locker, head down, deep in thought, she ran right into Leland Howard. Shocked, they both tumbled to the floor in a heap.

"I'm so sorry, so sorry," blurted Ellie as she scrambled to her feet.

"Uh . . . uh . . . oh . . . excuse me." Leland could barely speak. "My fault . . ."

"No. No. Totally my fault. I'm so sorry." Ellie's mind raced. She knew Leland, but they traveled in different social circles. A senior like Harland, Leland's demeanor tended toward quiet, even shy. Studious and always in the background, Ellie and the rest of the girls rarely noticed him. Now Ellie looked at him closely as they both got back to their feet.

Leland had a country-boy way about him, which Ellie found oddly attractive. She studied him carefully. *Only a few inches taller than me, but that will have to do.* A full head of light brown hair hung straight and shiny around his kind face. His worn clothes fit him well, and Ellie noticed his strong arms and weathered hands. Leland Howard did not constitute good boyfriend material, but he definitely made good husband material.

"You're Leland Howard, right?" Ellie put on her come-hither smile and tilted her chin down a bit so that she looked up at Leland through her long eyelashes.

"Uh, yes . . ." The fact that Ellie knew his name came as a surprise to Leland.

"Well, Leland Howard, I think I owe you an apology. How about you walk with me to Woolworth's after school and I'll treat you to a Coca-Cola?"

"You don't have to . . ." Leland broke into a fine sweat.

"Oh, but I want to! Please say you will."

"Uh, okay, but . . ." Leland's face flushed, and his breathing became shallow. He seemed to focus intently. "But, are you sure you want to . . . ?"

"Why, of course I'm sure, Leland. I'll see you then."

———

Leland stared after Ellie as she sashayed away, his heart pounding rapidly. The girl he had had a silent crush on for two years had literally knocked him off his feet and asked him out. He refused to let disbelief quell his excitement.

———

Ellie courted Leland with enthusiasm and determination. In a matter of days she seduced him into making love to her, not that it took a lot of urging. For Leland, however, intimacy at that level constituted a sacred act, and it confirmed what he had known since he had laid eyes on Ellie the very first time. He loved her. He loved her with his heart, his soul, every single part of his being. The unexpected news of her pregnancy filled him with happiness. How could she know so quickly? That question puzzled him, but his awareness of his overwhelming good fortune at having found his soul mate banished his doubt to the deepest corners of his mind.

Marie Eleanor Vance and Leland Samuel Howard married in a small ceremony in Ellie's backyard on the Saturday after Leland graduated. Seven months and three days later, she gave birth to their first and only child.

TEN
1939

This will do very nicely, thought Harland Freeman as he surveyed the plot of land in front of him.

His house—no, his masterpiece—would perch at the top of the rise. The hill would need to be cut back a bit and supported with a retaining wall of fieldstone. Little jewels would adorn the ledge at the top of the wall. Not jewels actually, but the drops of cobalt and sea green and silvery gray glass he imagined would be a nice addition to the natural colors of the stone.

The steps up from the street would have to be shallow, not as deep as those of the other houses in the neighborhood. He detested having to walk up steep steps. It just seemed wrong to him that one should have to suffer through physical strain before entering the elegant edifice he planned to build. He wanted all of his visitors, and he expected there would be many, to enter gracefully, a befitting introduction to the soirées he would host.

Harland Freeman did not enjoy popularity in town, but he was an important man. A pompous man who put great stock in appearing to be in control of all aspects of his life, he kept secret his disappointment about how things had turned out for him.

Well, this house would finally seal his position among Asheville's business elite. They would no longer be able to snigger behind his back, wondering when he would make some fatal error that would land him in bankruptcy, put him out of business and make it possible for them to get away with publicly deriding him. Maybe they didn't like him, but they would have to respect him once he built his house. They would attend his parties and thank him graciously for having been invited, and they would hide any contempt they had for him behind their smiles and friendly chatter. He would see to that. The shame he harbored for the place he had grown up, only blocks away, would finally be dispelled by the house he planned to build here.

Childhood memories always made Harland feel sick. Now, even while envisioning his new home sitting atop the sloped hill, his stomach churned as images pushed to the surface of an old shanty on a junk-filled patch of land at the edge of Stumptown. And he remembered Mazie. Mazie, who had saved his life in more ways than one. Mazie, whom he loved and hated in equal amounts. Mazie who these days crossed the street rather than speak to him.

Mazie gathered her apron in her hands and stepped into the morning sun splashing across her small stoop. She breathed in the fresh, wet air. Dew glistened on the small plants pushing their way through the damp earth in her small garden, and her chickens clucked and pranced in their hutch beside the house.

"Thank you, Lord, for this beautiful morning." She started and ended every day in the same way—giving thanks for what she had and asking the Lord to watch over her and hers. "I don't ask for much, Lord, just enough to feed my family, a warm place for us to sleep, my loved ones to come home safe and the chance to do your work here on Earth."

Depending on how one defined God's work, Mazie had plenty of it to do. She kept her own house, tended to the needs of her family and also worked in the homes of the rich folks in Montford who sought her out, in particular for her cooking. Her exceptional skill with everything from roast beef to apple raspberry pie gave Mazie more freedom than most of the women in Stumptown who worked from dawn to dusk cleaning, washing, ironing, scrubbing floors and doing any other task assigned to them by their employers.

Two families employed Mazie, both of them within a mile of her small place in Stumptown. Every day but Sunday she went to the Milners' in the late morning where she prepared lunch and put dinner on, to be finished and served by the kitchen maid. She then walked three blocks to the Raskins' to prepare their dinner, the leftovers of which would be used for the next day's lunch. When she got home she fed her own family and tended to her daily chores. She filled her mornings before work with feeding the chickens, cooking for her own family and getting her husband off to the mill and her children to school.

Mazie liked her routine. She enjoyed her work and her employers generally treated her well. What she didn't like was surprises. And as she stood on the stoop that morning in the warm sunshine, she spied a surprise coming up the street toward her.

"Well I'll be . . ." She shaded her eyes and squinted to get a better look. "Who's that scrawny little white boy toddlin' up my street?" She walked down the steps as he approached.

Harland had learned to walk only a few months earlier, and he had taken to it quickly. Whenever he got out of the house, he headed off in one direction or another, often wandering around for hours, looking for scraps of food and whatever else he could scavenge until his path crossed his mother's— who did her own roaming—or someone else brought him back home. Today he had meandered into Stumptown and found Mazie. He took one look at her, then walked right up and threw his little arms around her thick calf, hugging her tight and smiling into her dark face.

"Who are you, little boy?" She expected no answer, so surprise caught her again when he spoke.

"Harland hungry!"

"What? My word, chile . . ."

"Hungry!" In fact, Harland was ravenous, but he did not know that word. He knew "hungry" and he repeated it now as he did frequently in his search through the neighborhoods around his home, having learned that saying it often enough would usually result in someone giving him food.

"Okay, chile, let's get you somethin' to eat." Mazie took him inside and sat him down with a chunk of cornbread and two fried eggs, which he gobbled down without chewing.

"More!" he demanded. Mazie saw the fear and desperation in the boy's eyes, and her own filled with tears.

"Well, Lord, you sure done give me a chance to do your work today!" She spoke aloud as she gave Harland another piece of cornbread.

Mazie noticed the dirt and grime covering the boy's body, so she heated up a kettle of water and pulled the tub out from under the stoop. Then she stripped off his dirty pants, tattered shirt and the ragged shoes no longer big enough for his growing feet. She scrubbed him from head to toe and dressed him in clothes and shoes her own sons had outgrown long ago. Once clean, the child's thick, black hair gleamed and his dark eyes no longer showed anxiety.

"Now that's better!"

"Better!" Harland mimicked with a big smile.

Mazie surveyed the boy and wondered what she would do with him next. She had to go to work. She could not be responsible for this stranger. Where did he live? Why was he wandering around Stumptown?

"What you doin' with Crazy Eulah's boy?" Cora Jenkins called from the street.

"This little boy? He come up here looking for food and I give him a bath, too. He was filthy. You know his mama?"

"She live over there on Pearson, in the little shack back off the street behind the piles a junk. He be all over the place looking for food and a little love. He jus' now findin' his way to you?"

"I never did see this boy 'fore he come here this mornin'. I figure he be my God's work for the day!" Mazie laughed and Cora joined in with her rich trill.

"Well, you bes' be sendin' him on home. 'Ventually Crazy Eulah'll come lookin' for him, but no tellin' if that's today, tomorrow or when."

"You mean she let this chile roam 'round on his own? He jus' a baby. Can't be walking more'n a few months."

"Honey, he be wanderin' since he be crawlin'. Crazy Eulah leave him to hisself most the time. And his daddy ain't much better. Weren't for the kindness of strangers, that chile woulda starved or froze to death long time ago. You best fergit about that boy and git on to work."

"I'll be gittin' on to work, but I won't be fergittin' 'bout this chile. Somebody gotta love him, and looks to me like the Lord give me that job."

"Think twice 'fore you decide, Mazie. No way to know where takin' in a little white boy will lead."

Cora's good advice went unheeded. "No chile should have to fend for hisself in this world, not when he barely kin walk or talk. Not when I got a piece a cornbread and a egg to keep him fed, and not when I got arms to give him a hug and a voice to sing him a lullaby."

"Well, then . . ." And Cora walked off, shaking her head as she took one last look at Mazie and Harland.

63

"Come on now, boy. I gotta go to work." Mazie slipped out of her apron, picked up her bag and took the boy's hand. They walked together to the corner of Pearson Drive, and she pointed him in the direction of his house as she turned toward the Milners'.

"No . . ." he said and gripped her hand tightly.

"Yes," Mazie insisted. She loosened his hand and pushed him gently in the direction of home. "Go now." She bent down to give him a hug before motioning him on. He stood and watched as she walked away, huge tears rolling down his gaunt little cheeks.

—∿∿—

Harland found his way through childhood much the same way he had chanced upon Mazie. He rambled around the area surrounding the shack he shared with Eulah and his father, picking up the basics of survival along the way—food, clothing, language, craftiness—and in the process he developed a shrewd comprehension of the world around him.

As he wandered about his ever-expanding territory, Harland met the rich and poor alike. He quickly grasped that scrounging from the first group proved much harder than from the second. Those with plenty held to it tightly while people with little gave what they could freely. Experiencing such stinginess and generosity side by side proved a powerful influence on Harland's forming psyche. Avarice sank its roots in the fertile ground of the child's soul while the generosity of his most impoverished neighbors nurtured his growing body.

64

Harland's relationship with Mazie and her family deepened quickly. His visits became regular, and he grew to understand he need not beg from them. Mazie and her family provided not only food and clothing, but comfort and companionship. As the years passed, he became a regular at their dinner table and often spent hours at the little place, helping Mazie with the garden and chickens.

He would have lived there, gladly. Sometimes she walked with him to the corner on her way to work, and frequently she found him waiting on the same corner or on her stoop when she returned.

"Harland stay," he'd proclaim without budging.

"No, Harland, go home now." Mazie always responded the same way, the firm words coupled with a soft hand brushing back his hair.

"Stay!"

"No. Go home, Harland! I can't have no little white boy sleepin' in this house!" And he would reluctantly leave, only to return the next day.

Only when Harland entered school did he begin to learn the confusing social customs that dictated relationships between blacks and whites. Why could he sit at the dinner table with Mazie and her family but not play with her children in public?

This puzzled him, but even more so, it filled him with shame. He knew intuitively his ability to survive depended upon what people thought of him. How could he not have known about this taboo? Why had no one told him? And what was he to do now? Who would feed him, hug him and care for him if he couldn't go to Mazie?

Just as he had done from infancy, Harland adapted to the new circumstances forced upon him. He grew more secretive about his visits with Mazie and her family. Over time, as he became more autonomous, his visits to Stumptown became less frequent. Although he remained fond of Mazie, he put distance between himself and her. Sometimes he went so far as to pretend not to know her if he encountered her in public.

The critical gaps in Harland's development began to show themselves by his teenage years. Though self-reliant, he was not responsible. He did what he wanted, what he determined to be important based on his immediate needs. He was capable of handling whatever presented itself to him, but he had not developed the ability to think ahead, to plan or prepare for the challenges he would have to face as an adult.

When Eulah began including Stumptown in her daily sojourns, Mazie knew the time had come to teach Harland an important life lesson. She caught him one day as he left the tiny shack for school.

"Harland, we need to talk."

"What? Mazie, what are you doing here?" He looked around furtively.

"You gotta do somethin' about Eulah."

Harland caught his breath and bristled.

"It's none of your business, Mazie. Leave me alone."

"I'll do no such thing, young man. I took you in when you was starvin' and nearly naked. You growed up in my home more'n you did in this place." She glanced over his shoulder at the mess of a place he called home.

His face flushed with shame, Harland tried to cover by puffing himself up and jutting his chin toward her.

"I appreciate all you did for me, Mazie, but I'm a man now . . ."

"And a man has responsibilities, Harland. One a yours is your mother."

"She's not my problem! She never did nothin' for me, and I'm returning the favor!"

"I'm not axin' you to take care of her, Harland. I'm axin' you to take care of your friends in Stumptown, even though you pretend not to know us anymore." Mazie did not try to hide her disappointment. Much as Harland wanted to deny it, the force of Mazie's love held power over him. He felt his determination eroding as she held him in her gaze.

"What do you think I can do about her? She's crazy and you know it. She won't listen to anyone." Rarely did Harland feel helpless, but the idea that Mazie expected him to somehow control Eulah overwhelmed him.

"She's vexin' us all, Harland. She roams through the neighborhood in the middle a the night hollerin' and raisin' a ruckus. I know you can't do nothin' when you in school, or out there on the baseball field, but you gotta' do something to keep her home at night. I ain't wantin' to threaten, but she gonna' get hurt by somebody purdy bad if she don't stop."

For the first time in his life, Harland felt a burden of responsibility for others settling onto his shoulders. Not that he gave a hoot about Eulah. She could wander off into the night and never come back and it would be all the better for him. But he did care about his reputation and what Mazie thought of him. Harland truly owed Mazie his life. If she needed him to do this one thing, he would have to find a way to do it.

"I'll figure somethin' out, Mazie. I'll do my best," he conceded.

"Can't ask no more'n that. Please make sure your best is good 'nuf to let us sleep the night through, Harland."

And even as he resolved to pay his debt of gratitude to Mazie by dealing with his crazy mother, he also decided in the future to rigorously avoid ever owing anything to anyone.

Harland had little time to follow through on his promise. Barely three weeks later, some boys discovered Eulah's body in a patch of woods near the river, dead apparently of natural causes.

Harland was now an orphan, his father having died several years earlier. As the only child, Harland inherited the shanty and the land it sat on—valuable land on the growing edge of Montford. He took his belongings out of the shack, poured a can of kerosene on the floor and tossed a lit match inside as he exited for the final time. The place had burned to the ground before the fire department arrived.

There were questions about the fire, of course. No more than a superficial investigation, but still he had to talk to the inspectors. He stuck closely to the simple story he put together as he waited for the fire to be extinguished.

"I was trying to light the old kerosene lamp."

"When I struck the match, I knocked the lamp over and everything went up in flames."

"Don't know why I didn't get burned. Just lucky I guess."

"I jumped out of the way. I'm an athlete, you know. I can move fast and I did this time, that's for sure."

Eventually they left him alone sitting outside the smoldering ruins. He breathed in the acrid smoke, a smug, self-satisfied grin curling the corners of his mouth.

"Such a shame! That boy lost his mother and his house all at the same time." The sentiment echoed through town, voiced with a thinly disguised suggestion that it wasn't a shame at all.

Harland buried Eulah and, he hoped, his childhood with her. He was sixteen years old. He had a job at the hardware store downtown and friends he could stay with until he figured out his next move. That move, when it came, proved a major turning point in his life.

———

"You're Harland Freeman, aren't you son?" The well-dressed man asking the question had stopped Harland as he left work one day. "Didn't your mama die and your house over there on Pearson burn down a couple of weeks ago?"

Why is Mr. Howell interested in me? How come he knows so much about me? Harland should have been aware that everyone in town knew about him now—not only his name and where he worked, but many tidbits about his life before he became the talk of the town. Harland knew Mr. Howell owned the shop two blocks up from the hardware store. He had accumulated a sizable fortune as one of Asheville's most successful businessmen.

"Yes, that's me." Harland knew he would get more from Mr. Howell by placing the burden of the conversation on him rather than offering too much.

"Well I hope you're doing okay, son. Everyone has been pretty worried about you."

"Really? Why?"

This unexpected question put Mr. Howell on the spot.

"Well, you've got no family, and we just . . . we . . . we've been concerned."

"I'm fine. Thanks for asking, Mr. Howell." Harland flashed a big smile in the man's direction, a real sincere-looking expression, before turning to leave.

"Just a minute, son." The use of "son" annoyed Harland, but it also alerted him to the presence of an ulterior motive behind this seemingly friendly exchange with an influential man who had never spoken to him before.

"Yes?" And Harland waited.

"That land of yours has to be cleaned up, you know. Have you made plans to get it done?"

This caught Harland off guard. So glad to be rid of Eulah and the decrepit house, it hadn't occurred to him he had ongoing responsibility for the land. Unfortunately, not everything had burned, and huge piles of junk still filled the otherwise-empty lot.

"I haven't decided yet what I'll do with it." No hint of the discomfort he felt inside.

"You probably don't have much use for it, and it'll cost a good bit to clean it up. Don't suppose you have any money for that do you?"

"Well, I'm looking into a few things . . ." Harland lied.

"You know, I could take care of it for you. Buy the land and clean it up so you could get on with your life and not be bothered with it."

So that's it. Excitement quickly replaced the dread he had been feeling moments before. Mr. Howell's offer to buy the land came out of nowhere, and Harland's shrewdness kicked in immediately.

"Really? That might be good." Harland flashed the smile again.

"It's not worth much, of course. I could give you $300 for it."

"It's a big piece of land, I think, Mr. Howell. I'll have to check into it." Harland needed time to confirm his belief the lot measured nearly an acre and research the going price for that much acreage in Montford.

"Maybe $350. We'll get it taken care of in a couple of days, then?"

Too eager. It must be worth more than that. "I'll think about it and get back to you, Mr. Howell."

"Well . . . you don't want to wait too long, son. I'm doing you a favor by taking it off your hands, you know."

"Yes, sir. I understand completely." And Harland did understand, *completely.*

Harland had always made it his business to know who had money and who didn't. One of those with money owned the store where he worked. The next morning, he executed his newly formed plan.

"Good morning, sir." Harland maintained a friendly if reserved relationship with his boss. He followed orders, did the work assigned to him efficiently and occasionally asked for additional tasks so as to always appear industrious and occupied.

"Good morning to you, Harland. Fine day."

"Yes sir, it is . . . I suppose." The slight pause, the feigned uncertainty caught Mr. Wagner's attention.

"Something on your mind, Harland?" Mr. Wagner considered himself a beneficent man, and he welcomed this rare opportunity to prove himself helpful to Harland.

"Well, sir . . . if you don't mind . . . I wonder if you could offer some advice? Mr. Howell seems to want to buy my land over there on Pearson. He offered me $350 and that seems like a lot of money to me for such a little place, and all filled with debris the way it is. I'd like to have the money, but I don't want people to think I got too much for it—like I'm greedy or something."

The quick intake of breath on Mr. Wagner's part did not escape Harland's notice. *Just as I thought. I've got him.*

Mr. Wagner took a moment before responding.

"Three hundred fifty dollars must seem like a great deal of money to you, son." That word again. Son. Harland kept his irritation hidden.

"But it really is kind of low for the nice piece of land you've got there. How big is it? I think I heard somewhere it was an acre. Maybe in the paper after the fire?"

"I'm not sure, sir. About that I think." In fact, it fell barely shy of a full acre. Harland had already checked.

"Well then, you may be able to get more than $350 for it. Why, I'll take it off your hands and give you $400. How does that sound?"

"Sounds mighty nice, Mr. Wagner, but surely that's too much?"

"Not at all, son. I'd be happy to help a young man like you by paying him a fair price."

Mr. Wagner confirmed Harland's belief that he had a valuable piece of property. He spent the next day having much the same conversation with other local businessmen. He went back to Mr. Howell, who made a counter offer. He entertained an even higher bid from the owner of the men's store on Patton Avenue. He made the rounds, reporting back to each man about the higher offer from someone else. In the end, Mr. Wagner won the bidding war and paid hundreds of dollars more than the first offer made by Mr. Howell. Harland earned his nest egg and in the process gave birth to his reputation as a shrewd businessman.

Plato once said: "The direction in which education starts a man will determine his future in life." Harland's Stumptown education set him on a path that eventually led to the pompous, self-absorbed man standing at the curb, imagining his dream house on Chestnut Street. A man who had decided at a very early age it was better to be rich than poor, selfish than generous, haughty than humble. A man who Mazie, the only person who had ever truly loved him, ultimately counted as one of the biggest disappointments of her life.

Harland had slipped unwillingly into memories of his childhood, and he brought himself back now to focus on the sloped hill where he would build his new home. Harland's dream house would have turrets, sun rooms, an expansive wrap-around sleeping porch, winsome nooks and crannies to delight visitors of all persuasions and a glorious kitchen. The master bedroom would be massive in proportion and decorated with the finest handmade furniture, linens and carpets he could find. An elegant, expensive home with the relaxed comfort of a mountain retreat—Harland knew he could make his dream a reality.

Finding the right architect proved more difficult than he anticipated. Richard Sharp Smith had died years earlier. He would have been Harland's top choice. Instead he resigned himself to working with lesser beings and eventually the plans were completed. But only after two of the top architects in town had abandoned the project, unwilling to bend to Harland's demands for features out of character with the design styles they created.

Harland insisted on the best craftsmen to build his house, only those most in demand. For the door, one person stood alone at the top of the list. Leland Howard. It would have to be Leland Howard, even though getting that man to sign on would be an act of sheer will triumphing over plodding stubbornness.

ELEVEN
2004

Darcel Grimes' voice drifted from the television into the kitchen where Tate busied herself preparing dinner. She typically listened every evening to the six o'clock news on Channel 13, the local ABC affiliate, to keep in touch with the outside world.

"Plans to demolish a derelict mansion in the Montford historic district have neighbors taking sides as to the best use of the prime location on Chestnut Street."

Tate stopped cutting vegetables and dashed into the living room just in time to see a shot of 305 Chestnut Street illustrating the news story.

The brief piece highlighted the county's plans to seize the property for non-payment of taxes and auction it on the courthouse steps. A prominent local developer with deep pockets appeared on camera speaking about his desire to tear down the house and build eight small cottages on the site. The reporter interviewed two neighbors who favored the idea and looked forward to the removal of the eyesore which had blighted the neighborhood for decades. Another spokesman for the local neighborhood association objected to anything diverging from the stately single-family homes with spacious yards which populated the area. No one, it seemed, except Tate had any interest in saving the place.

This information could not have come at a better time. After her initial surge of interest in saving the house, Tate had reached what seemed like a dead end and her focus shifted back to the renovations on Maplewood. It had been a couple of days since she'd really thought much about 305. The story re-energized her. Tomorrow, she would dig in again, and now she had a new starting place. She'd have to check with Holly about the process involved in seizing and auctioning the property, but she expected she would have to move quickly or the place would be lost.

TWELVE
1917

Mary Alice Clayton entered the world in a small cabin in Asheville in 1878, the second of two daughters and the last child in the family to live past infancy. A quiet girl, given to retreating into fantasy when she was not occupied with the chores assigned to her, she asked little in the way of attention. "Not much trouble." When her mother talked about her youngest daughter at all, that's how she usually described Mary Alice.

The family lived a simple life. Mary Alice's mother tried to keep an organized home. Her father found work wherever he could. They had food to eat, beds to sleep in and a roof over their heads. Mary Alice dutifully went to school and studied reading, writing and arithmetic, gaining the skills necessary to succeed in life. Though intelligent, she rarely received encouragement or acknowledgment, and she excelled at nothing.

What energy Mary Alice's parents had available to engage in life beyond providing the basics went to her sister, Eulah Mae. Three years older, Eulah Mae had staked out her claim long before Mary Alice arrived.

However, the affection of their maternal aunt belonged solely to Mary Alice. Aunt Ida visited town infrequently, but when she did, she showered Mary Alice with attention, filling the child up with love.

On Mary Alice's 13th birthday, Aunt Ida visited and made a request the girl had been secretly wishing for most of her life. Could Mary Alice come to live with Aunt Ida and her husband? Uncle Fred had been badly injured in a fall. He could hardly get around anymore, and both of them felt age slowing them down. They could use some help with the chores, someone to look after them. If Mary Alice could be spared, they would be ever grateful. It did not escape Mary Alice's attention that her parents conferred only briefly before giving their consent. That afternoon, with her few belongings packed in a sack and a lightness of heart she had never felt before, Mary Alice set out with Aunt Ida to her new life.

She settled into a routine quickly. She made herself useful wherever she could. She provided help with the cooking and laundry, chopping wood, feeding the chickens and collecting eggs. No task proved too big or too small for Mary Alice, so long as she knew it would help her aunt and uncle. When they ran out of requests, she found ways to make their home better on her own. She gathered flowers from the small meadow to grace the wooden table. She mended curtains and expanded the garden. What she received in return held much more value than what she gave. In this house, Mary Alice slowly settled into the security of being loved.

Living in the mountains provided a tonic to Mary Alice's soul, and as she grew into adulthood, she came to know her surroundings intimately. She recognized the birds by their mating calls. She became familiar with the edible and medicinal plants growing in the wild and took great pleasure in watching the subtle changes occurring with each season. Frequently, with her work for the day completed and her aunt and uncle settled in, Mary Alice retreated to the woods. The peacefulness of the forest nourished her deeply. Weather permitting, she loved to lie down on a bed of soft pine needles in a patch of filtered sun and drift off to the lullaby sung by the wind wafting through the treetops. On such a day several years after her arrival at the mountain homestead, an unexpected meeting changed Mary Alice's life once again.

—⁓—

The ability to identify a good piece of timber before it had been harvested stood out as Arlen Howard's most highly developed skill. He knew wood intimately. He learned to whittle soon after he learned to walk, starting with simple stick figures carved from the leavings of the chairs and tables made by his grandfather and father.

The Howard men held a well-earned reputation throughout the region for their craftsmanship, and little Arlen followed happily in their footsteps. He loved the color of young cherry wood and the earthy fragrance of freshly cut maple. What schooling he had took time away from the forest, which he roamed from a young age in search of the best wood he could find to add to the stockpile in the family workshop.

The Howards' log cabin in the mountains just outside Asheville provided shelter and comfort for him and his older sister, their parents and their paternal grandparents. Although his sister eventually married and moved on, Arlen enjoyed his quiet mountain life. By the time he reached adulthood, he had become an accomplished carpenter, working alongside his father and grandfather, living each day as it came with little thought to the future.

So, the fact that Arlen found a wife at all came as a miracle. One afternoon as he moved quietly through the woods, he happened upon Mary Alice Clayton where she lay napping in a patch of sun.

Her rich, dark brown hair tinged with red fell in soft waves around her face. Her full black eyelashes formed soft curves on her cheeks, and her pink skin captivated Arlen with its paleness. Her simple dress rested in soft folds around her tiny frame, her small breasts pushing against the fabric and her full hips resting gracefully on the bed of pine needles. In her repose, Arlen sensed her receptiveness, her willingness to please.

Mary Alice awoke. No great revelation of love at first sight cast its spell over either of them. Rather, they were like-beings, and each recognized this quickly in the other. Neither needed to ask what thoughts occupied the other's mind or whether they made a good match for each other. Fate brought them together. They met in the woods one day, and not long after they married in the woods as well.

Mary Alice continued to care for her elderly relatives, and Arlen stayed in the cabin with them, returning to his family's home when necessary to help with the chores and collect supplies for his woodworking. When Uncle Fred died, followed shortly after by Aunt Ida, Mary Alice went home with Arlen to stay.

She found her place in the Howard clan as easily as she had with her aunt and uncle when she first moved to the mountains. She never questioned her life would continue in its quiet and predictable manner.

After several failed pregnancies, Mary Alice and Arlen's only child fought his way into the world in the spring of 1910. This first act of stubborn determination set the tone for his approach to the problems that emerged later in his life.

Leland Samuel Howard enjoyed several precious years at the homestead, learning to whittle and roaming the forest, just as his father had, before the Howard clan left for a vastly different life in the city. After his departure, the surrounding mountains forever held the tantalizing promise of a return to the peaceful life of his youth, but for the boy that dream remained undeniably out of reach.

The Howard homestead sat at the edge of the huge estate assembled in bits and pieces by George Washington Vanderbilt II. He visited Asheville in 1888 and immediately fell in love with the rolling Blue Ridge Mountains girding the city. He bought up 125,000 acres of land on which he would build a mansion the likes of which were unknown in the area. His acquisitions occurred with little fanfare, yet he single-handedly transformed tiny Asheville into a destination for the rich and famous, permanently changing the lives of its inhabitants.

These changes had little immediate impact on the Howards and other mountaineers like them whose land remained in their possession. Then Congress passed the Weeks Act in 1911. That legislation opened the door for the creation of national forests, and Mr. Vanderbilt saw the opportunity to sell off some of his property—more than eighty thousand acres of it. Although he died unexpectedly in 1914, his widow finalized the sale of the land, thus giving birth to the Pisgah National Forest. Several families with land near the Howards jumped at the chance to sell their property as well, leaving Mary Alice and Arlen more and more isolated.

As much as she loved the mountains, Mary Alice knew the time had come to move back to Asheville. When Arlen's parents died and only the three of them remained, she pressed hard until her husband reluctantly agreed to sell his heritage and relocate to the city. They sold the cabin where Mary Alice had lived with her aunt and uncle as well. Half the money went to help them set up a household in the city. The other half, with Arlen's permission, went to Mary Alice to keep in her own name.

They purchased an old, wood cabin on Cumberland Avenue with ample space in the front where Arlen and Leland could eventually build a more modern home, one suitable to city life. But the cabin in back seemed the best fit for all of them, a vestige of their roots in the mountains, and Mary Alice and Arlen remained in it for the rest of their lives. Simple lives, for the most part. Peaceful and productive lives surrounded by the noise of the city rather than the whispering sounds of the forest. They gradually adjusted to those changes, even Arlen and Leland, who previously knew only the secluded life of their mountain homestead. Arlen found ample work in the city to support them and Leland apprenticed with his father when not attending school. They grew accustomed to their neighbors, found a small church well suited to all of them and made new friends who they welcomed into their simple home. In fact, everyone felt welcome at the Howard household—everyone except Mary Alice's nemesis, her crazy sister, Eulah Mae.

THIRTEEN
2004

Eight years after her mother's death, Mazie Daniels finally pulled out the tattered box of memorabilia and began sorting through it. It overflowed with pictures, clippings and mementos, spanning the last century. She picked up a small, faded, black-and-white snapshot from near the top of the pile. A young woman perched on the stoop of a tiny house overlooking a verdant garden. A chicken coop leaned into the left side of the house, and a beat-up Model T sat out front. Alongside her stood a wiry girl, one hand resting on the woman's shoulder.

Mazie cradled the photograph and turned it over gently in her wrinkled hand. The scrawl on the back, barely visible now, read "Mazie and Baby 1932."

Memories of that moment came back to her clear as could be. She was 12 years old, and her family had just returned from church services. Cora Jenkins met them as they approached their house and, with great excitement, insisted they pose for a photograph she wanted to take with her new Beau Brownie camera.

"It's gonna be so beautiful!" Cora exclaimed. She had recently received the camera as a gift and she now went around the neighborhood taking pictures and selling them for five cents each.

"Don't fuss so," Mazie's mother had admonished, but she smiled and blushed a bit as Cora issued instructions on where and how they should position themselves. Moments later Cora snapped this picture, the first ever of Mazie, standing there with her mother on the porch of the little house in Stumptown where she had grown up.

Ancient history. God knows I never did think I'd get to be this old! And now I got this ol' box full of memories and don't know what to do with 'em all.

She continued sifting, item by item, sorting things into various piles. Pictures and souvenirs from the years of raising her three sons, various keepsakes of her own life from childhood through her married years and a sparse few reminders of her parents.

She kept coming back to the first faded image, reaching not only for the memories it held but also for the old feelings of happiness and hope. *Mazie and Baby. Mazie and Mazie, really. And I'm the last one.* She shared her name with her mother, her grandmother, great-grandmother and on back for at least six generations. By family tradition, the eldest female child of a Mazie became Mazie, too.

But her children were all boys, and while they promised their first girl would bear the family name, they had fathered only boys as well. From birth, she had been called "Baby," and the name followed her throughout her life within her family circle. Even her children called her by the nickname, though the outside world knew her as Mazie, a moniker she carried proudly.

She spent the next half hour hunched over the box and moving through the feelings elicited by the artifacts. Sadness, joy, grief, pride, regret, disappointment, surprise—they all lived there in the pictures and clippings and in her heart. Finally she stood up and stretched out her back and shoulders. She stepped gingerly around the clutter in the hallway on her way to the kitchen and put together a small lunch from leftovers in the refrigerator, then shuffled out to her long, narrow porch to sit in the sunshine. She leaned back in her chair and lifted her face to the light, allowing whatever thoughts came to drift through her mind unrestricted.

She awoke with a start when her plate clattered to the floor, and as she reached to pick it up, she heard Tate Marlowe calling up to her from the sidewalk.

"Mazie! Everything okay?"

"Must have drifted off. Old women do that, you know!" she chuckled. "Come on up, honey."

Tate climbed the steep cement steps slowly, favoring her left knee, which always felt like it might give out on her at any moment.

"Beautiful day, Mazie. See you're getting your sunbath in!"

"Yes, indeed." And they both laughed. Mazie's sunbaths had become a shared joke between them. For Mazie, anytime outside, regardless of the reason or the weather, counted as taking a little sunbath. "Got to keep my looks up for the gentlemen, you know." A sly wink always followed.

"The gentlemen, eh? How many of them are after you now, Mazie?"

"Only one special one. But I keep telling him I got no time to be flirtin' with him. I'm too old for messin' around anyway."

"Really? Just how old are you, my dear?" Tate arched her eyebrow, not expecting a straight answer from Mazie.

"Now a lady don't tell her age, Tate. You should know that." The wink again. "All I'll say is had black people been allowed to vote when I was comin' up, I would of happily voted for Mr. Truman."

"Well, that makes you older than me, Mazie." Tate smiled and sat down in the comfortable chair next to her friend. Both closed their eyes for a moment and took in the sun.

Their uncommon friendship had sprung out of mutual curiosity and close proximity. They met shortly after Tate purchased the two houses on Maplewood. Mazie lived in a rambling old structure just two doors down and across the street. Mazie initiated their contact, offering Tate a warm welcome and a glass of sweet tea as she moved into her new apartment. They chatted briefly the first day, and it quickly became routine for Tate to look for Mazie whenever she headed out for a walk.

They discussed everything from the weather to the state of Mazie's love life. She kept busy volunteering at Irene Wortham—a local agency providing a variety of services to children and adults with developmental disabilities—and she had more than one avid suitor at the place.

"I know I look old, Tate, but those mens still find me attractive. I don't understand it, but I like it."

"I understand it, Mazie. You've got a spark." Mazie's drooping old eyes twinkled, and a playful, almost cocky, look spread across her features.

"See, that's what I mean, Mazie. You always look like you're about to spring a surprise on me. You've got an impish quality about you that's quite fetching."

"Oh, I'm just playin' with you, honey."

"And that makes you interesting, Mazie. Really fascinating. No wonder the men are after you."

Tate shared with Mazie her disappointment that some of the neighbors seemed upset about her buying the duplexes and fixing them up. Her "For Rent" signs were routinely pulled down, and the woman directly across the street from Tate's place stopped speaking to her after Tate asked a long-time tenant to move so the current renovations could begin.

"You'd think they'd be grateful I moved the rabble-rousers out and the cops aren't here half the time in the middle of the night to break up knock-down-drag-out fights," Tate complained.

"Oh, honey, that Lester who used to live in your place? More times than not he'd fall down drunk in the street right outside his door and he'd still be sleepin' there in the mornin'. Can't tell you how many times he'd be rantin' and ravin' about somethin', fightin' his demons and wakin' me up from a sound sleep. I'm sure glad he's gone, and all his kind with him. All these neighbors 'round here be thinking the same thing, whether they say so or not."

"Glad to hear you say it, Mazie. The guy right next door to you? He told me one day it's too bad the people who grew up here in Asheville can't afford to live here anymore, because people like me are buying up property and forcing the price up."

"Well, he's got a point there, Tate, but . . ."

"'But' is right! I asked him where he's from and you know what he told me? Miami! And I found out he bought his place from a woman who owned it for only a year and sold it to him for twenty thousand more than she paid for it. Talk about hypocrisy!"

Mazie broke out into laughter and Tate bristled. "Now don't get me wrong, Tate. But you gotta chill out a little bit 'for you give yourself a heart attack!"

Tate looked hard into Mazie's face and noticed the slight grin and gentle yet firm gaze. *This is a woman who knows what she thinks and doesn't hesitate to say it. Just like me.*

"You know, Mazie. You're right. And don't start expecting to hear me say that very often!" Their mutual laughter rang clear, dissipating Tate's anger and softening her heart.

"You been pretty busy lately, Tate. What you up to? How's the work coming along over there?" She nodded toward Dave as he carried supplies from his truck into the apartment under renovation.

"Oh, much slower than I want, of course! His work is wonderful, and the place will be beautiful when it's done. I just hope that happens before the first snow!"

Mazie's laughter at the comment confirmed her ability to quickly pick up on Tate's sarcasm and dry humor, one of her most charming qualities as far as Tate was concerned.

"Actually, he's been working steady for the past couple of days. I've been on him, you know. He's finally putting the new windows in the kitchen. Hard to pin him down, but when he's there, he's working hard." Tate paused for a moment before changing subjects.

"But what's really got me going," Tate continued, "is an old house on Chestnut Street. Did you hear about it? It was on the news last night. They want to tear it down and build some cottages over there. It's a strange old place, empty a long time apparently, and . . ."

"You mean Mr. Freeman's old place?"

Tate gasped. "Mr. Freeman's place? Yes, a man named Harland Freeman built it decades ago, but how'd you know . . ."

"About Mr. Freeman? Why, honey, my momma mostly raised him when he was a boy. I growed up with him at my dinner table 'til he got too fancy to 'sociate with us no more."

"You *grew up* with him?" Tate struggled to comprehend Mazie's message. "You have to tell me everything you know, Mazie!"

They spent the next two hours locked in deep conversation, Mazie reliving her youth, Tate trying to keep up as Mazie told her fascinating tale.

Baby's birth coincided with the dawn of the Roaring '20s, setting the stage for a childhood filled with expectations that remained largely unmet. A happy and animated little girl doted upon by the rest of her family, she arrived seven years after the youngest boy. The one exception to the universal adoration of Baby visited frequently but did not live with them.

Harland had become a fixture in Baby's family by the time she arrived, and he openly resented the perceived lowering of his status triggered by her birth. At 10 years old, he had learned that with sufficient effort he could usually get what he wanted. And he wanted badly to maintain his position in Mazie's family.

He had always felt equal to Mazie's sons—two older than he, one younger. He had his own place at the dinner table, just like the others. The boys included him in their brotherly roughhousing and generally treated him as they treated each other. Of course, he had begun to understand his superiority, being white and all, but he hid that knowledge when in their presence, and his deceit seemed to go unnoticed.

The arrival of a girl changed everything in ways Harland could not comprehend. They coddled her, fussed over her, showed her off to everyone in the neighborhood. He had never been treated in such a deferential manner. Until then, he did not know what he had missed. Seeing her so joyful as she basked in the limelight ignited jealousy and anger.

Harland found a variety of creative ways to draw attention away from Baby and onto himself, once even going so far as trying to push his way onto Mazie's lap as Baby suckled. Sometimes his attempts garnered the desired outcome; other times they went unrewarded. Only when he became menacing did Mazie set strict limits on him. He remained welcome in their home, but he had to be kind to Baby.

Thus a tenuous truce established itself early on and held throughout the years. Baby wanted desperately to be loved by Harland, just as everyone else adored her. Harland wanted to retain the sustenance his life depended on, so he became adept at pretending he liked Baby. Every child has the innate ability to understand the difference between being cherished and being tolerated, and Harland's fake affection for her left a permanent scar on Baby.

Still, in those early years of Baby's life, most everything seemed possible. The country thrived in a period of economic prosperity that reached even into the corners of Stumptown. Baby's father skimped and saved until he had the funds to buy an old Model T from Mr. Milner, for whom Mazie had worked for nearly twenty years. The purchase put him in a position to strike out on his own, and he made a decent living for himself and his family hauling trash, cutting down trees for firewood, which he sold throughout the neighborhood, and performing a variety of other odd jobs. Work came to him easily, and his business continued to grow.

Then the crash of the stock market began eroding his success. Even before all the local banks failed about a year after the economic disaster, most of the jobs Baby's father depended on began to disappear.

The two oldest boys had already struck out on their own, but the youngest one scrounged for whatever work he could find to help support the family. Even with Mazie's wages and what the men brought in, Baby had to work. At the tender age of 11, she took on menial tasks at the homes where her mother worked and eventually found more work with the wealthy folks in Montford. Some of them had managed miraculously to salvage much of their fortunes. Not only had her childhood ended abruptly, but all her dreams had died in the process. A maid, not a jazz singer. A maid, not a teacher. A maid, not a hope in the world now of anything better.

"That's an incredible story, Mazie. Obviously things got better eventually."

"That's how my life worked. Can't do nothin' but let it be the way it is." A deep sigh said more about Mazie's feelings than her words.

"The first part disappointed some," Mazie said, "but the next part was purty good. My second husband treated me real nice. We had this big ol' house to live in and for my boys to grow up in. I married late the first time, you know, and had my babies late, so they was teenagers when we moved over here. We had a big yard for them to play in back then, 'fore they took most of our land to widen Broadway."

"Mazie, we can stop if you want, but I'd like to know more . . ."

"Honey, I can talk all day. Not many people around want to hear these old stories. My boys sure don't. My grandbabies listen to some, but they lose interest real quick. What do you want to know?"

"I still don't know how Mr. Freeman came to build that house over on Chestnut, or why it's been empty for so long. What happened to him, Mazie?"

"Well, Mr. Harland . . . now he had a way with money for sure. After his Momma died and his ol' shack burned down, he sold his piece a land for top dollar. Don't know how he did it, but he managed to keep all his money when everthin' crashed. Had a nice nest egg, and just kept on growin' it. Course he didn't need us no more then, so he just stopped comin' around. Broke Momma's heart, he did. He'd been like one of her own, then it got to the point where he acted like he didn't know none of us."

Mazie filled in some more of the puzzling gaps about Harland that Tate had struggled with ever since she first saw his old house. Apparently he climbed the social ladder yet never gained the status he longed for.

"But he was successful, wasn't he? I mean he had the money to build a mansion in Montford." Tate tried to reconcile the image she had of the man with what Mazie told her.

"I s'pose you could call him successful, yes. But he was a lonely man, I think. Musta been. Never got married, had no babies, no real friends to speak of. He had his business and a big ol' house, but that's not enough to make a life, is it?" Mazie did not wait for Tate to answer.

"Don't no one really know why he blowed his brains out, though."

"What?" Astonishment overtook Tate yet again. "He blew his brains out?"

"Sure did. Sat himself down on his porch in fronta that big old fancy door, stuck a pistol in his mouth and pulled the trigger. Did it day before Valentine's Day. Hadn't been livin' there mor'n a few months."

"Well, that confirms the story I've been piecing together. That's why he owned the place for only two years. He bought the land, built the house and then killed himself almost immediately. He sure had some demons!"

"Lotsa demons, goin' way back to being a tiny baby with a crazy momma and worthless daddy. I coulda' loved him but he wanted no part of me. Course that was a different time, and we couldn't a been together no ways. Still, I wanted him to love me and he didn't. Guess it was the good Lord's way of protectin' me from harm. Anyway, my life turned out good enough."

Mazie sat back and closed her eyes, exhaustion obviously weighing her down. Tate sat quietly for a few moments before speaking.

"I wish I knew what to say, Mazie. I can't thank you enough for sharing all this with me. You may not know it, but you've just given me a precious gift."

"You must be tired, listenin' to an old woman ramble on like this."

"Actually, Mazie, I'd like to talk more, if you don't mind. But maybe we'll do that tomorrow, after you've had some time to rest."

"We surely can, honey. You welcome to sit and listen to me goin' on and on any ol' time. You come back whenever you fancy." Then Mazie dozed off and Tate headed out for her walk.

After leaving Mazie, Tate made a quick stop to check in with Dave. A gaping hole in the kitchen wall greeted her, and she saw Dave's head peeking through from the outside.

"Hey, how's it going?"

"Pretty good. Got the old windows out and just need to add some bracing in here, then I'll install the replacements and it'll be good to go."

Tate saw shafts of light filtering through the exposed work area and realized no buffer of any kind separated the outer surface of the house from the inner kitchen wall.

"Can we put some insulation in there?"

Dave gave her a quizzical look. "Well, we could . . ."

Tate sensed his hesitancy. "Any reason we shouldn't?"

"No, but they never did that back when this house was being built. None of the other walls have it."

"Well, let's put some in there anyway. I know it won't make much difference if the rest of the place doesn't have any, but I'd feel better about it."

"Okay. Will do." Tate knew Dave considered her request wasted effort. *Maybe he's right. I don't really know anything about this stuff.*

"Thanks, Dave. You're very patient with me." Tate smiled at him, and Dave sent a knowing nod her way as she headed for the door.

"Hey, one other thing . . ." Dave called to her.

"Yeah. What?"

"These old windows are beautiful. It'd be a waste to throw them in the trash."

"I agree. They are nice. I like the waves and imperfections in the old glass. But what can we do with them? I've tried to think of things, like maybe using them as picture frames . . ."

"We could put them up on Freecycle and see if someone wants them. I bet they'd go fast."

"Freecycle? Never heard of it."

"It's a great website. Anything you don't want, you can post there and someone who can use it will come and pick it up. In fact, we could post all the old cabinets, the refrigerator . . ."

"That old refrigerator? Who would want that?" The previous tenant had left food in the decrepit appliance which probably dated back at least twenty years. Its surface, the color of split pea soup, sported a vast array of dents, scratches and pock marks. All the food left behind had rotted, leaving a smelly, dripping mess.

"Never can tell. But it's worth a try. Freecycle keeps stuff out of the landfill, and lots of times people are thrilled to get it. It may seem like junk to you, but it might be useful to someone else."

"How do I do that?"

"I can handle it for you. But if you want to know more about it, just Google Freecycle."

Just Google it. Tate chuckled to herself as she left the apartment and headed downtown, grateful for the beautiful weather on this early November afternoon. *Wasn't that long ago I railed against getting an answering machine, now I'm told to "just Google it," and I know exactly what he means!*

Her plan for the afternoon had been forming since she left Mazie. She had learned a lot about Harland Freeman, but she still knew virtually nothing about Leland Howard, the beneficiary of the trust that held title to the house on Chestnut Street. Her determination to find out more about who he was and how he came to own that property sent her back to Pack Memorial Library

FOURTEEN
2004

Tate's love affair with libraries emerged the minute she entered her first one at the tender age of 10. She could not remember what prompted that original foray into the world of books and her tentative search for heroines who spoke to her. Perhaps it had been a teacher or a schoolmate, but for whatever reason, she had embarked on a mission of discovery.

"Do you want me to go with you?" asked her mother.

"No." Tate had learned independence long ago out of necessity, and she refused to give up even a tiny bit of it now.

"Okay, honey. Pick out something, good." And with that Tate was released to explore on her own.

She hopped onto her bicycle and headed for the huge old house sitting atop a small hill at the other end of the village where she lived. She rarely traveled beyond the shops along Main Street so her eagerness for adventure propelled her forward. The hot summer sun burned through her thin cotton top and onto her bare legs as she rode.

The shade of the wide porch provided welcome relief once she reached her destination. Dating back to the late 1800s, the place had been the home of a wealthy couple, Charles and Agatha Putnam, who had no children. When they died, they left their home and a sizable collection of books to the town to serve as a lending library. A square, brick structure two stories tall, its long windows dressed in white shutters, the building seemed both inviting and intimidating. Tate took a deep breath to steady herself, pushed open the huge wooden door and stepped into another world.

Long shafts of sunlight filled with fat dust motes slid through the windows and came to rest on the dark, polished floor. Her footsteps seemed to echo through the enveloping quiet and she inhaled deeply, taking into her lungs the heady, musty odor of the unfamiliar sanctuary. She hesitated just inside, not sure what to do next.

A spare woman with graying hair pulled into a knot at the back of her neck approached from behind a desk which sat in an alcove of stained glass windows.

"Can I help you, young lady?" she asked kindly. Tate whispered her answer, mimicking the woman's own tiny voice.

"*Nancy Drew?*"

"Ah, yes. *Nancy Drew.* Of course." She took Tate's hand in hers and they walked through a tall doorway into the adjoining room. Floor-to-ceiling shelves covered every wall; ladders with wheels provided access to the higher rows of books; huge old chairs filled the center of the room. Tate had never seen anything like it.

"*Nancy Drew, The Hardy Boys . . .*" The woman gestured to a collection of books lining a shelf just at eye level to the right of the door. Awestruck, Tate tried to take it all in. "Just Nancy, thank you," she squeaked softly.

"Then I'll leave you to it. When you want to check out, see me at the desk." The woman bent close and spoke these hushed words into Tate's ear. The scent of lavender wafted behind her as she walked away, leaving Tate to herself in Wonderland.

Woozy with anticipation, Tate ran her fingers gently over the spines of the books before her. Tilting her head to the right, she read the titles without removing the books from their spot. Several caught her eye: *The Hidden Staircase. The Clue in the Diary. The Secret of Red Gate Farm. The Sign of the Twisted Candles.* There must have been more than twenty Nancy Drew mysteries available, and she wanted every one of them.

She stepped back to the alcove and whispered to the librarian: "How many can I have?"

"Only three at a time. But as soon as you bring one back, you can take out another."

"Okay, then." Tate went back to the row of books and eventually made her difficult choice.

"I'd like these." She delicately placed the books on the librarian's desk.

"Very good choices, my dear." The woman kept smiling at Tate as she opened the cover of each book, took a card from the pocket pasted to the inside front cover and wrote Tate's name down. She then rubber-stamped the due date on the slip in the book and on the card before placing the latter into her file. A few minutes later, Tate returned to the everyday world, clutching the precious cargo to her chest. *The Secret of the Old Clock. The Mystery at Lilac Inn. The Password to Larkspur Lane.* Those were her final choices and she could hardly wait to get home and begin reading them.

———

Pack Memorial Library, modern and well organized, air-conditioned and brightly lit, welcomed its patrons, but it did not transport Tate to another realm as did her visit to Putnam library decades ago. She stepped inside and headed to the North Carolina Collection, hoping to find a reference librarian to help her locate records related to Leland Howard.

She found a stack of Asheville City Directories dating back to the early 1900s. She selected several starting in the 1940s and took them to a nearby table where she could spread out. On her first try, she found the following notation:

HOWARD, LELAND, 8 CUMBERLAND AVE (MARIE) CABTMKR

"Wow!" Tate quickly hushed herself and gestured apologies to the people sitting in the reference area.

There he is! That was so easy. Tate looked at subsequent directories and found numerous entries for Leland Howard at the same address until he disappeared from the books in the mid-1960s. She also found one notation for Harland Freeman at 305 Chestnut Street, owner of Freeman's Mercantile, no spouse and no additional information. No further mention of him appeared after 1942, the year of his death. Gathering up her notes, she went again in search of help.

Carla Geoffrey came to her rescue.

"You can look over here in the biography clippings," she suggested. "And we can check for birth and death information. The full records are in the Registrar's office over at the Courthouse, but we have an index here."

"That would be great. Anything I can find will be helpful." Tate searched for biographical information but found nothing. The clippings file contained hundreds of biographies for a variety of professionals and artists, politicians and business owners, but nothing for Leland Howard or any other craftsmen, for that matter. She sought out Carla for help with the birth and death indices.

"I checked the archives at the newspaper office yesterday," Tate said, "and found a couple of references to Leland Howard. His wife died in 1962. Actually, she was murdered. And he was a craftsman—made furniture for wealthy folks here in town. The notation in the City Directory says cabtmkr—cabinetmaker. Think we can find anything about him?"

"We'll try. But birth certificates were not required by law until 1913, and then only within the city itself. So depending on when and where he was born, we might come up empty-handed."

Carla's prediction proved accurate. They searched the birth index—no more than a computer printout of the records housed at the courthouse—and found nothing about the birth of Leland Howard. Neither did they find anything for Marie Howard, but she would have had a different maiden name, so the dead end did not surprise them. The Ancestry.com database proved much more helpful. Details of the 1930 census had been released the previous year, and in it they found a listing for Arlen Howard. Living in his household were his wife, Mary Alice; his son, Leland; his daughter-in-law, Marie Eleanor; and his grandson, Clayton Samuel. For the first time, Tate realized Leland and his wife had a child born in 1927.

"Well, that's an exciting piece of information! But why would Leland himself be so elusive?" Tate mused. "Let's see what else we can find." Tate noticed Carla glancing at her watch. "Oh, I'm sorry! I've been monopolizing your time."

"It's okay. I can give you a few more minutes before I have to attend a meeting. I'm happy to help for as long as I can."

"Then let's look at the death index. I can search the Ancestry database on my own."

A tantalizing bit of information turned up as they continued their search in the death index: Marie Eleanor Howard had died, as Tate knew, on March 15, 1962. Her son, Clayton Samuel Howard, died the same day.

"Beware the Ides of March!" Tate exclaimed under her breath.

"I guess so!" Carla and Tate exchanged a look of amazement. "This is fascinating! Why are you looking into these people?"

"It all has to do with that old house on Chestnut. I really had no idea what I was getting into, but I can't seem to stop!"

"Oh, that old place has been a problem for ages. People have been trying to get it knocked down for I don't know how long!"

"Well, I guess I'm the only person alive who wants to see it saved, but I just can't let go of the idea that's what I'm supposed to do."

"It's a big task you've taken on. From what I hear, they are moving as fast as they can to finalize the deal with the developer and begin demolition. Of course they have to go through the whole legal process of taking possession from the current owner."

"Then I have to move fast, too. According to the tax records, the house is held in trust for a Leland Samuel Howard. The trustee is the law firm of Paige and Schmidt. I assume Mr. Howard is dead, but if so, why didn't he show up in the death index? Is there any other way to find him? Maybe something about surviving family? Hopefully he has living relatives somewhere."

"If he's dead, he would appear in the index."

"But he'd have to be in his nineties . . . and if he's still alive, why doesn't he show up anywhere?" Tate's growing frustration resided dangerously close to resignation. "I guess I'll head over to the Registrar of Deeds and see if they have anything there we couldn't find here."

"Sorry I have to leave, but I'll look further when I get back. How can I reach you if I find something?"

Tate gave Carla her phone number and headed home, exhausted. She completely forgot about going back to Ancestry.com, and the Registrar would just have to wait.

As Tate trudged home, she wished she had driven downtown instead of walking. Once there she brewed a cup of strong coffee and loaded it up with half-and-half, then settled onto her long comfortable couch. As usual in quiet moments like this, she looked around and began hatching plans for how she would fix her place up.

This couch has to go. Love it, but it's way too big for this tiny living room. Wonder how much replacement windows would cost for this place? Those sills are rotting and it's so drafty . . .

Just as she was about to drift off, the phone rang, yanking her back from dreamland.

"Hello?" She tempered her irritation. Few things annoyed Tate more than being jarred awake by a ringing phone.

"Miss Marlowe? This is Carla Geoffrey."

"Carla? Oh, Carla, yes, of course. What's up?" Tate planted her feet on the floor.

"I found something!"

"What? Tell me!"

"I couldn't stop thinking about how to find Leland Howard. It occurred to me he might be mentioned in places other than the clippings file since he was a well-known craftsman. So I searched some more, and I found a reference to him. He made a mantelpiece for the Princess Hotel during its renovation back in the 1950s."

"That's great, Carla! I wonder if they know anything about him over there?"

"Maybe, but the place has changed hands several times through the years. It's worth a try, anyway."

"Okay. I'm heading over there tomorrow. If I find anything, you'll be the first to know!"

FIFTEEN
1939

"I swear, Leland, you need to stop piddling around and get some real work done today," Ellie complained. Her search for Leland ended just where she expected, in the old log cabin at the back of their property. Once the home she knew and hated as a newlywed, it now housed Leland's workshop.

Leland nodded and continued carving a delicate pattern into the piece of birdseye maple in his hands. "I will, Ellie, I will. Just want to get this finished first."

"What you've got to do, Leland Howard, is get to work on that job Mr. Bloomfield gave you. You know we've got bills to pay and groceries to buy, and the boy has been asking for a bicycle for his birthday." Ellie heard the hardness in her own voice and felt the familiar twinge of sadness in her stomach.

She surveyed her husband as he sat in his rickety chair, turning the piece of wood lovingly in his hands. She had made her bed long ago, and she would lie in it for the rest of her life. She never questioned that. But sometimes he could be so stubborn, so difficult. She swallowed back her anger, turned on her heel and walked back to the house.

When she felt frustrated with Leland, Ellie often calmed herself by recounting all the reasons he made a good husband. His kindness. His dependability. His gentleness, loyalty, calmness, level-headedness, even his stubbornness . . .

Ellie continued to tick off Leland's admirable qualities as she went about her work in the kitchen. She had plenty to count, and they clearly outweighed the negatives, such as his occasional episodes of stubbornness, his lack of ambition and the fact that he loved her—probably his worst fault by far because Ellie's feelings for her husband fell far short of the intensity of his love for her, and that left her feeling guilty and resentful.

Ellie loved her husband, of course. But, she did not love him with the devotion Leland showered upon her. She had never felt passion for him, never had the sense her life would be incomplete without him. Once long ago she hoped for that kind of love, but Ellie learned at too young an age just how fragile hope is. One wrong move and her dreams had slipped away irretrievably. Everything from that moment on led her to this life, a safe and secure life with a devoted husband, a rambunctious son and not a single passionate dream for her own future.

Leland secretly longed to hear Ellie's voice tinged with the sweetness he remembered from their brief courtship. She most often spoke with a hard edginess these days, and her exasperation had cut through his reverie. Leland enjoyed nothing better in the world than moments just like this one, sitting in the sun and working on one of his own projects. Yes, paying work demanded attention, and plenty of it waited, but right now he wished he could just finish this one special thing for his own pleasure.

Leland watched his wife as she retreated to her kitchen. Her kitchen, his workshop. Her chores, his duties. The summation of those tasks and things that belonged to her and those that belonged to him added up to their marriage. They lived compatibly, occupying the same time and space. They even slept in the same bed every night, side by side, but they did not truly share their life together. No matter. Leland still considered himself blessed to have married Ellie, to hear her quietly breathing beside him in the early morning hours, to sit at the breakfast table while she cooked eggs just the way he liked them and to spend the evenings in their favorite chairs in companionable quietness. Those mundane activities did not quench the yearning deeply buried inside him, but at least they assuaged the pain a bit.

The one exception to their separate lives resided in the person of their son. Ellie shared the boy with him fully and without reservation. She expressed her love easily when the child served as the focus, and Leland allowed himself to imagine what it would have been like to grow up that way himself.

He had no doubt his parents loved him, but they had not demonstrated it the way he and Ellie did for Clayton. Clayton joined in everyday activities with each of them. At least in the early days he did, before he started changing. He worked the garden side-by-side with Ellie and sat next to his father in the workshop, often chattering away non-stop. Ellie had taught Leland how to cuddle and coddle their child, though Leland never became adept at it. Still, the two of them showered Clayton with attention and love at every opportunity, and Leland longed to experience the feeling of love like that.

As a child, Leland had wandered the woods on his own, often for hours on end. When with his parents, most often each of them focused on their own activities. His mother cooked, cleaned and did laundry. She held sole responsibility for the garden and the chickens, in fact for all household activities, and Leland ceased to be her helper as soon as he grew old enough to work with the men.

His father spent most waking hours in the workshop, first on the old homestead and then in the shed behind their cabin in town. In his youth, Leland served as his father's apprentice. Even though they occupied the same work space much of the time, each had his own solitary projects and social interactions rarely occurred.

Leland learned many things from his mother and father. He grew into a hard-working, trustworthy, reticent man who knew how to hold his feelings close to his chest. Yes, he could be stubborn at times—everyone knew that. But other passions of Leland's life remained hidden.

Timber rattlesnakes, though dwindling in numbers, still populate the forests of Western North Carolina. Their distinctive chevron markings make them easily identifiable while still providing excellent camouflage. This allows them to move inconspicuously through their habitat largely undisturbed as they go about their simple lives. Mild-mannered by nature, they avoid confrontation, always preferring an easy avenue of escape if one exists. Once cornered, however, they are fierce. Only the truly foolhardy will fail to back away once the warning rattle sounds, for the timber rattlesnake's bite is precisely aimed and potentially lethal to the unwary trespasser. The same held true for Leland Howard.

SIXTEEN
1944

Clayton Samuel Howard's propensity for trouble developed early and reached maturity long before he did. He had been hauled into police headquarters the first time at age 11, after bloodying the nose of Jimmy Boykins, who lived a few doors down from the Howard's. Jimmy Boykins, the local bully who had been harassing the neighborhood kids for years, made Clayton one of his favorite targets. He humiliated the boy with taunts and teases about his looks. Clay's good looks would develop as he matured. Until then he was a gangly, skinny kid with protruding teeth, arms too long for his body and raging insecurity, an easy target for any bully. Jimmy pushed Clayton off his bike, causing scraped knees and road rash on Clayton's right forearm that left a scar. He stole Clayton's scooter, wrecked it, then brought it back, leaving it broken on the front lawn. The pranks and damages escalated a bit each time until Clayton finally struck back.

One quiet afternoon, when Jimmy Boykins started taunting Clayton about his clothes, the boy turned quietly away as usual, face reddened with embarrassment at his weakness, tears filling his dark eyes. But instead of slinking away, he picked up a thick, fallen tree branch from the side of the road and walked up behind Jimmy Boykins, who now swaggered along laughing heartily. Without thought or warning, Clayton whacked his tormentor hard on the back of the head. The resounding crack filled the still air and sank into Clayton's very soul.

Jimmy Boykins fell face-first to the street, breaking his nose on the curb. He rolled over—groaning, dazed—and looked up. Clayton loomed over him, tree branch raised for the second blow, face a mask of maliciousness, the rage built up over years now spewing out through wild eyes. Jimmy cringed, raising his arms to cover his face, hoping the blow didn't kill him. He waited. He opened his eyes to see Clayton's face contorted in a vicious ear-to-ear grin as he slowly dropped the branch and sauntered away.

Clayton had found his power that day, or rather it had found him. In a perfect world, power is used for good, but Clayton did not live in a perfect world.

When Ellie and Leland picked up their son from the police station, they were solicitous and protective. They explained to the police in great detail all the grief Jimmy Boykins had rained down on their son, and how they were not surprised he had finally responded. Yes, perhaps he'd responded rather drastically. Yes, they did know Jimmy Boykins lay in the hospital with a severe concussion, broken nose and split-open eye. But Clayton had not hit him a second time when he could have, they argued. He had knocked down the boy who had been making his life miserable. He had done no more than defend himself. Too bad he had used the big branch, but please understand, they reasoned, Jimmy Boykins was three inches taller than Clayton and weighed at least twenty pounds more. Clayton had to make sure he hit him hard enough to knock him down, once he had decided to hit him at all.

Yes, yes, they would see to it the boy knew what he'd done was wrong. Clayton already showed remorse. They'd give him a good talking to, just as the arresting officer had done. They'd put him on restrictions and mete out the punishment he deserved.

As they walked home, their young son between them, both Ellie and Leland noticed the difference in how he walked. He stood up straight now, shoulders back, chin raised, facing the world head-on instead of shying away as usual—a good sign, they decided later as they rehashed the grueling day now behind them. A good sign. They were sure of it. Still, it nagged at Ellie that while Clayton seemed contrite, he also seemed smug and proud of himself in a quiet, secretive way.

Wishes die hard, especially those for a perfect child, those born deep in the fertile soil of a mother's heart, those fed by love and hope. Ellie's wishes for Clayton were of such a nature, and she held fast to them.

Her wishes for Clayton carried her through when she retrieved him from the police department the second time after he had broken three windows in the local grocery store for no apparent reason.

When the next incident occurred, Ellie reviewed all the wonderful things she remembered from the boy's infancy—his gleaming hair tinged with red in the sunlight, the big laughing eyes and the fruity smell of his tiny body when she lifted him out of the bath, the joy she felt as he laughed and squirmed in her arms. Ellie tried hard to remember every amazing experience with this boy from the moment of his birth and to squeeze out of her mind all the other things she had come to associate with him— the moodiness, the hard glint in those beautiful dark eyes when someone crossed him, the huddled tenseness ready to explode into some kind of mischief. And after every incident, Clayton became himself again—the sweet boy who loved his mother, a joy to have around.

Surely that's all it was—mischief—Clayton's way of getting even with the world he felt had let him down. And the world had let her child down in some very real ways.

Ellie knew that at least part of the blame lay with her. Keeping secrets always takes a toll on the ones you love. She had learned that lesson very well over the years.

She and Leland had forged a decent life. Of course, Ellie had wanted something different for herself, but she had to admit they had created a good existence. Leland provided for his family, though he never pushed himself to the level of success she envisioned for him.

A fine craftsman, one of the best in the entire region, his work graced most of the fancy homes in town. He held a notable reputation for his fireplace mantels, unique tables, comfortable chairs and a wide variety of one-of-a-kind furnishings. An ambitious man could have turned those skills into a great fortune, but Leland preferred a leisurely pace of work dedicated to meticulous detail. Ambition did not suit him.

"I'll get it done when I get it done." This response to being pressured to hurry up had become Leland's signature, and it irritated Ellie greatly.

Leland seemed content to stay in the little log cabin where he had lived with his parents, and then Ellie, since his boyhood. He had finally agreed to build a new house on the front of the property, but it had taken him almost five years to complete it. Ellie had not hurried him to finish the house because it disappointed her as soon as she realized what he had planned.

Her husband, despite being a master craftsman, had created for her one of the smallest and simplest houses on the block. A boring structure even before completion, it would never be more than the most basic of dwellings. In the beginning, she had tried to sway him to a grander plan, but he would have no part of it. Simple, solid, basic. He would provide his family with that. Pretentiousness belonged to the wealthy, not to simple folk like him and Ellie.

Simple folk. Ellie associated that description with people who had no aspirations, no gumption. Ellie had once dreamed of graduating high school and heading to the big city. Any big city would do. Having been isolated in the Western North Carolina mountains her entire life, Ellie knew of the outside world only what she read in her favorite magazines and gleaned from her conversations with visitors to Asheville.

Maybe she would go to Knoxville, or Atlanta, or maybe even New York City. She would find a way to leave as soon as she graduated, and she would go to a place where she could live a life as big as her imagination.

Harland Freeman could have been her ticket out of town—at least she thought so on their first and only date. Surely Harland would not want to stay in Asheville. He had big plans for himself, too, and together they could break free.

When Harland dumped her, Ellie ditched her grand plans. She picked Leland for her husband, married him and left school behind, but she did not give up her dreams. She just modified them. And she kept modifying them over the years to reconcile the chasm between living big and living simple. Her dream for a beautiful house had been transformed into the reality of the inelegant structure where they now lived. She had more space, and even better, she now had her own home since Arlen and Mary Alice chose to continue living in the cabin in the back. Still, Ellie had to resign herself to the house as she had done with so many other things since the day she was married. She made do with less than what she truly wanted.

At 17 years old, Clayton had become more than Ellie could handle. Yes, a mother could have dreams, but a child had no obligation to fulfill them. This knowledge crushed Ellie, who loved her child deeply. But even she had to admit that her love could not heal his wounds.

Clay, as he insisted on being called, slipped in and out of puzzling spells Ellie could not understand. In a bad spell, he kept the schedule he preferred, and no amount of limit setting by Ellie or Leland could control him. He continued to go to school, but only because he now held the title of neighborhood bully and school gave him ample opportunity to act out his new role. Even the older and the bigger kids steered clear of Clayton. He had no real friends, only a small group of weaker boys who attached themselves to him to avoid being his target.

Ellie began noticing small quirks in Clayton's behavior long before the full-blown pattern had emerged. The compliant, sweet child she knew so well seemed to slip away quietly and in his place Ellie faced a stubborn, demanding and angry version of the boy.

———

"Clayton, please . . ."

"Clay! I keep telling you it's 'Clay'!"

"Okay . . . Clay. I'm just trying to help. Tell me what's wrong," Ellie pleaded.

"Nothing! Everything! Leave me alone, Maw!"

Ellie cringed. "Please don't call me Maw, Clay. You don't like Clayton and I don't like Maw." She sought a fine balance between indignation, fear and motherly concern. Her son lay sobbing on the bed where he had hurled himself after bursting through the front door moments earlier.

"LEAVE ME ALONE! Get out! Get out NOW!"

His voice took on the threatening tone she had heard before, and it sent her scurrying out of his room, shutting the door as she left.

Ellie sank into her favorite chair and began weeping. Soon, maybe tonight, maybe in the next day or two, he would come back to her, meek and apologetic. He would beg forgiveness and she would give it, even though it became more difficult each time to do so.

Once it had been easy, back when he could be found working at her side in the garden or spending hours with her reading, baking and playing games they created just for the two of them. When he wasn't in school or with her, he could be found in the workshop with Leland, quietly whittling intricate figures from leftover wood and then proudly presenting them to Ellie.

His shyness came from Leland. He learned at his father's side how to be still in the presence of others, listening silently to what they said but saying nothing of his own. By the time he reached 6, Clayton could sit in a room with others and all but disappear. While charming behavior in a little boy, it seemed ominous in a brooding teenager.

And Clayton brooded a lot. "He's feeling tired," she would tell Leland when he asked why Clayton spent half the day in bed. "I think he's coming down with something." She tried to believe her own explanations, but doubt and worry kept gnawing at her.

When he beat up Jimmy Boykins, her concern escalated. She watched him more closely, looking for signs of trouble. She found plenty of them and busily went about searching for ways to counteract them. A bout of depression on his part prompted her to bake his favorite pie. His signs of irritation led to her efforts to soothe him. Sometimes it worked, sometimes it didn't. And as he grew older, her attempts became more ineffectual, leaving her feeling helpless and desperate, just as she did at this moment, sitting in her chair listening to the wracking sobs coming from his bedroom. Is it reasonable to remain hopeful when so much of one's experience points in a different direction? This life question surfaced for Ellie once again, as it often had in recent years when her son returned home in such a distressed state.

Clayton emerged from his room the following morning sheepish and tousled, still wearing his street clothes. Ellie expected as much. She had been awake most of the night herself while her son wrestled with his demons behind his closed door. He had finally quieted down about 3 a.m. and Ellie had slept fitfully before arising a few hours later.

"What happened yesterday, Clay?" Ellie blurted out the question even though she had intended to wait until Clayton offered an explanation.

"I'm sorry, Mom. Really. I messed up again."

"How? What did you do?"

"Really bad this time . . ."

"Clay, please tell me what happened." Ellie had seen her son through more scuffles than she could count. She recognized all of his common responses—remorse, indignation, sadness, justification—but this time she noticed something unusual. Fear.

"You're scaring me, Clay. Please . . ." Ellie pleaded.

"It's bad, Mom. You'll hate me . . ." She waited. The possibility of hating her son had ceased feeling foreign to her. She just now realized this and wondered when it had happened.

"I kissed that girl who lives down the street."

Ellie puzzled over this admission. Why should a boy of 17 be afraid because he had kissed a girl?

"You kissed who? Sheila?" The only possibility Ellie could come up with lived two blocks over. She knew Clay had a bit of a crush on Sheila which the girl did not share.

"No . . . not her."

What is he talking about? Who? Why was he so upset last night? Something's really wrong! Ellie took a deep slow breath, attempting to stem the panic she felt building. Clayton kept his head down, avoiding eye contact.

"That new girl who moved in a couple months ago."

Without warning, Ellie felt her body become leaden and anchored to the floor. At the same moment, her consciousness flew free of its bodily cage, swooped out of the room and down the street to the gate of the house four doors down. There she saw Emily Brown quietly playing in the front yard. She had built a small fort with lawn chairs and a sheet. Under it she sat with her cat and three dolls, having a tea party.

"That's a silly game for a 12-year-old," Ellie mused.

"What?" Clayton looked at his mother, surprised by the unexpected and seemingly unrelated response.

Ellie abruptly dropped back into her body and broke into uncontrolled sobs as the full import of what had happened—what her son had done—flooded over her.

"Clayton! No! She's only 12 years old!" The resounding smack of her open hand landing squarely on Clayton's face filled her with loathing and resolve.

Later that day, Ellie made her way to the Browns'. She apologized to her neighbors on behalf of her son, promised he would never bother their daughter again and begged their forgiveness.

"Oh, he won't be coming back here, that's for sure," offered Mr. Brown. "I made it clear to him it wasn't safe."

"What do you mean?" asked Ellie, alert to his threatening tone.

"I mean no disrespect to you, Mrs. Howard. Truly I don't. But I took your son by the collar when I caught him with my Emily and shook him up real good. I put the fear of the Almighty in him and told him if ever I see him within sight of my daughter, I'll shoot him dead. I showed him my shotgun so he'd know I mean business. Good day to you, and don't think I don't mean what I just said."

Ellie had no doubt Mr. Brown would keep his word.

SEVENTEEN
2004

Tate finally arrived at the Princess Hotel the following afternoon, even though she intended to go first thing in the morning. Discussions with Dave delayed her and just when she finished with him, she ran into Mazie again. They chatted for several minutes before Tate began filling Mazie in on what she had learned about Leland Howard.

"I 'member him, too," Mazie said. "Not very well, though."

"You're just full of surprises, Mazie!"

"Well, it was a small town back then. Everbody knew everbody."

"I guess so. Tell me about him."

"Don't 'member much, but I know his wife was kilt. Her son did it, or so I remember. Big scandal."

"Her *son* did it?"

"Yep. High on drugs, I think, or mebbe jus' crazy."

"This is getting to me, Mazie. Only yesterday I learned Leland had a child. His name was Clayton. He apparently died the same day Leland's wife was killed. I found that shocking, now you're telling me Clayton killed his own mother? My head might explode!"

"I don't know the details, mind you, but that Clayton boy was a hoodlum."

"How did he die? What happened to him?"

"I seem to 'member somethin' about him killin' hisself. I just know he died the same day and then Mr. Howard broke down and disappeared not long after."

"The more I learn about these people, the more I want to know. It's starting to drive me a little crazy!"

"You're like a dog with a bone, Tate. Can't let go, can you?"

"Nope, guess not. I'm gonna keep going until it comes to an end, somehow or another."

Tate left Mazie, intending to head for the Princess Hotel, when Holly called, inviting her to an impromptu lunch. Given Holly's busy schedule, Tate jumped at the chance, not knowing when the opportunity to get together would present itself again. They met at Rosetta's Kitchen and spent close to an hour together. Tate gave Holly an abbreviated version of everything she had learned in the past several days.

"You've been busy, Tate!"

"I have been, and there's more to do. I'm heading to the Princess Hotel right after this to see what I can find out. I hope it's not another blind alley."

"The man who owns the place now is a great guy. Took him two years to renovate. I haven't seen it yet, but I hear it's beautiful."

"Hopefully, Leland Howard's mantelpiece will still be in the lobby. I'd love to see it."

Tate got her wish and much more. Having finally reached her destination, she introduced herself to the receptionist and asked to speak to the owner.

"That would be me," the man answered. "How can I help you?"

"You're the owner?" Tate was confused.

"That's me. Our receptionist called in sick today, so I'm in charge. At least until my wife gets here. She's the real boss of the Front Desk." He smiled warmly and Tate took an immediate liking to him.

"Well, then. I guess I'm in luck." Tate turned and looked around the lobby. No fireplace. "Or maybe not. This will probably sound strange, but I'm looking for a fireplace."

"A fireplace?" The man looked puzzled.

"Well, a mantelpiece, actually. One made by a man named Leland Howard, sometime in the 1950s. I think this place was under renovation back then."

"Oh, *that* mantelpiece! It's one of our prize possessions!"

"You mean . . ." Tate took in a deep breath; her heart raced.

"Yes, it's here. Let me show you." The man led her through French doors and into a long sitting room off the main lobby. Beautifully appointed, with groups of comfortable seating, low tables, richly hued area rugs and a set of bay windows facing the street, it conveyed luxury and comfort all at once. Three large logs burned in a huge fireplace surrounded by an exquisite mantel gracing the wall at the far end of the room. They walked up to it, and Tate reached out to stroke the wood, running her fingers along the delicate carvings.

Tate's host gestured toward the mantel. "This is it. One of Mr. Howard's best, I think."

"What's your name?" Tate tried to focus on the man beside her, a difficult task given all the thoughts and questions that ran amok in her mind.

"Warren. Warren Wright."

"I have been searching for information about Mr. Howard for days now. I know a lot, but so much is missing. Do you know anything about him, about his work?"

"Actually, I know quite a lot. I did a great deal of research when I bought this place. Wanted to modernize it but keep true to its origins, you know, so I poked around in every corner I could find. There were plenty of them."

"And Mr. Howard? Please tell me. What did you find out about him?"

"That was not easy. He was an extremely talented craftsman, well known locally but never famous. Kept to himself. Apparently he was fussy about who he worked for, what he would build. This is one of only three mantels by him that I've been able to locate. He primarily made furniture but would sometimes do other things—desks for hotel lobbies, cabinetry, the occasional custom-designed door—"

Tate broke in. "Like the one on that old house on Chestnut Street?"

"Where?"

"The place on Chestnut? In the news lately? They want to tear it down?"

"Oh, that place. Yes, I heard about it. He did work on *that* house?"

"I wonder. According to the tax records he owns the place—owned it. Actually it's held in a trust of which he is the beneficiary. It has an unusual door. It's oversized with metal fittings like you'd see on a castle. So now I have to wonder if he made them. And if he did that one, then he must be responsible for the one on a little place I own. That's the only thing that makes sense . . . at least I think so . . ."

Tate looked into Warren Wright's warm brown eyes. "Oh, I just wish I could talk to him. I have so many questions. But he's dead, and there are no relatives, and . . ."

"He's not dead."

Tate faltered, unable to believe she had heard correctly. Warren Wright grabbed her before she lost her footing.

"You said he's . . . did you say he's . . ."

"He's not dead. I talked to him myself. At least I tried to."

"And you know where he is?" *Incredible! I can't believe . . . okay, wait . . . what I think is what I create. What I think is what I create . . .*

Tate chanted the mantra, willing herself to take in what she was being told. Leland Howard was alive!

"Yes. He's out there at Forest Glen. Unless he's passed on since I saw him. That was last year sometime."

"I've got to see him. Will they let me see him?"

"Don't know why they wouldn't. It's a retirement home, not a prison."

"Okay, I'm going to see him." Resolution replaced resignation, and Tate turned toward the door.

"Do you want to see the mantel?"

"What?"

"The mantel. You came here to see the mantel, and I'd love to tell you all about it."

"Oh! Yes, of course . . . I'm sorry, I was so shocked to learn he's alive, I forgot everything else!"

"If you appreciate his work, you'll love this. I'd hate to have you leave without really experiencing it."

Tate refocused. "Beautiful wood. Cherry? No . . ."

"Red Oak. A superb specimen and the craftsmanship is incomparable. Not many woodworkers took the time to focus on every aspect the way he did. He used only the finest wood he could find. Every detail is flawlessly executed. And he always added something special. Do you know about that?"

"Well, the whole thing seems special."

"Yes, but look at this."

Warren Wright stepped to the left end of the mantel, closed his eyes and ran his index finger gently along a row of delicately carved notches decorating its lower edge. Tate heard a faint click. To her amazement, a long, slim drawer dropped open, revealing a stash of chocolate-mint coins, each wrapped in silver.

"After dinner mint?" Warren asked, eyes twinkling.

"I'd absolutely love one!" Tate squealed, pure delight taking over.

EIGHTEEN
1940

Harland Freeman did not allow himself to feel uncomfortable when in the presence of others. Such undesirable feelings lay deeply hidden beneath his façade of self-confidence and tendency toward dominance in every situation. But at this moment, he squirmed in his own skin as the woman and her child walked along the street in front of him, obviously unaware he trailed just behind. He had to speak to Ellie, but not now—not in the presence of the boy.

Harland and Ellie crossed paths on occasion, but they never spoke, or even acknowledged each other, for that matter. In fact, Ellie uttered her last words to him as he left the park following their one mating all those years ago. Back then he feared she would pursue him after their encounter. He had many ways of sidestepping heartbroken girls, and he had prepared himself to use all of them with Ellie. But, the next day she walked right past him in the hall at school, her head held high, as if he didn't even exist. She surprised him even more when she became engaged to and then married Leland Howard immediately after the two boys graduated.

Ellie's refusal to acknowledge Harland did not bother him. The child caused his queasiness. The boy's birth occurred barely seven months after the rushed wedding, and Harland could not help but wonder if he watched his own son walking hand-in-hand with Ellie. And that name: Clayton—Harland's own mother's maiden name and his middle name— why had she chosen to pass his family name on to her offspring?

A handsome child, the boy sported black hair and dark, intense eyes, much like Harland's own. Never having met him face-to-face, Harland could not be sure, but he thought he detected in the child the same slightly bulbous nose and square jaw he saw reflected in the mirror each morning when he shaved.

Harland did not want children. He did not want a wife, a family, or even any close friends for that matter. Harland craved only respect. He secretly yearned for people to treat him the way they treated a successful man worthy of reverence and emulation. He imagined gaining status as the most important businessman in the city and people seeking him out as if the sole fact of being in his presence constituted a special event. Yet seeing the boy brought into question, if only for a moment, the value of living a solitary life, which in Harland's case had not yet come even close to meeting his expectations.

No offers came from professional baseball teams after high school, and the superficial popularity granted him as a star athlete melted away quickly after he found himself working as a clerk in the local hardware store, taking orders from a man he could barely tolerate.

Maybe his dreams had not materialized so far, but he continued to plot his way to the success he considered his due. It irritated him that even now as an adult he had to figure out how to please others in order to get his needs met, but he recognized that necessity, so Harland went to work each day. He meticulously organized the bins of screws and bolts, swept the floors and greeted customers with the bright smile he wore like a suit of armor polished up each morning before heading out into the world. *It's my way out.* This thought alone held Harland in check and stopped him from rushing out the door never to return.

He'd had a lifetime to grow accustomed to uphill battles like this one. He had spent his formative years living in that horrid cabin just north of downtown with his father, who eked out a living as a handyman working for rich folks, and his mother, Crazy Eulah.

Everyone knew his mother by that name, even beyond the boundaries of their little neighborhood, and once old enough to understand its meaning, Harland thought of her as Crazy Eulah, too. She gave birth to him at age 32—too old to have a child, as she told him countless times. His arrival strained her already tenuous hold on reality even further, and she retreated into herself to the point of sometimes losing complete touch with the world around her.

A neglected child must make a difficult choice early in life if he is to survive. He can cling helpless and childlike to the parents who have cast aside basic conventions such as feeding, clothing and protecting their offspring, or he can learn to fend for himself.

From birth, Harland insisted he would thrive, and his squalling determination pulled his reluctant mother from her stupor long enough and often enough that she fed and occasionally bathed him, though he often spent days clothed in nothing but a ragged diaper.

By the time he could crawl and even before he had acquired language, Harland had an acute awareness of the abandonment he would later describe as being estranged from God. How else to account for the fact that Eulah left him unattended in his crib for hours on end, or that his father failed to recognize Harland's need for touch and interaction, no matter how weary he may be after a long day filled with menial work?

People felt sorry for the scrawny boy with the thick black hair and sharp dark eyes, and he became adept at begging for his sustenance from them by the time he could crawl. Mazie saved him from careening headlong into the life of a tramp, drifting from mark to mark. She provided security, dependability and so much more. Through Mazie and her family, he acquired his social skills, and with their nurturing, by the time he entered high school, he had a veneer of likability and the athletic prowess necessary to become a star on the baseball team. Most of all, Mazie taught Harland how to love. Harland decided on his own that any emotion with the power to sway a man from his own calculated path must be carefully avoided.

Now he stood on the threshold of adulthood, and he had no doubt that with perseverance and cunning, the success he pursued would be his. He already had amassed what seemed like a fortune from selling the land on Pearson. He would continue to grow his savings, set himself up in business and build a fine house one day. His single-minded quest for respect blinded him to the slow death of his boyhood charm—the saving grace of his youth—and the emergence of the bitter, angry man lurking just beneath the surface.

—∿∿—

Harland struggled through the years of clerking at the hardware store and gaining the foundation he needed to move ahead in the business community. He worked his way up to the coveted position of manager and then, at the young age of 27, purchased his own business. Freeman Mercantile joined the many successful shops lining Lexington Avenue. He obtained the business in a distress sale that resulted from the collapse of all the local banks seven years earlier in the wake of the crash on Wall Street. He had squirreled away every dollar from the sale of the old family land on Pearson and then continued to build his fortune by diligently saving most of his earnings and making wise investments. His smugness about protecting his money during the Great Depression that swept the nation and broke the backs of many local business owners cheated him of the admiration he anticipated. Harland made things even worse by taking every opportunity to brag about his foresight and good timing, oblivious to the festering resentment of his colleagues.

He had turned himself into a powerful businessman, so they had little choice but to show him what passed for respect. One of them might offer him a ride across town when they saw him out walking, or vacate their seat on the trolley for him on the rare occasion he used that conveyance. But they didn't like him, and Harland knew that beyond a doubt.

Well, he didn't like them either. It didn't occur to him there might be a connection between these facts, an almost tangible chain of cause and effect. Harland Freeman did not waste time trying to understand the perspectives of other people. He had plenty else to think about. He had to keep the store running and make it as profitable as possible. He planned and plotted how to get the most work out of his staff for the lowest wages he could manage. If he could make a profit selling a mediocre product for an inflated price, that's exactly what he did. If the product could be obtained only from Freeman Mercantile, the price would be even more exorbitant.

He kept busy thinking about how he presented himself in public, always making sure his suit looked slightly better than the suits of the other store owners along Patton and Lexington Avenues, his shoes were highly polished and his shirts impeccably starched and ironed. But above all, Harland spent long hours laying the plans for the house he would build on Chestnut Street. After a few years of owning his business, the time had come to take another bold step. This house would be his crowning achievement, and he was certain he would finally be graciously welcomed into the ranks of the elite businessmen in Asheville.

"Oh, yes!" he boasted to Wallace Flanders, who owned the men's furnishing store two doors down and who lived on Cumberland Avenue in a second-hand house. "Yes, I bought the property on Chestnut. Don't know why such a prime piece of real estate hadn't already sold." He paused for the shortest moment then prompted, "Don't you think it's perfect for my mansion? Would you like to see my plans?"

"Nice to see you, Freeman," Flanders lied as he moved quickly out the door with his purchase under his arm.

Harland looked after him, and instead of feeling the anger or disappointment or rejection that stalked him, he puffed himself back up and strode off to attend to the next customer.

NINETEEN
2004

Asheville has been a traveler's destination through-out its history. It was originally the ancestral homeland of the Cherokee Indians; their footpaths crisscrossed the area. Those trails slowly grew into bigger crossroads as the white settlers arrived, and those new inhabitants attracted traveling tradesmen who came to barter pots, pans, knives, sugar and other hard-to-get-supplies for the deer, bear and beaver furs available from the local mountaineers.

The town had grown at a leisurely pace until the late 1800s when George Vanderbilt made his first visit. In addition to his French-inspired mansion, he built a village to house his craftsmen and supervisors and a church for the community.

Forest Glen Manor joined the varied accom-modations that sprang up in the early 20th century to serve the many travelers to the city. Tate recognized it as one of the nicer ones. It had been converted to a retirement center in the 1970s.

Besides a collection of small buildings set among the rolling slopes on a broad expanse of land on Hendersonville Highway, the grounds held several ponds and the landscaping accented the gentle ridges and well-worn, paved walkways winding through the four acres that housed the complex. Tate imagined it had been quite successful back in the heyday of cross country traveling, when automobiles were the conveyance of choice by families from across the continent. It enjoyed a desirable location, on a major thoroughfare and within a short distance from the Biltmore Estate, which had been opened to the public in the aftermath of the Great Depression.

Tate parked as close as she could to the entrance, grumbling about the number of empty handicapped spaces holding the choice locations. She felt a bit ridiculous for feeling this way, especially given the facility's status as a retirement home. But it always annoyed her to see dozens of rarely filled spaces designated for handicapped parking in all the parking lots in the world, it seemed. She laughed at herself as she approached the reception desk.

"Afternoon, honey. How can I help you?" Tate blanched at the unwarranted familiarity even though the woman's open smile signaled her eagerness to be helpful. Tate asked to see Leland Howard.

"Mr. Howard?" asked the receptionist.

"Yes, Leland Howard."

"Are you a relative?"

That's quite nosey of her. Tate felt her irritation building. "Do I have to be in order to see him?" she challenged.

"Oh, well . . . excuse me. No. No you don't have to be." The warmth in the woman's voice disappeared, replaced by a cold and clipped response. "I'll just get someone to take you to him." The receptionist scowled at Tate.

Serves her right. Tate sank into one of the worn chairs in the lobby. *Why do people have to ask such dumb questions?*

And why am I being so bitchy? She could feel the old Tate pushing her way to the surface, the Tate easily angered by the behavior of others when that behavior clearly had little or nothing to do with her. *I must watch that.*

The receptionist picked up the phone and dialed the extension in the Common room. "Someone here to see Mr. Howard," she said. "No, it's not a relative. I don't know who she is. She wouldn't say." Tate heard the sarcasm in the woman's voice, confirming she had been confrontational. *Clearly I still have a lot to learn about Southern charm and conventions.*

"Ma'am," called the nurse who entered the lobby moments later. "You're here to see Mr. Howard?"

"Yes." Tate rose and as she passed the receptionist, she stopped and said, "Look, I'm sorry for being rude. I shouldn't have acted like I did." The receptionist nodded grudgingly, clearly not willing to forgive. Tate bent close to her and said, "I've been learning about Mr. Howard's work, and I'm just here to meet the man who is responsible for so many beautiful things."

The receptionist softened. "Oh yes, he is very talented, isn't he? And he's such a love. It's so sad he never gets visitors, but no one's left anymore. He'll be glad to see you."

Tate followed the nurse into a large room filled with light from the expansive windows running the full length of the back wall. About a dozen people sat at small tables throughout the remarkably quiet room. No one there seemed willing to laugh out loud or speak in a full voice though many joined in on hushed conversations. Card players occupied two tables, one group engaged in a game of Hearts and the other in what looked to Tate like Hand and Foot. *I wonder . . . that's a pretty complicated game for old people.* She chuckled at her own stereotypical thinking.

Hand and Foot, a derivative of Pinochle, required a great deal of strategy to play successfully. With the large number of cards a player could be holding, it also required some physical dexterity that Tate thought could be difficult for old hands stiffened with arthritis. The four players involved in this game had card holders to deal with that problem.

"He's over here," said the nurse. Tate turned away from the card game. All the residents in the room looked clean and well groomed. Even those in wheelchairs appeared well taken care of.

In the far corner, Tate saw an old man hunched over a rectangular folding table filled with various chisels and pieces of wood—beautiful wood, not the cheap fragments of pine Tate would have expected to see in an arts and crafts room in a retirement home.

Even from a distance, she recognized some cherry and ambrosia maple. As she approached Leland, he focused on her with eyes of the softest blue she had ever seen. They sparkled, yet reflected an ancient sadness.

"Mr. Howard," said the nurse. "You have a visitor." Tate stopped beside Leland Howard and looked into the face of a man who, despite all he had lost, peered up at her with hope and curiosity.

"It's nice to finally meet you, Mr. Howard. My name is Tate Marlowe."

"Do I know you?" Leland searched her face hopefully.

"No, we haven't met before. I've been learning about your work, and I've seen the old house you own on Chestnut Street."

Tate saw pain hijack Leland's whole being as he took in what she said. He turned away, shutting her out, the light dimming in the sparkling blue eyes.

"Oh, Mr. Howard. I'm so sorry. I didn't mean to upset you."

He picked up the wood he had been carving and turned it in his hands, inspecting it closely and humming quietly.

What did I do wrong? I shouldn't have jumped right in like that. Now he'll never talk to me. Too abrupt.

Tate's visit had aroused the curiosity of the Forest Glen staff, one of whom hovered nearby eavesdropping on their conversation. As Tate stood in perplexed silence, one of the aides motioned to her.

"He doesn't talk about his past. I think he has a lot of bad memories and you may have stirred them up."

"I just wanted to meet him. I have so many questions, and I think he could answer them, but I never intended to cause him any pain."

"Well, he can be talkative and I'm sure he'd like to have a visitor now and again. We can't provide each of our guests as much personal attention as they'd like. Give him some time, then come back and try again."

"Do you think he'll give me another chance? I can be a bit of a bull in a china shop, if you know what I mean."

"Yeah, I know." The woman smiled at Tate and gave her a wink. Obviously the word had spread quickly about her encounter with the receptionist.

"Oh. Well . . . I guess I have more amends to make then."

"Don't fret about it. We're happy to have someone take an interest in Mr. Leland. He's such a darlin'. His sadness runs real deep, and we'd all like to see it lifted a bit."

"Do you think he might talk to me if I came back in a couple of days? Or maybe tomorrow?"

"Well, he loves to show off his woodworking. He makes wonderful little boxes with hiding places in them. Maybe you could start there. And I think he'd be even more inclined to talk to you if you'd bring along his favorite treat—peanut butter cookies. But he only likes the homemade kind, and he can definitely tell the difference. For an old man, his taste buds are in remarkably good shape!"

Tate left Forest Glen and spent the rest of the afternoon looking for instructions online and getting the ingredients necessary to make peanut butter cookies. She fought the urge to experiment with some of the updated recipes she found, opting for the original, simple version that harkened back to the days when people—when she—did not worry so much about things like high cholesterol, glycemic index and expanding waistlines.

These were my favorites when I was a kid. Sitting in the sun on the back porch with peanut butter cookies right out of the oven and a big glass of milk—that was Heaven!

Some of Tate's childhood memories remained crystal clear even after many decades, and often the most pronounced ones involved food. Her mother had taught Tate much of what she knew about cooking, and though Tate's diet had changed significantly over her lifetime, the skills she learned in her earliest years, standing on a stool beside her mother at the kitchen stove, still served her well now.

She had not baked cookies in ages. She couldn't remember the last time, but she could remember the first. She was about 5, and her mother was in a good mood. They pulled out the tattered recipe handed down from Tate's great-grandmother, scrawled on lined note paper in a spidery script. Then came the sugar, flour, eggs, peanut butter and the rest, which they mixed into a sticky, sweet dough. Tate rolled it into little balls between the palms of her tiny hands and then flattened the balls out by making crisscrosses in the top using a fork. She licked the stuff off her fingers and scooped up the leftover dough from the bowl, gobbling it down, too.

Her mother hugged her. They giggled. They made white spots on each other's noses with flour-dipped fingers. Easy laughter, sun-filled kitchen, chewy cookies, fleeting joy. Children do not forget moments like this, especially when they occur so rarely.

Tate savored this memory the next morning as she prepared cookies to take to Forest Glen. She baked three dozen, some crunchy and some chewy, sealed them up in plastic wrap and again set out on her quest for information.

TWENTY
1954

Rita Marie Thornton provided proof of the complexity of the debate regarding nature versus nurture. Did her problematic behavior as a child result from her genetic heritage or the circumstances of her family life? A powerful argument could be made for either side, and such debates took place frequently in the principals' offices and teachers' lounges of the various schools she attended in the many towns her family migrated through during her tumultuous formative years.

She arrived in Asheville in 1952 at the age of 15. With bad skin and limp hair, popularity proved elusive for Rita. But she now had new weapons. Her approaching womanhood brought with it the transition from skinny beanpole to voluptuous femininity, complete with firm full breasts, rounded hips and a bad attitude.

She embodied the definition of a girl from the wrong side of the tracks, and she embraced her status with enthusiasm.

Her clothing consisted mainly of cheap chemise dresses cinched in tight at the waist and worn shorter than the fashionable length of the day to show off her shapely legs. Occasionally she added a tight cardigan buttoned to just under her breasts, and she always sported an abundance of rhinestone jewelry from the 5 & 10 cent store.

She gained just the kind of attention she wanted. The bad boys began lining up, and within two months of her arrival, Rita had her pick of them.

Although she had no real friends to speak of, Rita's social calendar kept her busy every day and evening. She attended school sporadically, preferring to hang out under the bleachers with the greasers and smoke Lucky Strikes. The shallowness of her existence never occurred to Rita. She cared not who she dated so long as she had a boy on her arm every night and something fun to do every weekend. Then she met Clay Howard.

Almost ten years her senior, she considered him the sexiest man she had ever seen. From the first time she laid eyes on him, she set out to bed him. She put her hips in motion and sashayed across his path. He pretended not to notice her the first time or any of the many times in the following week she made it a point to be in his presence. Then one day she caught him giving her a sidelong glance as she passed.

"Hey there, handsome," she cooed, acting as grown up as possible for a 15-year-old. Clay had that unmistakable look of interest in his eye, so she pushed forward. "Why don't you buy me a pop?" Rita asked.

"What's a pop, little girl?" Clay tried to cover his confusion with swagger.

Rita's insecurity raged to the surface. She knew they called it "coke" down here. "Pop" had slipped out, an old habit. She pulled in her tummy, threw her shoulders back to make her budding breasts more prominent and stared Clay straight in the eyes.

"Oh, that's right. You *rebels* call it 'coke' don't you? Guess I figured a smart guy like you would know what a pop is."

Clay surveyed her up and down. Slow. Deliberate. "Oh, I know what it is all right," he announced, his voice smooth and silky.

Rita blushed and broke out in a fine sweat from ankles to hairline. But she never took her eyes off Clay.

"Now that we know what we're both talkin' about, you gonna buy me one or not?"

"Nah," said Clay. "You're jail bait for a guy like me." He chuckled and his perfect mouth curled into a sly grin. Rita felt herself melting, but she maintained her confident tone.

"Really? Jail bait is a good thing, ain't it?"

"Not unless a man wants to go to jail," quipped Clay. "I've been there, and it's not the place for me."

"Then we'll have to be careful not to get caught." Rita sauntered down the street, leaving him to watch every movement of her arms, her hips and her long, slender legs. Now that she had his attention, she would take her time reeling him in.

Four months later, Clay made it clear he had no intention of marrying Rita in spite of her pregnancy. So it came as a big surprise to Rita when his parents, whom she had met on a couple of occasions, invited her to dinner and gave her gifts for the child she carried. They made it known they cared about her and wanted to be a part of her life and the baby's life, no matter what their no-account son chose to do.

TWENTY-ONE
2004

The receptionist greeted Tate hesitantly. No "honey" this time. Just a "good afternoon."

"Hi. I'm here to see Mr. Howard again," Tate began, then she held out a package of cookies—her peace offering.

"I brought these along. I made some for him, and I wanted to give some to the staff as well."

"Now that's mighty nice of you, Missus . . ."

"Marlowe. It's Ms. Marlowe, but you can call me Tate."

"Ms. Tate. Very nice of you to think of us, too." Tate noticed her cool tone and the emphasis on "Ms.," but decided to let it slide. So many people these days still found it difficult, even distasteful perhaps, to address a woman by a title which did not signify marital status.

"Just Tate. No 'Ms.' necessary." She kept her tone friendly.

The receptionist paused briefly before giving a totally unexpected response.

"Okay, Ms. Tate. I understand you don't like our Southern ways 'round here. We call people 'honey' and we call 'em 'missus' even when we don't know if they're married or not. You pro'bly think we're uneducated or backwards, but that's not the case. We're polite. We're friendly, and we stick to our habits just like everbody else. We don't mean no harm, and we don't mean no offense. I'll bend to your way much as I can, but there's limits. So you decide. You can be Ms. Marlowe or Ms. Tate, but no way am I gonna address you by your given name and not put no title in front of it."

Tate stared agape at the woman whose fierce expression challenged her own indignation. *Whoa! What's going on here? I thought I was being polite!* She felt the flash of anger that warned of an impending meltdown, but instead of lashing out, she forced herself to look at it from the other side. *I'm pushy, bossy and demanding. I approach the world like everyone's out to get me. I take offense easily and feel justified in doing so.* These thoughts rushed through her mind in an instant and with them an overwhelming awareness of how caustic she could be. She felt the extremely rare sensation of shame flow over her. The next moment she found herself awash in a flood of gratitude. *This is exactly the lesson I need to learn.*

Tears formed in the corner of Tate's eyes as she took in the woman in front of her. Not just the face, not just the physical body, but the full spirit of the woman, her essence, integrity and dignity. She reached over and took the woman's smooth, dark, cool hand into her own.

Tate had failed to notice the woman's ID tag before, had not taken the time to put a name to the face, but now she did. *How appropriate. Ruby truly is a jewel.*

"I cannot thank you enough, Ruby. I rarely stop to think how I come across to others, and when I do, I usually make excuses for how it's their problem, not mine. I haven't been here long, and I still find Southern customs a bit perplexing, even annoying sometimes. Still, it's no reason to be rude, and I realize how abrasive I must seem to you. I'm really sorry. And I mean it when I say 'thank you' for pointing it out to me. Not many people are willing to stand up to me the way you just did, and it's truly refreshing, 'though I'll admit I'm embarrassed."

"I'm embarrassed, too," Ruby gasped. Tate noticed the flushing on Ruby's face and neck. "Don't know why I said that. I never talk to people that way. Somethin' just came over me."

"I have that effect on people sometimes!"

"But I should never have . . ."

"I get that you have to maintain your composure in this job. But no one heard you except me, and I'm so grateful to you right now, Ms. Ruby . . ."

"Really? For such shameful behavior?"

"Really. And I deserved it. I have to tell you, I needed to hear it. People just don't call me on my bad manners very often. They walk away instead, and I lose people without ever getting to see what part I played in it. You helped open my eyes in a way I couldn't have done on my own. You and I could be good friends."

"Well, Ms. Tate . . ."

"But you'd really have to stop calling me 'Ms.' outside of the work place!"

They broke into laughter, which filled the otherwise empty lobby just as someone entered from the door leading to the Common room.

Dorothy, the aide Tate had met yesterday, looked at the two women quizzically.

"You seem to be havin' a good time."

"We are," said Tate. "We're forging a friendship here based on mutual respect and brutal honesty!"

"And peanut butter cookies," Ruby chimed in. "Want one?"

"There are plenty to go around. I brought lots to share with the staff and the other guests. Any chance I can see Mr. Howard again, Dorothy?"

"They can't all have the cookies, you know. Some are diabetic and we have to be careful of allergies and what not. I'll take them and make sure everyone who can have one gets one," Dorothy volunteered. "And you keep some for you and Mr. Howard. I think he'll be happy to see you today."

Leland sat at the same table, looking out over the woods behind the facility, apparently deep in thought, absentmindedly fiddling with a small wooden box he held in his hands. Tate watched him from a distance for several minutes before approaching, which she did only after his attention returned to the work before him.

"Hello, again." She consciously softened her tone as she greeted him.

"Do I know you?" Same question. Same expression of curiosity. *I hope he doesn't remember me.*

"We met only once, very briefly. My name is Tate Marlowe."

"Marlowe is it? I don't recollect knowing any Marlowes."

"I'm fairly new in town. Wanted to come visit and bring you these." She placed the cookies on the table near him.

"Peanut butter?" He peeked up at her with child-like joy.

"Yep. Peanut butter. I hear they're your favorite."

"You bet!" He reached eagerly for the cookies then paused. "May I have one?"

"Of course. I made them just for you. Well, I gave some to the staff, too."

"Mighty nice of you, Missus . . ."

"Marlowe. Tate Marlowe."

He took a bite of the cookie and savored it for a moment.

"This is pretty good." Leland smiled at her mischievously. "You make 'em yourself?" Tate thought it might be a trick question.

"Sure did. I hear you're partial to homemade, and I also understand you're pretty good at telling the difference."

"One of my few remaining skills, I'm happy to say. Still have good taste buds." Leland spoke slowly and a bit haltingly. His thin voice quavered some.

"Well, how'd I do?"

Leland munched on the cookie and brushed the crumbs off his shirt front. "Not bad, but I like the chewy kind best."

"Well, you're in luck, because I made them both ways. Try this one."

Leland took the pliant mass from Tate and lifted it to his nose. After sniffing it, he gently pressed it between his fingers, testing the texture. Then he bit into it and broke into a big smile. Tate waited for the review.

"Mighty good cookie, Missus . . ."

"Marlowe. Just call me Tate, if that's okay with you."

" . . . Missus Tate." *No getting around it, I guess. Better get used to it, though the likelihood of that is remote!*

"Glad you like them. I haven't made them in years, so I was afraid they might not turn out so well."

"Why'd you make 'em for *me*?" The question caught Tate off guard.

"I . . . well, um . . ."

"Why'd you come to see me? Do I know you?"

"No, Mr. Howard, you don't. But I hope you'll let me visit so we can get to know each other. It may seem strange, but we have some things in common and I find you very interesting. I don't want to push, though."

He looked at her intently. "We have met before, haven't we?"

"Yes, I was here yesterday, and I think I upset you."

"You said something about a house and my work."

"I didn't intend to bring up bad memories."

"I'm an old man. I have good ones and bad ones. More bad ones than most folks, but lots of good ones, too. These cookies, for instance. They put me in mind of the ones Ellie would make for us. For me and my son, back before . . ."

Tate saw the pain overtaking Leland again, and she cringed thinking of the distress he must suffer. She knew about the death of his wife and son and that Leland had dropped out of sight soon after the tragedy. Now, miraculously it seemed, he sat in front of her. She prayed he would not close her out completely.

". . . back when we all lived together and things were still pretty good."

He's sharp. He remembers what I said yesterday.

"I'd like to hear about those days, if you're so inclined, Mr. Howard."

"You don't want to hear an old man's sad story, young lady, and believe me when I tell you I've got a sad one to tell."

"Actually, I do want to hear it. More than you could possibly know."

Why? Why is this so important to me? So there's an old house people want to tear down. Why can't I just let it be? It really has nothing to do with me. But Tate knew she would not let go until her questions were answered, whether it seemed reasonable or not.

———

Tate sat with Leland for almost two hours while he poured out a convoluted tale. As he talked, he kept his veined hands busy working on a beautiful piece of wood which gave off a faint, sweet aroma.

He shared snippets about his early childhood and his family's move from the forest to the city, interspersed with references to high school and other sharply remembered anecdotes spanning his long lifetime. At other times, he struggled as he tried to recover a lost memory that obviously still held significance for him. There seemed neither rhyme nor reason to what he related or in what order, so Tate did her best to piece together the disjointed tale, choosing to listen to whatever he wanted to share rather than butting in with questions of her own.

"Haven't talked about this stuff in many a year. Don't know why I'm talkin' to you now." He peered intently at Tate, as if searching for the answer to his question in her eyes.

"Maybe it was just a matter of time . . ." *I'm coming to love this old man. He seems to have suffered so much, and yet I believe he's still capable of loving.* ". . . or it could be the peanut butter cookies. I always thought they were kind of magical when I was a kid," Tate said.

Leland chuckled and she smiled back at him. He continued with his stories, like verbal snapshots of his life. But he didn't talk about his wife or son. Nothing about the house at 305 Chestnut Street. Guilt and impatience battled for Tate's attention. She wanted answers to specific questions, but she allowed Leland to set the pace and tone for their conversation, serving as his sounding board, getting vital bits of information for herself and hoping to give him respite from his loneliness.

Eventually the reminiscing took its toll. Leland's eyelids drooped and he seemed to dose off. Unsure whether to stay or leave, Tate looked around for help just as Dorothy approached.

"I can't believe he spent so much time talkin' to you. He usually keeps to himself and his work. Don't mix much with the others."

"I'm amazed. After yesterday, I didn't know if he'd even see me again."

"Those cookies must have cast a spell over him, just like they did the rest of us." Dorothy winked and Tate knew her amends to the staff at Forest Glen had been accepted.

Just then, Leland roused and began straightening up his wood and tools.

"You can leave it there, like always, Mr. Leland." Dorothy helped with the cleaning up. "It'll be right here when you come back." Leland lifted the piece he had been working on to his nose and inhaled deeply. Then he handed it to Tate and motioned that she, too, should smell it.

"It's beautiful. Such a sweet aroma. Really delicious." She took another deep breath, drawing in the richness of the wood.

"You ever work with wood?" Leland asked.

"No, never did. Maybe I should give it a try. It seems to bring you such great pleasure."

"Nearly the only thing in my life I could ever count on. That, and things changin' when you least expect 'em to." Once more, Tate had a sense of the deep and painful memories hidden behind Leland's comment, though she had no idea the extent of them.

"Could we talk again sometime, Mr. Howard? I'd like to come back if you'll let me."

"You come back whenever you want, young lady. I'm not much for company usually, but you're different. You bring homemade cookies!" The impish look on Leland's face made Tate smile.

"I thank you for the 'young lady' reference. I'm neither, really, but I'll take it nonetheless."

"Compared to me, you're young. I made an assumption about the 'lady' part!" Leland flashed a knowing look in Dorothy's direction, and all three of them burst into laughter. Leland's quiet, controlled reaction seemed unfamiliar to him.

"I'll come back in a day or two. Do you need or want anything else? I can be pretty versatile!"

"How about chocolate chip next time?"

"You got it." Tate still held the wood in her hand and she drew in its nourishing scent once more.

"Do you have enough wood? I could bring you more if you need it."

"No need. Mr. Price sees to it I have a good supply."

"Mr. Price?" *Who's Mr. Price? I thought there was no one left in Leland's life.*

"He don't come a visitin' no more. He's old like me. But he still takes care of things for me and makes sure I have enough wood. This here is rosewood." Leland took the specimen from Tate, seemingly unaware of the revelation he had just imparted. Tate maintained her composure, said her goodbyes and promised to return as Dorothy helped Leland out of his chair and they headed toward his room.

Tate went directly to Ruby's desk. "I know our friendship is brand new," she said in a teasing tone, "but I've got a big favor to ask."

Ruby looked at her, eyebrows furrowed, not sure what to expect.

"Mr. Howard just mentioned a Mr. Price. Says he takes care of things and gives him wood. Do you know who that is? Where I can find him?"

"Now you know I'm not s'posed to give out information like that, don't you?"

"Yes, of course. I didn't mean to . . ."

"Can't say just who that is. But don't see no harm in saying from time to time a van from Price Automotive comes 'round and drops off a package for someone here." Ruby paused, holding Tate's gaze.

"But anyone asks, you didn't hear it from me."

"Lunch is on me, Ruby! What's your preference?"

"If I had a friend inclined to do such a thing as take me to lunch, I'm mighty fond of that Uncle Piggy's place over by the high school. They got some barbecue that'll make your mouth water just thinkin' about it."

"Fact is, Ruby . . . sorry, Ms. Ruby . . . I've been hearing about that place lately, but I haven't been there myself yet. How 'bout I pick you up tomorrow and we check it out?"

"No need to pick me up. I'll meet you there at twelve o'clock. Be helpful if you go early and hold us a place. The line can be long sometimes, and I don't like waitin'." Ruby tilted her head slightly and smiled.

This woman is full of fire and sass! "I'll be there. Lookin' forward to it." And Tate was, indeed, looking forward to forging a new friendship. But she had another mission on her mind, too. As soon as she got home, she Googled Price Automotive and then headed back out immediately in search of more information about Leland Howard.

159

TWENTY-TWO
2004

"How can I help you?" The voice came from behind the counter as Tate entered the small lobby of the auto shop. The woman sported curly red hair, striking blue eyes framed with trendy glasses, and a no-nonsense attitude.

"I have what will probably sound like an odd question . . . ," Tate began as she took in the surrounding area. The desk was covered with a variety of mechanical puzzles, a few plants held tenaciously to life, and the walls sported funny sayings such as:

DON'T PUT YOUR CIGARETTE BUTTS IN THE URINAL.
IT MAKES THEM SOGGY AND HARD TO LIGHT.

". . . but then, this place is kind of odd, too!" she blurted out.

"Yes, we take great pride in being a bit odd here." The woman smiled and, never breaking eye contact, waited for Tate's question.

"I wonder if you know a Mr. Leland Howard. He's a resident out at Forest Glen."

"That would be my grandfather."

"Mr. Howard is your grandfather?" Tate gasped.

"No, my grandfather is the one who knows Mr. Howard. They've been friends for decades."

"Really? Then he's the one who sends the supplies for Mr. Howard's woodworking?"

"Well, he used to. He's in very poor health and doesn't get out at all. But he made sure Mr. Howard would continue getting everything he needs. He's Mr. Howard's guardian."

Once again, Tate found herself speechless. *A guardian?* "His guardian?" Tate asked. "I really need to talk to your grandfather! What's the chance of that happening?"

The woman took several moments to answer, all the while looking intently into Tate's eyes.

She seems to be sizing me up, Tate thought.

"I might be able to set that up, but what's your interest in Mr. Howard?"

"It's really complicated. He has a connection with an old house in Montford—the one they want to tear down. It's none of my business, really, but I can't seem to let go of the idea that I'm supposed to save the place. So I started looking for information and, in the process, found Mr. Howard, found you . . . every corner I turn leads to more questions. And I can't stand to leave a question unanswered. I'm quirky that way."

"Okay."

"Okay?" Tate wasn't sure what the woman meant.

"Yes. I'll put you in touch with my grandfather. In fact, he may be able to see you today, if you've got time."

"Plenty of it! Please set it up for me as soon as possible."

"But I need to warn you, he can be crotchety."

Two hours later, Tate Marlowe entered the library of Mr. Richard Price, a tiny, white-haired man ensconced in a wingback chair, who apparently had no time to waste on Southern hospitality.

"How do you know Leland Howard?" he asked before Tate even took a seat.

His granddaughter was right. He is cranky! Better not waste his time. Tate went right to the point of her visit.

"I recently learned he owns that old place they want to demolish over on Chestnut Street. I have this idea—maybe it's harebrained—that I'm supposed to save the place." She paused, wondering how much detail to provide. Sometimes less is more. Mr. Price did not stop her, so Tate went on.

"I tracked Mr. Howard down to Forest Glen. I spent a couple of hours with him earlier today. He told me a lot about his life, but I have so many more questions. And he told me you take care of him. That's why I wanted to meet you. It may not make much sense, but I'm very fond of him. I want to know more about him, his life, his work . . ."

"Why should I believe you? Leland doesn't talk to anyone anymore."

"I made cookies for him. He ate a bunch and talked 'til he dozed off."

"Why'd you do that?"

"Like I said, I'm fond of him. The staff said he liked peanut butter cookies, so I made them and took them to him."

"All of his work has been sold."

"What?"

"If you're looking for some of the pieces he made, they're all gone. Sold long ago."

"No, I . . . what pieces? You think I'm trying to . . ."

"Every once in a while, someone comes sniffing around looking for a table or a chest or anything he built. Think they'll find something priceless lying around and buy it for a song. Well, it's all gone."

"Oh! No! That's not why I'm here!"

"Then why exactly are you here, young lady?"

"Okay, let me start over. All I'm looking for is information. Last week, I took a walk along Chestnut Street and I happened upon the old place everyone is talking about. It's all over the news lately. I own a small house over on Maplewood that I'm remodeling. Both of them, mine and the one on Chestnut, have very similar doors . . ."

Mr. Price relaxed a bit. *He's willing to listen to me. That's a good sign.*

". . . and that got me to wondering how my little place could possibly have something in common with a crumbling mansion in Montford. So I started looking for answers. I found some. I learned Mr. Howard was a master craftsman. Then I found him, which seemed like a miracle, and he told me a lot. Now I'm here, talking to you, hoping for more."

"What do you intend to *do* with this information you want? Most people are just out to make a buck. Don't give a damn about who gets hurt in the process."

"You have every right to be suspicious of me, Mr. Price. You don't know me from Adam. I can assure you this is not about money. All I can say is my heart went out to Mr. Howard when I met him. For some reason I don't fully understand myself, I'm completely fascinated with him. All this started when I decided I have to save the old place on Chestnut. He owns it. That's a matter of public record. Yet he never mentioned it today even though I spent almost two hours with him."

Just as his granddaughter had done earlier, Mr. Price took his time appraising Tate. She sat quietly, squelching her urge to keep talking. In the background, she heard the clock in the hallway chime four times. As if on cue, Mr. Price began talking.

"I wondered why my granddaughter sent you to me, but she's real good at judging people. You stuck to your guns even when I told you there was nothing left to buy."

"Does that mean you'll talk to me?" She needed not ask.

"You see this old walking stick?" He leaned forward in his chair, hands resting atop a beautifully carved walking stick with what appeared to be an ivory handle. "A family heirloom, handed down through four generations. It came to me on my twenty-first birthday, and not two weeks later I managed to crack it badly. Thought I'd ruined it forever. A long time later I met Leland Howard, and he put it back to nearly perfect condition. Then I hired him to make the desk you see in the corner there."

Tate looked at the piece he pointed out. A simple design with a generally clean, spare appearance, five drawers and impeccable craftsmanship, the desk harkened back to the work of Gustav Stickley and Frank Lloyd Wright. But unlike their quarter-sawn oak or cherry, this desk appeared to be constructed of curly maple, and the lines were more flowing and delicate than the heavier Mission-style.

"It's incredible! I've never seen anything like it."

"That's the case with much of his work. Oh, he did common things for sure, but in an uncommon way. Everyone wanted something made by Leland Howard."

"He must have been very successful."

"Could have been. But he wanted a simple life. He wouldn't work for everybody, and he never worked any faster than he wanted to. He was definitely choosy about what he did, and his modesty tempered his success, I think. That's one of the reasons his work was so special."

"I saw a mantelpiece he made. It's over at the Princess Hotel."

"Ah, yes, I remember that one. Took him several months, way behind schedule. They were pretty upset about it."

"It's gorgeous, and the owner showed me a secret compartment."

"The desk has one, too. Think you can find it?"

"I can try! It's really okay?"

"Yes, of course. But it's not easy, I promise you."

Tate walked over to the desk and began slowly stroking the silky finish.

"This is incredible. Feels like it's brand new, and it must be fifty years old at least."

"Probably even older. It's one of his earlier pieces, before his work really caught on." Mr. Price turned toward Tate as much as he could but made no attempt to get out of the chair. She realized he must be in great pain.

She continued exploring the surface of the desk, under the knee hole, around the tops of the legs, every seam she could find. No luck.

"Pull out the bottom left drawer," Mr. Price instructed.

Tate followed his directions.

"Slide the whole drawer unit out. There's a small notch on the right interior." Tate found the spot and out came a frame that held both of the drawers.

"Reach in to the very back. There's a panel that slides out from under the desk top."

Tate removed the thin plate and searched under it. Nothing.

"Thought that was it, didn't you?" Mr. Price's eyes gleamed with playfulness.

"Where else could it be?" asked Tate, her frustration growing.

"There on the left, very bottom, right in the middle. Lift up on the sidewall."

Tate searched for the release point and pushed in lightly. The sidewall slipped out of position, revealing the secret compartment. No more than one inch wide, about three inches deep, and running half the length of the left side of the desk, it could easily conceal small treasures such as jewelry and coins.

"Oh! How clever! I love things like this." Tate surrendered to the joy of the moment and suddenly found herself lost in a memory from childhood.

Tate's love of secret places had grown out of necessity, and she had been teaching herself the art of self-protection for as long as she could remember. She learned to hide right alongside learning to crawl, and while she could not remember with images and sounds her tiny self under the sofa or behind the clothes in the closet, she knew that feeling of being surrounded by musty darkness and being safe in the moment.

One of her favorite hiding places as a child was under the sheltering bush at the edge of the yard by the little house her family moved into when she was five. The shrub grew tall, wide and untamed, with long arching branches radiating out from its center.

In the spring, Tate watched each little bud form along the boughs and push toward life. She carefully inspected the branches, sometimes pulling one or two into a different position to close any gaps. When the buds opened, tight clusters of white blossoms filled the willowy arms from end to end, and the little flowers put out a scent so strong it made her woozy if she breathed in too much of it. She loved that aroma—the sweet, sticky smell of it—and the fragile coolness of the white blossoms against her eyelids as she dipped down into the safety of the scent, knowing the little flowers would be followed quickly by thousands of tiny leaves, knowing behind those leaves there awaited a Tate-sized hollow, and remembering when hunkered down there she would find respite, albeit too brief, from a depressed mother and angry father.

"Miss Marlowe?" Richard Price's voice brought Tate's attention back to the library.

"Oh, I'm so sorry! I got lost for a moment." She felt the blush move quickly from her chest up her neck, then settle in on her face.

"Somewhere long ago and far away from the looks of it."

"Yes, that sums it up nicely."

"A pleasant memory, I hope?"

"A fond one. I just remembered hiding under a bush at a house I lived in as a child. Seeing the desk took me right back there—secret places and all that."

Mr. Price beamed at her, and Tate reluctantly reassembled the desk, then returned to her chair.

"Thank you for showing that to me. It just makes me love Mr. Howard more. He's much like the furniture he created, I think. He holds lots of secrets."

"That he does, but they are his secrets to keep or to share. It's not my place to tell you about his life."

Joy turned to disappointment quickly, and Tate let out a deep sigh. "Okay, I won't press you for more information. But I won't give up, either. You may find me sitting here again at some point, and I hope I'll be welcome."

"My favorite is brownies—with walnuts."

Tate laughed out loud at the old man, whose eyes twinkled with mischief.

"I'll take that as an invitation!" Tate said goodbye and made her way back to her truck. It had been a long, emotional day, and she wanted a nap more than almost anything. But on the way home, she took a circuitous route past 305 Chestnut Street.

"I won't give up!" she yelled out at the house as she cruised by slowly. At the same moment, she noticed an approaching pedestrian who gave her a quizzical look. *Now all the neighbors will think I'm a nut case. I really should learn when to keep my mouth shut!*

She spent the evening preparing turkey chili, which she devoured while watching her favorite TV show, *Wheel of Fortune*, followed by more television, dessert and a bedtime snack. In the back of her mind, she also thought through her eventful day.

Her social network had expanded significantly. Ruby would be a good friend, she was sure of that, and she would take the truck to Price Automotive for any work it needed in the future. Leland Howard would be on her schedule as often as he would permit, and she fully intended to visit Mr. Price again as well. *I can't get lost in all this. I've got to get the renovation next door done, find new tenants . . .*

She dropped into bed at 10 p.m. and descended into intricate, Technicolor dreams about travel to non-existent foreign countries, puzzles that needed solving but had no apparent solution and a fluffy brown dog that kept showing up in the most unlikely places.

TWENTY-THREE
1940

"I ain't about to do it," Leland said. He kicked a loose stone with the toe of his boot, keeping his eyes cast to the side and his thumbs tucked into the back pockets of his overalls. His rigid posture sent a clear message that he had no intention of budging.

"I need you, Leland." Harland kept his voice firm. Stooping to saying he needed someone humiliated him. Saying it to Leland made it even more aggravating, given that the roots of their fractured relationship went so deep.

"Nope." Leland's flat affect barely cloaked his anger.

"I'll pay you a bonus. You're the best woodworker in the region for doors, and I really want you to do this for me." Harland pressed on, determined to win this battle of wills.

"Nope," Leland repeated. "I ain't about to do it." He turned and quietly continued on his way home where he had been headed when Harland had stopped him.

Harland watched his retreat, his mind rushing furiously as he schemed how he would change Leland's mind. He didn't want to do it, but he had one more idea about how he might be able to get what he wanted.

——⟋⟋⟍——

Harland Freeman did not believe in heaven, and that was a relief. Because if you don't believe in heaven you don't believe in hell either, and most people would send him straight to hell for what he planned to do. It took longer than he hoped, but he forced himself to remain patient and vigilant. At some point she would pass his store and he would find a way to talk to her privately. Usually when she shopped she had the boy with her, and that would cause a problem. He had to talk to her alone, ideally not even to be seen with her.

Eventually, Harland got his wish. Ellie walked by as he rearranged the store's window display, no boy in sight. He followed her down the street and cornered her in an aisle at the fabric shop, sheltered by the tall stacks of wool, cotton and gabardine.

"Ellie."

Even though she had not spoken with him since their ill-fated encounter in the park so many years ago, she recognized his voice immediately and whirled around to face him. She stiffened as he stepped close to her.

"What do you want, Harland?" Had Harland been a man in touch with his feelings, he might have felt hurt by the chilling tone of her voice.

"I want Leland to make the door for my new house over in Montford," Harland said. His thin attempt to disguise his boastfulness failed miserably.

"Really, now why would you want him to do that?"

"He's the best woodworker in the region," Harland stated matter-of-factly, "and I want only the best."

"Did you ask him?" Ellie assumed Harland had not approached Leland directly.

"Yes, and he said 'nope.'" Everyone in town knew when Leland put his mind to doing something, or not doing it, there was no going back.

"Then the answer is 'nope,'" Ellie said. "I can't change his mind."

"I think you can, Ellie." Slipperiness had seeped into Harland's voice, and she felt a wave of nausea passing over her. She had first-hand experience with Harland's caginess, and she knew she wouldn't like what came next.

"It's for the boy's sake, Ellie. I see how fast he's growin' up now. Must be thirteen or fourteen, right? I know you and Leland both want what's best for him." Harland's mouth curled into the slightest smirk.

What a despicable man. How could I ever have . . .

"You want what's best for the boy, don't you Ellie?"

"Are you threatening me, Harland?"

"No, of course I'm not meaning to *threaten* you, Ellie." Harland held her gaze, conveying through his eyes the truth while continuing to speak his lie. "I'm just saying . . . we wouldn't want him to have a hard time in life, would we? If people knew the truth . . ."

The use of "we" made Ellie's stomach turn again. She had been in tight spots before, once because of this same man. She had persevered that time, and she would do so again. The strength of her shame fell far short of the power of her indignation, and in that moment she knew exactly how to assuage the humiliation she had suffered at the hands of Harland Freeman.

She placed her hand on the bolt of fabric closest to her and stretched to her fullest height, feet planted firmly. She tipped her chin up slightly, narrowed her gaze and looked her adversary straight in the eye.

"You are a despicable man, Harland, but I'll get that door for you. I only hope you're prepared to pay what it's gonna cost you."

"I thought you'd see it my way . . ." Harland's smugness waned quickly as the full impact of Ellie's message began to sink into his awareness. He shuddered as the coldness in her eyes and her menacing tone gripped him.

". . . what do you mean?" The fear in his voice sent a wave of pleasure through Ellie and she smiled at him for the first time since he walked away from her in the park so long ago. She held eye contact and waited. His breathing became shallow. Ellie stood firm as he began fidgeting.

"What do you mean? I told Leland I'd give him a bonus . . ."

"It's not what you'll be paying Leland. You'll pay him what he asks and not a penny less, and he won't take a penny more. It's what you'll be paying me that you're not gonna like."

Beads of perspiration broke out on Harland's broad forehead and the bridge of his pocked, bulbous nose.

This is wonderful! He's actually afraid of me. Maybe I'll wait 'til he cries! Ellie knew this time she, not Harland, would be the one getting exactly what she wanted. So she released him with the demand he meet her that evening to finalize her plan.

After dinner, Leland and Clayton went to the workshop while Ellie set out for her evening walk. She headed straight to the park and positioned herself behind a clump of rhododendrons where she could watch for Harland. He arrived on time for this encounter, looking around furtively as he approached the meeting spot under the tree.

He's got some demons following him, and I'm one of them! Ellie took great delight in this risky venture. It may have hatched itself in the aisle of the fabric shop earlier that day, but she knew it had been brewing in her subconscious ever since Harland abandoned her and their child a lifetime ago. Until that moment today, though, she never knew how she would even the score with him. After making him wait almost fifteen minutes, she sauntered into the park herself.

"You're late . . ."

"I'll do the talking, Harland. Sit down." As she issued the command, Ellie took a seat on the small bench at the base of the tree, forcing him to find a perch on the ground. This gave her a big advantage and increased his discomfort considerably.

"Surely you remember this place. 'Course there was no bench or swing back then, but it's pretty much the same otherwise, don't you think? You were very happy to see me the last time we were here, weren't you?"

"Ellie, I should have . . ."

"Like I said, Harland, I'll do the talking. I used to care about what you should have done, but I got over it. I've made a good life for myself, no thanks to you. But now you come to me wantin' something more. You're a greedy, contemptible man. You think the world owes you something you haven't earned. You demand respect from others even when you give them none in return."

Harland did everything he could to be indignant. How dare this woman speak to him in such a manner? But it didn't work. He hung his head as she continued.

"You could have had something good. We could have been a family. At least I used to think so, until I saw who you really are. I don't pretend to know what it was like for you growin' up with Crazy Eulah as your mother. But you're an adult and you've continued on a bad path when you didn't have to."

"Ellie, I . . ."

"People laugh at you, Harland. Behind your back they call you a buffoon. Still, you're an important businessman here in town, so they show you respect to your face. That's the most you'll ever get from them, no matter how fancy a house you build."

She studied him as she ranted on. She felt her own power, but also the meanness behind it. *I'm not a mean person. I'm just angry. I have a right to be angry. I have a right to get something out of him.*

"Here." She handed him a folded paper along with a notepad and pen. "You'll copy those words in your own hand and sign your name to it. That's what the door you want so bad is gonna cost you."

Harland read the note and looked up at Ellie in disbelief. "You can't be serious . . ."

"Oh, I'm plenty serious, Harland. You want Leland to do that work? Then you copy that out just like I wrote it."

"What are you going to do with it?"

"I'm gonna hide it away in a very special place. If you ever so much as speak to me again, or to my boy, you'll see what I do with it then. Leland will do the work for you. Then you will never speak to *him* again either. That note's my insurance policy you'll keep your word."

"How'll you get Leland to do the work? He said no."

"I got him to marry me when he barely knew me. He's stayed with me all this time. I've got some sway with him you wouldn't understand."

"How do I know you'll keep your word?"

"Common sense, Harland, not that you've got a lot of it. The truth could ruin me, too. You'll have to trust I'll keep the secret, just like I've done all these years. I guess your decision rests on just how bad you want Leland to do your work."

The solace of Harland's dreams for himself, and now for his perfect home and all it would bring him, had comforted him greatly throughout his life with its many difficulties and disappointments. It did not fail him now. How could he know for sure all those dreams and plans would turn out as he hoped? He couldn't, but giving them up would leave him bereft. With a deep sigh of resignation, he picked up the pen and wrote the note.

Ellie took it from him and rose from her seat. She fixed him with her gaze before turning and heading home, this time leaving him under the tree, shocked and confused, to fend for himself.

One chapter of their lives now closed while another opened. Neither had any notion of what they had conceived that day.

TWENTY-FOUR
2004

The time 9:47 glowed green from the clock radio as Cally slowly opened her eyes. The sunlight streamed into her room at the Princess Hotel, filling it with warmth and hope.

"Damn," she hissed as she looked at the clock. "I can't believe I slept so long."

She sat up, feet not touching the floor as she perched atop the high, old-fashioned bed. *No wonder . . . what a comfortable bed!* She stroked the silky soft sheets. The luxurious mattress and down pillows tempted her to slide into the soft warmth and drift back to sleep. But, she had things to do. She would dedicate her first day in Asheville to finding her Gamma's house. Gamma Ellie and Gampa Leland probably didn't live there anymore, but she would find the house and then figure out what to do from there.

Gamma and Gampa. She chuckled at the names she had given them as a little girl unable to pronounce the letter "r." Love and protection had surrounded Cally in their house, and her memories of the place brought her as close as she could come to what she imagined home to be like. Maybe the people weren't there, but surely the house remained, and she intended to see it again.

She took a shower, brushed her hair and climbed into clean jeans and a lightweight shirt. Shaking the wrinkles out of a jacket pulled from her suitcase, she headed downstairs. She scavenged a cup of coffee and a muffin from the remains of the breakfast buffet as the waiters cleared the dining room. Skimpy, but it would hold her until she decided what to do for lunch.

Asheville had changed greatly since Cally's mother spirited her away in the middle of the night all those years ago. Now she found it difficult to figure out where she needed to go. She remembered she and her mother had lived on Starnes Street and her grandparents' house stood close by. After some maneuvering around the new highway, she found her way to the corner of Starnes and Flint and parked the car. She would walk from here, she decided, retracing the path she had known by heart as a child.

Finding her way proved to be much more difficult than she could have imagined. Many of the landmarks she had used as a child had vanished. It took her several minutes to realize the huge blue tarp on the corner covered a crumbling foundation—all that remained of the old grocery store. After more intense scrutiny, she finally found her childhood home, now nearly unrecognizable. Had it not been for the stone wall bordering the sidewalk, she would have missed it. The sparse lawn where she had once played sported a maze of flowers and decorative plants laced with a beautiful brick walkway ending at a small fountain with water spurting from the mouth of a mermaid.

How pretty! She turned away, then suddenly flashed back on the last time she left the little bungalow.

"Come on. Get your things packed now!" The hard, demanding edge in Rita's voice scared Cally.

"But I don't want to," wailed Cally, her tiny face covered with streaming tears. "I don't want to leave."

"Get going now!" yelled Rita.

"But, Mommy, I want to stay with my friends and with Gamma and Gampa!"

"Calliope Ann. Do what I say right now. Gamma's gone and we're going too. We can't stay here no more." At 7 years old, Cally had known for a long time that when her mother invoked her full name, fighting back would be a hopeless cause. She stifled her tears as much as she could and slowly started putting her favorite things into her little suitcase.

"Where's Gamma, Mommy? Why can't I see her?"

"She's gone, Cally, I told you." Rita's tone softened a bit. "She . . . oh . . . she's just gone."

"But I want to see her!" Cally began wailing again.

"She's gone, Cally. You can't see her. Now pack!"

"Then I want to see Gampa . . ." Cally pressed on hesitantly.

"No, Cally. We have to leave now. Pack, or we'll leave everything behind."

Cally returned to the task, picking up her chisels and the pieces of wood she had learned to carve under her grandfather's watchful eye. "There's no room for that junk," yelled her mother, tossing it all onto the floor. "Just pack some clothes and two of your favorite toys."

"Okay, Mommy," Cally spoke quietly and kept her eyes cast down. When Rita left the room, Cally quickly picked the chisels and wood up and stuffed them under her clothes in the suitcase. She had no choice about going, but she would not leave her most precious belongings behind.

Less than an hour later, her mother pulled the packed car away from the curb and headed west.

—◆—

Cally pulled herself out of the memory and refocused on getting her bearings and finding her grandparents' house. She walked down to the next block, turned left and walked two blocks more. Some familiar details on the houses along the street convinced her she headed in the right direction, but the street then came to a dead end just before she expected to find the house on the next block. Instead, she faced a steep landscaped slope with a chain-link fence at the top, behind which the traffic on I-240 zipped by.

It had never occurred to Cally the house might no longer be there. In her mind and heart it represented permanence and love, belonging and hope. She had waited more than 40 years to come home again, and now she realized, with a sickening feeling, home had disappeared.

Cally stared ahead in disbelief. She lost all sense of her body and felt herself enveloped in a thick cloud. She tried to shake off the feeling by forcing herself to breathe deeply into her diaphragm. Her head spun and she heard ringing in her ears. Then she realized the ringing came from the church bells at St. Lawrence, the same bells her grandmother had used to teach her to count when she was a tiny child. The thought of her grandmother made her heart ache and she burst into tears. She sat down on the curb, wrapped her arms around herself and sobbed in despair.

Cally spent the rest of the day in a blur. She wandered around the neighborhood, deep in thought. She found her way to the shopping mall where she aimlessly strolled past the many window displays, doing little more than passing time. She managed to eat part of her lunch at an Indian restaurant and declined taking the leftovers with her when she paid her bill.

Eventually she went back to the hotel where she dropped into the comfortable bed and fell into a deep but turbulent sleep. She dreamed all night. About whittling little sticks of wood with her grandfather. About eating homemade applesauce in Ellie's sweet-smelling kitchen, and settling into Ellie's arms for a story before nap-time. About huddling in the back seat of a car hurtling its way to California in the dark of night. And about so many other snippets of her childhood she feared she might be going mad. Were they memories or dreams? Maybe both. It didn't matter. Cally spent the night wrestling with the past and despairing of the future.

"I love you Cally." Ellie's voice rang out clearly. Cally woke with a start and looked about the room. No one in sight. "I love you. You'll be fine." Ellie's voice again, and so clear, so real.

"Gamma?" Cally tried to pull herself fully into wakefulness. "Gamma? Is that you?"

And Cally realized the voice came from deep within, from the place in her heart where Ellie had always lived and always would live. Her tears fell softly as she nuzzled into the pillow, remembering the softness of Ellie's breast, the encircling arms and the warm sweet breath against her hair as she said again "I love you Cally. You'll be fine."

Hours later, Cally woke, refreshed and with a lightness of heart she found surprising. *I'll be fine, just like Gamma said.* And she headed out for a new day of exploration.

TWENTY-FIVE
2004

Tate arrived at Uncle Piggy's at 12 noon on the dot as Ruby had suggested. The weather had turned chilly and damp, and she huddled into her fleece vest, turning her back to the wind in an effort to stay warm as she approached the crowded entrance. The distinctive scent of barbecue wafted from the smokestack and filled the busy parking lot.

She joined the snaking line inside and immediately felt crunched in as more people entered behind her. Everyone chattered among themselves, filling the room with a buzz that competed with the annoying commentary emanating from the TV anchored to the wall above a row of picnic tables. The menu hung behind a tall counter and she scanned it quickly. Pork, chicken and starchy side dishes. She had been counting on something healthy and green to balance the barbecue ribs she planned on eating. Collard greens or a salad—any kind of vegetable would have been acceptable, but her only choice other than French fries appeared to be coleslaw.

Tate succumbed to the festering sense of irritation and disappointment that had emerged as soon as she'd stepped inside and looked around. *What a dump! Not what I was expecting since everyone says this is the best barbecue in town. And these people! No respect for personal space. I don't give a damn what you did last night. Just turn off the cell phone, shut up and stop bumping into me!*

Tate noticed her familiar, crotchety mood. Sixteen years in New York City had given her plenty of time to develop a strong intolerance for being crowded and subjected to the blathering of strangers in cramped spaces. The advent of cell phones, in her humble estimation, constituted a sign of the impending end of a civilized world. Strangers poured out the intimate details of their lives in full voice anywhere they happened to be with no regard whatsoever for who might be listening in.

She grumbled and fussed under her breath and side-stepped so she stood just slightly out of the line. She put her hand on her hip and stuck her elbow into the small gap she had created between herself and the man in front of her. She glowered at him as he continued his non-stop, animated conversation complete with theatrical gestures obviously meant to impress the man next to him. *If that oblivious idiot bumps me again, he'll get a sharp poke in the ribs.* Seconds later, Tate's wish came true. The Idiot backed into her jutting elbow and let out a loud yelp.

"Oh! My bad!" He glared at her as if she were the source of the problem. Tate hoped her wordless response conveyed the message that he should back off and pay attention in the future.

The stare-down with the man ended with Ruby's arrival. "My, my, honey," she called to Tate as she wriggled her way through the line. "Hope you didn't have to wait too long for me. Oh, it's unusually busy today."

"Hey, Ruby! Your timing is perfect." In fact, only two parties stood in line ahead of them.

"Been here long?" Ruby asked.

"Oh, just long enough, I think. I'll be glad to get out of this crowd and sit down." Tate sent a malevolent glance in the direction of The Idiot.

"Thanks for standing in line. I only have an hour for lunch, so I don't get over here as often as I'd like."

"Glad you took the time to meet me, Ruby. I just wanted to apologize again for being so rude to you."

The Idiot took notice of this and raised his eyebrow in an exaggerated Oh-you-being-rude?-I-can't-imagine-such-a-thing way. Ruby noticed the exchange and gave Tate a quizzical look.

"I had my hand on my hip and he bumped into my elbow. He seems to think it was my fault." Tate offered her excuse sheepishly.

"Oh, I see." Ruby turned to the man.

"Please excuse my friend here. She's just getting used to our Southern ways, and she's a bit of a slow learner."

Tate flushed from her neck to her hairline, partly from anger, partly from embarrassment.

"Yeah. I'm from New York. I don't like being crowded." An explanation, for sure, but definitely not an apology.

"Oh, that clarifies everything!" The Idiot smiled at Ruby and went back to the conversation with his friend.

Ruby turned back to Tate. "We're pretty acceptin' of folks around here, but looks like you may be givin' New Yorkers a bad reputation." The comment, offered with gentleness and a kind smile, landed on Tate with a thud.

"Am I really that bad? Tell me the truth, please."

"Honey, I believe we find what we're lookin' for in this world. And you jus' lookin' for someone to offend you."

"I don't think so. But maybe you're right. Living in New York forced me to develop a thick shell. Everyone does it to block out all the noise and constant commotion. You pull into yourself. For protection."

"Well, down here that shell of yours blocks out friendly folks and a whole lot more. Maybe you should think about givin' it up."

"Maybe I should. You know, Ruby, you have a way of going straight to the heart of the matter. That surprises me. And I appreciate it a lot."

"What I'm about to appreciate is a down-home barbecue sandwich. What about you?"

Tate studied the menu again. It didn't look any better the second time than it had the first. She had seen lots of food coming across the tall counter while she'd waited. It looked like everything was buried in thick barbecue sauce. *If I can't eat something healthy, then I'm gonna splurge on fries.* She decided on a rib and chicken combination plate with sides of coleslaw and French fries. They stepped up to the cash register to place their order.

"How you doin' today, Miss Ruby?" asked the cashier. Tate's mouth dropped open as Ruby responded.

"Jus' fine, and you?"

"Pretty good, but we're busier than usual today, so I gotta' stay on my toes."

"I see that. Hope you got enough food for me and my friend here."

"You know we do. You havin' your regular?"

Tate placed her order and paid for both of them. Moments later, their food appeared on the shelf across from the cash register. They picked it up and Tate followed Ruby down a hall filled with picnic tables on both sides. Business people in suits, grizzled old men in worn overalls and families from young to old filled the seats. Ruby continued toward a back room, Tate in tow.

"Do they know everyone by name here?" Tate asked.

"Most of us, they do, if we're regulars. I love this place. We've been coming here for family dinners most of my life. So many happy memories here." They reached their destination and Tate looked around at a room more depressing than what she'd seen out front.

Heavy, veneered tables surrounded by clunky, ladder-back chairs filled the large, windowless room. The far end sported an unlit gas fireplace set in a red brick wall. Ruby headed for one of the few open tables, a smaller one with four chairs, and Tate followed, fervently hoping this was not the kind of place where strangers plopped themselves down wherever they found an empty seat.

Ruby settled herself in and cut her sandwich neatly in half, making it easier to handle.

Tate tentatively took a bite of the rib meat which had fallen easily off the bone. Too sweet. She quickly tasted the coleslaw and a small piece of a hushpuppy. *Everything is too sweet.* She looked up to find Ruby watching her closely.

"Looks like this may not be your favorite kind of food, right?"

"I can't lie. I know a lot of people love this place, and I see why. It's obviously been here for ages, it feels like a friendly neighborhood here, the menu probably hasn't changed much over the years, the ribs are tender, juicy and smell wonderful . . . but I don't like so much sugar in my food. I was hoping for some collards or a salad of some kind."

"You're right. This is the same menu I been eatin' from since my family started comin' here thirty years ago. For me it's sort of like goin' to Grandma's house for Sunday dinner when I was a child. I can always count on things bein' just the way I like 'em."

"I can sure understand the appeal, then, and I bet most of the regulars here would say the same thing." Tate tried the broasted chicken and ate a French fry, both of which were delicious. "Next time, I'll probably stick with the chicken. It's really good."

"Yeah," Ruby interjected. "And make sure you eat those green veggies before you get here." They both laughed and continued with their meal.

Their conversation centered on getting to know each other. Ruby talked about her family, the recent loss of her mother, and her husband's illness. She took the job at Forest Glen several years ago in order to pay for her children's education. Her daughter would be the first person in the family with a college degree when she graduated in the spring. Ruby gushed with pride when speaking of the girl's achievement.

"She'll have her Bachelor's degree. She wants to teach and will try to get a job right away. But I think she'll go back for a Master's degree eventually. She loves kids. I hope she has her own. I want to be a grandma. But not right now. She's a good girl, real smart and determined. She'll teach social studies."

"She sounds wonderful. Seems like you're lucky to have all of them."

"Sure am. But it's not always easy. Still, I thank God every day. What about you? Is your family in New York?"

"Well, that's a long story." Tate evaded the question. "But first, can I ask you something about Mr. Howard?" She paused, hoping Ruby felt comfortable enough to talk to her. "How long has he been at Forest Glen?"

"I can't say much. But he arrived long before me. All I heard was that Mr. Price brought him."

"After I left yesterday, I went to meet Mr. Price. He's very old, but spry and friendly. I saw an exquisite desk Mr. Howard made, and it has a secret compartment in it!"

"Oh, that must be something. You know he makes all those little boxes, and some of them have hidden places, too. Don't know how he does it. He gave me one a couple years ago, and I keep my rings in it when I'm not wearing them." Ruby put her hands out, arching her manicured fingers to show off two beautiful rings, one with a ruby set in platinum, the other an embellished silver setting with a large lapis lazuli stone.

"I assume that one is a ruby. Your birthstone as well as your name?"

"No, just my name. My grandaunt's name, too. And this one, the lapis, my husband gave it to me on our second date. He said it was almost as beautiful as me."

"He sounds like a wonderful man."

"He is. I don't know what I'll do without him, but he's been goin' downhill for a few years now, so . . . but we were talkin' about Mr. Howard."

Tate took the hint and returned to the discussion about Leland Howard. "He simply fascinates me. I want to take care of him. I'm so glad he's out there at Forest Glen. You and all the rest of the staff seem to be so dedicated to your patients."

"Our guests, not patients. We love them. They're like our own family."

"Do you know where Mr. Howard was before he came to you?"

"The state hospital, I think. But you didn't hear it from me, understand?"

The state hospital! It all gets curiouser and curiouser. "No I didn't hear it from anyone. I promise." After they finished eating, they made their way out of the restaurant and paused in the parking lot.

"Thank you for this nice lunch . . . Tate." Ruby gave a wink in place of the missing title, and Tate laughed.

"Now we're getting somewhere. If you can lose the title, maybe I can lose the shell. It's been a true pleasure getting to know you, Ruby."

"Same here. Wish I didn't have to get back to work, but I do. What are you up to this afternoon?"

"Back to the library again. I want to take a look at a book they have that mentions Mr. Howard and his work."

"Can't stop diggin' can you?" Ruby asked with a big smile.

"Obviously not yet! I'll be back to see Mr. Howard again, so I'll be seeing you, too." They gave each other a friendly wave and headed to their cars. Little did they know their next meeting would occur so soon.

TWENTY-SIX
1942

Harland Freeman had been busier than usual. A practical and methodical man, he wanted every possible detail covered while he still controlled his own fate.

He secured the plot he wanted at Riverside Cemetery, the final resting place of Asheville's most elite. He sniggered quietly as he imagined the dismayed look on the face of Constance Ryland once she learned where he would be buried. He knew she would consider it an affront to her family name, but her anticipated horror constituted only one of the reasons he had worked so furiously behind the scenes to get his hands on that particular tiny piece of land. Just as he had been determined to live among Asheville's business titans in his beautiful house on Chestnut Street, he wanted to ensure he would rest at the top of the small knoll elevated slightly above most of them forever.

It did not occur to Harland that the dead are indifferent; the irony escaped him that he chased into death that which had eluded him in life. He could think only of how visitors to the cemetery would see his head stone and know he had been a wealthy and important man.

He commissioned his headstone and revised his will, an ironclad document that could not be challenged. His fortune would be used exactly as he intended after his death. He bequeathed $5,000 each to three local charities, ensuring his name would appear on the wall along with other major benefactors at organization headquarters. Everything he had accumulated during his troubled lifetime would go to good causes, but not all of them charitable. Harland left his mansion, his dream, to the one person who would want it the least, the one person who would recognize the gift as the insult and burden he intended it to be. Along with a sizable trust fund to ensure the upkeep of 305 Chestnut in the decades to come, Harland transferred his house and all his personal belongings to Leland Howard.

Harland thought about his life and how he had expected it to be different. *I'm not a bad man.* Even if spoken aloud, the thought could not ward off the nagging suspicion that he was, indeed, a bad man.

I'm a go getter. I'm determined and I persevere. That doesn't make me bad. It gave Harland little pause to acknowledge he had no friends or family. He had convinced himself long ago that he preferred being alone in the world. It freed him of having to make compromises and of dealing with someone else's need for attention or comfort. Harland didn't even have pets. He lived in his mansion on the hill on Chestnut Street as a solitary man, often padding around his library at all hours of the night. Of course he would never do such a thing, but if it pleased him to do so, he could even leave his socks and underwear on the floor of the bathroom with impunity—no one would speak a word of it to him.

A cadre of servants met his personal needs. The maid kept the house spotlessly clean. The cook prepared sumptuous meals for him. The gardener maintained the impressive landscaping around his property. A man needs only this and a healthy dose of respect and admiration—at least to Harland Freeman's way of thinking.

Harland's house had been completed close to on schedule, and he had moved in on a beautiful autumn day in 1941. The idea for his inaugural party began to form even before the contractors finished the last touches, so while he settled into his mansion, he busied himself with planning the event as well.

Barely two months later, he fussed with the final details prior to the arrival of his guests. Custom-designed invitations printed on parchment had gone out to more than 100 of the most prestigious businessmen in Asheville. RSVPs had arrived in large batches to the surprise and delight of the host. Almost 160 people would soon fill the magnificent rooms, and he expected they would all be quite impressed.

The Christmas decorations rivaled the best he had seen anywhere, with dozens of candles gracing the mantelpieces and tables. Opulent garlands of holly, mistletoe and evergreens covered every available banister inside and out, leaving openings at the newel posts so the intricate carvings in the wood could be admired. The sweet aroma of cinnamon and apple joined that of clove-studded oranges, filling the rooms and wafting out into the mild December night.

A ten-foot Christmas tree stood in the front window, glorious and gleaming with hundreds of tiny lights and one-of-a-kind ornaments. Harland didn't even like Christmas trees, but to omit one at a holiday party would be a social error of enormous magnitude. This event heralded the inauguration of his architectural masterpiece, and it had to be perfect. He spared no expense or effort to ensure his guests would praise it as the best party of the season.

The incident at Pearl Harbor barely a week earlier threatened to quell the festiveness of the event, but Harland would not change his plans nor lower his expectations simply because a war hovered on the horizon.

As the first guests reached the entrance, Harland took one last look around. He had built his crowning glory. It would quickly become his shame and, ultimately, his undoing, but as he surveyed his estate in that brief moment of joy, probably the only true joy he had ever experienced in his life, he found no hint of what loomed ahead. Moments later, he immersed himself in the prideful celebration of his new home.

"Lovely place, Harland."

"Beautiful, what you've done here."

"Exquisite!"

"A masterpiece."

The compliments flowed easily as the guests arrived, and Harland's pleasure nearly overwhelmed him.

"Thank you," he effused. "Thank you for coming."

"Oh, it's not that grand, is it?" he would say, assuming what he meant to be a humble attitude.

Most of the guests willingly put aside the destruction in the Pacific in favor of more comforting topics, and when the conversation inevitably turned in that direction, someone, often not Harland himself, would redirect it. They all seemed to be having a good time. Some of them chatted easily with him and seemed genuinely interested in what he had to say. Others smiled graciously and complimented him on the food, the cocktails, the furniture and the garden.

Harland floated from room to room engaging in social chit-chat with his guests. At one point, he passed the door to the drawing room. A small group of people had gathered there, talking about the house. He stopped, just out of sight, to hear what they were saying.

"Well, the place is quite grand, you have to give him that," said Constance Ryland, begrudgingly.

"Yes, I suppose you do. You know Smith's firm designed the place," said her husband.

"Yes, I know," chimed in another female voice, "but I heard he insisted they add some elements of his own design." Her tone suggested that had not been a good idea.

"Well, yes, and some of them work quite well, I have to admit," offered another.

Harland could not always tell who said what, but he beamed and leaned in a bit closer so he wouldn't miss a thing. He wanted to savor this night for a long time. He had sought recognition like this for most of his life. Tonight, it had finally arrived, and he reveled in it.

"That front door is quite something, don't you think? He made a point to show it to me earlier. He's obviously very proud of it, but it's rather ridiculous."

"What do you mean?"

"The Baroque design is totally out of place. Very ostentatious for a house here in Montford." Harland recognized the speaker in this case. Thomas Bristol was a local architect of note, and Harland had meant for him to be impressed by the grand door he had designed and which Leland had created exactly to his specifications. Harland pressed against the wall and listened closely as Bristol continued.

"It's fairly common in the Baroque style to use a pediment, and there are many different styles. Freeman added a swan's neck design which looks rather feminine coupled with those huge iron hinges and the lockbox. And there's the silly inscription he added."

"What inscription? I didn't see it." Harland could not place this female voice.

"It says 'A man's home is his castle!' How trite is that?" Harland felt a bit nauseous when he heard the guffaws and tittering coming from the room.

"Apparently he wanted a one-of-a-kind door, and he surely created that!" Bristol finished his monologue with a flourish.

"It's not really one-of-a-kind, though." Harland recognized the voice of Constance Ryland, who now spoke for the first time. "I noticed the door when I arrived," she said, "but it's not unique to this house."

Harland froze. What could she possibly mean? He had extensively researched door styles and used what he learned to create an exact design. He had drawn it out himself on paper and given it to Leland.

"Really?" said her husband.

"Yes, really," Constance continued. "I visited Ellie Howard a few days ago. Her husband recently put a new door on their house. The design is very similar. I'm not fond of the one on this house. It's too rough and boastful, but the one on Ellie's house is graceful, more finely rendered, and it doesn't have a pediment crowning the door. It's actually quite beautiful. But then I'm not an expert."

Harland gasped and went numb. His glass smashed to the floor. He became dizzy and lightheaded and grabbed the door jamb in an attempt to steady himself as the group came rushing out into the hallway. He knew he had gone deathly white, and his body seemed to be collapsing in on itself. He could barely remain standing.

"Are you all right, old fellow?" Mr. Ryland took his elbow to steady him.

"Yes . . . I think so . . . maybe I just . . . yes . . . I'll be fine." Harland reeled with the knowledge of Leland's betrayal.

"Really, old man, perhaps we should call for help . . ."

The women gathered in a huddle near him and made suggestions.

"Get him some water . . ."

"Loosen his tie and cummerbund . . ."

"Maybe he needs a brandy . . ."

The men supported Harland and led him to the midnight blue velvet settee he had procured from the same company used to supply furniture for the prestigious Kenilworth Inn. He sank onto the sofa and quickly grabbed his chest. It had just occurred to him he might be able to convince them he was having a mild heart attack. He rallied all the focus he could.

"I think I'm okay," he said. "Just some palpitations. Nothing serious, I'm sure."

"You look a fright, man, like you've had quite a shock."

"No, just some palpitations. I've been seeing my doctor about them just recently," Harland lied.

"We'll call him. Who is your doctor?"

"No need," said Harland. "I just need to rest. This has happened before. I just need to rest."

He persevered, and the men helped him up to his room, Harland feigning weakness and exhaustion all the way. They brought him a brandy and saw to it he settled in comfortably. He requested their assistance in informing his guests the party should continue in his absence.

The men finally left him to himself and he sat alone in his opulent bedroom, vacillating between rage, disbelief and mortification.

How could Leland have done that? What would possess him to make a door for his little shack like the one he made for Harland's stately mansion? Leland could not help but know an entrance like that was completely out of place on a working class bungalow sitting at the edge of the commercial district.

He continued to steam and brood while his guests slowly drifted out, eventually leaving the remains of the party behind. He had a vague awareness of the help cleaning up and letting themselves out. Finally he sat alone in the house. He imagined retribution, what it would look like, how good it would feel. He would sue Leland and ruin him. He would confront him face-to-face and beat him to a pulp. He would broadcast across town the truth kept hidden all these years and everyone would finally know. Harland knew he would never do that, add to his own shame in such a way, but he would find a means of landing a fatal blow to Leland. There must be a way, something so unthinkable it would make Leland suffer as he himself now suffered.

As he rambled through various scenarios, it suddenly occurred to him why Leland had done what he had done. And as much as Harland hated Leland for it, he knew he had deserved it. He did not accept it and he would surely find a way to retaliate, but he understood it, and in that same moment, he understood Leland had finally beaten him. His unassuming, self-effacing, plain and simple, much-despised cousin had won.

Leland had transformed his precious and beautiful creation—his castle entrance—into something ugly and spiteful, just as Harland had turned his own creation—the innocent child—into a tool to once again manipulate Ellie into giving him what he wanted! A fleeting moment of self-loathing flooded over him, then thankfully passed, and he resolved himself to getting his revenge regardless of his own complicity in the matter.

Harland's chance to confront the issue came a few days later when he cornered Leland at the hardware store.

"How dare you, Leland Howard! You intentionally humiliated me."

"What do you mean?" Caught off guard, Leland instinctively cringed as he turned to face Harland.

"I know what you did. Someone mentioned it at my party last week. You stole my idea for the door and put the same design on your pitiful little place." Harland loomed over Leland, fists clenched.

Leland mustered as much forcefulness as possible. "I take strong exception to your tone, Harland. Step back!"

"Not until you make a public apology! You'll not treat me with such disrespect and get away with it."

"You'll get no apology from me. I did the work exactly as you requested. You had no complaints when I finished the job."

"But you copied it! I wanted something unique, and you deprived me of that!"

Leland stood his ground. "Actually, Harland, I didn't copy your idea exactly. My door is a much better creation than yours—more artistic and finely done, more refined."

"You bast . . . you fool! You'll pay dearly for this, Leland, I promise you."

"Well, I guess I can rest assured you'll never again manipulate my wife into convincing me to work for you." An unfamiliar boldness had taken hold of Leland, and he seemed pleased as Harland's face flushed a deep crimson.

"You . . . you damn fool! You impudent bore! I tell you, Leland Howard, you'll pay dearly for what you've done. You wait and see!"

With that, Harland stormed out, leaving Leland to wonder what kind of revenge Harland had in mind. Lacking the imagination of a man like Harland, a man who had felt thwarted his entire life, Leland's idea of the impending revenge fell astonishingly short of its reality.

For almost two months following his last conversation with Leland, Harland worked diligently to finalize every detail of his plan. Now only one act remained to carry out his elaborate scheme. He carefully positioned the wicker arm chair with its thick cushions covered in royal blue duck cloth before his massive front door and settled into it. A strange mix of dread, excitement and self-satisfaction caused him to shudder as he placed the pearl-handled pistol into his mouth and quickly pulled the trigger. Blood and brain exploded out the back of his skull and splattered against the door. When the police finally arrived, the hand-tooled crevices of the door had soaked in the stain of Harland's short and pitiful life.

TWENTY-SEVEN
2004

Cally strolled down Haywood Street and stopped at nearly every window, peering in at the goods on display. *Maybe I'll take weaving classes.* The idea captivated her as she studied the huge loom in the window at Earth Guild. Pausing in front of Mobilia, just down the street, she allowed herself to imagine making a home in Asheville. *That white leather sofa would be great in a big open room with hardwood floors. Totally impractical. I want a dog . . . and maybe a cat, too. White furniture will never work. That contemporary look doesn't suit me anyway.* She thought of Laurel. Maybe if Cally stayed and her happiness returned and she didn't work so hard all the time, Laurel would come and join her. She breathed into the feeling of loneliness enveloping her. *I'll be all right. I just need to keep moving forward, not backward.*

She stepped into the recessed entryway of the store to get a better look at a table in the back. Something caught her eye and she looked down at the golden letters embedded in the floor. They jumped out at her.

J. C. PENNEY
COMPANY INC.

Cally gasped as she flashed back to being a very young child tracing those letters with her little fingers while her mother urged her to hurry up. The next day Cally would go to school for the first time, and her mother had agreed to buy her the shoes in the window at Penney's. Cally's fascination with the letters in the smooth floor quickly subsided in favor of the coveted red shoes.

The childhood memory had taken Cally completely by surprise. Until that moment, she felt like a visitor in Asheville, an interested tourist just like the hundreds of others enjoying the shops housed in the beautifully restored downtown. She sat on the bench outside Mobilia and willed herself to remember. Everything looked so different now, but the old department store helped her gain her bearings.

This used to be her neighborhood. Even as a little girl she roamed through town by herself, and she had spent many afternoons meandering home from school by way of the old shops on Haywood Street. She knew all the nooks and crannies back then, but most of them had disappeared or become unrecognizable. The stores she visited today had been reclaimed from the ruins of a defunct commercial center that had come close to being lost forever once the major businesses fled to the shopping malls on the outskirts of town. That had occurred after Cally had been spirited away by her mother long ago.

She stopped for tea and a scone at Malaprop's. She remembered this building. It once housed the Asheville Hotel, and she could still bring up the smell of the cigar-smoke-filled lobby. She bought scented candles and a yummy body wash at Sensibilities, imagining a long relaxing bath when she got back to the hotel.

Continuing down the street, she came to an abrupt halt in front of the library. *When did this happen?* She looked at the name on the building—Pack Memorial Library. She remembered that name from her childhood, but not this building. She stepped into the entrance and paused before continuing into the library itself. *I know I have it here somewhere. I always keep it with me . . .*

Cally fished around in her bag and pulled out the pouch containing all her membership cards. *Why do I have all this stuff? I rarely use any of it!* Finally, tucked away in a protected slot with a frequent flyer card from a long-gone airline, Cally found what she wanted. She had few mementos from her childhood in Asheville and she cherished them all equally. One was the tattered library card she pulled carefully from its hiding place. Clasping it close to her heart, she stepped across the threshold.

After more than an hour of rummaging through the library, she decided to head back to the hotel. She had enough reading material to keep her busy for a few days. The eclectic mix included an old classic, *My*

Antonia by Willa Cather, the most recent Harry Potter installment and a book about the history of Asheville. When her turn arrived, she approached the counter hesitantly, clutching her library card. *I hope this still works. I doubt they let strangers check books out.*

"How can I help you?" The librarian spoke softly. A web of tiny wrinkles encased her light brown eyes, accenting their long lashes. Her makeup consisted of only a bit of lip gloss. Light danced off the embellishments on her t-shirt, framing her face with dozens of glittery reflections.

"I hope you can. I have this, and I wonder if I can check these books out with it."

The woman took the yellowed card from Cally and studied it carefully for a moment.

"Calliope Ann Thornton?" The librarian enunciated each word beautifully, the space between them accented by the wavering tone of her voice. She looked up and studied Cally's face intently.

"Cally?"

"Yes . . . ?" Cally returned the intent gaze. On guard, she wondered why the woman acted so strangely. ". . . yes, my name is Cally."

"It is you! I can't believe it. Cally, it's me, Sally! Sally Barton. I mean Sally Simpson. You must remember me . . ."

"Sally? I don't think I . . . but that sounds vaguely familiar . . ." Cally felt herself tumble back through ancient memories again. And there she sat on the playground with her best friend at her side. She looked deep into the eyes of the woman in front of her and saw they still sparkled. "Oh! Yes! We used to pretend the rainbow ended over your head, because of the gold flecks in your eyes. Yes, Sally! I remember you!"

Her old friend came around the counter and she and Cally hugged each other tightly for the first time in decades, tears streaming down both their faces.

"I've always wondered what happened to you. You just disappeared."

"I know. My mother packed us up in the middle of the night and we went to California. I cried for weeks because I missed you and Gampa and Gamma so much."

"I want to hear everything, Cally. Why don't you come to supper tonight? Meet my family and we can talk about everything! We have a lot of catching up to do."

"We most certainly do. I'd love to join you. Oh, I'm so glad I found you!" Tears collected in the corners of Cally's eyes again.

"It's a miracle, really. I can't wait to sit and talk with you again." Sally looked around and realized another customer waited in line.

"Now what about these books?" Cally asked. "Can I still use this old library card?"

"No, but I'll get you a new one right now. Where are you staying?"

"At the Princess Hotel."

"Okay, we'll use that address."

They laughed and chattered on while Sally issued the new card and checked out the books her friend had chosen. As Cally stepped to the end of the counter to pick them up, they made their plans for the evening.

Cally stood quietly for a moment, breathing in the unique aroma of the library and letting the joy settle into her body. Sally returned to her station to attend to the next customer.

"Sorry I kept you waiting so long," Sally told the woman who had a curious look on her face. "She's a long lost friend who just turned up again. May I help you?"

"It's always nice to find an old friend again," the woman responded. "I'm looking for Carla in the North Carolina section. She helped me last week, but I don't see her there today. Interestingly enough, I'm trying to track down a particular book she found that references the Princess Hotel, where your friend is staying, and a local artisan named Leland Howard. Can you help me with that?"

"Why are you looking for my grandfather?" Cally screeched. Then she turned a blazing red from embarrassment.

Those were the first words Cally ever spoke to Tate. Sally and Tate stared at Cally, mouths open in disbelief.

"Leland Howard is your grandfather?" Tate asked.

"Yes, he is! Well he was . . . I assume he's gone now. I haven't heard from any of them in ages." Cally left her books on the counter and walked back toward Tate.

"Oh, honey. I've got some good news for you, then. He's still alive, and I know where he is."

Cally burst into tears. The words sank into her soul and searched out the deep pocket of grief she kept hidden from everyone, even herself. Her sobbing deepened and she nearly dropped to her knees,

209

weakened by the internal battle between disbelief and joy. Tate caught her and they stood there locked together by the common bond of Leland Howard, a man Cally had lost long ago and Tate had only recently found. Tate knew instantly she and Cally would be friends for a lifetime.

TWENTY-EIGHT
1940

Ellie left the park and walked home quickly. She looked out the kitchen window and saw Leland and Clayton just finishing up in the workshop. With a few precious minutes to herself, she went directly to the fireplace mantel, opened the secret compartment and slipped Harland's note into a corner.

She lifted her grandmother's antique tortoise-shell hair comb out of the drawer and caressed it gently. One of her prize possessions, it rested in its hiding place along with the bank book for the still-active savings account holding money Mary Alice had given her years before. The drawer also held the diamond ring her father had given her mother as a 45th birthday present and then passed on to Ellie after her mother's premature death the previous year.

These items comprised the totality of Ellie's dowry, accumulated only after her marriage, piece by piece. She clung to these valuable personal possessions, vestiges of possibilities she once imagined for herself. In different circumstances, Ellie would have thought of her collection as the financial means to launch her independent life. But over the years she slowly resigned herself to what she had, rather than what she wanted, and she came to think of her belongings as the nest egg she would eventually pass on to her son. She wished she had a daughter to hand them down to—a girl who would recognize the power and value the freedom inherent in having one's own money—not a boy who took the inheritance for granted. But her son would become the custodian for Ellie's accumulated goods and he would decide whether to use them or pass them on to his own children.

She pushed the drawer back into place just as her husband and son entered through the kitchen door.

"What's for dessert, Maw?" Clayton called.

"Clayton, I've told you a million times, don't call me 'Maw.' It sounds awful, and you just do it to aggravate me!"

"Okay, *Mom*, what's for dessert?" Ellie bristled slightly at Clayton's lack of apology and Leland's silence, but she kept her irritation to herself for the moment.

"Your favorite—rhubarb pie with vanilla ice cream. But . . . dinner first."

"Thanks, *Mom* . . ." Clayton put even more emphasis on the word this time as he bounded into the bathroom to wash his hands.

"He's getting worse, Leland, and you don't do anything about it."

"He's a good boy, Ellie. He's just testing the waters, trying to become a man."

"Testing the waters! Is that what you call getting into trouble all the time? We've had to haul him out of the police station two times already, and he's only thirteen years old!"

"Now, Ellie, that incident with Jimmy Boykins—Clayton had a right to protect himself."

"He had a right to stand up for himself, but not to give the boy a concussion and a broken nose, Leland. And what about the stones through the store window? What's the justification for that?"

"Boyhood prank, Ellie . . . just a prank."

"You didn't do things like that at his age . . ."

"No, but I didn't have Clayton's spirit, either."

"Spirit, is it? Or something else?"

"Ellie, he'll be fine. He'll grow out of it. Let's just give him some time."

If Ellie pushed any more, Leland would dig in his heels. She knew that. "I'll put dinner on the table okay?" she asked to end the argument.

"Yes, please."

After dinner, Ellie spent the rest of the evening tidying up the kitchen and thinking about how she would get Leland to do the work for Harland. She had extracted a choice prize from Harland. It had been sweet in the moment. Now she had to uphold her end of the awful pact she had forged with him.

"Leland, we need to talk." After a long night of fitful sleep, Ellie felt prepared to plead her case. Ellie rarely went into the workshop, but she believed Leland would be his most receptive to her request in the place he felt the happiest.

"Ellie, what are you doing here?"

"I've got to tell you something, and I'm going to ask you to do something you will not want to do. But it's important, Leland, more important than I can say. Will you hear me out?"

"I'll always hear you out, Ellie. What's got you so worked up?"

"I went to the fabric shop yesterday. I didn't find what I wanted, but while I was there Harland Freeman approached me . . ."

"He did what?" Alarms started sounding in Leland's head.

"He asked me to talk to you about the work he wants you to do . . ."

"Why on earth would he approach you when I already . . ."

"You already told him no."

"I told him NOPE! I won't work for that despicable man!"

Ellie waited while Leland fumed, pacing back and forth in front of his workbench, fists clenched.

"I'm asking you to do that work for him, Leland. As a personal favor to me."

"Why would you want me to do it, Ellie? I don't understand why you want me to work for that horrible man."

"Well, Leland, he is family."

"Ellie, it's not right to bring up family in regards to Harland. He may be blood-related, but he ain't family—not in the true sense of the word!"

"Whether we like him or not, Leland, family is family. Besides, it would be easy work for you. He would pay you a good wage and we can always use the money."

"We have enough money, Ellie. We don't need more. We're just simple folk."

Leland's words cut deep and went to the core of the biggest divide between the two of them. Leland relished being simple folk while Ellie found the designation intolerable. Rage engulfed her, and unable to control herself, she lashed out.

"You may be simple folk, Leland, but I am not! All my life I wanted things I didn't get. I wanted a life, a real life with adventure and excitement. I got you instead. I wanted to travel and see the world. I stayed here with you instead. I wanted freedom and independence. But what did I get? A husband and a troublesome son!"

Leland fell back, astonished at the force of Ellie's tantrum. He had never seen her this way, never heard these things from her before, and it terrified him.

Ellie felt all her long imprisoned dreams rising up, fueling the tirade. Once unleashed, her emotions poured out.

"Don't ever call me simple folk again, Leland! And don't ever think for a minute I don't notice all the things you do for others that you never do for me. You build beautiful furniture and help create fancy houses for all the rich people who want you. But when I asked you for a house, a real house instead of livin' in this old shack you love so much, what did you do? You built me a house all right. You built me the simplest, plainest house on the street. The most boring, basic house you could conjure up when you're the finest craftsman around. Why? Because you think of yourself as simple folk, not worthy of something special, and you think of me that way, too. I AM NOT SIMPLE FOLK, LELAND! I had wishes and dreams and ideas and plans just like everyone else. Big plans, big ideas. And I squandered them all in a moment of shameful passion!"

Wracked with emotion, Ellie could not believe the words she heard coming out of her own mouth. She stopped, tears streaming down her face, arms clutching her sides in an effort to regain some control. She sank, bent over, into an old chair and continued to sob. Leland, shocked by the scene in front of him, sat motionless and speechless on a stool, hands on knees, head hanging low, engulfed in panic.

Finally Ellie spoke again, this time more calmly. "Leland, I'm sorry for all that. Not for saying I'm disappointed about some things, but for saying it that way. And for trying to make it your fault. I chose this life with you. It is a good life in so many ways. But I'm not simple folk, Leland, and I wish you could see that and try to stretch more to my way of thinking."

"Ellie, I . . . I don't . . . you're . . ." Head still whirling, Leland searched for words. "You're right, Ellie. I always stick to the way I was raised. Not taking more than I need. Simple things are enough for me, and I didn't realize how vexing that is to you. I'm deeply sorry."

"You made me that beautiful fireplace, Leland. You made that special place just for me, and I love it so much. I guess I want more things like that. I guess I just want too much."

Leland paused before responding. "As far back as I know, the men in my family made wonderful things for other people. They never kept those things for themselves. We had our home, some basic furniture, all beautiful, of course, but not fancy, nothing more than we needed. The fancy things were always for others. You knew that when you moved here after we got married."

"I was just a child then, Leland, only 16. Your parents were good to me and I didn't want to stir things up. Then we had the baby, and we all lived in this tiny cabin. When you started building us a new house of our own, it seemed grand by comparison. But when I asked for nicer things, and I did ask several times, what did you say?"

"We just need a solid house, Ellie, nothin' fancy." Leland answered. "That's what I always told you."

"That's right. You said it so many times and I always gave way. And that house there? That's 'a solid house, nothin' fancy,' just like you insisted in your stubborn way."

"I never realized how much it disappointed you, Ellie. I truly never did."

"I came to terms with it, Leland. I'm comfortable there, and I've made it my own."

"But still, you should have what you want, Ellie . . ."

She looked at him, taking a moment to gauge his mood.

"And that brings us back to where we started, Leland," she said, matter-of-factly. "I want you to do that work for Harland and not to ask me any more questions about why."

Leland contemplated his wife and her request, both the things she said and those left unsaid. Her vehemence unnerved him, but his love for her persisted as strong as ever. She had a reason for asking what she did, and he wondered again what it might be. Leland was certain Ellie's moment of shameful passion had not been with him. And she had invoked family obligation which seemed odd since he had never had a familial attachment to his cousin and Ellie seemed to dislike Harland as much as he did.

He could think of only one possible source of the power Harland had over Ellie, one sole explanation for how he would be able to persuade her to do his bidding. Too awful to contemplate, Leland pushed the thought away just as he had done long ago the first time the idea occurred to him. Adrift in indecisiveness, a course of action suddenly popped into his head full-blown—a scheme so out of character for him it took him by surprise. But it would accomplish so many things, this unexpected plan of his. Harland would get his door, Ellie would get her fancier house, and Leland would prove to everyone, especially himself, he had a backbone. He resigned himself to his shocking decision.

"I'll do it, Ellie. Like you said, he's family, and maybe I understand just what that means a little better now than before. And I'm gonna make things right for you, too, Ellie."

"Thank you, Leland. And I'm sorry, really, for everything I said. You're a good man and I'm lucky to have you."

Leland thought about how much he loved his wife as he watched her retreat to her kitchen, and he reckoned Ellie saying she felt lucky to have him would be the closest he'd ever get to knowing if she loved him in return.

———

Leland screwed up his courage and went to Freeman Mercantile the next day. He listened to Harland boast about his house plans and how it pleased him Leland had come to his senses and agreed to do the job. Leland studied the sketch Harland had drawn for a Baroque-style door of massive proportions, discussed the type of wood he wanted, the time frame, the cost—all the details necessary to get the job underway. Not once during the conversation did Leland express his disgust for the man or the work, and not once did Harland seem to notice how Leland recoiled when he moved too close. When the conversation concluded, Harland unwarily put out his hand. Then, and only then, did Leland look Harland in the eye.

"I'll do this work, Harland, but I'll not shake your hand. That's what gentlemen do at the conclusion of business, and you're no gentleman." Leland took the drawing from Harland.

"I'll send along an estimate and you'll return a check for half the cost of the job. Once your check clears the bank, I'll get the supplies and begin the work, and you'll have your door by the deadline. Thereafter, don't ever speak to me, my wife or *my son* again." Leland turned on his heel and left the store without another word.

———

Harland stood in stunned silence as Leland disappeared from view. *Once the check clears the bank? Does he think I would write a bad check? How dare he* . . . Harland tried to shake off his indignation at the way Leland had spoken to him. *He'll do the job. That's what I wanted, and that's what I got. The end justifies the means.* Even as the note he had written at Ellie's command continued to haunt him, Harland hoped the old adage would hold true in this case.

———

A week later, Leland stood in the lumberyard, selecting wood for his upcoming projects. He meticulously inspected each piece for grain and texture, enjoying the distinct patterns and subtle color changes.

For Harland's job he needed cherry. Common and plentifully available in the Eastern United States, Harland had chosen it for its rich, warm hue; tight, wavy grain and satiny, lustrous finish. It would not be painted, like most doors, but left its natural color and sealed with varnish, highlighting Harland's design. When Leland found a perfect plank, he put it back in the bin. He methodically searched out those with tiny defects, faults almost imperceptible to all but the most highly trained eye, and he laid them out in a pile.

Once he had accumulated enough of the slightly flawed specimens for Harland's project, he moved on to the heart pine. It would blend with the floors in Ellie's house beautifully, its warm color ranging from reddish brown to pale yellow, adding to the appeal of the exterior. For her house, he chose only impeccable samples with gently curving grain and just the right amount of black sap staining. The heart pine would be fashioned into an impressive door to grace the entrance to the house he had built for her. It would be a much refined rendition of Harland's design, and the workmanship would far outshine that on Harland's house. Everyone who happened by would see that Ellie finally had the best work he could produce, better than anyone's money could buy.

While paying for and loading up his purchases, he tried to explain away the misgivings he felt in the pit of his stomach as a case of indigestion.

TWENTY-NINE
2004

The whirlwind encounters in the library finally ended with a plan. Cally, Sally and Tate would share dinner at a local restaurant where they could talk without the interruption of Sally's family. On Sally's recommendation, they found a table at Anntony's in the Grove Arcade. Tate loved the ornate Arcade and the outdoor seating at the restaurant, even though she found the food there disappointing. Still, the menu took a distant second to the opportunity to spend time with these two fascinating women.

"Okay, I have a question before anything else gets discussed," Tate said as they took their seats. "Cally and Sally? Is that why you were best friends—because you have almost the same name?"

The two women broke into laughter. "They called us the Bobbsey twins," Cally said. "We were inseparable."

"We lived around the block from each other," Sally added. "So our back yards joined and from the time we could crawl, we were like little homing pigeons. We just wanted to be with each other all the time."

Cally chimed in. "One time when we were maybe 3 years old, we were playing in the back yard and crawled under a big bush, curled up together and fell asleep. Our mothers were frantic looking for us. They even called the police because they thought we'd been kidnapped!"

The two reminisced some more while Tate sipped a glass of chardonnay. Dinner arrived just when Sally asked the question she had waited most of her life to have answered.

"What happened to you, Cally? Why did you disappear from Asheville?"

Cally's face tightened and her eyes began filling with tears. "Damn, I'm not going to cry again." She took a deep, grounding breath and squeezed her eyes closed while she willed the tears away.

"Truth is, I just don't know, Sally. Something happened, something bad. I never knew what. I asked Mom countless times and she always said 'It's better you don't know.' Whatever it was it scared her. I came home from school one afternoon, and she had packed up most everything we owned. What wouldn't fit in the car got left behind. A week later, we were in Los Angeles, sleeping on the couch at her cousin's place. She would never talk about it, and she would never come back, no matter how much I begged her. Finally I just gave up, and eventually I pretty much pushed away all memories of this place and all the people here. Thinking about them was just too painful."

Sally and Tate listened intently as Cally poured out her tale. With the words came the pain and frustration, and most of all the deep, untouched sadness. Cally had been torn away from everything she loved for reasons she had never understood.

How does someone survive that? How do you go on when you lose everything? As Tate puzzled about these questions, she noticed a clutching sensation in her solar plexus. It spread slowly through the center of her body, a constriction progressing from her stomach up the path of her esophagus to her throat where a huge lump formed, restricting her breathing. She felt light-headed and unfocused and realized her own eyes were filling with tears. Through the haze she saw Cally and Sally staring at her.

"Are you all right?" Cally asked, as she reached over and took Tate's hand. "Tate?"

In a flash, Tate remembered. She knew only too well how someone can survive what Cally had. She had done it herself. The memory of her brother's sudden death flooded her with grief. She wanted desperately to collapse into it, to fall in a heap into her bed and cry for two weeks like she had back then, twenty years ago. But Tate didn't cry anymore. She no longer allowed grief and despair to swallow her whole. And she certainly would not do so now, in a public place in front of two strangers.

Tate took a gulp of water and forced herself to breathe. The constriction eased, her head cleared, and she pulled herself out of the steep dive into emotional turmoil.

"Yes, I'm okay," she lied. "I just had something stuck for a moment." That part was not a lie.

———

Over dinner, the old friends shared other memories. Tate listened quietly most of the time, enjoying their laughter and joining in only enough to conceal her own pain. They shared desserts and coffee and then decided on a last glass of wine. Throughout the meal, Tate was aware Sally seemed a bit on edge, like she was holding something back. She wondered if Cally had noticed.

Sally opened the discussion about the past again. "Cally, I think I know why your mother left," she began hesitantly.

"Really? Tell me!" Cally's excitement lit her face up for a moment before she saw the grim countenance of her old friend. "Oh! It's bad, isn't it? Just like I always thought."

"Yes, it's bad. Maybe it really is best not to know, like your mother said."

"I HAVE to know! Sally, please tell me. No matter how bad it is, it can't be worse than all the stories I've made up about it my whole life."

"I'll tell you, Cally, but not here. Let's go back to my house. We can sit in the backyard, and I'll tell everyone to leave us alone."

"I think that's my cue to take off," Tate said. "I'll leave you girls to it."

"NO! Please come with us, Tate," Cally pleaded.

"But I would feel like an intruder. We just met."

"Maybe we just met, Tate, but I feel like I've known you all my life. You know my grandfather, and I have so many questions about him that we haven't gotten to. I'm not letting you go until I get answers to all of them."

Tate had told Cally in the briefest terms what she knew about Leland as they left the library earlier that day. But there was much to be shared, and Tate had plenty of questions of her own. She agreed to continue on to Sally's house with her new friends.

Tate's decision to spend the rest of the evening with them pleased Cally greatly. Her attraction to Tate had sprung up almost instantaneously when they met only hours earlier at the library.

How could she not be attracted to her? If Cally had noticed only Tate's physical characteristics, she would have seen a plump, medium-height woman who appeared to be in her early 50s—much younger than her actual age of 58—a woman completely unpretentious about her appearance. Tate seemed totally comfortable in jeans and a t-shirt, like she wore them every day. No make-up or jewelry save a large silver and turquoise bracelet on her left wrist, and no watch. Cally couldn't imagine going without a watch, given that she slept in hers and took it off only when showering.

Surveying Tate with only an academic interest, Cally would have taken note of her shoulder-length, naturally wavy hair—a shining mass of wash-and-wear chestnut brown tinged with sun streaks. She could not see Tate's eyes from that distance, but she expected they would be intense and beautiful.

But, Cally was not an objective observer and Tate's physical appearance was not the source of the profound impression she made on Cally. Every movement of Tate's body conveyed self-assurance. Her resonant voice suggested courage and resilience. The power of her gaze seemed magnetic, and when she'd wrapped her arms around Cally and held her tight there in the library, it had been like sinking into a familiar and safe place Cally had never known existed. But now, having rested there briefly and been deeply nourished, she had no desire whatsoever to leave.

—◌◌◌—

Sally still lived in Montford but not in the house where she had grown up. Cally and Tate settled into the comfortable chairs on the back deck while Sally brought out a bottle of wine and glasses. Tate realized they were only a couple of blocks from the house on Chestnut. She'd have to ask Sally about the place at some point and share with them what she had learned recently.

Sally poured wine for each of them. Still hesitant to cause her friend any pain, she asked again, "Cally, what I have to tell you is going to be hard to hear. Are you sure . . ."

"Absolutely sure, Sally! I'm tough. I can take it, whatever it is. Just spit it out."

"Okay. I don't think I knew back then what everything meant. I was a little kid, just like you. But eventually I put the pieces together."

Sally had come home from school one afternoon to find her mother very upset, though she wouldn't say why. She kept the doors closed and locked, which was unusual, and that evening Sally's parents excluded her and her brother from their huddled conversation. The next day in school, Sally heard Ellie Howard had been murdered in her own home and that her son, Clayton, was also dead. She wished so much she could be with her best friend, but Cally did not come to school and Sally never saw her again.

Cally listened solemnly without interrupting.

"Clayton was your father, wasn't he?" Sally asked.

"Yes. I didn't know him very well. He only came around once in a while. Mom always sent him away."

"Then maybe you didn't know he was a drug addict. He had violent mood swings. My mother told me all this a long time later."

"You know, I figured that out myself quite awhile ago." Cally spoke slowly and deliberately, and Tate realized she was exerting a great deal of effort to keep her composure.

"I remember Gamma Ellie keeping him at a distance from me. I visited her and Gampa a lot, but if Clayton was around, she would always send me home."

Tate watched Cally closely. "I know this is hard stuff to hear, Cally. How are you doing?"

"You know, I'm doing okay, Tate. It is hard to hear, but it's also a huge relief. I've spent my whole life wanting to know, and now I do. I can finally figure out how to move on."

"Well, I remember other fun stuff, too," Sally chimed in. "Want to hear some of that?"

"Yes, some fun stuff would be just the thing." Cally smiled and shifted to a more comfortable position.

"I remember the day you carved your initials into that old fireplace at your Gamma's house. We giggled the whole time. I tried calling you Cat after that, but you insisted on Cally."

Cally's brows and forehead puckered as she searched for the memory. When she found it, she squealed with delight.

"Oh yes! My initials spell Cat, but I didn't like that nickname. Oh, I loved that beautiful old fireplace. Gampa made it, and I spent hours sitting in the corner there and reading or coloring."

Tate went on alert. "You mean Leland? You had a fireplace made by Leland?"

"Yes, at their house. I loved it so much. One day I took a nail and carved my initials into it. When he found out, I thought he would be so angry. You know what he did?"

"What?" Tate asked.

"He took me out to his workshop, gave me a beautiful piece of wood, a small knife and a chisel, and he taught me how to carve." Cally paused for a moment and savored her memory.

"Where is he Tate? You said you knew."

"He's out at Forest Glen Manor. I can take you to see him tomorrow if you like."

"I would like that very much."

"You know, Cally, it's strange," interjected Sally. "Your Gamma's old house is gone. I thought they'd torn it down when they destroyed that block of Cumberland to put in I-240. But I was driving over on Maplewood the other day, and I could swear it's now sitting over there. It looks a lot different. It has white siding on it, and they're working on the inside. But I saw that old door, and I'm sure it's the same house."

Tate gasped. "That's my place! Do you mean to tell me Leland Howard owned my house?"

"Well, if it's the same building, then he not only owned it, he built it!" Cally said.

Tate turned to Cally and felt every cell in her body crackle with electricity as their eyes met.

THIRTY
2004

Tate greeted the next morning cheerfully, bouncing out of bed and into the kitchen to put food out for Pocket, who appeared moments later, stretching from paw to tip-of-tail and yawning deeply.

"You look like a little yoga cat, Babycakes," Tate cooed. "You know what they call that move you just made? A downward dog! Maybe we should get a dog. Whadda ya think?"

Pocket ignored Tate's chatter, choosing instead to sit in the patch of sunlight on the kitchen table and clean behind her ears.

"Okay, so maybe that's not such a great idea afterall. How about another cat instead?" No response from Pocket, who methodically licked between each toe of her left paw. Once that side was clean, Pocket yawned and started on the right paw.

"So it's the silent treatment, is it? Guess we're on our own then, just you and me." Tate put a small dish of fishy smelling cat food on the floor near the table and headed for the bathroom. She heard a soft thump as Pocket jumped off the table to gobble down her morning meal.

Thirty minutes later, Tate headed downtown to meet Cally. They had laid out their plans the night before as they sat drinking wine in Sally's backyard. First, they would have breakfast at Over Easy, a popular café on Broadway, then head to the library for more research and finally on to Forest Glen to see Leland Howard.

Hope the place isn't too busy. I'd love to get the little table in the back corner so we aren't squished in. Tate visualized herself and Cally sitting exactly where she wanted, with plenty of room around them and a friendly, attentive waitress. She reviewed her preferences in her mind several times as she walked the half-block from where she had parked. Just as she entered the small restaurant, she saw the party at the favored table paying their bill. She felt a familiar rush of glee, looked around and realized she was first in line, having arrived only seconds before the folks behind her. The waitress swiped the table clean and motioned to Tate just as Cally arrived.

"Thank you!" Tate glanced skyward as she uttered the gratitude under her breath.

"Hi, Tate!" Cally sang out. "I'm so happy to see you again." She threw her arms around Tate and squeezed tightly. Cally wore tight jeans, a waist-length leather jacket and a handwoven teal and purple scarf.

"Hey, Cally." Tate pulled away quickly. "We have a table."

"Wow, I thought we'd have to wait. Sally said this place is always packed."

"Well, I called in some help."

"Oh, they take reservations?"

"No, not really . . ." Tate pondered how much to share. ". . . a different kind of help."

"That sounds mysterious," Cally commented as they took their seats. She looked around at the clustered tables. "This looks like the best seat in the house. You must be really lucky."

"You could say that." Tate hesitated momentarily, then blurted out, "It's actually my runners."

"Runners? What do you mean?"

"Damn! I didn't mean to say that. You'll think I'm crazy!"

"Too late! It's out. So what, or who, are runners?"

"Well . . . here goes. Runners are spirit guides of sorts. Whenever I'm wishing for some amenity, like a great parking space, a perfect table, an empty cashier's line— you know, the things that make life feel magical—I call on my runners. They go ahead of me and get what I've asked for. At least most of the time they do."

"Okay . . . ?" Cally seemed skeptical. ". . . I'm not sure I know what you mean. These runners are like fairy godmothers?"

"That's another way to look at it. I probably shouldn't have told you about them. Like I said, you'll think I'm weird."

"I wouldn't say weird . . . maybe 'different' is a better word."

"I'll accept different! And lucky." But Tate knew luck had little to do with it. She knew faith and gratitude created the little miracles that showed up in her life frequently.

Over omelets, hash browns and strong coffee, Tate filled Cally in on what she knew about Leland Howard.

"He's been out at Forest Glen for several years. I don't know the details. You can't say I told you this, but one of the staff members there told me he had been in a state hospital before coming to their facility."

"Gampa was definitely not crazy. Why did they put him in a . . . a mental institution?" Distress contorted Cally's face.

"I'm sorry to tell you these things, Cally. I wish I could answer all your questions, but I can't."

"I know. I just hate to think of him alone in a place like that."

"He's being well cared for now. You'll see. The staff at Forest Glen loves him."

"Okay. What else do you know?"

"Well, he was a great craftsman—much sought after here in town apparently, but quite private. I found references to him in a few public records—not much really, other than the notice of your grandmother's death. He seems to just disappear right after that. I want to check further through Ancestry.com. Maybe we can find out what happened to him."

"But you said you met him. Didn't you ask him?"

"My first visit didn't go well. I mentioned his work and the house on Chestnut and he shut down completely. I thought he'd never speak to me again. So on my second visit, I just let him talk."

Cally listened but said nothing, so Tate continued. "A man named Richard Price seems to be the one pulling the strings. How that happened isn't clear. But he's the one who got Leland to Forest Glen, and he and his family continue to be involved."

"There was a Mr. Price who lived not far from us. A rich man with a big house in Montford."

"I think that's the guy. I met him recently. He's quite old now and has trouble getting around. He showed me a desk your grandfather made—one with a secret compartment!"

Cally closed her eyes and struggled to pull up a memory, the mental effort written all over her face. Tate waited.

"Secret compartments . . . that sounds familiar for some reason. I can't seem to . . . it's right there, at the edge of my memory . . . oh, I don't know! Tell me more. Why did you start looking for him?"

Tate sighed deeply. "This is feeling like an old story to me. I've told it so many times in the past week."

"Once more, please," Cally pleaded.

"Well, there's a huge old house not far from where Sally lives. I meant to ask her about it last night but never got around to it. It's abandoned and they're going to tear it down and build little cottages instead. Little cottages would be nice, I think. I'd probably even like to live in one of them myself. But ever since first laying eyes on the place, I've felt compelled to save it. So I started hunting for information, and I found out . . ." Tate stopped abruptly and her fidgeting put Cally on alert.

"What? What did you find out?"

Tate stalled. *I don't want to cause her any more pain. I want to take care of her, not hurt her.*

"Tate, please. Is it bad? Why won't you tell me?"

"Cally, I don't know what it means. I just have this feeling . . . I found out the house belongs to your grandfather."

"Gampa owns a falling down house in Montford! Why?" Cally struggled to make sense of it all.

"I wish I knew, Cally. Truly I do."

They sat quietly for a moment, Cally apparently lost in thought, Tate watching her for signs of what to do next.

"More coffee?" The waitress brought their attention back to the meal.

Tate waited for Cally to answer.

"No, thanks. I think we'll go now."

"Okay. Separate checks?"

"One check. I'll take it," Cally said before Tate had a chance to answer.

"Cally, please don't do that." Cally's gesture made Tate uncomfortable.

"Don't be silly, Tate. You can treat the next time."

"So, there's a next time, then?"

"I certainly hope so," Cally answered brightly. She dropped twenty dollars on the table and got up before the waitress returned with the check. As they walked out the door, Cally looped her arm around Tate's elbow and they headed for the library.

An hour and a half later, they had learned a few tantalizing details. A search of Ancestry.com produced two references to Leland Howard in the United States Census data. In 1920, he was ten years old and lived with his parents at 8 Cumberland Avenue. A decade later, the household had grown to include Ellie and Clayton. Because of a seventy-two-year rule, no more specific census data could be located. They found records showing birth and death dates for Ellie and Clayton. Most interesting was the marriage certificate for Ellie and Leland.

"Look, Tate." Cally pointed to the marriage date. "May 15, 1927."

"Yes?"

"May 1927. Remember Clayton's birth date? *December 1927!*"

"Yeah . . ."

"Gamma must have been pregnant when they got married!"

"Oh! You're right, Cally. He was born barely seven months later."

Cally sank back into her chair, mouth agape, staring at Tate. "Gamma always seemed so prim and proper. I'm having a hard time imagining her doing something like that in 1927."

"And let's do more math, Cally. They were both teenagers—only 16 and 17—when Clayton was born."

"Okay. So, in 1927 they are both in high school. They hook up and Ellie gets pregnant. They rush to the altar in May. Maybe Leland graduated, but Ellie couldn't have, could she? Not at 16."

"Probably not. But it wasn't important for girls back then. They were all destined to get married and raise a family."

"And the census shows them all living with Gampa's parents—my great-grandparents. They stayed in that house from the time they got married until Gamma and Clayton died. Then Gampa goes somewhere else for a while and finally ends up at Forest Glen. And the house somehow ends up on Maplewood."

"That sounds right. So, we know the whens and wheres—at least most of them. I still want to know the whys. And how does the house in Montford fit into all this? There's no indication of any connection between it and your family. Except, of course, that Leland owns it. Why didn't they live there? Why has it been vacant for decades?"

"Let's take one thing at a time, Tate. Right now, I'd like to see Gampa . . ." Cally stopped, a shocked look on her face.

"What? Cally, what is it?"

"What if he *wanted* us to leave? What if that's why Mom took me away? Maybe he hated us. Maybe he won't want to see me! I never considered that before." Huge tears formed in Cally's eyes, and Tate wrapped an arm around her shoulder for comfort.

"One thing at a time, like you said. Let's head out there and see what happens. Can we do that?"

"Yes . . . yes, okay. I just panicked for a minute. I'll be fine. Let's go."

THIRTY-ONE
2004

"You must think I'm a real wimp!" Cally turned to Tate as they sat in the parking lot outside Forest Glen.

"Why would I think that?" Tate noticed the effort Cally put into not crying, but small tears had formed in the corners of her eyes.

"I'm not usually like this—so emotional! What if Gampa doesn't want to see me?"

So we're back there, then—fear and insecurity. Tate reached over and put her hand on Cally's shoulder, giving it a gentle squeeze.

"Cally, I've only met your grandfather twice, but I can tell you for sure he's a loving and gentle man. I can't imagine he would not want to see you."

"But it's been so long! I was a little kid when Mom took me away. Maybe he's forgotten about me . . ."

"His mind is sharp, Cally. He may have buried his memories of you to protect himself, but I doubt he's forgotten you."

Cally sat staring at her hands in her lap, her shallow breath clearly an attempt to control her emotions. Tate waited a few moments before speaking again.

"So, my dear, I can pretty much guarantee you're never going to feel better by sitting here in the parking lot. We can leave and come back another time, or we can go inside. What's your preference?"

"I want to see him. I have to know."

Tate summoned her cheeriest voice, determined to do whatever she could to ease Cally's concerns. "Okay then. Let's go!"

They walked the short distance to the entrance and arrived in the lobby where Ruby stood ready to welcome them.

"Well, *Ms.* Marlowe. I never did think I'd be seein' you again this soon! And who's this with you?"

"And good afternoon to you, too, Ms. Ruby!" Ruby acknowledged the formal greeting with a huge grin and a wink.

Cally noticed the playful tone of the conversation and wondered what it meant. She'd have to ask Tate about it later.

"Ms. Ruby, I'm happier than I can say to introduce you to Cally Thornton . . ." Ruby waited through Tate's dramatic pause. ". . . Leland Howard's granddaughter!"

"Mr. Howard's *granddaughter?*"

Ruby's gasp caught the attention of Dorothy as she entered through the door behind the desk. She echoed Ruby's astonishment: "You said his *granddaughter?*

We thought he had no family left. *He* thinks all his family is gone!"

"She was gone for a long time," Tate said as she put a steadying hand on Cally's back. "But she's here now, and she would love to see Mr. Howard if you think he's up to it."

"He's busy carving some Christmas ornaments, but he always likes to have visitors," Dorothy offered as she escorted them into the common area.

Leland Howard sat in his usual spot by the windows, head bent over his work. Cally stopped short of approaching him. "I need a minute," she said. Tate and Dorothy stood quietly to the side as Cally took her time. She had yearned for this meeting for more than four decades. She would not rush now.

"Where did she come from, Ms. Marlowe?" The nurse whispered the question.

"California is the easy answer, but there's so much more to it than that Dor . . . Ms. Dorothy."

Dorothy gave the slightest giggle. "That 'Ms.' doesn't come naturally to you, does it, Ms. Marlowe?"

"Absolutely not! But, I'm learning to adjust to Southern customs, with Ms. Ruby's help."

"I had some trouble with that when I came to the South, too. When I'm at work, I always use the title when I greet someone. Informal situations, I tend not to use it. You know, at the store, with friends . . . but I always use it around older folks. It really is kind of confusing. I go by the better-safe-than-sorry rule!"

"Good advice, Ms. Dorothy. Thanks."

"We thought he was all alone. So, where did she come from?" Dorothy asked again as she nodded in

Cally's direction. They both noticed how still Cally stood and how intently she stared at her grandfather.

"She'll have to decide how much to share. But she was taken away as a child and just found her way back. She thought he was dead, and I think she's having a hard time taking it all in herself. I can't imagine what it will be like for him."

Cally turned to Tate and whispered "Okay." Dorothy took a seat nearby as Tate led Cally to her grandfather's side.

"How are you today, Mr. Howard?"

Leland looked up from his work and smiled broadly upon seeing Tate. He searched to see if she had a package with her. "No cookies today?"

Tate chuckled. "No, sir. No cookies today, but I did bring something very special with me." She indicated Cally. He turned his attention to the stranger as Cally knelt beside him, took his hand in hers and said: "Gampa, it's me. It's Cally."

THIRTY-TWO
1962

Leland left the workshop and headed for the house. Ellie would have lunch ready soon and his hunger had been building steadily as he worked all morning without a break. The chickens were fed, the garden patch tilled and ready for planting, and he'd made steady progress on the dining room table and chairs commissioned by the University president.

He noticed two broken plant pots on the floor as he entered the kitchen.

"Ellie?" He heard scuffling coming from the bedroom and Clayton screaming: "Give it to me! Where is it?"

Ellie's voice seemed odd—strong and determined, yet terrified. "It's for the girl. You'll never get it. I swear you'll never get it."

"What's going on? Ellie! Clayton!" Leland yelled as he headed through the living room where furniture

243

lay helter-skelter like a small tornado had just roared through.

He heard Clayton bellowing "I want it, Maw . . ." followed by a thud, a whimper and some whispered words from Ellie. Then Clayton stumbled out of the bedroom. His face contorted with rage, eyes ablaze, he paused in the middle of the room as if lost, head jerking from side to side, body twitching, scanning the room as if looking for something or trying to get his bearings. He froze when he saw Leland, and they stared at each other for a split second.

"I kilt her, Paw," he said before bolting out the front door and disappearing.

Leland stood anchored to his spot. *He killed her? What is he talking about?*

"Ellie! Where are you?" he called again, anxiety building, making it hard to speak at all. Fear propelled him to the bedroom where he found Ellie lying on the floor clutching her chest and gasping. He cradled her in his arms.

"Ellie. I've got to call for help."

"Too late . . . I'm goin'."

Leland began weeping, recognizing the truth in Ellie's words. She had only moments to live.

"I always bothered you about your hobbies, Leland. I'm sorry for that."

"Don't you worry about that, old woman," Leland said as he rocked her gently.

"Thank you for making that special place for me and the girl." Her words came in gasps as she struggled for breath.

"You're not gonna die, Ellie," he lied.

"I'm goin', Leland. Give Cally her things . . . promise me you will."

"What things?"

"From the mantel . . ."

"Ellie . . ."

"Clayton wanted them . . . drugs . . . they're hers . . . promise me." Ellie's words were barely audible.

Leland held her close and spoke in a hushed tone. "I'll see to it, Ellie."

Ellie took her last breath lying in her husband's arms, the husband she had chosen so long ago, the one who had stood by her through everything good and bad and whose loving face she now smiled into as her body went limp and she closed her eyes for the final time.

Incapacitated by grief, Leland sat holding and rocking Ellie until his sobbing finally subsided. He lifted her to the bed and gently laid her down, then went back to the living room, picked up the phone and dialed a familiar number. It rang three times before someone answered.

"Price residence." The voiced seemed to be coming from a long distance.

"Mr. Price, please. Leland Howard calling."

"Mr. Price is occupied. May I take a message?"

"Please tell him I'm very sorry to inconvenience him, but this is an emergency and I need him to come to my house immediately." Leland took care to manage the tone of his voice, to enunciate each word clearly, but the urgency he felt must have come through.

"Just a moment, please. I'll get him." Leland's thoughts bounced and tangled while he waited.

Shortly thereafter Richard Price's voice brought him back to the moment.

"What is it, Leland?"

"Ellie's dead. I need help, if you can, Richard. I can't seem to . . ."

"I'll be right there."

Leland walked slowly back to Ellie, lay down beside her and wrapped her in his arms for the last time. Breathing in her scent provided him a strange comfort in sharp contrast to the turmoil surrounding him.

Leland became aware of Richard Price standing quietly in the doorway of the bedroom several minutes later. The disarray left no doubt there had been a brutal fight. Splashes of blood covered the rug beside the bed. Glass from the shattered vanity mirror lay strewn about along with Ellie's hairbrush and combs, magazines from the night stand and items from the top of the dresser, which stood askew.

"Leland?" Richard called quietly.

No response. Just an almost imperceptible shudder and the sound of soft weeping.

"Leland? I'm so sorry. What happened here?"

"She's gone." Whispered, as if he could not bear to speak the words aloud.

"Leland, we have to call the police. Shall I do that?"

"Tell them not to hurry. I don't want them to hurry."

Richard Price left the room. Time passed. Not enough time. Not enough time to grieve, to allow oneself to believe the unbelievable. The police arrived. The ambulance. Someone took Leland gently by the shoulders and moved him off the bed and into the living room.

They asked him questions, silly irrelevant ones, like "When did this happen?" and "What do you remember?" and "How did you discover her?" They didn't ask the most important question, the one he had been asking himself since he'd walked into the bedroom and found Ellie dying. They didn't ask, "How are you going to survive without her?"

He answered the ones he could and asked some of his own.

"Sometime around lunch. What time is it now?" and "I came in from the workshop" and "Clayton looked at me and said 'I kilt her, Paw,' then ran out the door. Where is Clayton?" and "Is Ellie dead? I think Ellie is dead."

He watched them wheel the stretcher out the door and knew the answer. No matter how ardently he wished otherwise, that fact would remain unchanged.

Finally everyone left except for his friend. Richard brought him a cup of tea. "Are you hungry?" he asked.

"Not now. Not anymore."

"Let's get some of your things together, Leland. You can stay with us until we figure this all out. Claire and I will be happy to have you."

Claire? Leland found it difficult to pull his thoughts together. *Claire? Richard's wife. He still has his wife.* "I should stay here."

"Why, Leland?"

Isn't it obvious? Yet nothing was obvious to Leland. He had no reason to stay, but the thought of leaving, sent his mind reeling. "Can I stay here?"

"You'd be all alone, Leland. It's not good to be alone at a time like this."

"What time is it?"

"Let's get some things together for you, Leland."

A knock at the door interrupted them. Richard Price answered, and Leland heard him speaking in hushed whispers with the visitor. Then he returned, crying.

"What?" Leland asked, anxiety and hope rushing to the surface of his emotional quagmire. Maybe Ellie didn't die. They came to say she made it through after all.

"Leland, I don't know how to say this . . ."

"Is Ellie alive?"

"No, Leland . . . no. It's Clayton. They found him over in the park . . ."

"Is he coming home?"

"Leland, I'm so very sorry. Clayton hanged himself."

The two men sat together until the sun faded from the sky, Leland sinking deeper and deeper into a chasm of anguish from which he would never fully emerge, his friend sitting quietly at his side, praying fervently for guidance on how to prevent that inevitable outcome of so much tragedy.

THIRTY-THREE
1927

Ellie Howard thought the task of finding a suitable husband on short notice would be the most difficult challenge of her life, and it had been, up until she found herself firmly stuck in the roles of wife, daughter-in-law-in-residence and mother. Mary Alice, though gentle at heart, could be fierce when overseeing Ellie's induction into the Howard homestead—the small, cramped cabin on the edge of downtown Asheville. Mary Alice insisted things be done just so, and the old mountain ways of the Howard clan differed greatly from the city life of Ellie's childhood where her mother had shouldered the main responsibility of caring for the family with dutiful efficiency, freeing her children to pursue their own interests.

Mary Alice would have no part of the likes of Bisquick or Steero bouillon cubes or Minute Tapioca, modern conveniences Ellie thought essential. So at her mother-in-law's hands, Ellie learned to cook from scratch. Mary Alice considered canned goods from the corner store wasteful and inferior. She preferred to tend the huge family garden from early spring to late fall and preserve ample food to carry them through the year in her own kitchen, laboring over her beloved wood stove. Ellie reluctantly apprenticed in the garden. She became skilled at baking in the wood-fired oven. She collected the eggs, tended the chickens, even learned to wring their necks and prepare them for Sunday dinner, a task she found thoroughly disgusting.

Mary Alice also oversaw Ellie's mothering once the baby arrived. Ellie scrubbed dirty cloth diapers in the metal tub out back and hung them on the clothesline to dry in the sun. Mary Alice forbade the use the popular evaporated milk formulas so Ellie breastfed, and though her mother-in-law chided her for being shy, Ellie refused to feed the baby sitting in full view of anyone who happened to be in the cabin. Instead, she sat face-to-the-corner wedged between the masterfully crafted cradle and the end of the small bed she shared with her husband, a hand-woven shawl draped over her head and shoulders for privacy.

The months passed slowly, and Ellie felt herself slipping dangerously close to deep despair, an intolerable condition for a young woman who had lived most of her life buoyed by her optimism. Refusing to relinquish all hope, Ellie began forging a new path for herself in steps so small she sometimes barely noticed them—a path based on her desires rather than her circumstances.

Gently at first, she prodded Leland to build her a home of her own, and though his progress was exceedingly slow and frustrating, the house eventually emerged at the front of the lot facing Cumberland Avenue. She began exerting her will in opposition to Mary Alice as well, focusing on small areas where she expected the least resistance.

She loved Mary Alice and Arlen. They had graciously and lovingly accepted her into their family and their home. They had made room for her when they had precious little to spare. Still, she would not be swallowed up by them. She would not allow that to happen. She needed her own routines, her own rituals, and she intended to create them with her son and husband. She had not wanted the child, had not planned for him, and his arrival had set her on an unexpected and uncharted course. She resolved to restore vestiges of her former life where she could, and she would start with the tree in the park, the very spot where she had lost her way.

Ellie had passed that tree en route from one place to another her whole life. She loved its ancient spreading branches heavy with thick, green leaves in summer, rich with reds and oranges in the fall as it prepared for another season of rest, barren and majestic against cloudy gray skies in winter, and then again full of vibrant new life each spring. Since her tryst with Harland Ellie had avoided going anywhere near the tree she loved. Harland had stolen that from her, too, and she set herself the task of reclaiming her territory.

One afternoon in late August, Clayton's first summer, Ellie carefully dressed him in the little sailor suit her parents had given her when the baby was born. She encased his feet in the tiny white leather shoes that would one day be bronzed and displayed on the mantel her husband would build, put him in his buggy and headed to the park. Mary Alice came around from the side of the cabin as she was leaving, a laundry basket full of neatly-folded, dried clothes balanced on her hip.

"Where you goin', Ellie?"

"To the park, with my son."

"There's this ironin' to be done, ya know."

"I know. And I'll do it when I get back."

"Don'cha think ya should be tendin' to ya chores?"

"No. I think I should be taking my son to the park to enjoy this lovely afternoon."

"Ya got responsibilities, Ellie . . ."

". . . and the most important one is my son, Mother." Ellie did not like calling Mary Alice Mother, but she used the deferential moniker spoken in the most appeasing tone she could muster while still setting the limits she intended.

Mary Alice tilted her head to the side, shaded her eyes from the sun with her weathered hand and held Ellie's steady gaze. Ellie did not flinch. "Well then, don't be takin' too long. Woman's work is never done, ya know."

"Never done, maybe, but a break from it never hurt anyone." Ellie nodded to Mary Alice, pleased with herself for holding her ground. "I'll be home soon, Mother." And with that, Ellie took a huge step toward her own liberation.

She set out at a fast clip and arrived at the entrance to the park ready for her encounter, emboldened by her recent success with Mary Alice. She paused only for a moment, took a deep breath, straightened her spine and pushed the buggy ahead of her down the steps to the base of the tree. She stood motionless, heart pounding, eyes closed, and willed herself to remember the last time she had been there.

She had been a child, filled with unfettered fantasies of a grand and adventurous life with a dashing young man. She had been Ellie Vance then, and the world seemed to beckon her to greatness. As best she could, she conjured up those old feelings of excitement, anticipation, hopefulness, joy. But standing here now, shame beat down passion, guilt held happiness at bay, outrage gave way to resignation.

Yet, sheltered by the tree, she felt a hint of comfort. She took Clayton from the buggy, placed him on his back on the blanket she had spread out, and sat down cross-legged beside him. She shook his favorite rattle above his head, and he reached his tiny hand out and grasped her thumb. He giggled and held tight, pulling her hand and the rattle toward his perfect mouth. Ellie felt the rush of love for her beautiful child flood her body, and she unexpectedly burst into tears.

"It all started here, baby," she cooed. Clayton squealed as the rattle tinkled. "You started here and that made it a bad place for me for a while. But we are going to make it a good place again. We'll do that together, okay?"

She searched her child's smiling face, his shining brown eyes, and saw there only love, unquestioned trust and innocent joy. She realized how easy life could be, how focusing on joyful things could overpower darkness and regret, and she believed in that moment she could find her way back. She knew she would at least try her best to do so. With her child, she would create a good place where she could thrive and be happy again.

Ellie carved out time every few days to take her sojourn to the park. As Clayton got older, the buggy was replaced by a Radio Flyer wagon her friend Connie gave him for his first birthday. Sometimes Clayton would toddle along beside her, or Ellie would carry him. Eventually he graduated to a tricycle, then a two-wheeler. However they traveled, they always ended up at the base of the huge tree where they spent their time telling each other stories, reading from Clayton's favorite books or sharing a picnic lunch. Sometimes they would nap, the little boy wrapped safely in his mother's arms.

In those early years, the two of them were inseparable, but Ellie made it a point to include Leland as well. Whenever he had the time, Ellie encouraged Leland to join them in the park, and she paid special attention to nurturing the relationship between her husband and son. The family grew up under that tree as much as Clayton did, and no matter the season, they sought the place out for a respite from their daily routines. Other families did the same and over the years, the place slowly changed. At Leland's urging, the fathers hung a big rope swing from a strong lower branch. He made a simple bench of red oak and placed it on the opposite side of the thick tree trunk so parents could sit somewhere other than on the ground while they watched their children play.

With each visit, every little change, Ellie felt more secure, and eventually the new memories she so intentionally forged eclipsed those of her brief moment with Harland. That event from so long ago became submerged, leaving Ellie to mistakenly believe she had finally freed herself from it and from Harland Freeman.

———

Like all little boys, Clayton Samuel Howard knew what he wanted to be when he grew up. He would be a fireman, or a cowboy, a lion-tamer in the circus, maybe even a famous baseball player. From as far back as he could remember, his mother encouraged him to dream big. She showered him with love and he clung tightly to her. Many of his best childhood memories were of lying cradled against her as she read to him under the huge tree in the park. *Winnie-the-Pooh* and *Curious George* were his favorites until he could read by himself, and then he favored *My Friend Flicka* and *Bonus Kid*.

The day Clayton turned on Jimmy Boykins marked the death of a sweet little boy and the birth of a man who one day would kill his own mother in a fit of drug-induced rage. It was not a simple path from one existence to the other, nor was it an easy one. It started with the thrilling sense of power he felt as he loomed over Jimmy Boykins, weapon raised for another blow. Seeing his former nemesis cowering on the ground with a bloody nose sent an adrenaline rush through Clayton, and he inhaled the resulting sense of invincibility deep into every cell of his being. He wanted more, and he determined in that moment to find it however he could.

Clayton first sought his power by becoming the local bully. He swaggered. He boasted. He threatened and demanded. The neighborhood kids had heard what he did to Jimmy Boykins and they didn't want any of the same, so they either steered clear of him or buddied up with him. Clayton and his little gang roamed the neighborhood stirring up trouble here and there—mostly minor offenses in the beginning— but as he gained confidence, his behavior escalated and he ended up in trouble with the law on more than one occasion. Each time, Ellie or Leland bailed him out. He always offered apologies and promises to change his ways, and each time his parents chose to believe him rather than see the truth that lay beneath his compliant façade.

When bullying lost its luster, Clayton turned to vandalism. When breaking windows and defacing property failed to provide the rush he sought, he turned to drugs. Marijuana was easy enough to get, but it proved too mellow for his taste. He tried LSD, alcohol, amphetamines, even cocaine. Clayton would try anything once. By the time he reached his twenties, he had lost control of his life and from then until the end, he spiraled deeper and deeper into an abyss from which he would never escape.

He had moments of clarity when he realized what he had become, what he had given up in exchange for so little. He remembered feeling love for others and being loved by them. Flashes of the past would break through to the surface, usually when he was coming down from a high or sobering up after a drinking binge. He remembered whittling wood in the shop with his father, helping his mother bake or working with her in the garden. He especially remembered the spot under the tree—the "good place" his mother called it. He relived for a precious moment the peace of nestling there in her arms as she read his favorite stories and the joy of her pushing him high into the air on the rope swing his father had made for him and the other kids. And when he remembered, he wept. Then he would go in search of his next fix, whatever it might be, just so he could forget all the good things he'd lost, just so he could feel invincible again even for a little while.

The day he killed his mother he was in search of oblivion, or at the very least, cessation of his immediate pain. The clawing withdrawal from heroin drove him hard. His heart raced, he hadn't slept in at least two days, he was plagued with vomiting, cold sweats and muscle cramps so intense he felt his bones might snap.

She'll help me. That thought raced through Clayton's mind as he barged into the house and demanded money. She had money, he knew that. Or at least she had things he could exchange for drugs. The antique comb from his great grandmother—she'd shown him that once, and her own mother's diamond engagement ring. He believed there were other valuables as well, and she always had a little cash put away somewhere for emergencies. This was an emergency. Surely she'd see that and she would help him. She loved him.

But all she said was: "You'll never get it. I swear you'll never get it." She ran into the bedroom and locked the door. He went wild, smashing everything he could get his hands on, then kicking in the bedroom door and demanding again.

"It's for the girl! You'll never get it! I swear you'll never get it!" Her refusal reverberated through his head, clashing so hard against his belief she would rescue him that he couldn't make sense of her words.

When he did, when he understood she would not give him what he asked for, he stood staring at her dumbstruck. Anger surged through his veins just as the heroin had, but instead of reaching nirvana, he exploded in rage. And then he hit her, hard. And kicked her. And she collapsed and he knew he'd killed her.

As painful as his withdrawal was, it paled in comparison to the anguish that flooded over him as he saw her in a heap on the floor. Her beautiful eyes, which used to look at him with such love and adoration, now radiated only fear and disappointment. He shrank away from her and ran as fast as his broken body would carry him out of the house and along the familiar path to the park, to the good place. Maybe he would find the peace he pursued there.

The ancient old tree welcomed him as usual. No recriminations, no judgments. He pulled the weathered bench over to the old swing, climbed up and wrapped the thick rope twice around his neck. He spoke his final words into the clear, sweet air as he stepped off the bench. "I'm sorry, Maw. I tried to be good. I love you."

THIRTY-FOUR
1962

Richard Price handled funeral arrangements for Ellie and Clayton who were buried side-by-side on a sloping meadow in Riverside Cemetery. Leland attended the services, still in a daze, and said his final farewell to Ellie while standing on the exact spot where he would one day rest beside her. But contrary to his wishes, much time would pass before he joined her there.

All members of the Price household rallied to create a sanctuary for Leland, who, despite their best efforts, refused consolation. He slept fitfully in the luxurious guest room, roamed restlessly through the verdant gardens and consumed only the barest minimum of food and water.

None of those things that sustain life seemed relevant to Leland, whose internal battle between putting a decisive end to his keening grief or living in unabated sorrow raged on for several days. Ultimately, his final promise to Ellie tethered him reluctantly to survival. He must see to it that Cally got her things. Then he would find his way to Ellie. With his mission clear in his mind, he could finally begin formulating a coherent plan.

The next day, Leland rose early, bathed and put on clean clothes for the first time since leaving his own home. Exhausted by the effort, he sat in the courtyard, listening to the early morning songs of the birds and dozed in and out until his friend joined him, followed shortly by the housekeeper carrying a breakfast tray for the two of them.

"I'm hungry," Leland said in an unsteady voice. This revelation surprised both of them, though it pleased only Richard.

"That's a good sign, Leland. And I see you put on different clothes today—another good sign."

"I'll have some coffee," Leland said as the strong aroma whetted his appetite. He took a small bite of scrambled eggs. Weakened by days of little sleep or food, Leland's hand trembled, prompting Richard to pour the coffee, taking care to fill Leland's cup only halfway.

"I want to go back to my house today."

"I hoped to get the place cleaned up before you went back, Leland. Why not stay with us? You're welcome here for as long as you want."

"I need to get some things for Cally. I promised."

Richard Price's stomach churned. He had dreaded this moment ever since he learned Cally was gone, too.

"Can't that wait awhile, Leland? You need to get your strength back."

"I promised Ellie." Three simple words, yet they weighed heavily on Leland. Not just any promise—his *last* promise, and he intended to keep it. "I'm going today. It's not far. I'll walk over."

Leland had no idea if he would be able to walk the half mile to his house, but he sensed Richard's reluctance to help. He would go on his own if he must. Cally would get her things. And he wanted to see her, to try to explain. *How do you explain death to a seven year old?*

"What things, Leland? I could pick them up for you and get them to her." Richard didn't know how he would accomplish that since he didn't know where to find Cally. He'd just heard all the rumors racing through town about the tragic events surrounding Ellie's and Clayton's deaths, among them that Rita and Cally had abruptly left Asheville the following day. He had avoided telling Leland for obvious reasons.

"I can do it, Richard. I don't want to stay there. I'll get the things, take them to Cally's house, then come back here." Leland had eaten a few more bites of breakfast. He took a sip of coffee and rose to go, determined to carry out his task.

"Leland . . . I need to tell you . . ." Richard's voice cracked as he choked back tears.

"What?" *What now?* Alarm shot through Leland's whole being. Something was wrong. *How could anything else be wrong?* ". . . Richard?"

"I'm so sorry, Leland. I didn't want to tell you. Cally is gone. Her mother took her away."

261

Aghast at the news and the sudden prospect of not keeping his word to Ellie, Leland took a step backward, clipping his heel on the chair leg. He tumbled to the flagstone landing, hitting his head on a huge earthenware planter on the way down, and passed out. When he finally regained consciousness, he found himself lying on a small bed in a ward in the state hospital.

<center>~~~</center>

Years accumulated into decades. Leland Howard played little part in his own life, if one could call it a life, signing over the right to make all decisions on his behalf to his friend, Richard Price, who recognized with the help of the doctors that Leland would remain at risk of suicide if left on his own.

Leland never returned to the house he built for Ellie, visited the gravesites of his family nor reestablished an active existence. For those in the community he had once called home, he seemed to simply disappear, leaving behind ever-mutating stories about the dramatic events of March 15, 1962. Even they eventually faded into oblivion. He also left behind an unassuming house with a grand door and a workshop full of beautiful, one-of-a-kind works of art, demand for which sent their value skyrocketing. Fortunately, he had a dear friend who managed his estate and his care with dedicated devotion, flawless integrity and financial acuity.

As for Leland, he spent the years sequestered, first in the mental hospital where he underwent treatment for severe depression, including electric shock treatment,

262

and then Forest Glen where he eventually settled into a quiet life. Over time and with great effort, he successfully sealed up his memories and buried them deeply in his subconscious, allowing him to live around the edges of the overwhelming emotions they contained.

But today, as he sat working small pieces of basswood into intricate ornaments ready for hand-painting and sale at the upcoming Christmas Bazaar, the veils between those two worlds—one carefully constructed over the ruins of the other—fell away with a few words uttered by a stranger.

"Gampa, it's me. It's Cally."

THIRTY-FIVE
2004

It had been the most eventful three weeks in Cally's life. She had let Lauren go, left Los Angeles and her career, driven herself across the continent, searched for her roots, not found them, then met Tate and found not only her roots but so much more. She had found her grandfather. She had found home.

It is often said in Asheville, by those who leave and then return, that once you live in Asheville, you always come back. The city affects people that way—captivates them, draws them in, makes them its own. Asheville chose Cally as much as she chose it.

Though she loved the little city, she had nearly forgotten about it during those long years in California. Her grief over leaving her grandparents had eventually faded, and with its passing, the peaceful days of her childhood spent with them retreated to a dusty corner of her mind. She had left them locked away there to appease her mother, who refused to talk about anything related to their old life in the mountains.

Of the few memories Cally retained from her childhood, the night they left Asheville remained the most vivid. Rita packed only those belongings that would fit into the back of their beat up VW Beetle, secured Cally in the passenger seat and headed west.

"Where are we going?" Cally asked.

Rita gave no response. She stared into the night and drove silently for several minutes while her daughter waited. When she spoke, her voice sounded different. Had Rita been willing to name it, she would have said terror, bewilderment, disbelief—maybe all of them— had taken hold of her. But she would not name the pandemonium raging inside her, not to her child, not even to herself. "We're never going to talk about this place again, do you hear me?"

That night, the mother Cally had known all her life vanished, and Rita would never seem the same to Cally again.

Cally attempted the next day, as they continued west, to get Rita to take them back home. "Momma, I want to see Gamma . . ."

Rita glared at her. "I told you we were never going to talk about it again, Cally."

"But, Momma, I want to see her so bad my heart hurts!" She broke into ragged sobs.

"I said NO!" Then the new mother lifted her hand off the steering wheel, swooshing the back of it menacingly close to Cally's face as if to strike the little girl who instinctively crouched against the car door.

"You listen to me, Cally," Rita hissed. "I told you last night we are never going to talk about any of those people back there again. I just can't bear to do it." Her voice softened as she saw the fear and misery in her child's eyes. "Cally, we can't . . . I just can't talk about them no more, please . . ."

"I miss them, Momma. I miss them so bad." Cally finally acquiesced and stopped asking to go home. Even at 7 years old a child can understand when something changes forever. She may not know what, she may not know why. But she can know something special is gone and will never return.

"I know," said Rita. Then she turned her attention back to the road stretching out before her—dry, dusty and barren—hoping with each mile she and her child would survive what laid behind and what lay ahead.

By the time they reached Los Angeles, Rita had tucked all her feelings about what had happened in Asheville away in a chamber buried somewhere deep inside herself. She spent the rest of her life keeping the door to that chamber tightly closed, using alcohol, mind-numbing work and a series of irrelevant men as guardians to her secrets. In the process, she would also close out her child, who nonetheless held as closely to her as Rita would allow.

—⁓—

Rita's untimely death at age 54 shocked everyone but surprised no one. Her decades of heavy drinking resulted in cirrhosis of the liver which buddied up with diabetes and heart disease to create a direct path to an early demise. Cally had begun preparing herself to deal with a sickly and aging mother while still in high school many years earlier. It never occurred to her Rita might go suddenly rather than lingering on to suffer the indignities of a deteriorating body and mind. Being hit by a bus after stumbling half-drunk into the street proved a much better way to go, really, and Cally felt only a bit guilty for being relieved when her mother died in exactly that way.

In the days and weeks following Rita's death, Cally did her best to take care of tying up the remaining aspects of her mother's broken life. She arranged for the funeral and notified the few people who called Rita "friend," all the while dealing with the cleaving pain of having no relatives to call with the news.

Much of what she found in her mother's cramped and cluttered studio apartment went directly into the trash. Anything with value she packed up and carted off to Goodwill. *There are no memories for me here. Nothing to keep. Nothing to cherish.* Those thoughts predominated, leaving Cally in despair as she moved methodically through her mother's house, cleaning out all remnants of a barren life.

She worked in spits and spurts, knowing she need not rush. She could afford to pay the rent on the place until she got it emptied out. After devoting her life to keeping her mother as close as possible, refusing to let Rita drift away, it never occurred to Cally she could hire someone to clear out the apartment rather than doing it herself. This chore, awful though it was, represented her last physical connection to Rita. So she dragged herself through the task with no expectation other than eventually finishing it.

Cally loaded the last box for the thrift store into her car and then felt compelled to do one more walk-through before locking the door for the final time. She peeked into the medicine cabinet, checked out all the cupboards and opened the closet door to take another look. Strong, late-afternoon sunlight streamed through the picture window illuminating the usually dark space, and light bounced off something stuck far back in the corner.

Cally stooped down and pulled a battered wooden cigar box from a depression in the back wall. A flood of memories rushed over her as she pulled it close to her chest and began sobbing uncontrollably.

She clutched the box and savored the thought of what she knew she would find inside. The earthy, musty fragrance of old tobacco would be there along with the rough finish and the yellowed inscription:

LEWIS' SINGLE BINDER 5 CENT CIGAR

spelled out in fading letters. And it would have treasures in it. It would hold memories. This old box had always contained her mother's most cherished possessions. Cally instinctively knew it still did.

She cried herself to sleep there on the floor of her mother's vacant apartment. She woke to an incredible sunset, the sky streaked with clouds tinted purple, pink, orange and gold, and Jacob's Ladders glinting off the distant ocean. Her arms remained tightly wrapped around her unexpected prize.

Cally stood and opened the west-facing windows, letting in the cooling evening air, then sat leaning against the wall, cradling the cigar box. After several minutes, she lifted the lid with shaking hands and began sorting through the items one by one, taking her time with each.

Some of them she remembered. A tiny bracelet given to her mother as a child, which she herself had been allowed to wear on very special occasions; some old greeting cards from Rita's boyfriends; a decrepit rabbit's foot on a thin ball chain; a report card with an "A" in Reading and scrawled beside it in Rita's hand "my first A!" She remembered her mother showing her the report card and admonishing Cally to "do good in school, like I never did."

She did not expect what she found next. She pulled out a picture she had never seen before—a barely recognizable Ellie as a happy and vibrant girl, her face aglow with a huge smile. Her frothy hair stood atop her head, secured there with a fancy scarf tied rakishly over her right ear. She wore a simple cotton dress with a fitted bodice and pleated skirt.

As she stared at the picture, Cally reached back in time trying to connect with her grandmother. She did not know this exuberant young woman, the teenaged Ellie in the photo. She had known only the matronly Ellie, the subdued woman who smiled but never laughed out loud, the one who rocked a tiny Cally to sleep at naptime, and who later taught her to crochet doilies and bake brownies.

The next item surprised Cally even more. Tucked behind the picture she found an aged, folded note with her name penciled on the front. A strange sensation flooded over her as she reached for it. She felt spacey, her breath quickened, and her heart began pounding.

The corner of the room seemed to fill with a misty, white light with no obvious source. *It's so fragile.* This thought rolled through Cally's head as she opened the note carefully so as not to damage it. It read:

> *There is always something waiting for you where the home fire burns.*
> *I love you dearly and forever.*
> *Gamma*

Emotions engulfed Cally in huge waves—grief, joy, rage, disbelief, confusion. *Where did this come from? Why didn't Gamma give it to me herself? Why did Mom hide it away all these years? I'm so glad I found it. It's a miracle I didn't leave it behind . . .*

And then, gratitude and love surfaced, filling every cell in Cally's body. Her heart overflowing with thoughts of her mother, who, for reasons Cally could not comprehend, had both hidden and preserved this precious gift from her grandmother, she spoke aloud through her wracking sobs: "Thank you, Mom. Thank you so much for keeping this for me." The light in the corner glimmered brightly before receding. Rita's final gift had been found. Cally waited until her crying subsided, then gathered up the box along with all its treasures and left the little apartment for the last time.

THIRTY-SIX
2004

Leland Howard's life had always been defined by family. First his parents and grandparents when they lived on the homestead in the mountains, then Ellie and Clayton, and later Cally—all of them made Leland Howard the person he was. Rather, the person he had once been. In the wake of the loss of his entire family in a matter of days, nothing could have persuaded Leland to continue participating in his daily life, so the accident in the courtyard that led to his brief coma and subsequent hospitalization proved to be a blessing. The injury, coupled with his unremitting depression, provided a reason no one could question for him to slip out of reality and never return.

It proved less of a blessing that his mind remained sharp and his memories kept trying to claw their way back into the light of day. He kept them caged by focusing only on his daily activities—making the little boxes from wood supplied by his dear friend, Richard Price; bantering with the staff at Forest Glen; and occasionally sharing some of his carefully selected memories such as he had done with Tate Marlowe recently.

Of course, rummaging through his mind for recollections of happy events threatened to pull him deep into the abyss of grief awaiting him, so he rarely ventured into that territory. The presence of this young woman claiming to be his granddaughter created a critical decision point for Leland Howard. Keep her out, and he could remain in the relatively comfortable world he had constructed. Let her in, and he would . . . what? What stood on the other side of that possibility?

Leland Howard did not know what he would find if he chose to acknowledge the woman. He knew only that he had searched her face and found his sweet, little granddaughter with tears in her eyes and in need of comforting. He had searched his heart and unearthed the anguished aching, long in need of healing that only family could provide. *She called me Gampa.*

He reached his hand out into the past, into the present, and gently touched Cally's cheek. He chose family, willing to face whatever horror that choice might unleash.

He felt a bit dizzy and put his hand on the table to steady himself as if he were about to rise out of his chair. Then he sat back and took a deep breath.

"It's me, Gampa. Do you remember me?"

He sat quietly with eyes closed, mind racing, slipping in and out of coherent thought. It couldn't be Cally. *Cally is gone. They're all gone.* The woman squeezed his hand and pulled it gently to her cheek again. He felt her tears on his fingers.

"Cally is gone," he muttered. "They all went away and left me alone."

"I'm right here, Gampa. I came back. I thought you had died, and I came back and found out you were still here. It's me. It's Cally, all grown up."

Leland shook his head, trying to unscramble his thoughts. He looked again into the woman's eyes. And there she was—little Cally. He heard the faint echo of her laugh, saw her dancing around the living room of the old house in her princess dress, eyes twinkling as she waved her magic wand.

"Are you a princess or a fairy?"

Cally puzzled over this question. She looked to Tate for help.

"I think he's confused, Cally. This is probably pretty shocking for him."

Dorothy joined them at Leland's side and placed two fingers on his wrist to check his pulse. She noted his shallow breathing. "His pulse is racing. This is very stressful for him."

"I should leave . . ." Cally said, hesitantly, looking to Tate and Dorothy for confirmation.

"Are you a princess or a fairy?" Leland smiled as he stared intently into Cally's eyes.

"I don't understand, Gampa . . ."

"You have a princess dress and a fairy's magic wand. Which are you?"

The shared memory flashed into Cally's awareness, and she gasped as she remember that day in the living room at the old house. She responded just as she had so very long ago: "I'm a magic princess, Gampa!"

"Indeed you are, Cally. Indeed you are!"

They wrapped their arms around each other and began sobbing. Tate and Dorothy retreated to the edge of the room, leaving them to find their way back to family.

THIRTY-SEVEN
1942

Valentine's Day approached, and Ellie had agreed to help stage the annual party for the teen group at church. She hoped Clayton would attend. He showed no signs of outgrowing his wildness, and she sought any means possible to turn him in a positive direction.

Constance Ryland arrived at the same time. She and Ellie fell into a familiar banter as they began pulling decorations out of storage and catching up with each other. Their friendship, which began in grade school, remained solid through years of volunteering together even though they now lived very different lives.

Connie—Ellie was one of few still to call her that name—had married a wealthy man, but she came from working-class roots. Although it took a long time, she had eventually secured acceptance in her husband's social circle. With that acceptance came a challenge. Abandon her past or embrace it? She struggled to do both and eventually found balance. She remained involved at the church of her childhood through her volunteer work but now attended services with her husband at his place of worship. What many people interpreted as haughtiness, Ellie saw for what it was—Connie's way of straddling two worlds and remaining true to herself. Sure, she wore fancy clothes and expensive jewelry, but she never acted superior, at least not to Ellie.

"It's so good to see you, Ellie! I've missed you."

"I missed you, too, Connie. You've been out of town, haven't you?"

"Yes, we went to Palm Beach right after New Year's. We intended to return in March, but Phillip had a business meeting in Washington, so we came back early. I would have preferred to stay longer. You know I don't like the cold weather much."

"You never have, Connie. This winter has been pretty mild, though. No major storms so far and we've had some spring-like days already. Of course, it could turn bad again with little notice. We've all seen five or six inches of snow arrive in a single day in April or May."

"Well, it's good to be home, even this early in the season. And I've always loved this Valentine's dance. Remember? We'd come every year hoping to meet Prince Charming and end up being wall flowers all night!"

"Oh, yes, I remember. But Prince Charming finally found you, Connie. Quite a catch, that Phillip, and not only because he's rich."

"I have to agree with you on that, Ellie. I still wonder what I did to deserve ending up where I am. Don't you?"

"I know exactly what I did." Matter-of-fact. Nothing more needed saying.

"Oh, right." Connie blushed at her misstep. Ellie had never shared the details of her pregnancy and marriage, and Connie had always respected Ellie's decision not to discuss it.

Connie quickly changed the subject. "Well, what have you been doing to keep busy while I've been away?"

"The same stuff really. Nothing interesting. I cook, clean, do the laundry, try to keep my son out of trouble and my husband happy. It's not a bad existence, really."

"Your life sounds appealing to me sometimes. I get tired of the whole society routine everyone expects of us. I think Phillip would like to leave it all behind, too."

"Seems like all those parties would be fun. Don't you meet interesting people?"

"Sometimes, of course. There's the occasional celebrity—a couple of years ago I met Helen Forrest, who sang with Benny Goodman—but quite often it's just the same crowd discussing the same things. Everyone trying to impress everyone else. I find it quite tiresome. But I have to go, whether I want to or not."

"It's really that bad?"

"Let me give you an example. We went to the grand opening at Harland Freeman's house just before Christmas. You must remember him—such a bore in high school. Everyone wanted to see that place, you know? It's really quite garish, but if all your friends are going . . . well, as bad as it sounds, I didn't want to miss out." Connie chuckled at her own inconsistency. "So we went. Everyone was being polite and commenting on the place, discussing anything, really, just to not think about the War, and someone brought up the door that Leland made."

Ellie tensed up, not sure she wanted to hear what came next. "Really? People noticed it, then?"

"Oh yes. They noticed all right. Harland made a point to brag to Thomas Bristol. Anyway, everyone thought the design was unique, and then I told them about the door on your house."

"You didn't!"

"Of course, I did! Yours is really much prettier, I think."

"Did he hear you? Does he know?"

"Ellie, you're upset . . ."

"Oh . . . no . . ." Ellie tried to act nonchalant. ". . . no, I just wondered what he said when he heard your comment."

"I'm not sure he heard it. He wasn't in the room. In fact, just then he had some kind of episode in the hallway outside. The men took him up to his room and helped him settle in. We all left soon after."

Ellie paled.

"Come to think of it," Connie went on, "maybe that party wasn't so boring after all!" Connie's lighthearted laughter did little to dispel the worry building in Ellie's mind as they went back to preparing for the dance.

—⚬⚬⚬—

As if in response to Ellie's prediction of the previous day, fat, wet, heavy snowflakes began falling copiously early in the afternoon on February 13, 1942. They formed the last image to register in Harland Freeman's brain before he closed his eyes and pulled the trigger of the gun in his mouth. Moments before that irreversible act, he fleetingly considered delaying his suicide because of the unanticipated storm, but Harland had never been a man to second guess himself once he made a decision. A modicum of foresight would likely have swayed him, but the only accommodation he made for the unexpected weather was to cover himself from foot to armpit in a warm woolen throw after carefully positioning his chair before the front door of his mansion. The blanketing snow muffled the sound of the gunshot, which thus alerted no one to his demise other than the squirrels, already scurrying for cover from the encroaching blizzard.

Snow fell for twelve hours straight. By the following morning, it had transformed the neighborhood into a hushed winter wonderland, with willowy hedges bent low, shrubs camouflaged as snow drifts, and streets and sidewalks swathed in pristine, untrammeled snowy splendor. For nearly a full day after his death, Harland's body remained undiscovered.

The sun finally dispersed the thick cloud cover and broke through by mid-morning on Valentine's Day, revealing the streets as ideal paths for cross-country skiers and kids on sleds, along with bundled-up neighbors walking their dogs. Several such adventurers passed by Harland's house but took no notice of anything out of the ordinary. Harland's poor social skills and generally unfriendly style had resulted in everyone who lived nearby avoiding him whenever possible, so the fact his body went unnoticed for so long came as little surprise to anyone when news began spreading about his death later in the day.

Luckily for Harland, who had never liked dogs, those four-legged creatures do not squelch their natural curiosity and joy like their human counterparts do, nor do they parcel out their love grudgingly. So it happened that a frisky young Labrador retriever finally brought attention to the dead body sitting on the porch of the house at 305 Chestnut Street.

Sensing the chance of a new playmate, the dog broke loose from the middle-aged woman on the other end of the leash, bounded across the lawn and up the steps, stopping just short of jumping into Harland's cold lap. Yelping and wagging its whole body, the dog refused to leave Harland's side, forcing the woman to make her way up the treacherous walk to fetch him, apologizing all the way to the unresponsive Harland for intruding on his privacy. She wondered why he would be sitting so still in such inclement weather, until she realized as she reached the steps that Harland was dead. She grabbed for her dog, but the pup remained by Harland's side, licking his hand and pawing at him, showering all his love and attention on the still, cold body in those last moments before the world knew Harland Freeman as a corpse instead of a man. The woman finally pulled the dog away and rushed back to her house to call for help, barely able to contain herself long enough to do so.

The police eventually arrived, and in short order a crowd had gathered on the street.

"How long has he been there, do you think?"

"Someone killed him, right?"

"Why's he sitting out there like that?"

"Was he murdered? Surely not!"

"More'n likely he deserved it."

"I hope he went quietly."

"He was a mean man. Prob'ly just got what was comin' to him."

"Oh, I don't like to think he suffered."

"When did it happen?"

"Why did it happen?"

"How did it happen?"

Of course, most of those questions would remain unanswered for quite some time, opening the door for wild speculation on the circumstances leading up to the highly unusual event. Numerous theories and spurious facts emerged as the news swept through the city. Few if any who heard the story felt saddened by Harland's abrupt and dramatic departure. Some worried about their jobs at Freeman's Mercantile; others schemed to purchase the successful business before someone else could swoop in ahead of them. No one knew of surviving family to whom one could offer false condolences or press for information. There would be no funeral, no final goodbyes, no mourning period.

At least not for most. For a very few others, the suffering which began the day news arrived of Harland's death lasted in one form or another for the rest of their lives. But each of them would grieve in isolation and for very different reasons.

For Leland Howard, induction into the tiny group took place a week later and came in the form of a visit from a member of Paige & Schmidt, the legal firm responsible for handling Harland's estate. At Ellie's urging, Leland finally let the man into the house. The tone for the unwelcome meeting established itself quickly.

"Mr. Freeman's will is explicit, Mr. Howard. The house at 305 Chestnut Street is now held in a trust of which you are the sole beneficiary."

"That can't be. I don't want the place. I want nothing to do with anything involving that despicable man." This level of anger surprised even Leland.

"Now, Mr. Howard, you're speaking about a dead man . . ."

"Dead or not, doesn't change who he was when he was alive!"

"Leland, please. I know this is upsetting, but please don't lash out so." Ellie sat in the background and had not spoken until this moment.

"I don't care, Ellie. He had no right to burden me so. What did I ever do . . . this is an act of hatred on his part, not kindness. You know that man never had a generous bone in his body."

"Mr. Howard, he was your cousin, was he not?" the attorney pleaded.

"Being blood relation don't make somebody a good man. Our mothers couldn't abide one another, and neither could we. We never had what you would call a family relationship."

"Didn't you help him build that house? I seem to remember him mentioning so when we were drawing up his will . . ."

"NOT! BY! CHOICE!" Leland uttered this response with controlled rage, all the while staring angrily in Ellie's direction.

"Leland, I'm sorry . . ."

"Not by choice . . ." Leland said in a more measured tone, ". . . but yes, I did do some of the work on that place. Still, it doesn't mean I want anything to do with it now. It's a cursed house, and I don't want the aggravation."

"What do you mean, 'cursed'?"

"Well, he killed himself there, didn't he? What would you call it?"

The attorney took a deep breath and struggled to maintain his composure. He had a job to do. He had been sent to deliver the details of Mr. Freeman's will to the beneficiary. He never expected it to be fraught with such resistance and difficulty.

"I'm sorry, Mr. Howard. I can see this is not welcome news. Still, the will is, as I said, explicit. The house is held in trust for you."

"Well, then, I'll give it away just like he did! Ellie, who should I give that place to? It's rightly your decision, don't you think? You're the one insisted I do that work for him."

Leland directed the full force of his anger at Ellie for the first time in their entire life together. He wanted this to be her fault. Hers or Harland's, but not his, definitely not his.

Leland's precisely aimed fury landed squarely on its target, shattering Ellie's emotional armor instantly. She began sobbing uncontrollably. Leland immediately backed down, shocked at his wife's crying, something he had seen on only the rarest of occasions and never with such abandon.

"My god, what am I doing? Ellie, I'm so sorry! Please—don't cry." Leland moved to console Ellie, who sat hunched up, hands covering her face. He saw before him a vulnerable girl, not the tough and distant wife he had grown accustomed to over the years. He kneeled down, wrapped his arms around her shoulders and pulled her in close, cradling her and rocking gently. Together they wept, finally letting go of the festering suspicions, regrets and disappointments built up during the course of their marriage—wounds, big and small, now revealed without naming, and finally exposed for healing.

The attorney, ready to bolt from the overwhelming display of emotion, nonetheless held himself in his seat and waited for it to pass. When it did, Leland gave Ellie a gentle kiss on top of her bent head, returned to his own chair, blew his nose loudly into his handkerchief, then addressed the lawyer.

"As I was saying, I'd like to give the house away myself. How do I go about doing that?"

"Well, you won't be happy to hear you can't."

"Of course, I can. If I own it, I can do whatever I want with it."

"Not in this case, I'm afraid. The trust Mr. Freeman created will stay in effect for as long as you're alive. You cannot sell the house or in any other way convey it out of the trust. You can do whatever else you want with it, but it belongs to you until you pass. You have the right to pass it on to whomever you please in your own will."

"What if it burns down?" Leland blurted out this possibility even before he became aware of the plan hatching in his mind.

"I must caution you, Mr. Howard, not to make such suggestions."

"I'm not . . . no, not suggesting I'd burn it down. I'm sorry. That came out wrong," he lied. "I mean, what if something happens to the house and it's not there anymore?"

"The property would still belong to you, Mr. Howard. The terms of the trust are ironclad."

Indignation and disbelief finally took their toll on Leland. He sank back into his chair, feeling trapped and helpless. Ellie, still pulled back into herself, sat staring blankly at the knotted hands in her lap.

"Maybe I have no choice but to own it, sir, but I can tell you this," Leland continued, "I won't have nothin' to do with that house. Not now. Not ever. It can sit there and rot on its foundation for all I care."

"I understand what you're saying, Mr. Howard, but it won't rot. Mr. Freeman made arrangements for it to be taken care of regardless. He left a sizable fortune which also comes to you as his beneficiary and only surviving relative. Along with the house, the money will be held in a trust and used to maintain the property. If there is any money left when you pass, what remains will be part of your estate."

"There's no escaping then?"

"No sir. I'm sorry. It's yours, like it or not."

Leland sat in silence, contemplating the unavoidable impact of his inherited prison, as the lawyer found his own way out.

Ellie remained quiet, choosing not to educate the attorney about Harland's surviving relatives.

───✦───

Leland spent the following days secluded in his workshop, trying to make sense of the vindictive nature of the terms of Harland's will. He wanted desperately to find himself innocent, undeserving of such diabolical retribution. *What did I do that was so bad? I should never have made that door. I said nope then went back on my own word. Maybe I deserve this after all. I should've stood my ground. Maybe Ellie was right. Ellie was wrong! She made me do the work after I said nope. It's her fault, then, not mine.*

These thoughts, among many others, fought their way back and forth through Leland's mind, sometimes convincing him he had been wronged by Harland, other times persuading him of his own culpability in the matter. And throughout it all, Ellie remained a constant. His attempts to hold her responsible, to hate her for her role in his misery, always fell apart, rendered impotent by his enduring love for her.

Eventually, Leland resigned himself to his fate. He owned the wretched house on Chestnut Street. Even if he could not change that fact, he would do his best to forget about it and continue on with his life as it had been before his unfortunate change in circumstances. What made his intention virtually impossible to achieve was the door that greeted him each time he entered his own humble abode. The door with the carved fittings and scrolled panels so much like those on his loathsome inheritance, yet so much finer. The one he had meticulously constructed and installed on the house he built for Ellie in an act of defiance unlike any he had ever committed before.

Harland's words came back in a rush: "You'll pay dearly for this Leland, I promise you." Harland had carried out his threat. Leland *would* pay dearly, and he could do nothing about it.

He now cringed at the sight of that door, intuitively knowing he himself had struck the fatal blow that led to a wintery end for a cold-hearted man—a man whose death resulted from humiliation much more than from the bullet which shattered his skull.

From that day forward, Leland never again entered his own home through the front door.

THIRTY-EIGHT
1942

It is often hard to know where the paths we forge will lead us. Our intentions are usually clear, but every decision, mundane or monumental, alters our course. At any moment, we may find ourselves lost in unfamiliar territory with little idea how we ended up there. For Marie Eleanor Vance Howard that moment occurred after the attorney from Paige & Schmidt retreated and her husband left her alone in her living room.

She sat there awash in a flood of emotions she had kept deeply buried her entire adult life. Most perplexing of all, she found joy romping freely amid the turbulence. A wave of despair or grief or rage would threaten to pull her under, and then joy would pop her back to the surface. She would descend into disbelief, fury, guilt—and then unbidden, irrepressible exuberance would save her again. She was astonished when she finally realized the source of her elation. Ellie loved her husband!

Over the course of almost fifteen years together, Ellie had developed many feelings for Leland. Originally it was little more than a marriage of convenience, but Ellie had come to appreciate him; she had grown dependent upon him in many ways. She couldn't have asked for a better father for Clayton, especially now as the boy became harder and harder to manage. Leland's craftsmanship provided a good income for them; his even-temperedness contributed to a peaceful home life.

However, not all her opinions about Leland were favorable. She also saw him as meek and compliant—always the follower, never the leader. This left her in charge, a state of affairs she simultaneously nurtured and resented. If he had not been so willing to do whatever she asked, he would never have taken the job for Harland, no matter how she had tried to convince him. Maybe none of this would have happened if he had stuck to his refusal to work on that damnable house. *He just had to put that same door on our house! I told him not to. I knew it would lead to trouble. If only . . . no, this is not his fault. I shouldn't have made him do it.* Back into guilt and resentment and then, again, her heart flew open and love rushed in! *I truly love him!*

Ellie had wanted to be in love for as long as she could remember. Bits and pieces of her girlhood dreams floated back to her, and she pictured herself singing on a Broadway stage, or traveling the world with a dashing partner, or swimming in silky Caribbean waters under a full moon—all versions of the exotic life she once imagined. But regardless of where she found herself or who accompanied her in these fantasies, she was always in love.

Her unexpected pregnancy shackled her, and long ago she had turned to romance novels to assuage her longing. She kept her "books in brown" hidden away in the back of the closet, along with her shame. Eventually the routine of her daily life subdued the yearning, and she convinced herself she was content.

But now the force of Leland's rage had shaken her to the core and obliterated her pretensions. She saw his hidden strength for the first time. Not just his stubbornness—yes, he could be stubborn—but also strong and vital, with dignity and character. A truly good man, an honorable man. And she had done him a wrong he might never excuse. The thought of losing Leland struck a debilitating fear in Ellie, and she prayed fervently for his forgiveness.

—◊◊◊—

Three days later, Ellie found the chance she had been hoping for. She called Leland to the house for lunch, and he actually emerged from the workshop, taking off his work apron and dropping it on the chair outside the back door before entering the kitchen—just like always. Ellie breathed a quiet sigh of relief. She put a bowl of steaming, beef vegetable soup on the table for him along with butter and freshly baked bread. She sat down opposite him with her own meal.

"Leland, we need to talk. Can we please talk?"

"What's to say, Ellie? I'm not changing my mind."

"I know, Leland. I'm done trying to get you to do things my way. I've been bossing you around for much too long."

Leland looked up in surprise but said nothing.

"I realize what a burden I've been to you all these years, Leland. Having to take care of me and the boy, when you're not . . ."

"Don't say it, Ellie . . ."

"You know when we married I was already . . ."

"Hush, woman! Don't say it! Don't ever say it out loud. It don't need to be said."

"But that's how Harland . . ."

"I knew, Ellie, but I didn't know who. I guessed it was him when you insisted on me doing that work for him. But it never mattered to me then, and it don't matter now. The boy is mine, for better or for worse, just like the promise I made to you in your mother's back yard."

"He's been so vexing to us, to you . . . and you've never complained."

"Why would I complain, Ellie? I love the boy and I love you beyond words. I loved you long before you ever asked me to go with you to Woolworth's for that Coca-Cola. How could you not know that?"

"But I dragged you into this marriage and you . . ."

"I what? Went along blindly? Unwillingly? Is that what you think?"

"I . . . yes . . . I thought you married me because I wrangled you into it, not because you . . ."

"I married you because from the first time I laid eyes on you, you were all I ever wanted. That's never changed, Ellie. If you loved me even one iota as much as I . . ."

"I love you, Leland."

He stared at her while she continued. She had never said those words to him before. In fact, they had never talked like this before—openly, honestly and about things that truly mattered.

Ellie sighed deeply. "I've been so afraid these last few days you would leave me, and it made me come to my senses. I've always thought I could do without you if I really wanted to. But now I know how wrong I was about that."

"I . . . I wish I could believe you mean that . . ."

"I love you, Leland Howard. I didn't know it myself until a few days ago. I mean I had come to love you, but I'd never allowed myself to see the real you, your strength, and when I did, I thought it was too late, that I'd lost you. You were so angry."

"I lost control . . . I'm sorry, Ellie."

"Don't apologize for that, Leland. Harland did a terrible thing, and my part in it was horrid, too. But it woke me up. And I realized I'm in love with you. I don't just love you, like I love this soup or my favorite pair of slippers. I'm in love with you. I never felt this before, and I always wanted it, always missed it. And it's been right here in front of me all these years. Only I couldn't let it in. I couldn't let myself be in love with you because then you could . . ."

"I'd never hurt you, Ellie. Never abandon you."

Soft tears fell from Ellie's eyes as she took in the man sitting across from her. She felt passion for him building inside her, an unremitting desire to fall into his arms and meld with him. *But can I do that? Can I let myself go like I did that one time, like I've always dreamed of doing?*

Leland stepped around the table and pulled her into his arms. She relaxed into his embrace, buried her face in his shoulder and breathed in his enticing scent—the earthiness of the wood from his shop and the staleness of dried sweat on his work shirt, mixed in with his personal aroma, reminiscent of a fresh spring breeze— his own unique fragrance, which she had never let herself enjoy before.

"I'm so tired, Leland. These last days have been terribly trying."

"For me, too, Ellie."

They walked into their bedroom and lay down on the bed. Had they been young, had they felt this way about each other on their wedding night, their eagerness would have taken over. Instead, they wrapped themselves up in each other's arms and cried themselves to sleep. Both now trusted that passion would be there when they awoke.

THIRTY-NINE
2004

Tate had not been to the gym in over two weeks and as she looked outside at the drizzling rain, she knew she would not be returning today. The past several days with Cally and Leland had been mentally and emotionally stimulating, but her aching body craved exercise.

She took her coffee to the living room and sank onto the sofa, intending to read for a while. But her mind kept returning to yesterday's reunion between Cally and Leland. Although it had lasted less than half an hour, it left a profound impact on everyone involved.

Tate and Dorothy had excused themselves from the conversation once Leland recognized Cally, so Cally brought Tate up to date as they drove home.

Cally had chosen to sidestep painful questions about Leland's past, focusing instead on his daily life in Forest Glen, his favorite foods and other neutral areas. He told her about the peanut butter cookies Tate had made for him and Cally had promised to bring brownies on her next visit. In return, he promised to save the prettiest of the Christmas ornaments for her. Leland also asked after her health and her family, unaware of the pain that particular question would cause her. She had easily moved the conversation to another topic.

Tate had noticed that throughout the visit, Cally kept physical contact with Leland. She patted his forearm, or held his hand, touched his cheek, gently brushed his shoulder. Leland never took his eyes off Cally, searching her face intently as if determined to commit every aspect of her image to memory. They shared a hug and mutual tears when they parted.

Tate listened to Cally's report with interest as they drove back into town.

"It sounds like a great visit, Cally. I assume you want to go back."

"Absolutely. The sooner the better. Maybe we could discuss when over dinner tonight?" Cally had turned to Tate and gazed at her in a way that made Tate a bit uncomfortable.

"Sure, dinner would be nice. Did you have anything particular in mind?"

"No, not really . . . other than just getting some more time with you . . ."

Tate instantly picked up on Cally's thinly veiled message, and her defenses kicked into high gear. "Oh . . . well . . . I meant any particular food, but sure. Let's have dinner. But if you don't mind, can we do that tomorrow? I've got a bunch of things to get caught up on at home."

"Oh . . . sorry. I guess I'm taking up too much of your time."

"No! I didn't mean that, Cally. I just have some deadlines to meet. I can go tonight, but tomorrow would work better for me."

"It's a date then!" I'll just have to occupy myself 'til then with shopping and beautifying myself. Maybe a facial and a mani-pedi. Any idea where I can find a place for that?"

"On Haywood, just down from the library, but believe me, Cally. You really don't need to be any more beautiful than you already are." Tate gulped. Matter-of-fact honesty came easily to her, but the spontaneous compliment had slipped by all her filters. She feared it had revealed too much, perhaps hinted at a promise she knew she could not keep or exposed a personal wish she herself had not previously recognized.

"Why thank you, Tate. That's very nice to hear. So just drop me off on Haywood Street, okay?"

"Sure. You're welcome." Tate's pulse pounded and she knew her face was flushed. "I didn't mean anything by that remark about your beauty . . . I mean it sounded too personal . . ." Tate felt Cally pull back emotionally. Her smile vanished just as they pulled up in front of Malaprop's. "Uh . . . okay, then. I'll pick you up around seven tomorrow it that works for you.

Cally opened the door, then looked back at Tate. "Well, I'm not going to take any of that personally."

With that, Cally jumped out of the truck and gave a cheerful wave, leaving Tate alone to figure out the meaning of Cally's parting remark.

I have to stop this. Tate willed herself to quit rehashing yesterday's conversation with Cally and focused on the book she intended to read. Regardless of how hard she tried, she found herself unable to settle, especially since her body still felt so sore and tired. She rose from the couch and looked out the back window into the empty parking area behind the house. *Good—no one home.* She turned on the boom box and started looking through her CDs as WOXL 96.5 burst through the speakers.

You've always won, every time you've placed a bet.
You're still damn good, no one's gotten to you yet . . .

The bouncy tune filled the room and Tate sang along, humming the parts she didn't remember until she found her Disco CD and popped it into the slot.

You're still the same, baby, baby still the same—

came to an abrupt halt and The Weather Girls started their slow build to a jumping chorus of

It's raining men! Hallelujah! - It's raining men! Amen!

Tate turned up the volume and started dancing, slowly at first, then with more enthusiasm. She sang along gleefully. "You can't carry a tune in a bushel basket," she chanted to herself, then raised her voice and sang even louder, laughing as she did so.

She danced and swayed and shook and shimmied all the way through *It's Raining Men*, then *YMCA* and *I*

Will Survive. By the time she was halfway through *We are Family*, she panted heavily and sweat rolled down her face and back. Flushed and ready to collapse, her body felt energized and tingly.

There had been a time in Tate's life when she had danced with abandon whenever the urge hit her. Now, she allowed herself that freedom only in solitude, aware of how her aging body no longer looked appealing gyrating across a dance floor in tight jeans and high heels under black lights. Besides, Disco had died long ago, and other than a cheek-to-cheek slow dance with a sexy partner, or a synchronized line dance to twangy country music, Tate saw no sense in dancing at all if she couldn't dance to Disco.

The music ended and she fell onto her couch spent and happy. Though she would have preferred to nap, work awaited. She had to check in with Dave next door and pick up groceries for the next few days. And she had plans to meet Cally for dinner.

Dinner. Not a trip to the library or another visit with Leland, but dinner, just the two of them. Tate had suggested inviting Sally, but Cally had nixed the idea quickly. *Is this a date?* The thought left Tate with a queasy feeling which she pushed aside by heading over to see Dave.

"Yucky day to be working, isn't it?" Tate's greeting caught Dave by surprise and he looked up from his work on the new windows. Still under construction, the apartment remained unheated and drafty. The temperature had dipped significantly, leaving the room cold and damp.

"I don't mind. Being indoors is way better than some of the other things I could be doing today."

"You always have a positive attitude, Dave. I appreciate that about you."

"Even though I'm slow as a snail sometimes?" Dave's sheepish grin signaled his attempt to apologize for the many delays in getting the job completed.

"Looks like things are moving along, though," Tate countered. *Why do I do that? Always let him off the hook like that, even when he acknowledges messing up?*

"Yeah, and I've got a surprise for you." Dave motioned for Tate to follow as he headed down the hallway. "Look!"

Tate stepped into the bedroom on the left and saw that the new half-bath had been installed in the space that used to be a small closet.

"Wow! That's great. When did that get done? I thought the plumber was busy elsewhere."

"He had an unexpected change in his schedule, and he came over yesterday and finished it up. Thought you'd be happy to hear it, but I haven't seen you in a couple of days."

In fact, Tate had not been around for more than a few minutes here and there for the past week. Everything was behind schedule, and she had postponed the carpet installation as a result.

"Yeah, I'm happy all right. Sorry I haven't been around as much, but I've been busy looking into that old house over in Montford."

"What old house?"

"The one with the fancy door. I told you about it, didn't I?"

"You mentioned a house with a door like that one," Dave said as he gestured toward the open entryway, "but that's all."

"I can't believe I haven't chewed your ear off already. I've been obsessed with it for almost two weeks!"

"Nope. What are you obsessing about?"

"Okay." Tate sighed. *Here I go again.* "There's an old house over on Chestnut. The County plans to seize it for non-payment of taxes and they're going to sell it on the Courthouse steps. Some developer wants to tear it down and build a bunch of cottages. But I found the man who owns it. Everyone thought he was dead, but he's living out at Forest Glen and then his granddaughter showed up a couple days ago. I met her at the library, but she thought he was dead, too. I took her out to meet him yesterday and now I'm still trying to figure out how to save this old house even though he doesn't seem to care about it."

Dave's puzzled look finally brought Tate's outburst to a halt.

"Sorry, Dave, it's just such a long story, and I've been living and breathing it for so long that I think everyone should automatically know what I know about it. In a nutshell, this old place is going to be torn down if I don't figure out how to save it. And I have to save it. I just have to!"

"I know that place—over on Chestnut, sitting up on a hill, right? Been in the news recently?"

"Yeah, that's the place."

"I've done a lot of work on the old places in Montford. Years back I worked on the house next door. Someone used to take care of it. It's only been in the past ten years, give or take, that it's gotten so run down."

"Do you know who took care of it?"

"I never talked to anyone, but I'd see them over there on occasion. I still see the guy who used to mow the lawn around sometimes."

"Seriously? You still see him? Where? When?"

"Well, I don't have his schedule written down . . ." Dave grinned and Tate couldn't help but laugh.

"Okay, I know I can get intense sometimes! Any ideas on how I might track this guy down?"

"I've seen him working over there at the Black Walnut. Maybe they know something."

"Thanks, Dave!" Tate turned to leave then caught herself. "Wait, I almost forgot. Fill me in on what's happening here."

"Thought you'd never ask! The plumbing inspector is due in this afternoon, and assuming everything is all right, I'll be able to start the finish work on the bathroom first thing tomorrow."

"That's great, Dave. Any idea when I can start painting? I need two days and then you'll be able to install the bathroom fixtures and the cabinets and countertops in the kitchen . . ."

"Let's take it a step at a time, okay? I'll finish the bathroom tomorrow, and that includes the laundry area on the other side of the new wall. Next step will be the vinyl flooring, then the painting."

"Okay. Sounds good. That gives me a couple of days to work on a plan for saving that old house."

Tate took a quick shower then went directly to the Black Walnut Inn, an elegant bed and breakfast establishment occupying a house designed by Richard Sharp Smith and dating back to 1899. After accepting the hostess's gracious invitation to tour the Inn, she left not only with the name of the gardener, but also a generous sample of the homemade pastries being prepared for that afternoon's tea.

She jumped into her truck and immediately dialed the number for Scott, the gardener. He was working only half a mile from the Black Walnut and agreed to talk to her if she had time to stop by. *You bet I have time.* In fact, Tate could hardly wait. Minutes later, she greeted an aging skinny man in overalls with a pronounced limp and a wad of chewing tobacco tucked into his cheek. A blue merle Australian Shepherd trailed along a few paces behind him.

"I'm Tate Marlowe. Thanks so much for seeing me."

"Yessum. Scott's my name and this here is Blue." Scott nodded at the dog and tipped his battered cap to Tate, but he did not shake her outstretched hand. The old dog ambled up to Tate and sniffed her carefully.

"Friendly fella, that's for sure." Tate scratched behind the old dog's ears.

"You got dogs?"

Caught off guard by Scott's question, Tate wondered why that was important. A test of some sort. She answered carefully. "No, no dogs. I have an old cat, though, and I have friends with dogs."

"Well, ain't nothin' like a dog." Tate noticed how the Shepherd leaned into Scott as the man reached down to stroke its head.

"I can see getting a dog. Maybe someday, if my cat approves."

"Why you lookin' for me?" Tate was surprised that his directness unnerved her a bit.

"Well, a guy who's renovating an apartment for me says he used to see you mowing the lawn over at 305 Chestnut. Says there used to be people who took care of the place, you being one of them. So I'm hoping you can tell me what happened over there, why it's gotten so run down."

"Now why would you care? Don't nobody care 'bout that place no more."

Tate noticed a hint of anger in Scott's voice. "Sounds like maybe *you* do."

"Mebbe I do. Don't matter though. I can't work for nothin', and that's the only way anythin's gonna get done over there since they stop payin' for the upkeep."

"Who's 'they'?"

"Them damn lawyers, that's who. They had plenty money, far as I know. But they jus' walked away from the place. Prob'ly kep' the money theyselves. Jus' let the place fall apart. Stop paying me, the maintenance man, everone who kep' the place in shape."

"When was that, Scott?"

"Oh, mebbe eight, ten yars ago."

"Up until then, who paid you?"

"Lawyers, like I said. Name a Page and Smith, or sumpin' like that. Checks stop comin' but not me. Kep' on workin' for months, waitin' ta git paid. Finally

303

tracked 'em down where they office was, but they long gone from the looks of it. Empty buildin', paper tacked ta the winders . . ."

"So, that was the end of it? Did you ever hear from anyone again?"

"Nope. Heared nothin' and got nothin'. They still owe me hunderds a dollars."

"I'm sorry to hear that, Scott. Sounds like you took good care of the place until that happened."

"Yep, did best as I could. Funny ole place, that one. Sad, ya know?"

"Sad how?"

"Man who built it kilt hisself right there on the front porch. My daddy were his lawn man. I usta work with him when I were a boy. It was purdy fancy when Mr. Harlan' first built it, but always strange, you know. Like all the things on that house don't go together."

"Yeah, I noticed that, too."

"And then when he were dead, the neighbors was real mean 'bout it. Like he were a bad man or sumpin'. He weren't no bad man. Jus' a man livin' in a big ole house by hisself, tryin' to get by like the res' of us. 'Cept of course, he had way more money!" Scott chuckled to himself. "He weren't 'xactly good, but he weren't bad neither. He were near nice to me sometimes. Give me a li'l money a my own when I worked there with Daddy."

"Sounds like a nice gesture to me. He didn't have to pay you extra, did he?"

"Didn't have to, no. Jus' seem like he knew it would mean sumpin' to me, you know, to have a li'l bit a money a my own. And he made sure ta tell my daddy the money were mine ta do as I please."

"Did you ever meet the man who owns the place now? A Mr. Leland Howard?"

Disbelief flashed across Scott's face. "Somebody own the place?"

"Yes, but I don't know how he came to own it . . . or why."

"Far as I know, no one done owned it since Mr. Harlan' shot hisself." Scott looked perplexed. "Why that man let it go fallow?"

"I wish I knew, Scott. Now the City wants it torn down and I want to save it. I hope what you just told me will help me do that."

"Seem like a big task, ma'am. Don't know why you care, but if it kin be saved, I hope you save it."

"Thanks, Scott. I'll keep in touch, if that's okay. I have some property over on Maplewood and I'll be looking for someone to tend the lawn come spring."

"Always glad for work, ma'am, leas' so long as ole Blue here's welcome, too."

"Your dog is more than welcome on my property, Scott."

They parted ways, Scott waving a goodbye, Blue gently wagging his tail and Tate highly motivated to track down "them damn lawyers."

Tate went directly to the library and immediately sought out Carla for assistance. Tate found her at her desk in the reference room.

"Hi, Tate. What can I help you with today?"

"It won't come as a surprise that I need more information, right?"

Carla smiled. "No, it won't. And that's what I'm here for, so what can I do for you?"

"Well, at some point in the past there was a law firm in town named Page and Smith. I checked directory assistance for them but there's nothing there now, so I figured I'd come straight to the expert for help!"

"What else do you know about them?" Carla turned to her computer and started typing.

"Not much, really. I have an idea they were still practicing law ten years ago, but around that time, they apparently closed up shop."

"Is this related to that place on Chestnut Street?"

"Of course! I've been living and breathing that place since I saw you last. That's what led me to Page and Smith. They used to pay the gardener for taking care of the lawn, and then the checks abruptly stopped coming to him eight or ten years ago."

Carla continued searching her data base as they chatted. "I'm not finding Page and Smith. I'm spelling that P-A-G-E. Is that right?"

"I think so, but I only heard the name spoken. I've never seen it written. Are there other possibilities?"

"P-A-I-G-E is worth a try. Aha! Here's something!" Carla pointed to the monitor and Tate read over her shoulder. "Okay, if that's them, then its Paige and Schmidt. Let's see . . . according to this article, they closed the practice in 1996, and it looks like they may have been in trouble . . ." Carla summarized the piece, which focused on a complaint by a client that someone in the firm had failed to file paperwork with the court on a timely basis, resulting in the client's case being dismissed. That client had filed a lawsuit claiming malpractice and won a huge settlement.

"I wonder what was going on," Tate mused. "Sounds like someone let things slip. That may be what happened over on Chestnut."

"What do you mean?" Carla seemed genuinely interested, so Tate continued.

"Well, I tracked down the man who used to do the lawn work over there. Apparently there were caretakers in place for several decades after Freeman's suicide. This guy, Scott is his name, says his father was the gardener and there was a handyman. I'm guessing the taxes were paid, too. Is there any way we could track that down? Wait . . . I'm sorry. I'm rambling again."

Carla seemed completely content to let Tate go on unabated. "No, it's fine, Tate. Really. I've been a librarian for a long time, and I don't remember ever working with someone as fired up as you seem to be about this . . . what is it? A project? A passion?"

"A puzzle! I've loved them all my life, ever since my sister started making up word games to play with me when I was only 2 or 3. And this is a big, huge puzzle! Everything I learn seems to create more pieces, more questions. You're right, I am fired up!"

"Okay, so tell me more. What else did you learn?"

"Well, Scott took over when his father passed and kept the lawn and garden in good shape. The lawyers paid for his services, and there was no problem until suddenly the checks just stopped coming. He finally went to the office only to find it had been closed for some time. The place was vacant. No forwarding address, no way to contact them."

"What'd he do then?"

"He had to stop doing his work at the house. He couldn't work for free, even though I got the feeling he loved the place. From the looks of it, the same happened with the caretaker and the taxes. Seems like the law firm just walked away from the place. And I wonder if they were letting it slip a long time before that. The façade is in bad shape. I doubt it has been painted since it was built."

"Let's look further, then," Carla suggested.

After close to thirty minutes of searching, they had formulated a speculative timeline for the rise and fall of Paige and Schmidt. Established in the heyday of the mid-1920s, the firm quickly gained a reputation as top-notch specialists in real estate law and estate planning. Both original founders retired in the early 1940s and their sons took over. The second generation of Paige and Schmidt continued as active partners for another two decades even after their offspring, also sons, assumed stewardship in the late 1960s. During that time, the firm's reputation began to fade.

Carla and Tate found two articles hinting at the eventual downfall. In one case, a junior partner was arrested and convicted of drug use; in the other, a major malpractice suit against the firm was dismissed, but in the aftermath, Paige and Schmidt quickly shrank from five attorneys down to two—the great grandson of the original Schmidt, and the great granddaughter of the original Paige. She married a wealthy Frenchman and moved out of the country, leaving the firm in the hands of the only remaining descendant of the founders. It was under his watch that the firm folded, following the law suit that apparently bankrupted it.

"So where do you go from here?" Carla's question echoed Tate's own thoughts.

"Where do I go from here? Good question. Maybe I can find someone who can tell me more about these lawyers. And there was a trust fund . . . rather there is a trust fund. Where is it? How do I find out more about it? Who has control of it . . .?"

"Looks like you may be heading back to the courthouse, no?"

"I think you're right, Carla. As usual, you've been a great help. I owe you!"

"It's my job, but I have to say you make it more interesting than usual, so I owe you, too."

"Well, when I get this all sorted out, we'll have to celebrate."

"I'd like that very much, Tate," Carla said, smiling broadly.

Her inviting response surprised Tate. "Oh . . . okay, then. Well . . . thanks again, Carla."

Tate left the library and headed for the courthouse, where she learned that the only trustee on record for the property held in Leland Howard's name was the defunct law firm of Paige and Schmidt. Indeed, they had just closed up shop and walked away.

FORTY

2004

Tate had been so busy thinking about the ramifications of what she had learned through Scott and Carla about Paige and Schmidt that she had little time left to prepare herself for the evening with Cally. That also meant she hadn't had time to worry about her dinner with Cally. Now she stood before her closet, searching for what to wear and wishing she had nicer choices than her usual jeans and t-shirts. She finally settled on the one pair of black slacks she owned along with her favorite lightweight jacket. Then she shoe-horned her feet into her black cowboy boots with the silver toe and heel guards. The final touches included small gold earrings and dabs of her signature essential oil blend at her wrists and behind her ears.

So much for this not being a date! "Well, it isn't a date," she insisted to the image in the mirror as she gave her hair a quick brushing. "I don't do dates anymore!"

Why not? the image seemed to ask. She locked the front door and headed for her truck, refusing to follow that path of inquiry into the past.

———∿∿∿———

Tate pulled up in front of the Princess Hotel at the appointed time and found Cally waiting for her at the entrance, dressed in an outfit of tailored slacks in slate gray with a hip-length, belted, black leather jacket over a white, cotton shirt, the high collar flipped up behind her neck and accented with a silk scarf in crimson. *Stunning! What a gorgeous woman!* Tate felt her pulse quicken as Cally climbed into the passenger seat.

"You look great!" Tate smiled self-consciously as she greeted Cally.

"You too, Tate! I've been looking forward to seeing you all day, especially after that visit with Gampa yesterday. Do you think we could go back tomorrow?"

"Sure, I can work that into my schedule easily."

"I hope I'm not keeping you from important work. I fear I've been monopolizing your time ever since we met."

"Well, I'm the only boss of me these days, so I make my schedule whatever I want it to be. You don't need to worry."

"Okay, then. Tomorrow it is. But I don't know where I'm going to get good brownies. I promised him, you know."

"There are a couple of great bakeries in town. We should be able to find something. But don't expect to fool him that they're homemade. He has a remarkable ability to tell the difference!"

They had agreed to have dinner at The Corner Kitchen, so Tate decided to take the route through downtown on their way to Biltmore Village.

"This is such a beautiful town, and so much different from when I lived here as a child. I'm so glad I came back—came *home*! And meeting you is a big part of that for me. It's like we were destined to meet . . . at least it feels that way to me." Cally had not taken her eyes off Tate since getting into the truck, and Tate felt a bit uneasy under the intensity of her attention.

"I know what you mean. I'm not surprised, though. Spirit had some reason for getting me tangled up with that house in Montford. Like maybe I found it so I could help you find Leland or something. I don't know. Does that sound weird?"

"I've never been all that religious or spiritual, so it does sound a bit . . . unusual to me. But you clearly feel a connection to things like that—Spirit as you call it, your runners . . ."

Tate welcomed the opportunity to divert Cally's focus from her. "Yeah, my runners! I'm hoping they'll find us a good parking space down in the Village." The two continued to chat amiably, but Tate felt herself pulling back a bit whenever Cally moved the conversation into personal territory.

Thanks to her runners, Tate believed, they quickly found a space within a block of the restaurant and were seated less than ten minutes later. The Corner Kitchen occupied a quaint house dating back to the late 1800s, one of the many original cottages in Biltmore Village, which sat at the entrance to George Vanderbilt's magnificent estate. They had a choice table near the fireplace in a small dining room across the hall from the open kitchen.

"Do you have any favorites?" Cally asked as she perused the menu.

"I've only been here once before, and everything was delicious. I'm thinking about the trout, but the steak sounds good, too. What about you?"

"Yes, the fish, I think."

They ordered an appetizer to share, and Cally ordered the fish along with a perfectly paired Riesling, while Tate settled on steak and a smoky chardonnay.

"I know I'm supposed to drink red wine with steak," Tate offered preemptively.

"Really? Why?"

"Well, red wine with red meat, and all that. There are lots of rules, aren't there?"

"It all depends. Do you like red wine?"

"No! Every time I've tried it, I ended up with a massive headache. I've been told by people who seem to know about these things that I must be drinking cheap red wine. I think it doesn't matter. Me and red wine don't mix."

"Then there's no reason to drink it, is there?" Cally took a sip of her Riesling and waited for an answer.

"That kind of surprises me. You seemed to choose your wine carefully, and only after you decided on what you were having for dinner. Me, I always order something white, regardless. I bet you're one of those who know a lot about wine."

"In my business, I'm expected to entertain clients, and to do so lavishly. The firm has a huge budget for wining and dining, and they even sent me to wine pairing classes so I could court new top-tier clients. So, yeah, I know a lot about it. But if you don't like something, you don't like it, no matter what the experts say."

"That's a refreshing attitude. And a relief!" Tate laughed as she tipped her glass in a salute to Cally. "So what is your work, exactly?"

"I'm a publicist. I work in a prestigious firm in Los Angeles, and I have a variety of clients, but mostly I represent companies and people who provide services, like accountants, doctors, hairdressers to the stars . . ."

"Do you like what you do?"

"I'm good at it, let's leave it there. I fell into it. It's not what I planned for myself."

"What did you plan?"

"Nothing, really! I earned my bachelor's degree in psychology. Then I went to work as a receptionist just until I figured out what I wanted to do next. That was ages ago, and as the years passed I learned more about the business, moved up the ranks, and they were about to make me a partner before I left town."

"When do you go back?"

"Honestly, I'm not sure I will."

"Really?"

"It feels like there's nothing there for me anymore. My mom died not long ago, my girlfriend left me . . ."

"I'm sorry, Cally. Sounds like you've had a rough time of it."

"You know, I thought so, too, until I spent three weeks driving across the country. That's plenty of time and distance to get some perspective on your life, and that's what I did. It's pretty clear to me that I don't want to go back, and there's really no reason to."

"So what would you do instead?"

"Stay here—move back home. I should be able to find some kind of work here. I have enough money to live on for quite a while, so I could take time to look around. Maybe go back to school. I have a lot of ideas running around in my head, but so much has happened I'm having trouble sorting through all of them."

"Well, there's more to add to the mix. Want to hear the latest news regarding that house in Montford and your grandfather?"

"Yes, but I'd also like to get to know you better, Tate."

Alarms started sounding in Tate's head again. She paused and took a sip of wine before responding. "I'm sure we'll get to that, but let me tell you about these lawyers . . ." and she launched into the story of meeting Scott and researching Paige and Schmidt. Cally listened, and by the time dinner arrived, she seemed content to focus on the quest for answers about 305 Chestnut Street rather than pressing Tate for more personal information.

"This trout is outstanding!" Cally offered Tate a taste and Tate reciprocated with the steak, which had been cooked to perfection.

"I'm as impressed this time as I was on my first visit. This may become one of my favorite treats when I'm feeling extravagant."

"I bet you have a lot of favorite places, don't you?"

"Not all that many, really. I mostly cook for myself, but occasionally I go out for brunch with friends. I like AnnTony's as you know. And Over Easy. Wait! You've already been to most of my favorites with me!" Tate hoped offering these superficial details of her life would satisfy Cally's curiosity.

"Then I guess we'll have to find some new favorites together." Cally seemed completely unselfconscious as she said this.

"Uh, well . . . yeah, we'll have to try some new places." *She's not going to give up.* Tate tried to cover her discomfort with a weak smile and another sip of her wine.

Cally paused and studied Tate closely before responding. "Yes, we'll try a bunch of new places, and maybe we'll both find some favorites."

Tate thought Cally's response could mean more than just favorite restaurants, but she decided to let the innuendo pass without comment. Over dessert and coffee, each shared details about her life, but Tate continued to shy away from anything remotely romantic when Cally headed in that direction. Eventually, Tate won out. Cally's demeanor shifted slightly, her intimate tone receding even though she remained upbeat and friendly. Tate recognized that Cally's disappointment counterbalanced her own sense of relief.

They used the drive back to Cally's hotel to firm up their plans for visiting Leland the next day.

"It was so good to see him, but I'm still nervous about going back," Cally offered.

"What worries you? The visit yesterday seemed to go really well."

"I know. It did go well. But it was stressful, and I just hope it wasn't too much for him. And, there are so many things I want to know. What happened to Gamma? Where has he been all these years? Why didn't he contact me? Those are hard questions, and maybe I won't like the answers I get, assuming he will—or even can—answer them."

"You can drive yourself crazy with the worrying" Tate said, "or you can just let things unfold as they will." Cally stiffened a bit and Tate realized after the fact her comment sounded a bit harsh.

"Oops! Sorry for being so abrupt. Let me rephrase that. In my experience, we can make things worse than they really are by dwelling on everything that might not work out the way we want."

"Of course, you're right, Tate. I'm just so eager to know these things, and . . . but I'll be patient, I promise. At least I'll try to be patient."

"Well, if anyone knows about patience, I think its Leland. His work is so detailed. I mean he's in his nineties, and he still sits all day and makes those delicate ornaments and sweet little boxes of beautiful wood. You didn't get to see them yet. Some of them have hidden compartments in them—"

"You mentioned that the other night—hidden places—and it seems so familiar . . . I wish I could remember . . ." Cally closed her eyes and concentrated intently.

Tate gasped as an idea flashed into her mind. "Oh, Cally! I just realized something! Have you seen the

317

fireplace at the Princess, the one in the sitting room just off the lobby?"

"Sure, it's beautiful. Why?"

"I'll show you why as soon as we get inside. You're going to love this!"

Tate had just pulled up to the entrance of the Princess. Instead of dropping Cally off as planned, she quickly parked the truck at the side of the drive. They went inside, and Tate steered Cally directly to the fireplace and gestured to the mantel.

"Does this look familiar?"

"No, why?" Cally seemed puzzled.

"This mantel is Leland's work, Cally."

Cally stared at Tate wide-eyed. "No!"

"Yes! Leland made this mantel. I was here last week, and Mr. Wright, the owner, showed it to me. It's *very* special."

"Yes, it's quite beautiful . . ."

"I mean *special*, really special, Cally. Look . . ." Tate hoped she would be able to find the trigger mechanism. She carefully moved her finger across the notched lower edge of the mantel as Warren Wright had done. Her first pass yielded nothing, so she tried again, slowing her movement, closing her eyes, tuning out the background conversation, even holding her breath so she could focus totally on finding the right spot. Then, a faint click and the hidden drawer dropped open.

"Oh! That's just like the one at Gamma's house!" Cally burst into tears and laughter simultaneously as Tate bowed formally and offered her an after-dinner chocolate. Cally threw her arms around Tate's neck and began sobbing.

"Whoa! I didn't mean to make you cry, Cally."

"It's okay," Cally choked between sobs. "Okay . . . so happy . . . miss Gamma . . ." The other hotel guests excused themselves, leaving Cally and Tate alone as they sank onto a comfortable couch beside the fireplace. Tate waited until Cally quieted.

"Wow, you must think I'm a real cry baby! Honestly, I think I've cried more in the last few days than I have since the night Mom took me away from Asheville."

"It's all right, Cally. You've been through a lot, and crying is a good thing, really . . . though I must admit I rarely do it myself."

"It's just like at Gamma's . . ." Cally once again seemed to struggle with a buried memory.

"What do you mean, Cally?"

"That's what I kept trying to remember. The secret place. 'This is our secret place.' That's what Gamma told me when she showed it to me. I was real little, maybe 5 or 6 . . ."

"Ellie showed you a compartment like this one?"

"Yes! In her house. In the mantel Gampa made for their house. The one I carved my initials in. Remember? We were talking about it with Sally . . ."

"Wait. You mean the house I own now? The one I'm renovating?"

"Well, yeah, if that is, in fact, the house Gampa and Gamma lived in over on Cumberland."

"Now it's my turn to be shocked and surprised. So you're saying . . . wait. I was talking to Dave about the house—he's the one doing the work for me. I remember him saying something about a fireplace.

He has to patch the floor where it used to be in the living room . . ."

"Oh, I wish it were still there, Tate. I'd love to see it again. Gamma only showed it to me one time, but it was magical. There were things in there she was saving for me."

"What things?" Tate had trouble staying focused as her mind raced between trying to attend to Cally, then to questions about the missing fireplace, on to her own grief about precious things once meant for her which were taken by others, and then back to the present conversation with Cally.

". . . and a comb . . ."

"I'm sorry, Cally. My mind wandered for a minute. I have so many questions. Tell me again, please."

Cally seemed unperturbed and started over. "One day I was with Gamma, and Gampa was in the workshop out back. She told me she had something special to show me. Then she went to the mantel and opened the secret drawer. I remember being so happy. I jumped up and down and danced all around."

"It must've been wonderful, especially for a child."

"Oh, it was! She showed me everything, but only after she made me promise I wouldn't tell anyone. I realize now how big a promise that was to ask of a child, but somehow even then I knew it was truly something between her and me, and I never told anyone."

"What was in it, Cally?"

"There was a comb—a beautiful tortoise-shell hair comb. She told me who it had belonged to, but I don't remember. It must have been passed down through her family for generations, though. And a diamond ring. A few other things. There was a little book of some kind. I don't remember much more than that."

"And she said it was your secret place? Just yours and hers?"

"Yes, that's what she told me. She was keeping those things for me. I wonder what happened to them. I never saw them again."

Tate's own memories grabbed her full attention, and she remembered sitting with her great grandmother as they looked through a trunk of clothes in the upstairs bedroom of the old farmhouse. The musty smell of the room with peeling and stained wallpaper on the slanted walls and threadbare rugs covering creaky wooden floors filled her nostrils. She saw where her own father had punched a hole in the wall just above the feather bed, and the huge Christmas cactus in its pot in front of the east-facing window with the cracked pane. She felt the soft brush against her cheek of the woolen fabric in the long skirt and matching, fitted jacket with whale-bone stays that her grandmother promised would one day be hers—a broken promise that still caused her pain a lifetime later. She squeezed Cally's hand and willed herself back to the present moment.

"Are you okay, Tate?"

"Yeah . . . yeah, I'm okay. I just got hijacked by my own memories for a moment. You said you never saw those things again . . ."

"No, only that one time. I don't know what ever happened to them. I wish . . ." Suddenly, Cally gulped and turned pale. The color left her face, and Tate thought for a moment she may pass out.

"What? What is it, Cally?"

"Tate, they're still there. She left them for me, and they're still in there!"

"How do you know that, Cally? How could they be? I mean that was decades ago and . . ."

". . . because she told me so!" Cally exclaimed as she began a frantic search through her handbag. She fished for the leather pouch, pulled out the old library card that she'd slipped back into its place after her visit to the library, and from behind it she retrieved the yellowed, penciled note written in Ellie's hand. "Look!"

Cally handed the note to Tate, who unfolded it carefully and then read the words:

> *There is always something waiting for you*
> *where the home fire burns.*
> *I love you dearly and forever.*
> *Gamma*

Tate suddenly felt chilled as goose bumps popped up over her entire body, and for a fleeting moment, she had the sense they were not alone in the room after all. She looked into Cally's face and found a combination of excitement and grief.

"What is this, Cally?"

"I didn't know until this instant, Tate. I found it in a box of keepsakes when I cleaned out Mom's apartment. She had it hidden away. She never told me about it." Cally paused as if trying to get the courage to say the words aloud that pounded inside her head. "I think Gamma wrote this note for me just before she died," she whispered.

"Really? Why do you think she did it then . . . I mean why not some other time?"

"Why write it at all, unless she thought she wouldn't have a chance to tell me herself? And why so cryptic? 'Where the home fire burns.' Why not say 'there's something for you in the secret place?' Or, 'look in the mantel and you'll find your things?' No, I'm sure of it, Tate. She wanted to give me this message, but she also wanted to make sure only I would understand it. And now I do."

"That all makes sense, Cally, but still, it's speculation, don't you think? And in any case, the fireplace is gone."

Desolation quickly replaced the excitement on Cally's face. She began weeping again. "Of course . . . of course. It's all gone. You're right, Tate. How silly of me to think . . ."

"No, Cally, not silly. Not silly at all. You may not have the things, but you have the memory. You know she loved you, and nothing can erase that truth."

"I know . . . but it would have been nice . . . it was nice for a moment to think . . ."

"She loved you, Cally."

"Yes . . . and it would be nice to have something to touch, something she cherished and passed on to me. It's one of the things that's always been missing in my life. You know, the feeling of connection you get when you can hold something close to your heart. Memories are wonderful, but to have something physical, that would be . . ." Cally sighed deeply and squeezed Tate's hand. "I'm exhausted, Tate. I'm gonna call it a night. Do you mind?"

"No, of course not. Do you think you still want to visit Leland tomorrow? We could do it another time."

"Tomorrow, yes! I'm going to let myself sleep as long as I want, but I'll call you in the morning, and we'll decide what time then, if that's okay with you."

"That's fine, Cally. I'll see you tomorrow." Tate gave Cally a big hug and bid her goodnight, then headed home. She realized she was exhausted, too, more from the emotional seesaw she had been on for most of the day than from the fact she had been on the go for more than twelve hours straight.

She crawled into bed at a much earlier hour than usual and spent the night rummaging endlessly through debris scattered across her dreamscape in search of precious items lost long ago. Just when she thought she had found what she was looking for— she wasn't quite sure just what it was—it would slip away, and she would find herself back at the beginning determined to continue the search. *I'll find it. If I just keep looking, I'll find it.*

FORTY-ONE
2004

Tate woke to the ringing of the phone the following morning and jumped out of bed, heart racing, to answer it.

"Hello?" Groggy, pressured, demanding an answer.

"Tate! It's Cally. Are you okay? You sound weird. I hope I didn't wake you up."

"Uh, yeah . . . hey, Cally. I thought you were sleeping in."

"I did. It's 8:30 already."

"You call that sleeping in?" Tate exhaled and tried to ease the tension in her voice. Being awakened by a ringing phone always triggered panic for her—a the-sky-is-falling response she couldn't control. "You sound cheerful."

"I am! I slept like a rock and had wonderful dreams about Gamma. I miss her like crazy, but I realized when I woke up that I felt wrapped up in her love. I just can't always remember that, especially when the pain of missing her takes over."

Tate knew exactly what Cally meant, but she wasn't about to say so. She also chose not to share with Cally her frustrating dream of the night before. "Glad you had a good night after all. You were pretty upset when I left you."

"I hate crying like that, but it really helped. I think I cleared out a lot of emotional stuff I've had buried forever."

"That's good, Cally. Listen, I'm gonna need some coffee and breakfast before I'm fully functional. How 'bout you?"

"I'll get something downstairs. They have a nice breakfast layout here, and I think I'll read a bit. When will you be ready to head out to Forest Glen?"

"Give me a couple hours. I've got to check in next door before I leave."

"No need to rush. Maybe it would be better if we get there just after lunch. What say you pick me up around 12:30?"

Tate breathed a sigh of relief. That would give her plenty of time to ease into the day rather than rushing. Tate knew most people did not consider it *rushing* to be out of the house before noon. She was not most people, though. Even after a lifetime of forcing herself to adhere to a schedule set by others, she showed no signs of ever becoming a perky morning person. "That sounds perfect, Cally. You promised Leland some brownies. I could pick some up on my way to you, if that's okay."

"Actually, I have a better idea. I'm going to ask the chef here to make a batch for me. If that doesn't work, we'll find some on the way."

"Great idea, Cally. I'll see you later, then."

Tate turned the burner on under a saucepan of water, pulled the Melitta cone, coffee beans and a filter from the cupboard, then peered into the refrigerator looking for breakfast. She decided on eggs and toast for herself, put out some food for Pocket, then settled on the couch with her coffee and a pile of paperwork. She paid some bills, wrote out a to-do list of things to discuss with Dave and errands she could no longer put off, then bathed, dressed and headed next door.

She glanced at the clock on her way out. Only 10:20! *Amazing—I feel ready to go!* Cally's early morning call had set the stage for a grumpy Tate, but instead she felt energized, a curious reaction that puzzled her. As she contemplated her mood, she felt an unfamiliar stirring in her solar plexus. She realized the thought of seeing Cally made her happy, and that made her very uncomfortable. *Don't be foolish. There's no future there, and even if there was, I'm not ready.* The silent reprimand had little impact on the insistent excitement that pushed to the surface of Tate's awareness.

———∿∿∿———

Cally bounded out of the Princess Hotel lobby as soon as Tate pulled up to the entrance. The small package she carried filled the truck with the enticing aroma of warm chocolate and cinnamon.

"So, the chef came through, huh? Those smell yummy!"

"Yeah, she sure did. I love this place, you know? Everyone is friendly and helpful. Dawn, the chef, even let me help make these. She had a recipe from her mother, and we added some cinnamon like Gamma taught me to do. So they're homemade after all. I hope Gampa likes them."

"I'm sure he will, Cally. Are you ready for this?"

"More than ready. I love Gampa so much, and even if I don't get answers to my questions, at least I have him again. He's really old and I want to spend as much time as I can with him."

They chatted amiably during the short drive and a few minutes later, Ruby greeted them as they entered Forest Glen.

"Oh, Mr. Leland will be very happy to see ya'll again so soon!"

"Hi, Ms. Ruby. You look lovely today." Cally seemed to have no problem with the Southern traditions.

"Ms. Ruby . . . nice to see you again." Tate tipped her head slightly in Ruby's direction. The greeting and gesture earned a big smile from the receptionist.

Cally interrupted: "Have they finished lunch? Is this a good time to see him? I brought him some brownies!" She spoke more rapidly than usual.

Ruby quickly reassured her. "It's a good time, honey. They finished lunch half an hour ago. Dorothy'll take ya back to him."

Leland sat in his usual spot and appeared to be totally engrossed in his work on the ornaments for the Christmas Bazaar.

"Hi, Gampa." Cally's soft voice filled the space between them and Leland looked up at her. He studied her face carefully, and Cally worried that he didn't recognize her. "It's Cally, Gampa. I brought you brownies just like I promised."

Leland turned his gaze to Tate and Dorothy, then back to Cally. Without speaking, he slowly rose from his chair and reached for a hug from Cally. "I didn't know if you'd come back. I thought it was a dream."

Cally wrapped her arms around the frail old man and held him gently. Tears filled the eyes of both as they shared an embrace five decades in the making.

Dorothy excused herself to break up a squabble between two residents on the other side of the room, and Tate found a seat a discreet distance away, giving Cally and Leland their privacy.

Cally pulled up a chair close to Leland's and leaned into him as they talked. Old people develop a particular aroma, often unpleasant, but in Leland's case, he smelled much like the wood he so carefully worked—a hint of age, yes, but also a sweet, earthy mustiness that at first reminded Cally of hiking through the northwestern forests with Lauren, but then took her back to her childhood. She remembered the workshop, remembered sitting in the old rocking chair, whittling away on little wood scraps Leland provided and being lulled to sleep by the rasping hum of sandpaper on wood as Leland created his masterpieces.

"I loved the workshop, Gampa. I miss it."

Leland continued working on the ornament in his hand. "That was a long time ago, Cally. Best not to remember too much."

"I wish I didn't, but I do. At least I remember as much as I can. Mom took me away and I didn't understand, never have until just recently. I know a lot about what happened now. And I have so many questions . . ." She waited, hoping Leland would offer answers. ". . . and I want to ask you about . . . Gamma, and . . . and so much. Can I ask, Gampa?"

"I'm an old man with a broken heart . . ."

"It hurts you to talk about it, doesn't it? Oh, I'm so sorry, Gampa. I didn't mean to . . ."

"Sweet child . . . you were always such a dear thing. Ellie loved you, we both loved you so much. You were her pride and joy, even more'n Clayton . . ." Leland grasped Cally's hand and blinked back tears.

"Don't talk if you don't want to, Gampa. I love you and I don't ever want to make you sad."

"Best not to remember too much. That's what I been doin' ever since . . ."

Cally waited quietly, holding Leland's hand.

Leland sighed. ". . . well, since Ellie . . ." He could not complete the sentence. "I don't remember the funeral. I know I was there, but I can't remember it. Richard Price would know."

"Is he that man who lived in the big house near you and Gamma?"

"Good friend. He took care of me after Ellie . . . I went to his house for a while and then I fell and . . . somehow I ended up here. This is a good place. How long've I been here?"

Cally feared the strain of their conversation was taking its toll on Leland, so she changed the subject. She picked up one of the ornaments he had finished. "These are beautiful, Gampa." Three had been completed with one more in process. All shared common elements of design while retaining unique features.

"They're for Christmas. I carve 'em and the girls paint 'em." Leland nodded to a table across the room where Cally saw two old women dabbing red, green and white paint on Leland's creations. Personally, Cally liked them better without the paint, but she kept her opinion to herself; then Leland spoke again.

"They're better without paint, but everone wants shiny things for Christmas."

Cally burst out laughing. "I was just thinking the same thing! They're so beautiful with the natural wood colors showing. This one looks like cherry, but those others are something else, maybe birch?"

"Pine. Some basswood, too, but mostly pine. But that cherry one . . ." Leland picked it up and turned it in his hands, holding it up to the light, sniffing it for the sweet scent. ". . . this one's for you, just like I promised. See, I don't forget everthing."

"It's beautiful, Gampa. I love it."

"Alls it needs is a clear finish, but wipe it on with a cloth so it don't drip."

"Oh, I remember seeing you do that when I was a very little girl! I'll do it just like you say." Even tiny flashes of her childhood, such as this one, filled Cally's heart with joy. "And I have something for you, too."

"You brought me a treat?"

"I sure did." Cally opened the package of brownies and Leland peeked in.

"I thought so. I could smell 'em. Wondered when you'd get around to giving 'em to me." He chose a brownie with no hard edges, picked it up carefully, inhaled its aroma, then took a small bite. His face lit up in a big smile, his blue eyes sparkled. "There's cinnamon in 'em—just like Ellie's!"

"Yes, I remembered Gamma teaching me that. Is it good?"

"Did you make 'em?"

"I had help from the cook at the hotel where I'm staying. We used her recipe, but I added the cinnamon. I haven't tasted them yet."

"Well, you should, and give one to your friend there." Leland pointed at Tate, who had dozed off in her chair in the sun.

Cally chuckled. "Do you think I should wake her up? I already did that once today."

"I bet she won't wanna miss out on brownies. Besides, I need to talk to her."

Cally approached Tate and called to her softly. "Tate, Gampa is asking for you."

Tate opened her eyes and stretched, cat-like. "I was snoozing. The sun coming through the windows here is delightful."

"I can see that. You looked quite peaceful."

"He's asking for me? Why?"

"He wants you to try the brownies and says he needs to talk to you."

"Mr. Howard, nice to see you again." Tate truly enjoyed being around Leland Howard. *He's like the grandfather I always wish I had.* Tate's grandfathers, both of them, had been mean men with abrasive personalities and harsh words for small children who dared approach them. She had learned early on to steer clear of them whenever her parents took her and her siblings for a visit.

"And you, too, Mrs . . . no, don't tell me . . ." Leland struggled to recall her name. ". . . Mrs. Martin?"

"Marlowe. Tate Marlowe. But you can call me whatever you like."

"Yes. Mrs. Marlowe. Now I remember. Have a brownie? My granddaughter here made 'em herself!"

"I know she did, and they smell wonderful." Tate bit into one of the soft, fudgy brownies and nearly swooned. "They're even better than I expected!"

"Why thank you, both of you." Cally beamed.

Leland began reciting the chain of events since Tate's first visit, looking to her for confirmation of each part. "You came here by yourself, then you brought me peanut butter cookies, then you brought me my granddaughter."

"That's right."

"Why did you come the first time?" Leland's directness never failed to catch Tate a bit off guard.

"Well, that's an easy question to answer and a hard one at the same time."

"Should be easy. What's hard about it?"

"I don't want to upset you again like I did the first time I was here."

"You asked about a house."

"That's right." Tate's eagerness to get answers to her questions proved difficult to control, but she held back, determined to let Leland lead the conversation.

"That house I built?" he asked.

Tate vividly remembered her first meeting with Leland Howard. She had asked about 305 Chestnut Street, not the house he had built, the one she now owned. So she lied. "Yes."

"Why?"

There seemed no alternative but to answer Leland's questions directly, so Tate continued with the deception, convinced it would eventually lead to some of the answers she sought. "I own it now."

"You own the house I built for Ellie?"

"Yes."

"Do you like it?"

"Well, yes. But I think it's a lot different now."

"How's it differ'nt?"

Leland's questions felt a bit like an interrogation, but his wavering voice and sad eyes eased her discomfort. "Mr. Howard, I'm not sure how much to say. I don't want to stir up anything for you that you don't want to talk about."

"I do want. I been fergittin' much too long. It's time to remember again."

"Well, it's different in lots of ways. It's been moved, for one thing."

"What do you mean, moved?"

"It used to be on Cumberland, right?"

"Yes. We lived at Number 8 Cumberland. In front of the old cabin, the workshop."

"That was before they put the expressway through."

"What expressway?"

"I-240. It's a huge highway. It goes right through where your old neighborhood was and wiped it out. But they moved your house over to Maplewood.

334

That's where it is now, where it was when I bought it last year."

Leland looked befuddled. He put his head in his hands and rubbed his scalp along the hairline, then pulled his palms slowly down over his face, covering his eyes and massaging his temples with his thumbs before looking back at Tate. "They moved my house?"

"Yes, sir. It musta been a real sight to see." Tate offered a smile, hoping to ease the shocking information.

"Yes, it woulda been that!" Leland smiled back, but behind the slight upturned curve of his lips lurked a tightness that Tate read as a combination of disbelief and sadness. Leland reached for her hand, and she pulled her chair closer to him.

"The workshop—did they move that, too?"

"I don't think so." Tate paused, dreading what she had to say next. She gently squeezed Leland's hand. "They probably tore it down."

Leland began weeping. "I grew up there." Tate could tell the news landed heavily on Leland.

Cally sat close by listening intently. "Are you okay, Gampa? You don't have to talk about this. We can come back another time . . ."

"I'm okay, Cally." He breathed a heavy sigh, letting go of the sadness a bit, and turned back to Tate. "How else is it differ'nt? Besides bein' moved?"

Tate made a point of speaking softly and slowly, hoping to minimize the impact of her message. "Well, from what I can tell, the inside has been changed a lot, too. The hallway was moved and it has three bedrooms. I think an old back porch was closed in at some point to create the third one . . ."

"Is that front door still there?"

Tate's mouth dropped open and she turned wide-eyed to Cally, who also looked astonished.

"It has a beautiful door, with an old lock and hinges and scroll work around the panels . . ." Tate could hardly believe Leland himself had broached the topic that had been plaguing her for what seemed like forever—why did her house and the one on Chestnut have such similar doors? She held her breath, waiting for his response.

"Beautiful, maybe. But a big mistake."

"What do you mean, a mistake?"

"That's not a story I can tell. I only did one mean-spirited thing in my whole life and that door was it." Leland hung his head and dropped his hands into his lap.

Tate and Cally simply stared at one another. Tate shrugged her shoulders, a gesture that said "I don't know what to do," and Cally did the same, as if to say "Me, neither." They waited.

"You have questions, Mrs. Marlowe, and you, too, Cally. I can't answer no more of 'em right now."

"Oh, of course." Tate patted Leland's hand. "We can go. We'll come back soon . . ."

"I can't answer 'em, but Richard Price can. He'll tell you what I can't if you want him to."

"Are you sure, Gampa?" Cally moved to stand behind Leland, her arms over his shoulders. She bent over and rested her cheek against his hair, then rocked very slightly back and forth, cradling him.

Leland cupped his hands around Cally's forearms and swayed with her. "Richard Price'll tell you. Secrets need to be told sometimes, and now's the time for mine. You go talk to him."

"He's so tired," Cally mouthed to Tate. "We should go." Tate nodded and said her goodbye to Leland, then stepped away as Cally did the same.

Tate motioned for Dorothy, who had been keeping an eye on them during their entire visit. "He's exhausted, I think. He told us a lot just now, stuff he's kept buried a long time. I'm a little worried that it may have been too much for him."

"Don't you worry. We'll take care of him." Dorothy looked at Cally as she joined them. "You come back again soon, please. He was so happy after your last visit. I know it means the world to him to see you."

"If it means even half as much to him as it does to me, then that's way more than a world! That's a whole universe." Cally reached for Dorothy who pulled her into the kind of embrace a mother gives her child.

Tate watched, perplexed. *How can anyone surrender to another so completely? And Cally barely knows her.* No one could explain that to her, not even Richard Price. But there were so many questions he would be able to answer, and Tate itched to ask them.

FORTY-TWO
2004

"Oh my god, Cally. That was amazing!" Tate sank into the driver's seat of the truck and turned the key just long enough to open the windows. A chill filled the sunny November afternoon and it felt invigorating.

Cally leaned her back against the passenger door and curled up in the seat. "Yeah! Astonishing. Incredible. Unbelievable . . . I guess that's enough superlatives, don'tcha think?" They both laughed.

"Do you have any more of those brownies? I need a sugar fix!"

"Nope. But I could use a strong cup of coffee right about now. Is there someplace close?"

"I think there's a little café in a strip mall just up the road."

"That'll do. Let's go." Cally straightened herself and reached for the seat belt as Tate buckled up, cranked the key and put the truck in gear. Tate had remembered correctly. She pulled into a parking space at the front door of the coffee shop. With the lunch hour well behind them, the café had only two other customers so they had their choice of seating. They slid into a booth near the plate-glass windows and looked at the menu.

"Did you see that display case on the way in? Those pies look yummy." Tate's mouth watered at the thought of a slice of the pumpkin or the Key lime pies she'd seen.

"Yeah, I did see them. But I think I'll go for some of that cheesecake. I can't believe I'm hungry."

While Cally seemed genuinely surprised that she wanted food in the middle of the afternoon, Tate felt long overdue for a snack even though she'd had a brownie so recently. The waitress took their order and within a couple of minutes delivered fresh pastries and steaming coffee.

Tate took a bite of pumpkin pie and found its rich creaminess satisfying. "Um, this is good. Just what I needed. I know I shouldn't be eating this, but really, that was an emotional whirlwind of a visit. I need sustenance!" Tate offered this editorial comment in a lighthearted manner prompted by her belief that the best defense is a good offense. It seemed to work, because Cally showed no interest in discussing Tate's eating habits.

"Whirlwind is right. He's a sharp old man, for sure. When we first got there, I thought he didn't recognize me. He studied me so intently, you know?"

"I saw that. I think he can't quite believe you've come back after all these years."

"Well, he can't be any more surprised than I was to learn he's still alive. Oh, Tate. I can't thank you enough. I don't think I would ever have found him if I hadn't met you. I believed they were all gone for so long I don't know if I'd have even thought to look for him, really."

"Your mom never talked about the people here?"

"She mentioned her mother sometimes. Nana— that's what I called her. She'd send cards and presents sometimes for my birthday and Christmas. I honestly don't know what happened to Mom's dad. I think he left Nana not long after we went to California. Mom never told me the whole story about anything."

"What happened to Nana?"

"She died a long time ago, fifteen or twenty years, maybe more. I tried to get Mom to come back for the funeral, but she wouldn't. Of course by that time she was pretty far gone herself, what with the drinking and all."

"I'm so sorry, Cally. You've had a tough time of it."

"Not any more so than most other people. My hunch is you've had your own challenges . . ."

Tate felt the familiar clenching in her stomach, the closing off.

". . . I know. You don't like to talk about it, so I won't press."

The tightness eased. "Well, we have plenty of other stuff to talk about. Richard Price for example. Do you want to go see him?"

Not only did Cally want to meet Richard Price, she seemed as eager as Tate to go that very afternoon. Tate put in the call and Mr. Price offered the hoped-for invitation. They finished their dessert and coffee. Less than an hour later, the housekeeper escorted them to the library where their host greeted them.

"I called Forest Glen right after I spoke with you, Mrs. Marlowe. The nurse, Dorothy, I think her name is, she checked with Leland and he did indeed give me permission to tell you what I know. I understand you have a lot of questions for me. But first, I want to hear from this lovely young lady." He turned his attention to Cally. "You're Cally, then?"

"Yes, sir. I'm Leland's granddaughter."

"Oh, I know who you are, my dear. Did you ever get the note I sent?"

"Note? I didn't ever get a note from you."

"Not from me. The note from Ellie."

Cally gasped and burst into tears. She rummaged through her bag, found the note and handed it to Mr. Price. "This one, you mean? You sent this to me?"

He took the tattered old paper from her and turned it over delicately in his hands, but he did not open it. "Yes, this one. I found it after . . . well, you know. I didn't know what happened to you. I gave it to your mother's mother and hoped she would send it to you. I never knew if you got it. I'm glad you did."

"I didn't know where it came from. I only found it recently, after my mother died. She had it hidden away with some other keepsakes. Will you tell me where you found it, how you found it?"

A pained expression filled Richard Price's face. He leaned forward, using his carved walking stick for support. "After Ellie was . . . after she . . ." He paused, tears forming in the corner of his eyes. ". . . after it happened, I brought Leland here. He was devastated, could barely speak, wouldn't eat . . ."

"He said you took care of him . . ."

"As much as he would let us do, we did. Part of that was to clean up the house, his house. He never went back there, you know."

"I didn't know. . ."

"Of course, how would you? Well, I went to clean up the house, put things in order. I found the note tucked under the pillow on the bed. I knew Ellie had written it, and I think she had done it just before she died. So I figured it was important to her that you get it."

"Oh, I had that same feeling! Somehow I just knew she had written it in her last minutes!" Cally barely controlled her tears.

"So it did mean something to you. Good." Richard Price handed the note back to Cally.

"You never read it? You don't know what it says?"

"Certainly not. It was intended for you, not for me."

"Mr. Price, it means more than I can say." Cally choked back the emotions flooding over her as she read Ellie's last words aloud. "I think it refers to the old fireplace in their house. It had a secret compartment, and she kept things in there, things she said were just for me."

"Ah, yes. Leland is fond of his secret compartments. He put them in most everything he built. Your friend here knows about them, too." He gave a nod in Tate's direction.

"And I love them! Can I show Cally the desk?"

"Please do. I'd join you but I'm too unsteady on my feet. Remember how to open it, do you?"

"I think so." Tate took Cally to the desk and after some initial confusion and a couple of hints from Richard Price, she revealed the secret compartment.

"Oh, that is so incredible!" Cally clapped her hands gleefully.

"You know, Cally, I think that desk belongs to you." Cally turned to Richard Price, mouth agape.

"What? No, of course not. It's yours."

"You're right. It has been mine for a very long time. But I don't have that long left, and it should go to someone who loves it as much as I have. I think that's you."

"Your children, your family—they should have it."

"There's no one left who'd appreciate it for anything other than its monetary value. It's a work of art made with love, and it deserves to be loved by someone who understands its true value, not the price it would bring at auction. Will you take it?"

Cally looked at Mr. Price, then at Tate. "Well, that settles it then. I have to buy a house and settle down here in Asheville!"

"That seems a bit impulsive, Cally. Don't you want to think about it?" Even as Tate voiced her words of caution, she knew Cally had already decided.

"I've been thinking about it, Tate. Ever since I got here, I haven't thought about much else, except Gampa. What I should do, where I would be happy, how I want to live the rest of my life . . ." She lovingly stroked the time-worn desktop. "Mr. Price, I would be honored to own this beautiful desk made by my grandfather. Can I leave it with you until we both agree the time is right for me to take it?"

"It will remain in my safekeeping until you're ready. Now, shall I tell you what I know about your grandfather?"

"Yes!" Tate and Cally uttered the affirmation simultaneously and they settled into comfortable chairs to hear his story.

FORTY-THREE
1942

Harland Freeman took special care to prepare himself for the next-to-last most important day of his life. He bathed and groomed himself meticulously, then dressed in his finest clothing. His muted blue, cotton shirt coordinated perfectly with his hand-tailored suit constructed of fine, homespun wool in Hoover Gray from the Biltmore Industries' looms. The color of the fabric had been created specifically for Herbert Hoover, and Harland had chosen it carefully. The double-breasted jacket with its thick padded shoulders narrowed at the waist, giving Harland the larger-than-life look he wanted. He added a matching vest, wide tie, black wing-tip shoes and engraved gold cufflinks.

Once dressed, he surveyed himself in the mirror. He posed with and without the black Fedora and decided the effect of adding the hat enhanced his overall image, especially when worn fashionably tipped over his right eye. Satisfied with his appearance, he descended the stairs, plucked his new walking stick with the large, silver, bird's-head handle from the stand just inside the massive front door and struck out for his destination.

He paraded along Chestnut Street, marking each pace by swinging his stick up to waist height then clicking the metal tip on the pavement on the down stroke. The pretentious nods he offered to the occasional passersby were met with mixed reactions, and one man, who he recognized as his neighbor from two doors down, actually crossed the street to avoid greeting him. Undeterred by the intentional slight, he continued on his way.

He entered the iron gates at Riverside Cemetery and paused, giving himself time to savor the view. The winter air smelled crisp and spicy, and he inhaled it deeply into his lungs. His eyes scanned the rolling hills and took in the vast array of monuments sweeping down the embankment to the industrial area hugging the banks of the French Broad River. Paupers rested forgotten in the insignificant graves strung along the bottom of the hill. Somewhere among them lay both of his parents. He had never bothered to search for their graves, and now he turned away in disgust.

He walked purposefully to the top of a knoll near the entrance, the favored final resting place for the likes of the Wolfe family—Thomas had been buried there a few years before—the Von Rucks, Westalls and other noted Asheville elite. A beautiful spot, surely, but not what he wanted.

He crossed the small winding road to an adjacent section of the cemetery. There on a gentle slope with an unencumbered view of the mountains, he found the Ryland family plot. He circled the area carefully, studying the headstones and monuments for their size, style, wording and craftsmanship.

Constance Ryland had shunned him since their high school days. Regardless of his rise in status, she had chosen a friendship with the lowly Ellie Howard rather than him. Constance had come to represent in Harland's mind every person who had ever shunned or scorned him, and she would be the one to pay for all their sins. She had stood with them in his library, at his party, drinking his wine when she uttered the words that decimated his life and ultimately led to his premature need for a burial site for himself. In that moment a powerful hatred for her invaded him and set him on his final path. Once carried out, his vengeful plan would even the score and tie her to him for eternity, and what made that such a perfect outcome as he saw it was the fact she could do nothing to avoid the fate he planned for her.

He lingered as he surveyed his surroundings, even resting briefly against the shoulder-high marker bearing the name of Constance's father-in-law, before he settled on his decision. Then he walked to the cemetery office and purchased three adjacent plots immediately in front of the Rylands. He would visit the funeral parlor the next day and finalize the plans for his burial.

Something close to joy overtook Harland as he walked home. He imagined Constance's horror when she realized what he had done, how outraged everyone would be by his final act of retribution. They had shunned him in life, but they would be unable to forget him in death. And finally, he wouldn't care a whit about what they said about him.

Upon his return home, Harland took great care to ensure everything was in its proper place. He returned the cane to the stand by the door, handle turned just so, and placed the cufflinks in precise alignment in the silk-lined case sitting atop his dresser. He hung the suit, vest and shirt in an emptied section of the closet where they would be easily found. He positioned his shoes immediately beneath the cuffs of his pants and draped the tie over the shoulder of the jacket. To guarantee his directions were followed exactly, Harland left a detailed note tucked loosely in one of his shoes. Unfortunately, Harland failed to anticipate the difficulty the undertaker would experience trying to make him look good in his casket once he had blown part of his skull and brain away.

———

"Well, I certainly didn't think I'd be dealing with this man again so soon." The funeral director held the note from Harland in his hand and spoke aloud as he sat alone in his office. Only four days previously, Harland had marched into his establishment asking questions about his services and prices.

"I'd like to make burial arrangements," he'd said.

"Oh, I'm sorry. Has there been a death in the family?" The Director assumed his most soothing tone, the one he reserved for the grieving.

"Not yet. I want to make plans for my own interment, when the time comes, of course." Harland made it a point to use the less common term for burial, an elitist choice apparently lost on the Director.

"We certainly can help you with that. Are you ill?"

"Illness has nothing to do with it, my man. I just want to make sure it's done right, so I'm making the arrangements myself. Can't leave an important thing like that to anyone else, now can I?"

"Oh, well . . . usually it is the family members left behind who take on that role, but . . ."

"Like I said, better to do it myself than take chances." Harland found no reason to tell the Director the true reason for taking matters into his own hands—there was no one else who would do it if he didn't.

"Of course. Well, then, let me show you around." The Director led Harland to one of two viewing rooms.

"We have two choices for visitation. This is the larger room, and there's another just here . . ."

"Won't be needing a viewing room. You'll just be seeing to my burial. There will be no funeral services."

"I don't understand. You'll want your family and friends . . ."

"There'll be no family, no friends, no clergy. Just your staff seeing to preparing me and getting me into the ground over there at Riverside Cemetery. I have a choice plot. Three, actually, and I'll be buried in the middle one, so there's one left vacant on each side of me."

"Yes . . . I see. It's common for plots to be set aside for family members who . . ."

349

"No family members! I don't like to be crowded, so I'm to be placed in the middle and the ones on either side will remain empty!"

"Uh . . ." Nonplussed by Harland's commanding style and highly unusual request, the Director fumbled for words. "Uh, I . . ."

"Well, man, can you do it or not?"

The Director inhaled deeply and rubbed his hand over his eyes. In his line of business, he typically dealt with people at the most vulnerable and needy times of their lives. They welcomed his comforting style and eloquent gestures of support. His melodious voice calmed them. They often wept, the women especially, and gratefully accepted his handkerchief to wipe away their tears. This man fell so far from the norm the Director had no tools to deal with him.

"Uh . . ."

Harland stared hard at the Director and seemed to relish his discomfort.

The Director took another deep breath and with it recaptured his composure. "Yes, of course I can do as you ask."

"Well then, let's discuss the details."

The Director spent the next hour with Harland as he chose his coffin—the most stylish one available from the highest-priced group—and ordered an extravagant and expensive monument. Now, only days later, he sat in his office, having just returned from Montford with Harland's body and his instructions.

A photograph of the Director's dearly departed mother rested on the corner of his desk. He fervently believed she watched over him from her vantage point in Heaven. He spoke to the image now, as he had the habit of doing when the strain of his work felt heavy. "At least this will be the end of it for me as well as for him. And I doubt you'll have to worry about dealing with him up there!"

———✺———

Harland's burial occurred as he had instructed, with no fanfare, no exequy or ceremony of any kind. That left the staff from the funeral home and the cemetery to search for alternate ways of getting the sense of closure usually provided by ritual. Having been denied that, they felt no connection to the person of Harland and little responsibility for the body of Harland. They put him in the ground and covered him with dirt. They laid the sod back down over him and saw to the placing of his monument. Having fulfilled their duties, they turned their backs and left him alone.

As per his instructions, a rectangular perimeter of stones reaching eight inches above the ground outlined the three plots where Harland lay. This well-defined border warned anyone who thought about stepping onto his land not to tread on private property. Long benches supported by small pillars spread out on each side of his pedestal monument, so the structure stretched the full length of the three spaces. While the seating invited visitors, the boundary shouted KEEP OUT!

Atop the monument rested a bronze urn draped with a laurel wreath. A polished text panel contained his epitaph, which read:

Harland Clayton Freeman
B: March 21, 1910 – D: February 13, 1942
I stand by all I did
Disapproval does not trouble me now I am dead

Harland could not know while composing his plagiarized sentiment that even in death he would pay the consequences he had earned in life.

───

Winter gave way to a dazzling spring, then an early and brilliant summer. Dogwood, poplar, ginkgo and ancient oaks dressed the hillsides of the cemetery in color. Always a peaceful place, Riverside Cemetery proved most beautiful in spring.

Harland's monument stood almost ten feet tall from its base to the tip of the urn. Nothing within twenty yards rose to this height, so it commanded the entire slope. Regardless of the sun's position in the sky, at some point during every day, the pedestal's shadow poked its way into the Ryland family plot, thus stealing a bit of the beauty of each day from them. This punishment would last even longer than that which he had settled upon Leland Howard. Leland would die one day and be released from the burden placed upon him, but no means of escape existed for the Rylands—at least none Harland could imagine.

Although Asheville is blessed with an ideal climate, it is not immune to occasionally destructive weather events, and it was exactly that—an unpredictable summer storm of massive proportion—that eventually rescued the Rylands from Harland's wrath.

The birds and squirrels sounded the initial warning as they scurried for cover. Human inhabitants of the city noticed the gathering storm when thick, white clouds, their bellies colored golden by the sun, began accumulating in the western sky in mid-morning on a particularly warm day in early June. By that afternoon, a towering thunderhead with an anvil stretching as far as could be seen marched steadily toward the city, spawning several tornadoes in Tennessee as it approached. Though the mountains proved disruptive enough to the rotation of the storm to prevent the formation of additional funnel clouds, they did not mitigate the heavy rain, golf ball-sized hail or blinding flashes of lightning.

The bolt that reached down from the sky to destroy Harland's avengement did what all lightning does. It sought out the high pointy object standing in the open field, attracted especially by the imposing bronze urn. The charge toppled the vessel and pierced the heart of the granite pedestal, leaving a deep fissure in its wake. Weather continued its work, filling the crevice with water, then freezing it during the cold winter that ensued. Amid the blazing color of the following spring, the stone finally gave way and Harland's monument, the one he intended to serve as an enduring reminder of his disdain for those who had shunned him, broke apart and tumbled across his grave. Decades later, when someone finally came looking for him, they found a thick carpet of deep green ivy obscuring the entire gravesite.

FORTY-FOUR
2004

Richard Price began at the beginning, telling Tate and Cally how he and Leland had met and the slow development of their friendship, about Leland's growing popularity as a craftsman, his lack of ego, his family life with Ellie and Clayton.

"I never knew a man who loved his wife more deeply than your grandfather loved your grandmother. Frankly, I never understood it. Always seemed to me that she was cool toward him."

"I remember her as loving and out-going," Cally countered.

"With you and your father, she was, until Clayton started getting into so much trouble."

"What kind of trouble? He used drugs, didn't he."

"I don't know the details. But yes, he probably used drugs. He was what they called a Greaser back then—

one of the bad boys—and seemed proud of it. Hung out with the wrong crowd, always getting into scrapes, got hauled off to jail more'n once."

"I don't remember him very well. Gamma always sent him away if he showed up at the house when I was there. In any case, he never tried to be a father to me."

"None of that mattered to Leland. He loved Ellie and he loved Clayton—stood by him no matter what kind of trouble that boy got into."

"Gampa was always gentle and loving. I scratched my initials into the mantel and instead of getting mad, he taught me to whittle."

"He was proud of that incident. Did you know that?"

"Proud? He should have been furious."

"Nope. He told me about it, even showed me your handiwork. Thought it showed a love of the wood and some initiative. That's what he said about it. Clayton never took to the woodworking. Leland saw a chance for the family tradition to continue through you."

"Mr. Price, will you tell me about the day she died. The day they died? And what happened after that?" Cally reached for Tate as she asked.

Providing comfort to others had always been one of Tate's strengths. She usually did it with words, but now she simply folded her hand around Cally's delicate fingers.

"Those are painful memories, but you deserve to know. He called me. I went to the house immediately, and he was lying on the bed with Ellie in his arms. I knew she was gone, but he continued to cradle her until the police arrived. They took her away, but he didn't want to leave. Before I could convince him to come with me, they came back and told us they'd found your father in the park where he'd hung himself."

"He killed her, didn't he?"

"Yes, he did. Your grandfather saw Clayton running out the door, and he admitted it."

"It must have been terrible for him, for both of them. You can't kill your own mother and not feel tortured."

Tate listened to Cally and marveled at her stoicism and the compassion she expressed for Clayton. Tate would never be so forgiving toward those responsible for the crushing losses she had suffered.

Richard Price continued. "I don't know what went on in his mind. And I had Leland to take care of, so I focused on that. He had been at my house for several days, and not doing well, as I said. He finally came out for breakfast one morning. He was intent on going back to the place to get some things for you. I'm not sure what, but it was really important to him. I had to tell him you were gone and I didn't know where. That's when he took a bad fall on the terrace. Hit his head and passed out. He went to the hospital, and it became apparent he was slipping into a deep depression."

The old man leaned back in his chair and breathed deeply. Cally and Tate exchanged glances and waited to see if he would continue.

"I talked to the doctors about bringing him back here, but they thought he was a suicide risk, so they sent him off to the state hospital. He languished there. They did their best to treat him, but he never pulled out of the depression completely."

"How did he end up at Forest Glen?" Cally tried to keep her questions to a minimum, since Mr. Price was already giving them so much information, but this one was important to her.

"Well, over the months it became obvious he'd probably never live on his own again. He didn't want to go back to work. I knew he couldn't stay in that hospital. I had to get him to someplace better."

"Forest Glen seems like a very nice place. The staff is good to him."

"It has always been one of the best retirement facilities. But he didn't have any money."

"I have been wondering how his care is paid for."

"Well, he was a master craftsman. You know that, don't you?"

"Yes. Tate has told me some about his work."

"He had a workshop full of finished pieces. 'My little projects' he always called them. He did his work for money, of course, but he spent a lot of time making the things he wanted to make, even if no one had commissioned them."

"I have very fond memories of that workshop. I'd sit with him. I remember lots of things stacked up along the walls, many of them draped with old sheets. There was all kinds of wood and sawdust all over the floor . . . he'd lay his tools out in neat rows and carefully put each one back in place when he finished with it. I think I learned my own sense of orderliness from Gampa."

"Well, those 'little projects' became highly valuable after he stopped working. People were clamoring for anything made by Leland Howard. Leland allowed me to take care of his financial matters. In fact, he was happy to turn it all over to me. I was able to sell everything he had made, put the house on the market, sold off most of their personal items . . ."

"I wondered what happened to their things." Cally teared up again.

"I'm sorry, Cally. I would have saved them for you, but Rita just whisked you away. Your Grandma Thornton wouldn't tell me where you were. She just said you were gone and never coming back. So I did what I thought should be done. I sold everything I could and invested the money for Leland's care."

"It's okay, Mr. Price. Really it is. I have the note from Gamma, some childhood memories, a few things Mom left. And now I have Gampa again. I really couldn't ask for much more."

Tate had chosen to remain quiet throughout the conversation until now. "I have a question, if I may." There was one crucial issue Richard Price had not mentioned.

"If I can answer it, I will. Leland told me to tell all the secrets."

"The house over on Chestnut Street. It's in Leland's name. Why didn't you sell it?"

"Well, Ms. Marlowe, that's a long story."

"We've got time, don't we, Cally? If you're up to telling us more, that is, Mr. Price."

"Yes, plenty of time!" Cally said.

"Well then. Let's have some tea. It's a relief to talk about this after all this time." Richard Price rang for the housekeeper, who took his request for strong tea and a 'little nibble,' both of which arrived a few minutes later as promised.

"Freeman was a contrary old scoundrel if ever there was one."

Cally turned to Tate, a puzzled look on her face.

"Oh, I never told you! The man who built that house was named Harland Freeman."

"How much does she know?" Richard Price put the question to Tate.

"Almost as much as I do. I just don't think I ever mentioned Mr. Freeman to her."

"Well, everyone found him unlikable, Leland more so than others. They were cousins, you know."

"Cousins?" Tate could not squelch her excitement. "They were cousins? How were they connected?"

"Leland's mother was Mary Alice. She left town when she was quite young. Went to live with an old aunt and uncle up in the woods. Leland was born on the old homestead, and they moved back to town when he was 8 or 9."

That's why I never found a birth record. Tate would fill Cally in on that later. "Who were Harland's parents?"

"Mother was Eulah Mae, Mary Alice's older sister. Crazy Eulah everyone called her. Father was a layabout most of the time. Worked here and there but never steady. When Mary Alice and her family moved back to town, she'd have nothing to do with Eulah Mae. So the boys, Leland and Harland, never spent time together. Leland's dislike for Harland was mutual."

Tate could not hold back her next question. "Then why on earth would he give the house to Leland?"

Cally sat back and let Tate take the lead. Tate's passion for the house on Chestnut clearly outweighed Cally's interest in the place.

"I'm not sure what all happened between the two of them. They had no use for each other, that's for sure. At least until Freeman wanted his special door when he was building that monstrosity . . ."

"It is a strange place, for sure. But not monstrous exactly . . ." Tate reminded herself not to interrupt again. "I'm sorry. Go on, please."

"Never could figure out why Leland did that work. He didn't want to, but somehow he felt pressured. I always sensed it had something to do with Ellie, though I can't imagine what that would be. Anyway, Leland took the job, but then he also put a door very similar to the one he made for Freeman on his own house over on Cumberland."

"I own that house now. I think I told you when I visited you the first time."

"Yes, I remember that. Same door, almost. Rumor had it at the time that Freeman was furious when he found out. Wasn't even a couple months later he shot himself. Transferred the house to Leland, but made it so it couldn't ever be sold long as Leland was alive. Leland felt like it was an anchor around his neck. He always hated the place and wouldn't even travel down the street in front of it anymore."

"Wow. He must have had a powerful aversion to it."

"No more'n his aversion to Freeman himself, I can tell you that."

Tate offered more information. "I met the man who used to tend the lawn over there a couple of days ago. He says there were some lawyers involved but they stopped paying him a long time ago."

"Paige and Schmidt. Those hooligans!"

"Hooligans? What'd they do?"

"Not much of anything in the last few years before they closed up shop. That was the problem. Let things slip and got sued a couple times. They finally shut the doors and left town. That was the last anyone heard of them."

"I went to the courthouse and saw the trust, the one holding the house for Leland. At one point there was money in it, too. Any idea what happened to it?"

"I should have done more about that when the lawyers dropped the ball. But I had a stroke—that's what left me like this." He opened his arms, hands palms-up in a gesture of helplessness, and looked down at his legs. "But Leland would never even talk about the place, and I wasn't ever involved. So I chose to stay out of it. Maybe a lawyer could help you figure out if there's anything left and where it is."

"That's a good idea. I could sure use some help. We could use some help, that is, assuming Cally wants to pursue it."

Richard Price locked his eyes on Tate and paused before speaking again. "You're intent on saving that old place. Why?"

"The place haunts me, pure and simple. But there's another reason, too, one I just realized. I have to save it because it belongs to someone." Tate turned slowly to Cally and touched her shoulder. "I think it belongs to you, now, Cally."

Cally hung her head and cried quietly. "That was just dawning on me, Tate. I think it's time for me to go see the place, don't you?"

"Yes, if you're up to it."

Cally turned to Mr. Price. "You've had a long afternoon with us here. You must be ready for us to leave."

"I've told you most of what I can, and it's a bigger relief than I expected. I think I'm ready for a nap. Old men need to rest a lot, you know." His impish quality peeked out through his watery eyes, and Tate was happy to see their visit had not worn him out enough to quell his playfulness.

"You have been so generous with your time, Mr. Price. I can't thank you enough for everything you've shared with us." Tate's words fell far short of expressing the extent of her gratitude.

As they left the library, Mr. Price called after them. "You'll come back again, won't you? Both of you?"

"I certainly will, if you'll have me. And I'll bring treats next time," promised Tate.

"Me, too!" Cally chimed in. "I'll come to visit you and my desk!"

As they walked to the truck, Cally asked to see the house on Chestnut Street. Tate drove by slowly and stopped at the curb. However, Cally made no move to get out and look around. Instead, she gazed intently at the old place then sighed deeply, as if a heavy weight pressed down on her.

"You don't want to see it?" Tate asked.

"Oh, yes, I do. But I'm exhausted. I want to see it when I can really take it in. Could we do that another time?"

"Absolutely. Just let me know when." As Tate pulled away, she glanced at the house through the rearview mirror. *I'll bring her back. I promise. A* sudden chill ran down Tate's spine and she had a strange sensation that the house understood.

A short drive brought them to the Princess Hotel. "I'll call you soon, Tate. Okay?"

"Okay, Cally. Whenever you're ready, we'll look at that house, and if you want, I'll show you my place, too. Ellie and Leland's old place."

"I'll *really* need to rest up then. All this is . . . it's wearing me out."

"Take your time. I'll be here when you're ready."

Cally looked at Tate a long time before speaking again. "You're probably the best friend I've ever had, do you know that?"

These words instantly sank roots deep into Tate's heart. "That's probably the nicest thing you could have said to me, do you know that?"

They smiled at each other. Tate noticed a feeling of deep satisfaction suffusing her body as she drove home. *I'm happy. I'm really happy!* She couldn't remember the last time she had felt this way.

FORTY-FIVE
2004

Tate reached down and gave the wheel a good spin. Her flipper landed on $450. "I'll take a 'T.'"

"Yes, there's one 'T.'" Pat Sajak smiled at her, and Vanna White touched the square on the puzzle board, illuminating the 'T.'

Tate spun again, this time landing on $1,500. *Oh, this is good.* "I'll have an 'H.'"

"There are two 'Hs,'" crooned Pat Sajak.

Tate had already racked up $3,450. Her palms left faint wet handprints on the counter in front of her as she made her next move. "I'd like to buy an 'E.'"

"There are *five* 'Es,'" Pat said as Vanna White quickly touched the squares and clapped her hands.

Tate spun again, landing on the $500 space. The lights on the wheel flashed brightly. Tate felt odd as if suspended in this place and happy to be here, finally, but not at all sure how it had happened. *Don't freak out. Just keep playing.* "I'll take an 'R,' please."

"Yes, there are two 'Rs.'" Pat Sajak smiled. "You're doing just fine." Tate's nerves made her freeze for a moment. "Spin or solve," coached Pat Sajak.

"I'll have to spin." Worry crept into Tate's voice. *I feel really wonky. Gotta stay focused.* She took a deep breath to steady herself. She stood on the platform behind the player's desk, yet she also felt like a spectator suspended above and off to the side of the scene. She reached down and spun the wheel again.

Pat Sajak and the audience oohed as the flipper caught on the $600 side of the peg and held, narrowly avoiding slipping over to the "Bankrupt" side.

Tate strained to make sense of the puzzle. It read:

    _ h e r e ' _ t h e _ _ r e _ _ _ _ e?

Where's the . . . Tate tried frantically to fill in the blank spaces.

Tate intended to call an 'S,' so she was horrified when she opened her mouth and said: "I'll take an 'L.'"

Pat Sajak paused, then pronounced: "Yes . . . there's one 'L.'"

As Vanna White illuminated the letter, Pat Sajak bought her some time by saying: "It's a phrase. Spin or solve or buy a vowel."

Tate hesitated. "I'll buy an . . . 'A.'" She couldn't shake the nauseating sensation of floating just above the floor.

"Yes, there's an 'A.'" Pat Sajak seemed amused as Vanna White made another square spring to life.

Stumped, Tate could not figure out the last word in the phrase.

Spin or solve, just don't panic. Tate hesitated. "I'd like to buy a vowel, Pat." *'I' or 'O'?* Tate struggled to decide. "I'll take an 'I.'"

Again Pat Sajak—and Spirit—smiled upon her. "Yes, there is an 'I.' That's the last of the vowels. Spin or solve."

Suddenly the puzzle sorted itself out and the missing letters popped into place in Tate's mind. "Pat! I'd like to solve the puzzle."

"Please do."

"Where's the fireplace?"

Tate struggled up out of the dream just as she was about to be congratulated in person by Pat Sajak. Vanna White's figure faded away, still happily applauding Tate's success, and Tate forced her eyes open. The clock read 8:45 a.m. and she felt hungry. She started laughing softly to herself. *Well, at least I finally made it to Wheel of Fortune! Wonder how much money I won?* As her feet touched the floor, a new thought flashed into her awareness. "Where's the fireplace," she said aloud. "Yeah! Just exactly where *is* the fireplace?"

The excitement of her dream quickly gave way to a thrilling idea. The fireplace may not be in the house next door, but it had to be somewhere—she believed without question that no one could possibly have destroyed a work by Leland Howard—and she set herself the challenge of finding it.

Less than two hours later, Tate and Carla walked through the stacks at the library, searching for *Cabins & Castles*, a book containing a historical overview and records of individual properties in Asheville and Buncombe County, mostly ones constructed prior to 1930. Carla had pointed them in that direction when Tate showed up asking for help in finding information about the house she owned.

"It's a great resource," Carla told Tate. "It may have something in it about your place." She pulled the book off the shelf and they sat down at the nearest table. Carla leafed through the book then turned it toward Tate, who sat across the desk. "Here. This is your place on Maplewood, right?"

Tate looked at the old black-and-white photograph of a fancy house with no resemblance whatsoever to the one she owned. She read the address printed in the caption—her address. "It's the right address, but it's not the same house." Tate read parts of the description in a hushed voice.

> . . . a story-and-half weatherboarded house on a high frame basement . . . intersecting gable roof . . . vertical boards in the gables, set inside a flat frieze frame, end in a sawtooth pattern.

"I don't know what much of this means since I don't speak Architecture. But this is definitely not my house." Tate slid the book back to Carla, who tapped the picture of the house that once occupied the lot on Maplewood.

"I wonder what happened."

"Oh! Of course—it couldn't be the same house, because mine was moved there!"

"Well, that clears things up."

"Sometimes I can be dense. I knew the house had been moved, but this book was published before that happened."

"Obviously it was published before the original house was torn down," Carla added.

"Okay, I know what to do next. I think I know who can help me."

"Who's that?"

Jim Kitching. I bought the place from him, and my bet is he knows its history. Thanks again Carla. You've been very helpful, as usual."

"Anytime you need anything, let me know. I'm always happy to see you."

"I'm sure I'll be back. In any case, I'll let you know what I find out, if you're interested."

"You know I'm interested, Tate." Carla's comment hung expectantly in the air, but Tate chose not to address it in the personal way it had been offered.

"Okay. You'll hear from me again, then."

Tate made two phone calls as soon as she left the library. Cally did not answer, so Tate left a message. Jim Kitching answered on the first ring.

"Hey, Tate. Haven't heard from you in ages."

"You said if I ever needed anything to call, so I'm calling. I have a kazillion questions about the duplex on Maplewood—the one next door to me."

"What do you want to know?"

"Well, I know you moved it. It used to be over on Cumberland Street, right? What do you know about the house, Jim? I mean before you relocated it. Like who owned it or anything?"

"Yeah. The short story is they were going to tear it down when they decided to put the Interstate through the middle of town. I bought it really cheap. Well, me and my partners. The old place on that lot had burned down a long time before that and . . . you know, Tate, this isn't going to be a short story after all. How about I meet you over there and we walk the property and I'll tell you what I know."

"Great! How about today? I'm renovating the place, and I have lots of questions, like I said."

"Well, sure, I guess I can come over today. Sounds like you're in a big hurry! What's up?"

"I'll tell you when you get here."

"Okay, then. I'm out picking up some supplies and I could stop by in about an hour."

Tate and Jim stood just inside the door of the apartment. Dave had made a lot of progress. The trim around the new windows in the kitchen area had been replaced. Oak cabinets and sparkling countertops now filled two walls. The dishwasher had been installed along with an up-to-date gas range, large refrigerator, a deep double sink and new lighting.

Jim looked around. "Jeez. This looks great! You've put a lot of work and money into this place."

"Whadda ya think? Am I doing it justice?"

"More than justice. Wish I could of done this when I moved the place here. But we had to make it livable on the cheap. We were working with a loan that required we create affordable housing, so I cut a lot of corners to meet the budget. If it wasn't essential, I didn't do it."

"Well, that explains a lot, then. When we pulled up the old carpet and vinyl we found these beautiful floors underneath. They're heart pine."

"Yeah, I remember that now. But they had been cut up so bad in some places, we just covered it up."

"I can understand why, after seeing what was under the stuff we pulled up. I'm putting carpet back down in the hallway and bedrooms, but I've decided to salvage the floor in this room."

"That'll be nice. I hated to put down that vinyl and carpet, but it cost half what it would have to resurrect the wood."

"I think it'll look beautiful when this area is refinished. That'll happen next week, I hope. Depends on how long it takes to get everything else done so we can begin the finishing up. I hope to have a new tenant in here next month."

"What happened to Kristin? Why'd she move?"

"She was a real trip, Jim. She couldn't stand me. In fact, most of the neighbors are ticked off because I started moving the old tenants out and fixing these places up. That surprised me, actually. I would've thought they'd be happy to be rid of the boozers and brawlers from downstairs."

"People don't like change, even if it's for the better."

"Mazie said basically the same thing."

"You've met her then?"

"Sure have. She came over offering sweet tea not long after I moved in, and now we're buddies."

"I'll have to stop by and say hello. Used to see her all the time when I was here taking care of the place. She's a sweet thing, isn't she?"

"Really sweet. I can only hope I'm as feisty and functional as she is when I reach that age."

"So what did happen to Kristin? I'm surprised she left. She grew up in this place and then when her mother remarried, she stayed here with her baby."

"Well, I finally asked her to leave. I don't know how she was with you, but she was really difficult to deal with. Demanding, complaining constantly about one thing or another. She wanted the place fixed up like I'd done with the other units, but she didn't want to pay more rent. She finally left, but not without leaving a mess behind."

"What kind of mess?"

"Personal stuff, a refrigerator full of moldy food, things like that."

"Sorry she caused you problems. She was a pretty good tenant for me, though."

Tate trailed along as Jim walked through the apartment, commenting on the work he had done to save the house from demolition, all the planning and preparation, building the new foundation which now housed the downstairs apartment, and the major production of loading the house onto a huge truck and hauling it from Cumberland to Maplewood.

"Sounds like a lot of work, Jim, but it also sounds like you had a passion for it."

"I sure did. I've lived here in Ashevull my whole life, except when I went away to college. I hated seeing the old places torn down so they could put that highway right through the middle a town. They did a lot of destruction in the name of modernization."

"Well that brings us right to the point of my asking you to come over here today. You know that old place over in Montford they want to tear down? Big house, up on a hill on Chestnut Street?"

"Yeah, I've been seeing that on the news lately. What's your connection?"

"Well, this house is actually the connection, though I've only recently figured that out."

"This place? How so?"

"This house was built by Leland Howard. He was a master woodworker back in the '30s and up until he dropped out of sight after his wife was killed. He's also the man who owns the derelict place over in Montford. I'm not going into the whole story—it's way too long and convoluted. If you want to hear it, maybe we could do that over a drink or lunch sometime. What I'm wondering about right now is what changes have been made to this place." They had finished the tour of the apartment and returned to the open living room and kitchen area. "What can you tell me about that?"

"Well, I did a lot of rearranging to make the place more usable. There used to be a doorway there." Jim indicated the wall with the new sink and stove. "And the bathroom was on the left down the hall. And there were only two bedrooms."

"Sounds like it took a lot of work."

"Yeah, and I did it all myself, pretty much. Maybe I should a kept 'em, but I got busy with other things and they took up too much of my time."

"You clearly loved them, Jim. I'm glad I bought them from you."

"I'm glad you got 'em, too, Tate. You're doing right by them."

Tate brought their attention back to the wood floors. She gestured to the small rectangular depression at the entrance to the hallway. "We have to patch that one spot. I wonder why the boards were cut out there, though."

"They weren't cut out. There used to be a fireplace there."

"I knew it! My carpenter said there was probably a fireplace here at some point a long time ago. What happened to it?"

"Yeah, there was a fireplace there, but we took it out. It was a beautiful old thing, with a slate hearth and a carved mantel. Shame to let it go, but we needed the space, and you don't want a fireplace in a rental unit, believe me."

"So you just ripped it out?" Tate's voice was edgy as she tried to hide her disbelief.

"Oh, no, we didn't destroy it! I would never do something like that!"

"So where is it?" Tate's heart raced. *It isn't gone. It may not be here, but it's somewhere, and I'm going to find it.*

"We sold it to an architectural salvage company, along with the original cabinetry."

An original Leland Howard mantelpiece. "What happened to it? Do you know?"

"Don't rightly know, but unless someone bought it, it's probably still at the salvage warehouse."

"What warehouse would that be?"

"Conservation Salvage, up in Weaverville. That guy has every kind of thing you can imagine from the old houses that were torn down."

"Jim, I can't thank you enough. I owe you lunch, for sure. Maybe we'll have it right here in this apartment once it's finished. I make a mean turkey and cheese sandwich!"

"I'll take you up on that. We'll have to invite Mazie to join us. I'm gonna stop over there now and say hello. See ya' around."

"You sure will, Jim. Thanks again."

Tate dropped down to the floor and leaned against the wall. She closed her eyes and let all the information she'd just learned swirl through her head. She began constructing her to-do list as she sat in the empty, unfinished apartment. *I'll go to Conservation Salvage right now. Maybe the mantel is still there. Please let it be there. Have to call Cally. Need to take her to see the place on Chestnut. What if I don't find the fireplace? What if I do find it? Will Cally's things still be in the compartment? Unlikely, not after all this time. She needs a lawyer to get control of that trust. We need to visit Leland again. I'm starving. I need to eat something before I head out.*

She pressed the heels of her hands into her eye sockets and massaged them slowly trying to slow down her racing thoughts. *One thing at a time. Lunch first, then Conservation Salvage, and I'll try Cally while I'm on my way there.*

FORTY-SIX
1921

Even though the calendar said Tuesday, Mary Alice Clayton Howard carefully laid out her Sunday-best dress on the bed. With her husband and son at work in the shed behind the cabin, she had privacy and quiet. She warmed a teakettle of water and poured it into the chipped porcelain washbasin, then quickly bathed herself. She took special care with her grooming, smoothing the fabric of her dress after slipping it over her head, cleaning the dust from her only pair of shoes and tucking stray hairs into the bun of coiled braid nestled at the back of her neck.

Once satisfied she had done all she could to make herself presentable, she went to the cupboard and took out her cherished sugar bowl. A long crack ran halfway down the side, and she cradled the vessel gently so as not to further the damage. The bowl came into the family as a wedding gift to Mary Alice's great-grandmother. It had been handed down through three generations of Clayton women before reaching her, and each one had treasured it. The last had been Aunt Ida—the only woman to actually mother her—and now it belonged to Mary Alice.

She lifted the lid and removed a small roll of bills. She spread them out on the table and counted. She still had forty-seven dollars and a few coins, about three dollars less than Arlen had given her when they sold her aunt and uncle's homestead in the mountains.

Her husband treated her well. Mary Alice smiled as she clutched the money to her bosom and thought about how easily he had agreed to split it with her right down the middle. No other man she had ever known would have done such a thing. No woman she knew had ever been the recipient of generosity like this from a father or a husband. She had been blessed to find him and blessed with all he provided her—not just this money, but safety and love and a beautiful son, too.

But the sugar bowl was not a bank and having the money so closely at hand proved to be a great temptation, an emotion Mary Alice deplored and had given into only once. Shortly after the family moved to Asheville, before Arlen had established his business and at a time when provisions had almost run out, she had succumbed and used almost three dollars to stock up on cornmeal, flour, beans, coffee and sugar. She did not feel guilty about the meal, flour and beans. She had used them along with the eggs from her chickens and the preserved vegetables and smoked meat they had brought with them when they moved to town to feed the family until Arlen found steady work. She could even justify the coffee. A pound brewed weak and the grounds used twice would last almost two months, and Arlen loved his coffee. The sugar, though, *that* was pure indulgence, easily done without by all of them. She should never have spent thirty-five cents to buy sugar. After that misstep, she vowed never to be led into temptation so easily again. It had taken several weeks to settle her mind about what needed to be done, and now she was about to do it.

Her decision had been hastened a bit by the appearance at her door only days before of her sister, Eulah Mae. Mary Alice did not recognize the unkempt, mumbling creature at first. Then Eulah Mae glared at her and demanded to be let in. "Show some 'ospitality to yer sister, Mary Alice!" she demanded.

Mary Alice flatly refused. "I want no part a you, Eulah Mae. Go away and don't come back to my door ever again." She had not been face-to-face with her sister since leaving for the mountains nearly thirty years earlier, but she had heard about Crazy Eulah and even seen her from afar while shopping downtown a few weeks earlier.

"Here ya are, livin' in this fancy house and me strugglin' fer a bite to eat and a warm place to sleep. Show some compassion, won'cha?"

"I gladly left ya behind all those years ago, Eulah, and I ain't about to pick ya back up now. Go away."

"Then gimme some money, sister. I bet you got some hidden away somewheres. Up in yer cupboard? That's whar Ma kept hers when she had some."

"You'll get nothin' from me, Eulah Mae." With that Mary Alice shut the door in her sister's face and dropped the latch on the inside. And she settled on the details of her plan to put distance between herself and temptation while simultaneously moving her money out of harm's way—said harm taking the form of her estranged sister.

Mary Alice took the bills from the table and put them in a hidden pocket in the seam of her dress as she left the house.

"You off, then?" Arlen stepped onto the porch just as Mary Alice closed the door.

"I am."

"Ya look lovely and determined, Mrs. Howard."

"That I am, Mr. Howard."

"And yer sure you'll go by yerself? You'll not need me to come along?"

"I'll not need yer company but I thank ya fer offerin'." No reason for Mary Alice to say she didn't want her husband's assistance, that she eagerly anticipated carrying her business out on her own.

"I'll see ya at suppertime then, I s'pose."

"And don' stay too late in that workshop. I'm cookin' up somethin' special fer ya."

Mary Alice chose the most direct route to her destination. She would make the necessary detours to pick up the few items she planned to purchase on her way back home. She walked briskly up Haywood Street and turned on Patton Avenue to reach the American National Bank building. She stood across the street for a few moments while summoning the courage to enter the lobby where she then waited her turn to see a clerk. She approached the window when beckoned by the teller and spread her money out carefully on the counter.

"I'm here to open me a savin's account." She stood straight and tall, weathered hands clasped tightly at her waist, shoulders squared as if she expected a fight.

"I can't help you with that . . ."

Mary Alice had been building up the courage to carry out her plan for weeks, and she waded into the fray before the teller could finish. "Why not? 'Cuz I'm a woman?"

"Oh! No, ma'am!" Mary Alice's unexpected forcefulness flustered the teller.

Mary Alice studied the young man standing behind the bars of his cage as she read his name tag. "Then why? My money's no good here, Mr. Meeks? Is that it?" The teller's face had reddened under her assault, highlighting the clusters of pimples on his flat forehead and broad nose. Limp hair the color of a field mouse hung in a clump over his right ear, having escaped from the slick layer of pomade meant to keep it under control. He wore an ill-fitting suit jacket on his thin, slumping frame. Mary Alice felt a bit sorry for him, but she meant to do the business she had come here to do and he would not stand in her way if she held any sway in the matter.

"No, ma'am. That's not it at all." The boy looked as if he may begin crying, and Mary Alice felt her resolve slipping. "I'm just a teller, ma'am, and a new one at that. This is my first day at the window by myself, so I wouldn't know how to help you even if they'd let me. You'll have to see the assistant manager to open a new account." The teller motioned toward a man sitting at a large wooden desk on the opposite side of the lobby.

Mary Alice felt the tears welling up in her eyes as she thanked the teller and turned quickly away, the money clutched in her hands. She felt remorseful for having spoken to the young man the way she had. Her mistaken assumption about how to open an account had led to the exchange between them and she felt foolish as a result. Her courage spent on the unnecessary encounter, she now approached the assistant manager hesitantly. He gestured toward the sturdy, leather-upholstered chair in front of his desk, and she quickly sat down.

"How may I help you?"

"Is a woman allowed to open a savings account in her own name at this bank?"

Mary Alice had intended all along to simply present herself as a valid customer like any man would do. Arlen had gladly given her the money and made it known it was hers to do with as she pleased. Why should she not be able to open an account? But she also knew banking was a man's world. She glanced at the other customers, all men, which proved her point.

"You are most certainly welcome to open an account with us, Mrs. . . .?" The assistant manager smiled at her, friendly like, and waited for her to give her name.

"Mrs. Arlen Howard. But I'd like the name on the account to be mine, if that's possible. Mrs. Mary Alice Howard."

"Of course it is! Let's just get this paperwork filled out, shall we?"

Less than half an hour later, Mary Alice stepped back into the sunlight with her new passbook. She opened it and read it slowly, brushing her fingers lightly over the writing where it said "Mrs. Mary Alice Howard" on the line at the top of the first page and "$47.32" in the column provided for a record of the deposits.

"Forty-seven dollars and thirty two cents! In my own bank account!" Mary Alice had never done anything like this in her entire life. She had heard about and seen women stepping out of the traditional roles assigned them and doing outrageous things—dressing in scandalously short skirts, dancing into the night, smoking cigarettes, doing business in a man's world—she'd heard about these things and while she considered most of them shameful, she also felt exhilarated to have joined the ranks of non-traditional women. Opening a bank account in her own name may seem small by comparison to, say, driving an automobile, but for Mary Alice it would be the greatest departure from convention she would ever undertake.

Her plan was clear. She would make a trip to the bank at the end of every month and have the interest her money earned posted to her passbook. The money would grow and one day she would have something valuable to hand down to the next generation—something in addition to a cherished, cracked sugar bowl.

Mary Alice's monthly ritual grew over the years. At first, she hurried to the bank to have the interest on her account posted, then rushed back home to hide the passbook away. Arlen never asked her about the money, and she offered him no information about it. She wanted this one thing for herself. Over time, she became more secure in her monthly trips, often stopping for tea or to do a bit of shopping, always after seeing the new amount printed neatly in the "Deposits" column. Mary Alice never took anything out of the account, so the "Withdrawals" column remained empty. By October of 1930, her $47.32 had grown to almost $75.00. Mary Alice could not have been prouder of her accomplishment, which made the fall, when it came three weeks later, all the more devastating.

In November of 1930, more than a year after the national stock market crashed, the collapsing economy flooded Asheville. Central Bank and Trust failed to open for business on November 20, and American National Bank followed suit the next day. Mary Alice's money simply disappeared. She believed her pride had led to her downfall, and she never again engaged in the world of money. Even when American National reopened its doors and began refunding some money to its depositors, her shame kept her from laying claim to what belonged to her. Even the pleading of her daughter-in-law, Ellie, did not sway her.

"Mother, why just let the money go to waste?"

"A man's world is not for a woman!"

"Money is not a man's world anymore. You have a right to what's owed you!"

"My pride in stepping out a my place brought me shame and regret. I wasted good money tryin' to git more. I'll not be doin' that agin."

Many versions of this conversation took place between Mary Alice and Ellie over the years until finally Mary Alice gave in. She would not have an account in her name, but she would make her claim and give the money to Ellie to do with as she pleased. It had been meant for the next generation anyway, and now that Leland and Ellie had a child, the time had come. The two women went to the bank together and left with half the money Mary Alice had lost six years earlier.

Ellie took the money as she had promised Mary Alice she would do and opened an account at Asheville Federal Savings and Loan. Following in Mary Alice's footsteps, she let the account slowly grow until she transferred it to her granddaughter's name in 1961.

The passbook took its place in the secret compartment along with Ellie's other valuable possessions, all the things she intended to give Cally one day. Ellie daydreamed about how she would present the gift. Perhaps she would wrap everything up in one fancy package and give it to Cally at her high school graduation. Better yet, she would save the precious items for Cally's wedding day. Or maybe she would give them to the girl one at a time on ordinary days and special occasions alike, until she had presented all of them—the diamond ring from her mother, the hair comb from her grandmother, the passbook with a tidy sum of money to usher Cally into whatever life she chose and, of course, the note which would shake things up so badly but which would also finally let the truth be known.

FORTY-SEVEN
2004

Tate decided to take the scenic route to Weaverville, so she headed north on Merrimon Avenue, which wound past a beautiful lake and park before the landscape turned into a smattering of tiny strip malls, family restaurants, tire stores and a variety of other shops that catered to the needs and fancies of the local population. She noted several places along the way that she wanted to visit, including a small Mexican *taqueria* and *tienda*, a farmer's market and a cheese store. Today would not be the day for meandering and poking into new and interesting corners of the city. Today her focus lay entirely on finding the missing fireplace.

Conservation Salvage occupied a small storefront on Main Street in Weaverville. Tate stepped through the door and into another era. There is a particular aroma that heralds the slow passing of time and this placed exuded it. Tate inhaled the heavy fustiness deep into her lungs. Just as pheromones attract potential mates in the animal world, this scent excites the senses of antique-lovers and bargain hunters, drawing them into the recesses of tiny shops and huge warehouses alike. Tate understood how one could get lost in the mysteries of a place such as this. At least a dozen old tables filled the shop, their entire surfaces covered with boxes and trays of old doorknobs, rusting hinges, crystals that had once adorned chandeliers and lamps, old tools—many rusting and all obsolete—and countless other artifacts of days gone by. Likewise, the walls held several glass-front display cases filled with salvaged items from another time. However, she did not see a single mantel and her heart fell at the thought that what she came looking for might not be here.

A man behind the counter looked up briefly before continuing his conversation with another customer. "I'll be with you shortly."

"No rush. I'll just look around." Tate studied the man quickly. Much like the merchandise filling his store, he had an aura of oldness about him. Though more than six feet tall by Tate's estimation, he stood slump-shouldered and head bent, thus giving the appearance of a much shorter man. Deep creases radiated out from the corners of his eyes and mouth and his thick, dark hair had been slicked back off his face. One chunk had fallen loose and rested against the edge of his black-rimmed glasses, which sat askew on his nose. Tate guessed his appearance belied his real age. *No more than 50, give or take a couple of years, I'll bet.* Having summed up the proprietor, she turned her attention to the array of objects on display until he turned his attention to her several minutes later.

"Looking for anything in particular?"

Tate noticed a surprising clarity in his deep blue eyes, which reaffirmed her conclusion about his age. "Actually, yes. Something very particular. I'm looking for a fireplace you would have purchased probably ten years ago or so."

"Well, that is very specific! Tell me more about it."

Without a moment's thought, Tate launched into her story. "I own a small house that was moved to its current location about a decade ago. It used to be on Cumberland Street in Asheville and now it's over on Maplewood. There was a fireplace in it when it was originally built, and the man who moved it sent me here. His name is Jim Kitching. He said you bought the mantel from him when they were remodeling the interior of the house."

The man watched her intently, and she stopped abruptly as she realized he did not need all the information she had given him. "Sorry! That's probably more than you need to know."

"No, it's fine. I have a lot of old mantels in the back. I don't recall a Jim Kitching, but I buy from so many different people I could never remember all of them. Let's look around."

He headed through an opening at the back of the room and into a wide hallway created by crude shelves along each side, which were filled with stacks of furniture, mostly wooden chairs in a bewildering variety of styles. The store front gave the impression of a small shop, and Tate had not previously noticed the entryway to the cavernous warehouse space in the back. Her hopes for finding the mantel were re-ignited. They had just stepped into the warehouse when a tinkling chime from the old-fashioned bell attached to the top of the front door announced another customer.

Tate noticed the proprietor's dilemma—continue on with her or return to the front of the store. "Seems to be a busy day for you. Is it always like this?"

"I wish it was! I'll be right back . . . if you can wait a moment that is . . ." The man hesitated, as if worried he would lose one customer by attending to another.

"No hurry. I'll need some time to look around. If you point me in the direction, I'll find my way."

"Are you sure? I can just see to them and come right back."

"I'm sure. I just want to poke around a bit. By the way, my name is Tate." She offered her hand and the man shook it gently.

"I'm John. John Hathburn."

"Nice to meet you, John."

"Likewise, Tate." He looked thoughtful for a moment then obviously decided she could be trusted on her own.

"Okay, follow this hall down to the end and take a right. You'll pass through the hutches and cabinets and then take another right and you'll find the mantels. There're probably a hundred or more back there."

John returned to the front of the shop and Tate headed in the direction he had indicated. *A hundred or more. This is going to be a challenge!*

As she walked through the conglomeration of artifacts lining the aisles, Tate flashed back on memories from her childhood. A heavy farmhouse table reminded her of a rambling kitchen with a wood-burning cook stove at her great-Grandma Marlowe's farmhouse. The unforgettable taste of sandwiches made of brown sugar heaped onto homemade white bread slathered with butter that she had helped her grandmother churn the day before jumped into her mind and made her salivate. Passing a china cabinet with peeling veneer, she heard the clink of heavy, cut glass candy dishes and cruets as her other great-grandmother, Grandma Strauss, placed them carefully on the delicate shelves of the breakfront in the cramped dining room after letting Tate hold them and run her tiny fingers over the etched crevices that created snowflake-like designs.

Along with these distinct recollections came the feeling of excitement and curiosity she had felt every time her family visited those precious old women. She freely explored their farms, climbed trees, spied on sows wallowing in mud and nursing piglets and watched a golden carp swim in the water tank where the horse took long draughts of cool, dark water. These images of her early life and dozens of others flashed and flickered through her consciousness and stirred up a deep yearning.

As she turned the corner that led to the collection of mantels, she stopped short and caught her breath. Stacked three or four deep on both sides of the corridor all the way to the back wall stood a dizzying array of fireplaces. "Wow! This could take the rest of the day!"

Tate whispered these words into the stillness surrounding her. A row of horizontal windows placed a couple of feet below the ceiling and caked with decades of dirt allowed thin shafts of sunlight to filter in slanted streaks to the floor below. Specks of dust filled the streaming light and floated about lazily like tiny feathers drifting along on imperceptible currents. As she exhaled, her breath sent them scurrying in fascinating corkscrews and swirls. She recalled exploring Grandma Strauss's cavernous barn, the scent of fresh hay, the crackling of straw, the creak of the old tractor as she climbed onto the metal seat—and the dust motes scattering frantically as she blew her breath into the beams of light filtering down through the cracks in the roof.

She allowed herself to live there in the memory for a few moments, as a child surrounded by wonder and amazed by her power to make things happen in the world around her. She blew her breath into the air again now as an adult who had grown into her power and also had learned not everything would bend to her will as easily as tiny particles of dust held captive in sunlight. She allowed herself to feel the beauty of innocence and the burden of experience all in the same moment. She watched the swirling vortex she had created and felt a sadness permeate both body and mind. They were all gone now—the people and places that had been her refuge as a child—so she breathed into the pain and refocused on the task ahead.

Tate spent a few moments surveying the dozens of mantels stacked against the walls. She began visually sorting them into groups. Big, small, fancy, plain, older, newer—and as she did so, her plan began falling into place. No need to look at the huge, ornate items constructed of mahogany or teak. Leland would have used wood native to the mountains around Asheville, and he would have designed a mantel to fit his modest home both in size and style. As she looked around, those criteria narrowed her search down considerably. Additionally, it made the search easier since all the oversized mantels hugged the walls and the medium and small-sized ones stood in the first and second rows. Tate did not claim to be psychic, but she often knew in advance when something was about to happen, and she had that sense now. She would find the mantel. It was right here, right in front of her, waiting to be rescued.

She began picking her way through the pieces on the left side of the aisle. She quickly assessed each one, passing up many for their simplicity or shoddy workmanship and looking more carefully at those she thought could have been made by Leland. Several promising possibilities ultimately proved disappointing. She continued her detailed search for close to half an hour, wishing she had the dimensions of the space in the floor where the fireplace once sat and also chastising herself for not having brought along a flashlight. When she reached the far wall, she turned and headed back, inspecting every promising item on the other side. She had nearly returned to her starting point when her heart began pounding rapidly.

Wedged in the second row and half-hidden by the broken specimen in front of it, she spied a dust-covered mantel about the right size and made of what she believed to be cherry. She stepped as close to it as she could, working her toe into a small opening so she could lean in even more. She brushed dirt off the top of the mantel and saw the distinctive color and grain of cherry wood. Inspection of the details along the rim revealed a design reminiscent of the one she had seen on the mantel at the Princess Hotel. She sucked in her breath and closed her eyes, both hands resting on the mantel. *This is it. I know it is!*

The problem lay in proving her belief. Only one thing would verify her find, and it would be extremely difficult to see. She stepped back and assessed the possibility of moving the mantel out of the tight slot it occupied. That would require clearing the space in front of it and swiveling it out so she could see the side. Just then, John Hathburn returned.

"You could not have better timing! This might be it. I have to see the side of it, down near the bottom. Can you help me?"

"That's pretty heavy stuff there. I'll get someone to come over and . . ."

"I'm strong, John. I'm really strong! If we work together we might be able to move it out just a little so I can see the side. Do you have a flashlight?" Tate realized her excitement may sound like bossiness to John. "I mean . . . oh! I'm just so excited. Can we try to do it ourselves? I can barely stand the suspense."

"Well, if I can move this one out first . . ."

"I can help! Let's do it together." Tate grasped one end of the obstructing piece and began lifting. John's eyes registered his surprise at her strength, and he quickly took the other end. In moments, they had shifted the first mantel out of the way. Together they worked Tate's prize out of its position and slid it part way into the aisle, its right side exposed. Tate dropped to her knees and, using the sleeve of her sweatshirt, wiped cobwebs and layers of dirt away.

"I knew it!" Her squeal reverberated through the huge room. "Look!"

John knelt down beside her and looked where Tate pointed. "C-A-T. Looks like someone's initials."

"That's exactly what it is—the initials of someone who will be ecstatic to see this again!" Then Tate burst into tears leaving John to stare at her in astonishment.

"What's wrong? Did you hurt yourself?" John seemed flustered and fidgeted around her as if looking for open wounds.

"I'm fine."

"You don't look fine. You're bawling like a baby!"

John's comment startled Tate and she began laughing through her tears, which seemed to confuse him even more. "John, I'm okay. Really I am. It's just that . . ." She sniveled and wiped away tears. ". . . I can't even explain what's going on with me right now, but it's all old stuff. Finding this just opened so many old wounds and memories, and I'm swirling in them right now. Can I just sit alone for a bit? I'll come out in a few minutes. Please?" Tate recognized the pleading in her voice and it increased her already extreme discomfort at expressing raw emotion in front of a stranger. She rarely did that even in isolation.

John stood his ground, unwilling to leave a crying woman sitting on the bare floor unattended. "Let me help you up."

Tate reeled herself back in as much as she could. "I know this seems really weird. I'm a complete stranger to you, but I'm okay, really. I just need a few minutes to collect myself." Tate's crying slowed and her laughter stopped completely.

"You're sure? You don't need help getting up or anything?"

"Absolutely sure."

"Well then . . ." and John started back down the aisle, turning a couple of times on his way, a puzzled and concerned look etched across his face.

Tate sat alone in the shadowed space and let her emotions run free again. They ran the gamut from grief to joy, touching along the way on the countless highs and lows of her life, the concessions she had made, the stands she had taken, the losses suffered, the battles won, all the decisions and actions—from tiny to life-changing—that had led her to this moment. They flowed over her and threatened to drown her, and as she had always done in the past, she resurfaced to find herself strong and vibrantly alive.

The cathartic experience left Tate feeling vulnerable. Given the opportunity, she would have curled up in a darkened room and slept, but she had important things to do that demanded immediate attention.

"I'll be back to pick it up soon," Tate told John as she paid for the mantle. It's a gift for a dear friend and I want to give it to her as soon as possible."

FORTY-EIGHT
2004

Cally climbed out of a deep sleep and dropped her feet to the floor. They barely touched, given the height of the bed, and she felt like falling back into the cozy nest. But she had already missed breakfast as well as the early morning hours, her favorite part of the day, so she pushed herself out of bed and into the shower.

Thirty minutes later, Dawn stopped her as she was heading out the door of the hotel. "Hey, Cally! How'd your grandfather like the brownies?"

"Dawn! Oh, sorry! I should have made it a point to stop by and see you when I got back yesterday. But I was exhausted! Will you forgive me?"

"No need to apologize, my dear. You look like you could use a cup of coffee and some breakfast."

"I could, but I'll get something outside. I missed breakfast by a good hour."

"Well, that works out just fine because we have the dining room to ourselves and we can chat for a while. If you have time, that is."

"I've got plenty of time, Dawn, but I don't want to put you out. You must be cleaning up and getting ready to leave."

"Yep, but I have time to fix an omelet and brew a fresh pot of coffee. I haven't eaten yet myself. Will you join me?"

Cally watched as Dawn prepared their meal. Starting with organic, free-range eggs, she dressed them up with sautéed red onion and portabella mushrooms, Havarti cheese and baby spinach, then a garnish of fresh, spicy, tomato salsa. They took their omelets, a carafe of hot coffee and toasted French peasant bread to the small café table on the back patio. Although chilly morning air greeted them, the women were bathed in sunlight. Cally sank back and took in a deep, cleansing breath and let out a long sigh as she exhaled.

Dawn watched as Cally settled in. "From the sounds of that, you need to decompress as much as you need to eat!"

"That's the truth! You're very perceptive."

"Vacation shouldn't be so stressful, Cally. Was it hard seeing your grandfather yesterday?"

"I wish this *were* a vacation! No . . . actually I don't wish that, but you're right. It has been stressful, and I'm not handling it all that well."

"Want to tell me about it? I'm a good listener as well as a good cook."

"Let me try the cooking first." Cally took a bite of the eggs. "Wow! That's one of the best omelets I've ever eaten. What did you season it with? I must not have been paying attention."

"That's one of my little secrets. I'll tell you when I get to know you better." Dawn poured coffee for both of them.

"Well, guess I'll have to stick around so I can learn the secret."

"Hopefully that isn't the only reason you'll want to be my friend." Dawn held Cally's gaze.

Cally felt a familiar tug in her solar plexus and quickly changed the subject. "This is all delicious, Dawn. Thanks for offering it. I planned to grab something over at City Bakery."

"Sounds like you've got plans for the day."

"I do. I'm going to look around an old house in Montford. Tate—you know, my friend who found Gampa for me—she found this place, which led her to Gampa, and . . . wait. I'm rambling.

"Rambling is fine. There's no place I'd rather be right now." Dawn's smile matched her sentiment.

"That's very generous of you, Dawn. Are you always like this with women you hardly know?"

"Only the ones I find especially interesting."

"Oh, I . . ." Cally didn't respond to the obvious come-on.

"So tell me about the place and about your visit yesterday."

As they finished breakfast and a second cup of coffee, Cally talked briefly about the old house in Montford and shared the highlights of the previous day. She emphasized how much her grandfather and the staff at Forest Glen had enjoyed the homemade brownies and thanked Dawn again for helping with them. Cally found herself relaxing into the conversation and enjoying Dawn's company, but she took care not to mention how emotionally draining the past few days had been.

"Sounds like you've been in quite a whirlwind."

"For sure. It's been up and down, but mostly up and filled with surprises. I can't even begin to say what it's been like to find Gampa again after all these years. That's probably the best thing that's ever happened in my entire life."

"I guess it'll be pretty hard to leave him when you head back to Los Angeles."

"Funny you should bring that up." Cally considered how much to share. "I may not be going back."

"Really?"

"This place feels like home to me. It *is* home. There's no reason to go back to L.A. At least not a good enough one to make me want to return."

"But what about work? And all your friends?"

"I don't need to work . . . at least not for a while. And it's obvious to me I can make friends here."

A broad smile creased Dawn's face. "I'm happy to hear that."

"I've only known Tate for a few days, and she's the best friend I've ever had. Sounds strange, but . . ."

"It doesn't sound strange to me. She gave you back your grandfather, and from what I can tell, you've been longing for a connection to your past your whole life."

Cally began weeping. She dabbed her tears away with her napkin and took a deep breath to help rein in her emotions.

"It's okay, Cally. You can cry in front of me."

"It may be okay with you, but it isn't with me. I'm a pretty strong woman . . . very strong, really. But I've been crying at the drop of a hat for days, and I'm getting pretty tired of it."

"Well, then. I won't encourage any more of it!" Dawn clapped her hands together twice. "Buck up, little cowgirl!" Cally burst into laughter and Dawn joined in.

"Now that's just what I needed. Thanks!"

"You're more than welcome." Dawn noticed Cally had not finished her meal. "Are you done with that, or would you like to finish it? I can brew more coffee . . ."

"I'm done. You have things to do, I'm sure, and so do I. But thanks, Dawn. This has been an unexpected pleasure."

"I'm glad you joined me, Cally. I hope we'll have more little get-togethers like this in the future."

"I'm looking forward to it. I'll see you again, soon, I'm sure."

Dawn sang a little song to herself as she began picking up the dishes and watching Cally depart.

—⁓—

Finding her way around Asheville became easier each time Cally ventured out on her own. Everything had seemed a jumble when she'd first arrived, but now she recognized the old streets from her childhood and had a good understanding of the new routes that had emerged when the Interstate cut a wide swath through town. She took her time, winding her way through the pretty side streets, checking out the trendy shops and restaurants that now occupied the old, restored buildings. Eventually she parked at the curb in front of 305 Chestnut Street.

Yesterday she'd sat at this same spot with Tate after the intense meeting with Richard Price, and she'd felt overwhelmed. Huge, dilapidated, ugly . . . those words flooded her mind then and she made a vow now that she would try to see the place as Tate saw it: a thing worthy of being cherished and brought back to life. It would be demolished unless someone took immediate action. But, try as she might, no vision of beauty materialized as she studied the tired, old house. She wanted to simply drive away and forget Tate's haunting words of the previous afternoon: "I think it belongs to you, now, Cally."

But those words had been spoken, and they had landed hard on Cally. She'd felt the truth of them reverberating through her body. *An unwelcome responsibility. That's what this place is. Why does Tate love it so much? What on earth will I ever do with it?* Those thoughts rolled around in Cally's mind as she left the car and reluctantly climbed the crumbling steps to inspect her destiny. Most often, life's challenges are immediately obvious. The same cannot be said for life's blessings.

Cally noticed everything wrong with the house and property at 305 Chestnut—its overgrown and ragged landscaping, tawdry bits of colored glass embedded in the retaining wall, moldy paint, missing cedar shakes, sagging gutters, grimy windows, pock-marked front door. Everywhere she looked she saw decay and sadness. She *felt* it, too, as if by stepping onto the property, she'd crossed an invisible boundary into a web of gloom and sorrow and left the living world behind.

A man passing on the sidewalk below noticed her car, looked up and saw her. A startled expression captured his face as he quickened his pace and hurried away as if he'd seen a ghost. *No one loves this place. They even try not to see it.* That thought broke through Cally's sense of dysphoria, and she remembered seeing people respond in a similar way to her mother. Rita had become invisible the deeper she sank into depression and alcoholism, and the world had shrunk away from her until only Cally remained. *Ragged, sagging, tawdry — they could all describe Mom, too.*

Anguish took Cally prisoner as the unexpected comparison between her mother and the old house exploded. She doubled over from a piercing pain in her solar plexus. Willing herself to move, she stumbled whimpering around the corner to the back porch where she dropped to the floor under the long row of kitchen windows. She curled into a fetal position and sobbed until her grief-induced flash flood of tears subsided.

Exhausted, she rolled onto her back, pulled her knees up and stuffed her bunched-up jacket under her head, then fell into a state of deep contemplation. She lay there for a long time, drifting in and out of awareness, revisiting times with her mother, both good and bad, the precious moments she'd recently spent with Leland, being read to while she rested in Ellie's arms and a raft of other memories and images. The slow motion chronicle floated through her awareness like a discombobulated version of the old television show *This is Your Life*, and she fell into it, reliving the ups and downs without judgment or remorse.

She may have slept, she couldn't be sure, but she came back to alertness when a ray of sunshine picked its way through the nearly bare branches of a huge maple tree and played along the surface of her face. She shivered in the chill, stretched out to her full length, sat up and leaned against the wall. She felt something poking into her back, and as she turned to see what it was, she spied the expansive kitchen. She caught her breath at the sight of it.

Cally's long-held-but-never-realized dream of becoming a gourmet cook sprang to the surface. She envisioned an array of colorful, fresh ingredients laid out on the white-tiled counter tops, pots bubbling on the vintage stove, the aroma of hand-crafted bread emanating from the oven, all of it crystal clear. And it surprised her to find Dawn standing beside her in the imagined domestic mecca rather than Tate.

Cally realized her earlier feeling of foreboding had vanished and been replaced by a sense of anticipation, perhaps even excitement. Maybe the place could be saved, *should* be saved, after all, as Tate believed. And just maybe she was the person to do it.

With renewed energy, Cally surveyed the house and grounds with an eye to how it could be restored to its optimal condition. She knew little about owning property or the various aspects of construction and rehabilitation. She would need experts, a trusted team to guide her and carry out the work. Tate would help with that. And she would need money. She had her savings and investments, a substantial retirement fund. She could sell the condominium in Los Angeles . . . but she had no idea if what she had would be sufficient for the monumental task of rescuing the house. *It will be my house, mine! I need to own it in my heart before I can even think about owning it on paper.*

Cally took her time walking the property, poking into corners and peeking into windows. She found a rusted glider languishing in the brush under the maple tree, a broken birdbath of blue glazed tiles buried under layers of moldering leaves, a wasp's nest cemented under the gutters of a second floor balcony. She sat for a bit on the edge of the old fish pond and absentmindedly pulled up some of the weeds growing there. With every new discovery and each small gesture, she took another step toward possession of the house. By the time she headed back to her car, the place belonged to her and she had fallen in love with it, even in its decrepitude. Now she would have to find a way to make her ownership legal.

Cally had lost all sense of time since she'd parked and climbed the steps to the house. When she reached the car, she realized with a jolt she had not called Tate as promised. She reached for her phone and remembered suddenly that she had left it on the nightstand. She returned to the hotel as quickly as possible and dialed Tate's number, eager to make plans to meet for dinner and share the day's discoveries and decisions. She just needed a few hours to herself to reconcile all the new plans forming in her mind.

FORTY-NINE
2004

T ate headed back to Asheville after making arrangements with John Hathburn to get the mantel ready for pickup. If Cally didn't want it, she would keep it.

Where is Cally, anyway? Why won't she answer my calls? Tate had tried to reach her three times since waking and Cally's lack of response worried her. But Tate also recognized another feeling hovering under the surface, one uncommon for her. She felt disappointed about not having someone to share this adventure with. That, piled on top of the swamp of emotions she'd just survived, added up to the beginning of a really foul mood.

A niggling resentment crept into Tate's awareness, and she tried to swallow it away. The letdown she experienced had grown out of her assumption that she and Cally would spend the day together even though Cally had made no such promise. *That's on me, not her.*

Accepting responsibility for her feelings did little to assuage them, so Tate turned her attention to her to-do list. Check in with Dave and then . . . what? Plenty of things awaited her attention, but none captivated her like finding the mantel. *Need to shake this off, get out of my head . . .*

The phone rang and Tate picked up immediately.

"Hey, Tate. It's me. How are you doing?" Cally sounded perky and that poked at Tate's already grumpy mood.

"Driving down the road. Shouldn't be on the cell phone, but I hoped it was you. Been trying to reach you all day."

"I know. I'm really sorry about that. I left the hotel without my phone and didn't realize it until half an hour ago. I meant to call much earlier." Cally sounded truly apologetic, and Tate felt her annoyance beginning to slip away.

"Oh. That makes sense. Where are you now?"

"Back at the hotel, just now. It's been an eventful day. Can we meet later, maybe for dinner, and I'll tell you all about it?"

Tate checked the time—3:45. "I've got a better idea, Cally. There's something I'd like to show you, and we can do it today if we leave soon. I could pick you up."

"That sounds mysterious, Tate, but I'm really exhausted. Can it wait?"

"Of course it could, but . . ." Tate's eagerness to show Cally the mantel overrode her ability to tune into her friend's reluctance. ". . . well, if you really don't want to go, then it'll have to wait." Snappish. Impatient. Not what she intended, but her comment had come out that way nonetheless.

"Sounds like it's important to you, Tate. Want to tell me where we'd be going?"

"Not unless you insist. I promise it will be a nice surprise." She tried to tone down her attitude.

"Another surprise? I'm too tired to cry like a baby again, and it seems that's all I've been doing lately when faced with surprises."

"I can't guarantee you won't cry, Cally, but I'm ninety-nine percent sure you're gonna love it."

"Then I guess I can't refuse. I'll wait for you downstairs." Cally did not sound enthusiastic.

"I'll be there in ten minutes, fifteen tops. See you shortly."

Tate should have known better. Her nerves were raw and her mood irritable. Together they created a volatile cocktail that usually triggered the anger she so arduously tried to avoid. She should have headed directly home and isolated herself until she felt more in control. She should not have pushed Cally or herself into another emotionally charged situation. But once she set her mind on something, even common sense could not divert her.

—◦◦◦—

Cally seemed quiet as Tate drove back to Weaverville. Although she chatted about the weather and delicious breakfast with Dawn, she side-stepped revealing what had kept her so busy all day, even after Tate made a couple of attempts to open that conversation. Cally made her own effort to discover the nature of the impending surprise, but Tate remained tight-lipped.

Tate found Cally's behavior confusing. *She's withholding something. I hate it when people do that. Give me a hint of something important, then I'm supposed to guess what it is or live with the suspense.* Ever since they'd met, Cally had been open and easily shared her feelings and thoughts. Now she slouched in the seat and closed her eyes, making herself even more inaccessible. Tate sat with the uncomfortable silence and fought against her urge to withdraw into anger. Disappointment reared up again, nearly extinguishing her excitement about finding the lost fireplace. By the time she parked the truck in front of Conservation Salvage, Tate felt completely deflated. She also realized she had pushed Cally hard to make the trip even though Cally had made it clear she wanted some down time.

"We're here?" Cally roused herself as Tate pulled into a parking space.

"Yeah, this is the place."

"What is it? Looks like an antique shop."

"Something like that. Listen, Cally. I'm sorry. I pushed you to come here when you obviously didn't want to. We can come back another time. I'll take you back to the hotel."

"No, Tate. Don't do that. I'm just wiped out, and I have so much I want to tell you, but I need some time to process it for myself before I share all of it with you."

"Is that why you've been so quiet all the way here? That's so unlike you."

"Actually, it is like me, at least a lot of the time. But I haven't been like that with you, and I think it scares me a little."

"I scare you, Cally?"

"No, not you specifically. Just that I opened up to you immediately and that you know so much about me, about all the things I've lost and how hurtful it's been and . . . I just don't share that stuff with people easily."

"Well, it would have been hard to avoid, don't you think? Given how we met and each of us having such a strong connection with Leland and all?"

"Point well taken, but still . . ." Cally closed her eyes again, took a couple of deep breaths and let a few tears roll down her cheeks. ". . . I'm emotionally raw, Tate. I feel like I'm caught in a whirlwind and being sucked into quicksand all at the same time. I can't find my balance. I feel like a wimp, a crybaby, a basket case. And I really don't like being like this or having you see me like this."

Tate took it all in. She could see the toll the past several days had taken on her new friend. *New friend.* Hard to believe she had met Cally only four days ago. It seemed like they'd shared a lifetime already. She could keep that to herself, or she could follow Cally's lead, open up, share herself with another person.

"I know how you're feeling, Cally." She managed to squeeze the words out, guiding them carefully past her resistance and the lump forming in her throat.

"I'm not sure you do, Tate. *You* don't cry every time something crosses your path."

"No, I don't. That's because I've spent most of my life learning to keep my feelings to myself, with a few notable exceptions."

"What would those exceptions be, exactly?"

"Anger, for one. That's the biggest one. I'm not proud of it . . . actually, I probably am, as sick as that sounds!"

"Proud of being angry?"

"Well, yeah. I guess that would be one way to describe it. Anger isn't pretty, Cally, I'm not saying that. But it protects me and keeps me moving forward."

"Really?" Cally stared at Tate wide-eyed.

"Really. Instead of getting scared, or anxious or depressed or . . . almost anything, I get angry. That energizes me, I get really focused, and I push through whatever it is. At least that's usually what happens. Of course, it pisses other people off and they avoid me like the plague—but that's really the only downside I see!"

Cally started laughing, and Tate followed suit. "I love to hear you laugh, Tate. But I wonder if that's another defense?"

"Well, it's a way of defusing my own anger. And I do have a wicked sense of humor that I'm pretty proud of, too."

Cally reached for Tate's hand and gently kissed it. "I love you, Tate Marlowe. I truly do. I've only known you a few days, but we're going to be friends for the rest of our lives."

"Even if I get angry with you sometimes?"

"I'm way tougher than you may think. And I don't scare easily."

"That's good to hear."

"And don't be surprised if I call you on that anger, should you ever direct it at me."

"I would really, truly appreciate that, Cally, more than I can say. Most people just walk away from me when they see that part. It never occurs to them that underneath the anger is a lot of pain."

"Now I know, Tate."

"Yes, you do. And that's scary!"

"Good. Then we're even!"

"We are, and we're even in another way, too."

"How's that?"

Tate hesitated. She didn't like revealing herself, but in some way she felt she owed it to Cally. "Well, I had my own meltdown today—right here, as a matter-of-fact." Tate nodded toward the storefront.

"You had a meltdown in an antique store?"

"I sure did. I think the owner was about to call the paddy wagon on me."

"That's hard to imagine. You're so strong and I've never seen you even a little bit out of control."

"Then you wouldn't have recognized me a couple of hours ago, Cally. I sat on the floor and bawled like a baby. And I have to say I felt a lot better afterwards."

"I bet you did."

"But it's exhausting. I rarely cry, but when I was here, I saw several things that reminded me of my childhood—good memories, wonderful ones—but gut-wrenching at the same time." Tate began tearing up and quickly wiped her eyes dry.

"It's okay, Tate."

"Ahhhh . . . I have to stop! I hate this!" Tate took several deep breaths followed by long sighs, regaining a bit of control with each round. Cally sat quietly and waited.

Tate's composure returned and she shook herself a bit then took the keys out of the ignition. "Okay, I think I'm ready to go. How 'bout you?"

Cally let out a long sigh of her own. "I guess so. Let's see what the big surprise is."

———

John Hathburn looked up as Tate and Cally entered the shop. "Hi. Didn't expect you back so soon. It's not ready yet."

"No problem, John . . ."

Cally interrupted them. "What's not ready yet?"

"I brought the friend I mentioned, John. This is Cally. Can we go back there?"

"What's not ready yet?" Cally insisted.

"I found something, Cally. Something incredibly special."

John watched the two women, noticing the tenseness building in Cally as well as Tate's efforts to maintain her own composure. "Go on then. Want me to go with you?"

"It's okay, John. Actually I'd prefer it be just the two of us, if you don't mind."

"Sure. Go on back. Call if you need me." He hoped he would not have to witness another storm of emotion from either of them.

Tate headed for the door into the warehouse and motioned for Cally to follow. They worked their way through the aisles of old furniture.

"How'd you find this place, Tate?"

"Long story. I'll tell you later."

"Why'd you bring me here? What'd you find?"

"I had a dream last night. I was on *Wheel of Fortune*, and just as I woke up, I solved a puzzle . . ."

"Very interesting, but it doesn't answer my question!"

"Don't you want to know what it said?" Tate enjoyed building the suspense. Cally, however, wanted no part of it.

"NO! I want to know why I'm here, Tate."

Tate persisted. "The answer to the puzzle was 'Where's the fireplace?'"

Cally glared. "Where's the fireplace? *What* fireplace?"

"Exactly! The fireplace that used to be in my house. Leland and Ellie's old house."

"You mean . . ." Cally stared at her wide-eyed.

"You know, Cally. There used to be a fireplace in my house and it's not there anymore, remember?"

Cally dropped her head into her hands and shook it several times. "I remember, yes, I remember. But it's gone, you told me that."

"It *was* gone, Cally."

"It *was* gone, and now it's not gone? That makes no sense!"

"It was gone and now it's found."

"Found?"

"Found!"

"Here? You mean you found it . . . here?"

"Right here, where it's been ever since they took it out of the house, ten, maybe fifteen years ago."

Cally propped her hands on her knees and began taking deep, slow breaths. "I . . . am . . . not . . . going . . . to . . . cry!" She uttered one word each time she exhaled. And she did not cry. She stood up and declared: "Show it to me!"

"I thought you'd never ask!" Tate grabbed Cally's hand and began trotting toward their destination.

As they approached the collection of mantels, Cally immediately noticed the one sticking partway out into the aisle. She rushed over, brushed off some of the dust and rested both hands on the top.

The laying on of hands. The thought hit Tate as she watched Cally, head bowed, eyes closed as if communing with a living being. *She's healing it. They're healing each other. And me.*

Cally turned to Tate. "This is it, isn't it."

"Yes."

"Gampa made this?"

"Yes."

"And my initials are here? You're sure this is the right one?"

"Yes."

Cally knelt down and searched the wood panel with her fingers for the scars she had etched so long ago. She found them and the tears refused to be held back again. Tate sat down on the floor with her and waited for several minutes.

Cally finally spoke. "I can't believe it, Tate."

"It's true."

"How'd you find it?"

"When I woke up from that dream this morning, I just knew the fireplace was somewhere, that it had not been destroyed. So I went to the library and . . . no!" Tate stopped abruptly. "Short version!" She hissed the command aloud, looked at Cally and started again. "I called the guy I bought the house from. He came over. He told me he sold the fireplace. To John. After he moved the house to the current location. I came here looking for it. I found it. Here we are!"

Cally grinned. "That's the shortest version of anything I've ever heard from you."

"Thank you! It was a monumental effort."

Tate reached for Cally's hand and they sat quietly for a few moments. "You know there's one more thing to do, Cally . . ."

"I know, Tate. I'm working up my courage."

"A part of me wanted to look when I was here earlier, but I just couldn't."

"I appreciate that."

"I'm not known for restraint any more than I am for succinctness . . ."

"It must have been torturous for you . . ."

"Hard, difficult, but not torturous. She left it for you, not me."

"Do you think it's still in there?"

"Only one way to find out."

"Only one way. And I have to know, even though it may break my heart."

"Okay, then. Want to look now?"

"I have to."

They stood up and Cally faced the mantel. She began running her finger along the underside of the top piece, listening carefully for the faint click heralding success. She reached the other end without the hoped-for reward and turned to Tate. "You try."

Tate knew instinctively she could not honor Cally's request, that to do so would diminish Cally's experience of finding the gift awaiting her if it was still there. "No, Cally. You try again."

"Please, Tate . . ."

"Tell me, Cally. Do you remember watching your grandmother open the compartment?"

"Yes, oh yes. It was magical!"

"Think back to that moment. See her doing it. Where does she put her finger? How does she move it? Do it just like she did."

Cally started again. She placed her index finger on the mantel and paused, deep in concentration, then adjusted her position slightly, moving her touch a bit lower on the edge of the mantel. She traced carefully along the surface, feeling each groove of the carved design. They both held their breath. The only movement in the warehouse was Cally's searching finger and the dust motes floating in the air. Then . . . the click . . . echoing through the silence. They gasped in unison as the secret compartment fell open.

Cally stood on her tiptoes and peered in. She threw her hands up to her mouth. "There's something in there!" She wrapped her arms around Tate's neck and they jumped up and down together, weeping and laughing all at the same time.

"It's still here, Tate! I can't believe it!" Cally reached into the drawer and pulled out a small velvet jewelry pouch. She upended it and a diamond ring dropped into her open hand.

"This was my great-grandmother's! Gamma showed it to me." Cally turned the tiny ring over and held it up to a shaft of light so it sparkled.

"It's beautiful. Does it fit you?"

"I don't know. It's so small . . ." Cally tried to slip it onto her ring finger but it wouldn't move past the first knuckle. "Nope. But I could wear it on a chain . . ."

"That you could."

"There's more stuff in there, Tate." Cally looked frightened, like a small child who had been caught dipping into the cookie jar without permission.

"It's all yours, Cally. I already bought it and I'm giving it to you."

"No! Really?"

Yes, really. So it's okay to look."

"I know, but it seems . . . strange. Seeing these things again, whatever they are. Gamma was the last person who touched them."

Cally took a moment to brace herself, then reached back into the compartment. She pulled out a tortoise-shell hair comb. "Oh, I remember this, too. It belonged to Gamma's grandmother, so that's my . . . great-great-grandmother! I've never touched anything so old."

Tate bent close to see the comb. The magnificent piece measured nearly the full length of her hand and about two inches wide. It sported dark brown and orange blotches scattered on a pale amber-colored background. She knew nothing about antique combs, but she imagined this one to be quite valuable. "It's beautiful, Cally."

"I remember it. Gamma kept it, but I think it made her unhappy."

"Really? Why?"

"Something about turtles dying for the sake . . . something. I had no idea what she meant, but I remember her saying it and looking so sad."

"Oh! Of course. Real tortoise-shell is probably illegal, like ivory."

"You mean owning it is a crime?"

"Well, probably not. If this is an antique, it could date back to long before laws banning it were passed."

"Gamma must have kept it because it's a family heirloom."

"You could get it appraised, Cally. Have an expert look at it and give you some advice."

Cally held the ring and the comb close to her chest. "Yes, that's a good idea." She seemed pensive.

"How you doin'?"

"I'm okay . . . actually, I'm frazzled. I had a long day before coming here, and there are more things in the drawer . . ."

"Do you want to leave them there for now?"

"I can't. I know they've been safely hidden for decades, but now that I've found them, I'm terrified of losing them again." Cally took a deep breath and removed two more items.

The first was a blue bank book with gold lettering and worn edges. She opened it slowly. Inside she found her name in flowing cursive in the varying shades of black and gray typical of fountain pen writing: *Calliope Ann Thornton*. Speechless, she handed the book to Tate.

"Ellie must have opened this account for you." Tate pointed to the date of the first deposit. "Look. Over a hundred dollars in 1961. It's probably inactive now, but I bet you can still claim the money somehow."

"It's priceless, no matter what." Cally gently tapped her own chest above her heart with the palm of her hand. "*She* left it for *me*."

417

"She obviously loved you, Cally. She took care to leave you these precious things." Tate noticed that Cally held one more item in her hand. "What's that?"

"I don't know. It's a letter . . . or something. It scares me."

"Why?"

"It just does. I don't think it's from Gamma. I'm not sure I want to open it."

"You don't have to, Cally . . ."

"She left it for some reason . . ."

"But still . . ."

"She wanted me to read it, whatever it is."

"Still . . ."

Cally couldn't know she was about to discover a secret Ellie had kept even in death. She slowly slipped the folded note paper out of its yellowed envelope and read it aloud:

> My Confession
>
> My name is Harland Clayton Freeman. I was born on March 21, 1910. I am unmarried and the owner of Freeman's Mercantile in Asheville, North Carolina. I am a very successful businessman and I have accumulated a sizable fortune. I think this makes me important, but really I am a cad. When I was in high school I used my popularity as an athlete to bed as many girls as I could. I didn't care who they were, and I paid no heed to the consequences my behavior might cause them. I bragged to my friends about my conquests because I thought

it made me popular. Now I know it made me despicable. Regardless of my success as a businessman, I am a complete failure as a human being. In March of 1927, I seduced Marie Eleanor Vance and fathered a child with her. Then I walked away and denied all responsibility for the child's existence. The boy's name is Clayton Samuel Howard. Ellie married my cousin, Leland Samuel Howard, who is raising the boy as his own and is a far better father to him than I ever would have been.

I would never have admitted to this except that I'm a greedy man who will do whatever I must to get what I want. I want Leland Howard to build a fancy door for my new house and he said no. I won't accept no for an answer, so I cornered Ellie and threatened her so she would convince Leland to change his mind. In exchange, she demanded I write this confession, and I do so willingly since getting my way is of utmost importance to me. I have no wife and no children born legitimately at this time, and I do not expect to acquire such burdens in the future. Therefore the only person with the right to claim my fortune when I die is Clayton Samuel Howard, the child I fathered with Ellie.

Signed: Harland Clayton Freeman
December 19, 1940

FIFTY
2004

Neither woman seemed able to speak when Cally finished reading Harland's note. Until that moment, he had not been a main character in the story Tate had pieced together about 305 Chestnut Street, even though he had built the place. Now everything had shifted.

The world's tipped sideways. Somehow, Tate understood that Ellie had secured the confession and that it had been a high price for Harland to pay.

Tate watched Cally closely. After placing the note back in the envelope, Cally had stuffed all the items from the secret compartment into her jacket pocket, closed the drawer and stepped a few paces away. She now sat cross-legged on the floor with her back to Tate, rocking herself gently.

Tate stayed put and sat quietly while several chains of thought fought for dominance in her busy mind.

Fragments of the puzzle banged into each other and began arranging themselves in appropriate alignment with the other pieces, spreading out in a vast, shifting, three-dimensional tableau. Ellie, Harland, Leland, Clayton, murder, love, desperation, anger, revenge, suicide, doors, secret pacts, facts, conjecture . . . all of them falling into place and fitting together finally into a comprehensible whole. She did not know all the details. Nonetheless, Tate began to understand the saga from beginning to end. But putting it into words . . . how could she possibly do that? Maybe in the end it wasn't even important. Each of the players had done what they'd done. They made decisions and set themselves on a path. A path that led to this moment. None of it mattered except Cally. And Leland. And the house at 305 Chestnut Street.

And me. I matter, too. At least I should. But why? None of this really has to do with me, does it?

Cally rose and turned to Tate. "This changes everything." She said this quietly then turned and walked back toward the shop entrance.

Both women took the ride back to town in near silence. Tate drove on auto-pilot as she rambled through memories from her childhood.

As a child, her family had visited the farms of her two great-grandmothers several times a year. She had been allowed to wander those farms alone, meandering through the pastures and outbuildings, often for hours at a time. During those visits Tate had experienced a freedom and adventure missing from her usual home life.

In Grandma Strauss' barn, strips of wood nailed to support beams formed a steep ladder up to the hayloft. After scaling to what seemed like a dizzying height, Tate would sink into the scratchy, sweet hay and bury herself, with only her nose and eyes still visible. Lying there, she listened to the rhythm of her own breath, to the chirps and buzz of birds and insects, the creaking of old timbers and the rustling of small animals scurrying through the dark corners of the cavernous building.

Cally's voice broke through Tate's reverie as they reached the outskirts of Asheville. "You seem really far away."

"I was." Tate sighed, but did not speak.

"Away where?"

"My grandma's house. Grandma Strauss, actually my great-grandmother. I was at her farm, laying in the hayloft in her barn. It was one of my favorite places."

"What did you like about it?"

"Pretty much everything. The smells were amazing. Cow manure, decaying straw, weathered wood, old leather yokes and saddles . . ."

"You liked the smell of manure?" Cally's question signaled her disbelief.

"Well, yeah. I did. I know that sounds weird, but fresh cow manure has this pungent, earthy aroma that has a way of anchoring you to the land, if you know what I mean."

"Sounds yucky, but it's obviously a fond memory for you. What else do you remember?"

"It's odd. I don't have a lot of memories about my childhood, just some snapshots of different places and events. I remember the outhouse. I clearly didn't like that! It was spooky to have to use it for a bathroom, especially at night. But she had cows and a horse, pigs, barn cats, a huge garden. The old water trough for the horse had a big fish swimming in it. It was a magical place for a kid. You learn a lot about life being on a farm even briefly, and we visited often."

Cally shifted in her seat a bit and seemed to visibly release some of the tension she had been holding ever since Tate had picked her up earlier that afternoon. "I've only lived in Asheville and Los Angeles. In fact, I don't remember ever being on a farm. There was a neighbor near Nana's house here in town who had chickens. I got to help them collect the eggs once. That was fun."

"Well, then, sounds like a trip to a working farm should be in your future, Cally."

"I can't think about going anywhere just now. I'm exhausted. Tell me more about your grandmother's farm, please."

Tate thought about Cally's request. Should she tell more of her pleasant memories from childhood or dip into the tightly held stories buried in her past? Tate did not easily open herself to others, but the possibility of doing so now, with Cally, kept creeping into her awareness. And after the revelations Cally had just endured, Tate's secrets seemed small in comparison, but they loomed large for her.

"What if I told you about something awful I did once? Would you hate me?"

Cally had not been fully engaged in the conversation until now. She sat up straight and stared at Tate. "I would love to hear about it, though I can't imagine you ever doing anything awful."

"We all have a dark side, Cally. Or at least memories of things we wish we could take back."

"Yeah, I guess we all do."

"I usually learn from my mistakes and move on. I don't hang onto things much, you know? But there's this one thing that happened at Grandma Strauss' farm that I'm still ashamed of to this day."

"I want to know all of you, Tate, not just the good part, which is what I see all the time. Tell me, please."

"Well . . . I . . . when I was little I . . ." Tate cleared her throat and her grip tightened on the steering wheel.

Cally waited quietly for Tate to continue.

"When I was maybe 9 or 10, we were visiting Grandma Strauss. I went out to the barn like I often did. There was a new litter of kittens, maybe a couple of months old. We weren't allowed to have pets at home, and I wanted to play with one of them really bad. Barn cats are only semi-tame. I'd tried to catch one many times before, but they always got away. That day, I saw one playing with a half-dead mouse, and I pounced before it could scramble out of reach." Tate could feel the lump growing in her throat and the heat of shame rising up her chest and covering her face. "This is hard to tell."

"Take your time." Cally had never seen Tate so upset.

Tate took a couple of deep breaths before continuing. "So, I grabbed this little kitten and held her tight. She was a gray tabby, really tiny, and so cute. I remembered someone telling me that cats always land on their feet, and I wanted to see if that was true. I threw her up in the air as high as I could and it was just like they said. She flipped in the air and landed right-side up. I found this thrilling. As soon as she hit the ground, I grabbed her and threw her up again, even higher."

Tate glanced quickly at Cally. She saw in her friend's face anticipation and concern—and enough acceptance that she felt willing to continue.

"I think the kitten must have been scared nearly to death and disoriented, because this time she landed squarely on her nose and it began bleeding. I thought I had killed her and I tried to pick her up again. I think I wanted to cuddle her, you know, rock her and soothe her the way a mother does an injured child. But she got away, and all I saw were the little drops of blood she left behind." Guilt coursed through Tate's body, transporting her back to the instant the kitten had hit the floor of the barn and sprinted away. She tried unsuccessfully to stem the tears forming in her eyes.

Cally touched her arm gently. "That must have been awful."

"Way past awful. I don't know which was worse— feeling sick that I had hurt an innocent animal or being terrified that my dad would find out and I'd get a whipping."

"You got a *whipping*?" Cally seemed shocked.

"No, not that time. He didn't find out about the kitten. I don't think anyone did. I snuck back out the barn a couple of times to look for her, but I never saw her again."

Cally did not ask about the whipping. Instead, she let Tate finish her story. "Do you think the kitten died?"

"Probably not. At least now, as an adult, I imagine she just got bruised and more than likely healed just fine. Every time I remember that day though, I still get this sick feeling in my stomach, this overwhelming feeling of shame and guilt, just like I had in that moment. I've never told anyone about it before."

"Thank you for telling me, Tate."

"You don't hate me? Think I'm an awful person?"

"You were a kid. You were as innocent as that kitten. You didn't intentionally hurt her."

"No, it was definitely not intentional, but that didn't change the impact on the kitten. I've carried that lesson through my whole life."

"It made you a better person, I think."

"I hope it did, but I'm not always so sure."

"What do you mean?"

"Well, I don't intentionally go around hurting people. I learned that day to think about what I do and that my actions may impact others in ways I can't predict. But I also believe other people are responsible for how they feel about something I may have done that they find aggravating."

"I'm not sure I follow. Give me an example."

Tate thought for a moment before answering. "Okay, so say I'm having a really bad day. I'm in physical pain or I've just gotten some distressing news . . . something like that. You call me up and I answer and snap out a greeting that oozes with my frustration or whatever it is . . ."

"Okay."

"... and you don't understand why I'm snapping ..."

"Yeah ..."

"... well, a situation like that could go in a bunch of different directions. You could assume I'm having a bad day and ask me what's wrong. You could assume I'm angry at you and you could get angry right back at me. You could take it as a personal slight and silently add it to the list of grievances you're collecting against me. Or any number of other responses, right?"

"You think I'm collecting grievances?"

"No, of course not. Maybe once you've known me for longer you might. I hope not, but . . . people do collect grievances, don't they?"

"Okay, I see what you're saying ..."

"So, all I did was express what I was feeling in the moment, unfiltered. You hear what I say, how I say it, and you make an assumption about what it means to you or about you. And if you take it personally, you may get annoyed with me and then blame me for upsetting you. But if you do that, it really isn't the result of what I said or did, it's the result of the story you made up about it and what it means to you."

"You really believe that?"

"I really, truly do."

"But you snapped at me for no reason. Hypothetically."

"See, that's just it, Cally. I snapped. I didn't snap at you in the sense of targeting you with my bad mood. I just expressed my raw feelings and you happened to be the one who heard them. If I hadn't answered the phone in this scenario, or if you hadn't called, or if someone had knocked on my door unexpectedly . . . it could have been anyone or no one who heard that expression of whatever I was feeling. I didn't do anything other than not greet you in the friendly way you would have liked me to."

"So what if I said that to you? 'Tate, you didn't greet me the way I wanted you to.'"

"I would recognize the truth in your words and apologize. And I probably would explain and beg your forgiveness!"

"So no matter what happens, it's not your fault?"

"No, that's not what I'm saying. Sometimes I do things even when I know they'll come to a bad end, or when I should be aware of that possibility. Still, I do them anyway. And if that's the case, I take responsibility. Like this afternoon. You made it clear you wanted time to yourself, but I talked you into going to the salvage company with me."

"But I'm glad you did. Now I am, anyway."

"But you didn't want to go, and I knew that, and still I pushed my agenda. That was putting my needs above yours. We all do that, and sometimes, like this one, it works out okay. But if it hadn't, I'd be apologizing all over the place to you right now for having pressured you into going."

"I'm glad you pushed me, Tate."

"Okay, thanks for that. But there are other times when I do something and realize after the fact that I should have thought it out better first. I hurt someone, and it wasn't intentional, but it still resulted from my actions. I own it when I do something like that, and I try to make amends."

"Well, I think I understand better than when we started this conversation. You don't intentionally do hurtful things most of the time. When someone gets upset and you didn't do anything wrong, you don't let them put it on you. You sometimes are pushy and you own it. And sometimes you should think more before you act. Have I got it right?"

"Pretty close! And I don't kowtow to many of the social conventions about being nice and sweet and all that crap, either."

Cally noticed the tight smile beginning to curl the corners of Tate's mouth. "So, I guess we're done being serious, right?"

Tate's smile morphed into a grimace. "Yeah. I can only handle self-disclosure in small doses, and this has been a really big one!"

"Thanks for opening up to me some. It helps me to know you better."

"I trust you in ways I don't trust many people, Cally. That says more about you than it does about me."

They lapsed back into quiet for the remainder of the trip. Tate thought about how easily Cally had understood the point she was making about one person being held responsible for another person's feelings. If how one feels is the result of what she thinks—and Tate had no doubt at all that was the case—then what one feels about any particular situation lies directly in her own control. Change your thoughts and you change your feelings. Change your feelings and you gain control of your life.

Tate had done just that with years of practice, and she found it puzzling that so many people chose to hang onto the belief that they would be happier if only other people treated them the way they wanted. In Tate's world, if you don't like how someone treats you, you simply stop hanging out with them. Undoubtedly, that accounted for her shortage of close friends.

—⁓—

Tate eased the truck into the crowded drive in front of the Princess Hotel. "How are you doing, Cally?"

"I can't really tell. I'm pretty much of a mess, I think."

"That trip to Conservation Salvage was an emotional roller coaster for me. I can barely imagine what it was like for you."

"And that's only part of it."

"Really?"

"Yeah. That was the end of what had already been a very full day for me."

"Oh, right. You never told me what you did today."

Tate expected an answer that did not materialize. She waited, her anticipation building steadily. "Cally?"

"I went to that house today, Tate. I know time is running out."

"Oh! Wow!" The news rocked Tate to the core. "And then I forced you to find the fireplace and its contents! I'm so sorry, Cally."

"Actually, it's okay, Tate. I wouldn't have chosen it, but I'm glad I . . . I'm glad you found it and took me there. It's just that . . . I don't know . . . I always imagined somewhere in the back of my mind, in my heart, all the good things Gamma left for me. It never occurred to me that I'd find them after so long and . . . and it wouldn't be only good things. That note was so . . . shocking. I'm not sure . . ." Cally trailed off into thought.

"Not sure of what, Cally?"

"I'm not sure . . . who I am. I guess that's it. Leland is not my grandfather. This man named Harland is. And what he said in that note. Why would he say all that? And why would Gamma hide it away for me to find someday?"

Tate felt herself gearing up to come to Cally's rescue. She would reframe the situation, point out that Leland was, in fact, the grandfather Cally had known all her life and maybe he hadn't been Clayton's biological father, but he had been his real father, and he had been and still was a wonderful grandfather to Cally. She felt all this gathering and about to burst out of her mouth in a rush when she remembered that sometimes the kindest thing she could do for another person was to let them feel bad. Allow them the time and space and support to move through their feelings at their own pace. So she sat back, took Cally's hand in hers and allowed her friend to cry.

Several minutes passed before Cally spoke again. "You're not going to believe this, Tate. I don't . . . but I want to do one more thing today. Actually, two more things."

"Really? What?"

"Well, I haven't eaten since Dawn fixed me breakfast this morning, and I'm starving. So I'd like to get some dinner. Something quick and easy. And . . ."

"And . . .?"

"I want to see Gamma's house. Your house."

FIFTY-ONE
2004

Unexpected memories of being taught to read and write by Lee Lou filled Tate's thought as she carved out a picnic area in the living room of the house that once belonged to Leland and Ellie—the house Tate now called her own and the one that served as the closest thing to a real home Cally could remember.

Their plans had been formulated quickly as they sat outside the Princess Hotel. Cally wanted time to shower and change clothes. Tate wanted the same as well as leeway to prepare the apartment so that Cally would be able to look around without stumbling over equipment and materials.

Cally arrived just as Tate finished, and the aroma of Chinese take-out filled the open space when Cally entered toting two large bags of steaming food.

"I have to confess. I was so hungry I gobbled down an egg roll on the way here!" Cally offered the bags to Tate who began unpacking them and spreading the boxes of food out on the recently installed countertop.

"It's a little chilly in here, but I brought a couple of extra space heaters over, and it should be warming up pretty soon. Do you want a wrap?" Tate offered Cally one of the small throws she had picked up from her house next door.

"No, I think I'm okay, but thanks." Cally stopped and looked slowly around the large, open living and kitchen area. "This is so different from when Gamma and Gampa lived here. Are you sure it's the same place?"

"Yeah, it is. I know it has been changed a lot . . ." Tate pointed to the main entrance. "But I'll bet you remember that."

Cally walked over to the massive door and slowly traced the delicate scroll work that framed the panels with her finger. "Oh yes, I remember this very well. Gampa made it, but he never seemed to like it very much."

"Really? That surprises me. It's an amazing piece, and he obviously took great pains to construct it."

"Yes, but remember what he said? When we asked him about it? He said the door was a mistake and the only mean-spirited thing he'd ever done."

"Oh, you're right. I'd forgotten that. I wonder what he meant."

"I don't know, but it is beautiful. Much more so than the one on the other house."

"Okay, Cally. I know you're starving and I'm pretty hungry myself. Let's have some of this food, and I want to hear all about it."

Over a spread of egg rolls, hot and sour soup, vegetable lo mein, chicken with mixed vegetables and brown rice, Cally related the events of her day to Tate. She shared her awareness of the similarities between her mother's deteriorated condition from alcohol abuse and depression and the old house on Chestnut Street.

"I didn't *want* to want the place, Tate. I went there to confirm the decision I'd already made not to try to claim it. I knew that would disappoint you, but it just seemed so overwhelming and, really, that place is kind of weird. You know that, don't you?"

"Yes, of course. Weird, but compelling, too. At least for me, and I hoped it would be for you as well."

"I walked around it. I noticed how a neighbor on the street scurried away when he saw me there. That's when it hit me that people treat that house like they treated Mom. I had another one of my crying fits, right there on the back porch. When I finally sat up and saw that kitchen, it took my breath away!"

"Yeah, the kitchen got to me, too!"

Cally paused and pushed some cold food around on her plate with her chopsticks. "Well, I started looking at it differently then. I knew it would be mine one day, like it or not, and I left there ready to do whatever was necessary to keep it."

Tate noticed that Cally sounded resigned, not excited. "You don't seem so happy about that decision, though."

"I was when I left there. Until I read that note." Cally leaned back against the wall and released a deep sigh.

"When we were at the salvage company you said 'this changes everything.' What did you mean?" Tate braced herself to hear an answer she hoped would not come. *Please, Cally, help me save that house.* This thought surprised Tate, since she rarely wanted help from anyone.

"Well, Leland is not really my grandfather. I can't even begin to make sense of that!"

"But he is, Cally, in every way that's important. And from what that note says, he was a good father to Clayton as well."

"That house . . . I had hopes for it before . . . now it feels, well, *haunted!* I don't think I could live in a place where a greedy, arrogant man—one who happens to be my biological grandfather, no less!—killed himself. And why did he give the place to Leland? That just seems cruel since they obviously hated each other."

Tate took time to respond. She looked around the room where they sat and reviewed in her mind how it differed from what she had purchased less than a year earlier. "I'm not going to try to sway your decision, Cally. But I believe a house reflects the character of the people who live in it. This place for example. You know what it was like when you were a child and Ellie and Leland lived here. You loved the place. You still think of Asheville, and even this house, I bet, as home, right?"

Cally surveyed the room. "Well, yes. Sort of."

"That's the spot where the fireplace used to be." Tate indicated the missing floor boards at the hallway entrance and the space just to the right of it. "And you sat right about there when you carved your initials. It was a much different place, then, wasn't it?"

"Yes, it was. It was home, like you said."

"And then Ellie and Leland were gone, you were gone, other people lived here, and the place took on an entirely different feel. When I bought it, this place was a dump. The people who lived downstairs had filled the backyard with broken down trucks and cars, discarded furniture, at least a dozen old tires and I'm betting a thousand beer cans and bottles they'd thrown into the bushes."

"No way!"

"Yes. It was awful. They got into drunken brawls in the street all hours of the night. The cops were here routinely breaking things up. This place would have scared the pants off you."

"Why did you buy it?"

"Because I saw immediately what it could be. Just like I did when I saw the place on Chestnut. And I knew I could make it a happy, peaceful place again."

"And you have."

"And I have. And someone could do the same for Harland's house. Whatever unhappiness it has soaked up since it was built, in all those decades that it has sat empty and unloved, it doesn't matter. It can be a happy, vibrant place filled with joy if someone makes it that."

"But he must have been a horrible person. I hate being related to him. If a house can hold a person's energy, then that place reflects all his negative traits, doesn't it?"

"Cally, we can't ever know what drove Harland Freeman. But I truly believe that each and every one of us, even the most detestable among us, does the very best he can at any given moment. Why not give him, and the house, the benefit of the doubt?"

"I wish I knew more about him. You really think he had good qualities, too?"

Tate suddenly remembered her recent conversation with Mazie. "Actually, I know someone who can tell you a lot about Harland Freeman. Her name is Mazie and she lives right across the street! I'll take you to meet her if you want."

"Now?"

"No, not now. Mazie is up there in years and is likely asleep by now. Or nodding out in front of the TV. Soon, though. If you want."

"Yes, I think that would be good. But, Tate. I still don't really understand why you seem so gung ho about that old place."

"Actually, it is routed in my very earliest years. I was just thinking about it before you got here."

"Tell me, then."

Tate shared her memories of Lee Lou and her own personalized Head Start program with Cally, and as she did so, she felt her heart open a bit more to this woman whom she had met only days before.

Tate's closeness with Cally and her willingness to share such personal parts of herself came as a surprise. A lifetime of believing she could depend on no one but herself had ensured that Tate would have countless experiences to confirm that tightly held conviction. The permeable barrier she had constructed to protect herself allowed support to flow in one direction only. Tate could reach out and care for others but she would rarely accept the same from them. She had diligently devised numerous ways to deflect nearly every offer of help she saw coming, and those defenses had become so much a part of her that she no longer recognized them as things of her own creation.

Cally willingly shared some of the most painful aspects of her life with Tate. She cried openly, laughed easily and seemed to flow through her emotional landscape without much resistance. Tate could not imagine doing the same, but as she became more comfortable with Cally, she felt herself softening.

Tate moved slowly from her thoughts back to the room as Cally took her hand and laid her head on Tate's shoulder.

"You seemed a long way away for a minute, Tate."

"I was just thinking about how the Universe brings people together. A few days ago, you didn't exist for me, and now you're changing how I see life."

"Really? How so?"

"I'm so independent. Have been pretty much all my life. I don't let many people in beyond the surface, and I certainly don't look to others for support when I'm going through something difficult."

"Yeah, that's pretty obvious."

"But it feels different with you, Cally. I feel different. I tell you things about my life and it feels good to do that. Maybe that's why we were thrown together, so we could heal each other. And Leland, too."

"Yes. And maybe that house."

"Yes, Cally, that house. We could heal it, too."

FIFTY-TWO
2005

Cally parked her car on a side street and entered Riverside Cemetery on foot. Having suffered through what seemed like a brutal winter to her, especially after living in California for most of her life, she felt grateful for the warm February sun and unseasonably mild temperature. Still, she wrapped the cashmere scarf more tightly around her neck and tucked her gloved hands into the pockets of her puffy, thermal jacket to protect against the cold breeze rustling through the barren shrubs at the entrance.

She followed the path taken by most first-time visitors and history buffs who seek out this expansive memorial to Asheville's history—a loop around the Wolfe family plot, past the Von Ruck mausoleum, along the winding paths girdling the rolling hills that contain the final resting places of Asheville citizens dating back to the early 1800s. Cally had learned that some of the remains interred there even predated the establishment of Riverside in 1885. As the city's need for space grew, the bones of the dead had been moved from the burying grounds surrounding the churches in the heart of town and relocated to the new graveyard established on the edge of Montford.

Cally resisted the pressure she felt to hurry to the cemetery office for help in finding the gravesites she had come looking for. Instead, she strolled past headstones with names like Clingman, Vance, Patton, Merrimon, Rankin, McCormick—monikers that lived on as names of the streets, structures and geography of Asheville and Western North Carolina. Finally, after exploring for more than an hour, she felt ready to find her grandparents.

The office occupied a squat brick building adjacent to the Jewish section of the cemetery. As Cally entered, she was greeted by a middle-aged man dressed in jeans and a flannel shirt.

"How can I help you?" He offered his hand and Cally shook it, relieved to find a friendly, outgoing man rather than the ashen, somber creature she had imagined would hold the position of Cemetery Manager.

"I'm looking for a grave. Actually two of them."

"Names?"

"They're my grandparents . . . but they're not buried together . . ." Cally suddenly felt nervous.

"No problem. I just need to know their names."

"Well . . . my grandfather was Harland Freeman . . . I mean he was my biological grandfather, not my real grandfather . . ." Cally stopped abruptly and turned to leave ". . . never mind. I think I'll just go."

"Doesn't matter. I can still help you find him."

Cally hesitated at the door and took a deep breath to steady herself. "Okay. Sorry about giving you all that personal information. Just their names, then. Harland Freeman. He was buried here in 1942. And Ellie . . . Marie Eleanor Howard. In 1962."

Cally left the office ten minutes later, map in hand, and headed toward Harland's grave. She made a couple of passes through the area where she expected to find it without success. Then she remembered part of her conversation with Mazie Daniels. Tate had taken Cally to meet Mazie the day after they found the mantle.

After telling Cally about Harland's earliest years, Mazie related how he had been ostracized by the business community he hoped would accept him. "Anyone who didn't hate him 'fore hated him after they saw that awful tombstone he put on his grave."

"Why did he do that?"

"Can't say why. He left his life with my family behind long 'fore that. People didn't like him 'cause he was pompous and self-centered, but he thought it was 'cause they held his past against him. Maybe they did, but even so, he wasn't a likable man. Everthing he did just pushed everone farther away."

"What about you, Mazie?" Cally had liked Mazie immediately and recognized that telling Harland's story still stirred up emotions for the old woman.

"He pushed me away, too. I tried not ta turn my back on him, but . . . anyway, he put that huge tombstone right up in front a the Rylands' plot, and it overshadowed 'em. I think he prob'ly did that on purpose. But then it fell down and people started fergitten about him. That house of his over on Chestnut is the only thing left and it's an eyesore. Folks can't wait to be rid of it. Most of 'em ain't never heard a Harland and don't know that was his place."

Thinking of Mazie brought a smile to Cally as she retraced her steps and found the Ryland family plot. From that vantage point, she easily located the crumpled monument, overgrown with ivy, which sat a few paces along the slope. She looked across the gentle hills of Riverside, the afternoon sun in her face, and thought what a beautiful resting place Harland had chosen.

Unfortunately, the peaceful view proved no match for the swirling emotions that enveloped Cally. Sadness, anger and confusion fought for dominance, but Cally's resolve won the battle as she approached the fallen marker. She tugged thick vines away from the stone until she had uncovered most of the old granite. Then she sat on one of the moss-covered benches that bracketed Harland's grave.

"You don't know me, but I'm your granddaughter." Cally's words came out in a ragged whisper, and she looked around to see if anyone had heard her. Harland certainly couldn't, but Cally spoke for her own benefit, not his.

"Mazie told me about you. You were a pretty despicable character from what I understand." Cally rubbed debris off the headstone so she could read what had been inscribed. "Even that epitaph. 'I stand by all I did . . .' What was that about, anyway?

442

"I wanted to hate you like everyone else did. But I know you had a difficult childhood. I know about Crazy Eulah, the old shack, all of it." Cally thought about her own childhood—the losses she had suffered, the challenges of growing up with an alcoholic mother, being ripped away from her home and her loved ones. Her experiences had shaped her and Harland's had shaped him. Everyone, even Harland, deserved forgiveness. And Cally was the only one left to provide it. As this awareness flooded over her, Cally's heart began to open.

"I wish things had been better for you. But I'm also glad I was born, and that wouldn't have happened without you. So I've decided not to hate you. I think you've always wanted to be accepted. So now you are, Grandfather. By me."

As Cally spoke her thoughts and feelings aloud, the anger and sadness she had carried for so long began draining away. She ran through all that had changed for her since hearing Mazie's story about Harland's tombstone. That tale had set her on the path to Riverside Cemetery. It had also sealed her decision to remain in Asheville and help Tate save Harland's house.

In the months since, Cally had moved from the Princess Hotel into the apartment that had once been Leland and Ellie's house. She planned to stay there until renovations were completed on the house on Chestnut Street. She liked living next door to Tate, and though Cally thought it unlikely they would ever become romantically involved, their friendship had deepened steadily as the weeks passed.

With the help of a savvy lawyer, Cally had gained control of the trust Harland had created and the sizable amount of cash that remained in the trust's bank account. She used some of the money to pay delinquent taxes, thwarting the neighbors' hopes for demolition. Scott returned to work on the property after Cally paid him much more than what he was owed from his work a decade earlier. He immediately began clearing the land around the house of dead vegetation, and the yard now awaited new plantings which would arrive as soon as the weather permitted. Cally expected by mid-spring the house would be fully renovated and ready for move-in.

It had not all been easy though. The challenges of working with architects, adhering to city laws governing work in the Montford historic district, trying to make friends with the neighbors who resented her squashing their hopes for new development on her land—all of it proved to be exhausting and frustrating at times. Still, her plans continued to move forward and she inched steadily closer to creating a new home for herself in Asheville.

Cally now understood what Tate had known when she first saw the house on Chestnut Street, that new life could be breathed into it and it could be a happy and welcoming place. It could—and would—become Home. Cally told all this to Harland, and as she did so, she felt herself settling deeper into her new life.

But more of her past remained to be found, and it lay down the hill. A few minutes later, she sat on the ground in disbelief staring at twin headstones:

Marie Eleanor Howard   Clayton Samuel Howard

1911 – 1962   1927 - 1962

Beloved   Beloved

Wife and Grandmother   Son

—⁓—

As Cally left the cemetery, she called Tate. They now sat on the porch of Cally's apartment, soaking up the last rays of winter sun.

"It just never occurred to me that Clayton would be buried there, too!" Cally had done her crying in the car on the way home. What remained was shock and anger. Clayton had always been a shadowy figure in Cally's life. Rita actively avoided him, and he hovered on the outskirts of Cally's relationships with Ellie and Leland. As far as Cally could remember, they had never even spoken to each other more than a handful of times.

Cally never thought of Clayton as *father*. In fact, for most of her life after Rita took her to California, Cally hadn't thought of him at all. That is until she and Tate had discovered his role in Ellie's death. Finding him interred next to Ellie had left Cally dizzy and nauseous as she tried to make the connection between the man who had murdered her grandmother and the one lying under the marker emblazoned with "Beloved Son."

"How can I help, Cally?" Tate squelched her urge to jump in with a pep talk.

"You just being here is support enough, Tate. If I hadn't met you, who knows what I would have done. I may have gone back to my condo, my job, my empty life in California. But now I have all this beauty and hope and possibility in my life."

"You seem really happy, Cally. I'm glad you're coming to terms with Harland."

"Me, too. I'm going to put a new marker on his grave. Nothing so intimidating as the original. Just something that acknowledges his life, you know?"

"I do. I think Harland is finally getting what he always wanted—love and respect."

"I told Gampa. I don't think he's able to forgive Harland, but he gave me his blessings nevertheless."

Tate still joined Cally for visits to Forest Glen occasionally, but she hadn't been in over a month. "I need to get back out to see him soon. How's he doing?"

"He's slipping a little. He hasn't fully recovered from that bout with the flu last month, and they say he may not."

"How does he feel about you moving into Chestnut Street?"

"He seems relieved. He'll own it till he dies, but his will leaves it to me, so he said he was finally untethered from it!"

"You've had an eventful day, Cally."

"That I have! I'm feeling better, though. I guess if I can find it in my heart to forgive Harland, then I'll eventually be able to do the same for Clayton. I better, because it's not like I won't be seeing him again."

"Yeah, I guess so . . . him being there beside Ellie . . ."

". . . and eventually Gampa, too."

The two women sat in companionable silence and watched the sun color the bellies of the clouds pink and gold before disappearing behind the mountain ridges.

FIFTY-THREE
2005

Tate left home without breakfast or coffee. She walked briskly and didn't slacken her pace until the house came into view. Formerly so dilapidated and sad, it now bustled with activity as workers finished the final steps of the renovation.

So much had happened since Tate first stumbled upon 305 Chestnut Street all those months ago. She had learned a great deal, not just about Cally and her relatives, but also about herself. Cally had found a place to call home and transformed it into a nurturing haven. Tate had not done the same for herself, and she wondered if she ever would, if she even could.

Tate walked around the house and into the backyard. Soil had been turned and planting beds prepared for the meditation area Cally planned for the far corner of the property. The fish pond would be reborn as a water garden. Within weeks, the yard would be ablaze with color and abundant life.

Tate dropped into a deep wicker chair with soft cushions near the old fish pond and wrapped her wool barn coat snuggly around herself. She would always be welcome here, she knew that. But it would never be hers.

Still, meeting Cally and forming that immediate and tight bond, joining forces to save the house, allowing herself to develop real connections with people as diverse as Leland and Ruby and Richard Price . . . these experiences had changed Tate.

"Someday." Tate allowed herself to sink into a vision of the life she wished for, one filled with richness and possibility. "Someday I'll have my happily ever after, too."

ACKNOWLEDGMENTS

No book is written by the author alone, and this one certainly wasn't! My initial interest in writing grew out of the high praise I received from Mrs. Palmer, my twelfth-grade English teacher, who thought my book report on *Giants in the Earth* far exceeded all expectations. That same interest was dashed to the ground by an unnamed professor at Miami-Dade Junior College who had no appreciation at all for the feminist perspective and told me I should focus on doing something that would earn me a living.

Many story ideas have lived in my head for years, some for decades, but until now, this is the only one that has actually been written. I owe that accomplishment largely to my dear friend Tracy Coates who has believed in Tate Marlowe since I first introduced her to Tate in 1999. It is also Tracy who told me about National Novel Writing Month in 2005. My participation led to the birth of *Final Rights*, which then sat untended for years.

Letting a story lie in fallow ground is familiar to many writers, especially, I think, those who attempt to produce a finished piece for the first time. There are all kinds of excuses: I don't have time, I have writer's block, I don't like what I've written, I have great ideas, but I don't know how to get them down on paper . . . the list goes on.

I would likely still be stewing in those excuses if it were not for my extremely good fortune in having found Micki Cabaniss Eutsler and the staff and editors at Grateful Steps. Over the course of dozens of meetings, Micki read every word of my story aloud with me sitting next to her. I saw and heard in the moment her reactions to the characters I had created and their experiences. Her feedback is the best education I could have asked for as a new author. Her encouragement and guidance have made this a much better story than it would ever have been without her.

When I needed answers to questions anchored in the real world rather than the one I was creating, I called on several people who were gracious and helpful. The staff at Pack Memorial Library in Asheville, NC, and Putnam Library in Nashville, MI, provided me with a wealth of information and memories that have influenced this story. Zoe Rhine and Ann Wright at Pack Memorial Library helped me obtain the cover photograph. My research into the workings of real estate in Asheville led me to Annika Brock, a local attorney, and Devorah Thomas of City Real Estate, a savvy broker and good friend. Kathryn Scott, architect, helped create the door that sparked Tate's interest. Tom Ross, professor of Weather and Climate in the Blue Ridge Naturalist Program, assisted with the destruction of Harland's grand monument.

Over the years of wanting to write, and then writing this book, I've had ongoing support and encouragement from my family, in particular my sister, Linda Frank Lodovice, and from a cadre of friends including Cheri Britton, Ann Paige, Kathie Schmidt and the members of my two book clubs.

My heartfelt thanks to all of those named here and many others who have cheered me on. And you can expect me to be calling on you as I dive into the next Tate Marlowe mystery!

CPSIA information can be obtained
at www.ICGtesting.com
Printed in the USA
FFOW01n1751081114

8567FF